DAVID BARBAREE
THE
EXILED

ZAFFRE

First published in Great Britain in 2019 by
ZAFFRE
80–81 Wimpole St, London W1G 9RE

A CIP catalogue record for this book is
available from the British Library.

ISBN: 978–1–78576–338–0

Also available as an ebook

1 3 5 7 9 10 8 6 4 2

Typeset by IDSUK (Data Connection) Ltd
Printed and bound in Great Britain by Clays Ltd, Elcograf S.p.A.

Zaffre is an imprint of Bonnier Books UK
www.bonnierbooks.co.uk

Cast of Characters

PARTHIA

The Kings of Parthia

King Vologases, ailing ruler of Parthia, king since A.D. 51, sparked civil war naming youngest son, Pocorus II, as his heir

King Vologases II, eldest son of Vologases, one of three sons vying for the throne

King Artabanus III, second son of Vologases, faring badly in the civil war

King Pocorus II, youngest son and heir of Vologases

Loyal to King Artabanus III

Zenobia, wife of King Artabanus III

Darius, satrap of Bactria, advisor to King Artabanus III

Meherdates, aka the Toad, Latinized son of Parthian hostage in Rome, ears shorn off by King Gotarez (aka the Butcher), after failed coup

Himerus, Chief Eunuch of the King's Harem

ITALY

The Flavians

Vespasian, deceased, emperor of Rome, ruled from A.D. 69–79

Titus Caesar, eldest son of Vespasian, former soldier and general, named emperor after his father's death in June A.D. 79

Domitian, second born son of Vespasian

Domitilla, eldest daughter of Vespasian

Vespasia, second born daughter of Vespasian

Imperial staff and courtiers

Ptolemy, slave and Imperial secretary to Titus

Jacasta, loyal and long serving maid to Domitilla

Livia, maid to Domitilla

The house of Secundus

Plinius Secundus, aka Pliny the Elder, admiral of the Imperial fleet, soldier, author and close advisor to emperors Vespasian and Titus

Gaius Caecilius, shy, bookish nephew to Pliny

Spartacus, secretary to admiral Pliny

Zosimus, slave to Gaius

The house of Ulpius

Lucius Ulpius Traianus, blind wealthy senator from Spain

Marcus Ulpius Traianus, nephew to Lucius Ulpius

Theseus, one-eyed freedman and former gladiator

Cyrus, freedman to Ulpius

Elsie, elderly slave, like a mother to Marcus

Senators and patricians

Cocceius Nerva, senator fallen out of favour with the Flavians, has network of spies throughout the empire

Sulpicius Peticus, recently returned from Syria, owner of gladiators, brother was put to death under Nero

Cerialis, general and friend of the emperor Titus, engaged to Domitilla

Tascius Pomponianus, lives near Stabiae on the Bay of Naples

Eprius Marcellus, deceased, senator under Nero and Vespasian, conspired to kill and overthrow Vespasian

Caecina Alienus, deceased, former commander during the civil wars, implicated in Marcellus's conspiracy to overthrow Vespasian

Valerius Festus, arrogant member of Domitian's entourage

Soldiers and Praetorian Guard

Virgilius, recently named Prefect of the Praetorian Guard and Titus's right-hand man

Manlius, centurion charged with watching Parthian hostages, Barlaas and Sinnaces

Catullus Messallinus, legate in the Praetorian Guard and good friend of Domitian's

Parthian hostages

Carenes, deceased, general and satrap of Mesopotamia, supported Meherdates in failed coup to overthrow King Gotarez

Barlaas, warrior of royal descent, co-conspirator with Carenes in the coup to overthrow King Gotarez

Sinnaces, son of Carenes, born in Italy

Parthian emissaries

Arshak, leader of Parthian emissaries, short with miscoloured eyes

Farbod and Farhad, brothers, tall and noble in appearance

Atropates, old translator who wears a Scythian cap

Gladiators and hunters

The Batavian, legend of the hunts, owned by Nerva

Minnow, gladiator, Myrmillo class, owned by Sulpicius Peticus

The Spear of Sogdia, warrior brought by Parthian emissaries to Italy

Locals in Reate

Plinius Pinarius, undertaker, seeking an audience with Domitilla in Baiae

Sextus Pinarius, son of Plinius Pinarius, expected to take over family business

SYRIA

House of Ulpius

Nero, deposed emperor, posing as Spaniard Lucius Ulpius
 Traianus

Marcus, former slave, now posing as nephew of Ulpius

Theseus (aka Spiculus), former favourite gladiator of Nero

Doryphorus (aka Cyrus), former freedman of Nero, actor and
 master of disguises

Local patricians

Commodus, governor of Syria

Sulpicius Peticus, senator from Rome, owner of gladiators,
 brother put to death under Nero

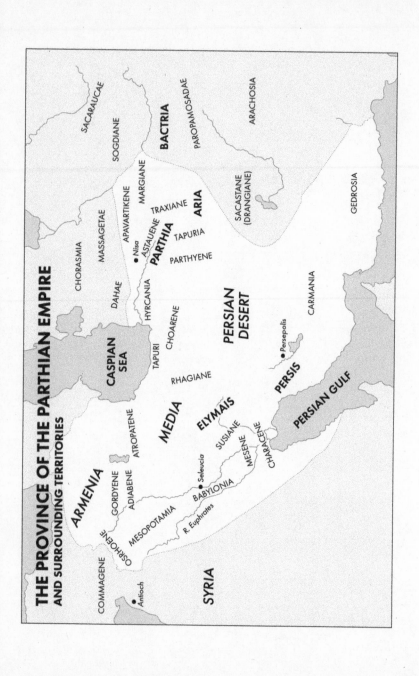

THE PROVINCE OF THE PARTHIAN EMPIRE
AND SURROUNDING TERRITORIES

COMMAGENE

ARMENIA

OSRHOENE

GORDYENE
ADIABENE

MESOPOTAMIA

SYRIA

Antioch

R. Euphrates

BABYLONIA

Seleucia

MESENE

CHARACENE

SUSIANE

ELYMAIS

MEDIA

ATROPATENE

RHAGIANE

TAPURI

CHOARENE

CASPIAN SEA

HYRCANIA

DAHAE

MASSAGETAE

CHORASMIA

SACARAUCAE

SOGDIANE

APAVARTIKENE

MARGIANE

Nisa

ASTIAUENE

PARTHIA

TAPURIA

PARTHYENE

TRAXIANE

ARIA

BACTRIA

PAROPAMOSADAE

ARACHOSIA

SACASTANE (DRANGIANE)

GEDROSIA

CARMANIA

PERSIAN DESERT

Persepolis

PERSIS

PERSIAN GULF

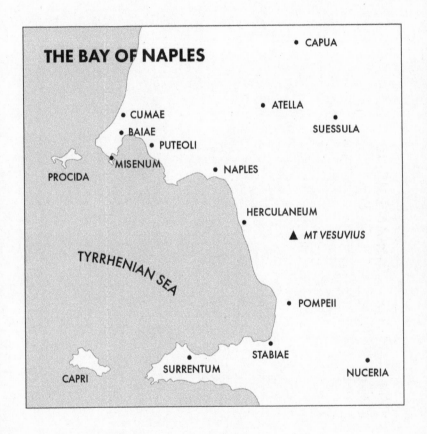

THE BAY OF NAPLES

- CAPUA
- ATELLA
- SUESSULA
- CUMAE
- BAIAE
- PUTEOLI
- MISENUM
- PROCIDA
- NAPLES
- HERCULANEUM
- ▲ MT VESUVIUS

TYRRHENIAN SEA

- POMPEII
- STABIAE
- SURRENTUM
- CAPRI
- NUCERIA

Author's Note

Parthia was ancient Rome's rival for more than two centuries. It stretched from the Euphrates, past the Caspian Sea, to the Hindu Kush mountain range, and south to the Persian Gulf. It was comprised of modern day Iran, Iraq, and parts of neighbouring countries, including Turkey and Afghanistan.

When not at war, the two great empires engaged in the ancient equivalent of a cold war. Pretenders to the rival's throne were backed. Hostages were exchanged. Concessions by one were used for political victories at home.

We know little about Parthia's internal political history, particularly during the second half of the first century A.D. Between A.D. 77 and 80, following Vologases I's thirty-year reign, there are references in the record to three different successors – Vologases II, Pacorus II and Artabanus III – which suggests civil strife, but this is only guesswork.

In Rome, Nero, the last of the Julio-Claudian emperors, fell from power in A.D. 68. Vespasian was the last man standing after a short but bloody civil war. He reigned for a decade and established the Flavian Dynasty, which would last another twenty years under his sons, Titus and Domitian.

Under the Flavians, at least three men claimed to be the deposed emperor Nero. Not much information has survived about these so-called False Neros. We know they were thorns in the side of the Flavians and that one sought refuge and support in Parthia during Titus's reign, but little else.

This book is the second in a series inspired by the False Neros. It is set during A.D. 79 and 80. The extant historical record for this period is mainly comprised of accounts written decades or even centuries after the fact, by men who brought their own personal and political biases to the task of recording history. It is therefore difficult to sift fact from political fiction. Thankfully, novelists do not need to adhere to the same rules as academics. This is a work of fiction. I have taken liberties novelists allow themselves. But I have also strived for a story that is true in its own way, one that fills the gap scholarship cannot, and explores the historical record's inherent biases and unexplained contradictions.

Prologue

The general arrives in the afternoon. Half the city is there to greet him.

'Shall we begin?' he asks.

The question is rhetorical: the general sets the agenda, not the other way around. But the priest – a local man, and ignorant of the Imperial protocol – lacks the deference one is expected to show the second most important man in the empire.

'We must wait,' the priest says bluntly, 'until the sun has begun its descent.'

The general grumbles. 'Wait?' But the priest is merely a proxy, charged with conveying Apollo's will. Who is the general to argue?

So, he makes camp. He waits.

Caesar would have come himself. But Caesar is not well; he hasn't been for some time. Bedridden, rumour has it, never to rise again. The senate decided to send his son, the famous general. After all they collectively thought but didn't dare say aloud, it's only a matter of time before the son is named emperor, once Caesar has breathed his last.

At the anointed hour, the general walks through a forest of ancient pines, up a steep hillside, to the Temple of Apollo. The building is more than a thousand years old – older than Rome itself. North African marble façade, grooved columns, and two podiums, separated by a flight of stairs; a hearth burns on the first, day and night. Nearby is a cliff overlooking the Tyrrhenian. The island of Ischia lies in the distance, a shadowy black peak, rising from the sea.

By torch light, the general sacrifices three black bulls and an ox. The animals' necks are slit and a sea of blood pours onto the dirt; puddles form, gelatinous and black. Acolytes recite ancient verse while the priest, on his knees, with blood-stained forearms, from finger tips to elbows, removes and inspects the beasts' entrails, running his thumb along each liver, like a seamstress confirming every stitch. Once certain there are no anomalies, he takes the general through the forest, down a narrow dirt path, to the entrance of a cave.

The general's companion, a white-haired soldier, is told he must wait with the acolytes.

The priest ducks into the cave; the general follows.

The passage is narrow and dark. The priest leads him into a small room. Torch light slowly illuminates the room and a human size heap in the corner begins to move.

The Sibyl.

She sits up, leaning her back against the rugged wall of the cave.

The priestess is tiny, all bones and sinew, with filthy black hair. She is only a girl, eight or so. But with her pale skin and black eyes, she has the look of an old woman, with one foot in the grave.

'Speak and she will answer,' the priest says.

The general hesitates.

As a soldier, he never hesitated. He smiles and thinks, What's wrong with you? Is this little priestess of Apollo more fearsome than a German horde or a Sicarii assassin? Remember: this isn't for you. It's for the priests back in Rome, and the god-fearing Senate. Ask the questions you came here to ask and then go do something productive.

The general clears his throat. 'The Oracles tell of a calamity for Rome if the last of the Trojans crosses the Euphrates.' He cannot bring himself to say the man's name. It would give the imposter too much credence. 'We have heard rumours of someone claiming to be such a man amassing an army in the east. He could cross the river any day. He may have already. Tell me what I must do, for the good of Rome.'

The Sibyl's voice is an empty whisper. 'Fear not. Every empire must fall.'

'Tell me, priestess' – the general's voice is louder as he grows more confident – 'what must I do to protect the Principate and to prevent war?'

The priestess's head tips back, her eyes begin to oscillate, as though she is watching the erratic flight of a bee, and her voice becomes as deep as a man's. She says:

> *'When the last of the Trojans is west and east, mountains will fall and black ash will fill the sky.*
> *When the seed of Aeneas crosses the Euphrates, the heart of the wolf will burn, and a plague will take root.*
> *Beware of a mother's curse. It follows the guilty, even through death.*
> *Beware of the curse of Remus. You are no Romulus.*
> *Beware of Strength. He is your greatest weakness.*
> *When the golden-haired children are gone, a slave shall rule.*
> *Apollo keeps his word.'*

She falls to the floor and retches black bile, then curls up into the heap they found her in.

The general is pale when he exits the temple, though later he will claim it was the moonlight, not colour draining from his face – not a sign of fear. He retires to his tent with his grey-haired companion. They drink wine until morning. They talk of war, of women – anything to distract from the oracular bag of bones that the general spoke to.

The white-haired soldier thinks: this was supposed to be a function of tradition, to appease the empire's superstitious soul. Has it become something more?

Finally, he asks, 'what did the Sibyl say?'

The general recites what he can from memory. When he's done, he forces himself to laugh. He is, after all, the great general who ended the siege of Jerusalem. What does he care for the predictions of an eight-year-old girl?

'Mountains will fall,' he says to his friend. 'As though the gods could topple mountains.'

I

Tremors
A.D. 79

Zenobia

1 April

The harem of Artabanus IV, Parthia

The message comes after sunset. The king's eunuch, Himerus, delivers it. There will be no battle, he says. Not tonight.

Collectively, eighty-eight women – on edge since the foreign army was first spotted this morning – breathe a sigh of relief. Beside me, the queen, who is eight months pregnant, begins to sob tears of joy. The harem is not ready for another fight. The scars of Persepolis – the lives lost and the brutal, long march north that followed – have yet to heal.

The news comes as a surprise, but I don't share their sentiment. I feel – disappointed. Yes, tonight there will be no battle. But we are at war. The battles will come. A fight, at least, could have ended our exile; a fight could have led to a proper roof over our heads, rather than the smoke-stained canvas I stare at every evening as I wait for sleep.

Himerus concludes the speech with platitudes for our king, reminding us of his unparalleled intellect, his magnanimity, the righteousness of his cause. The flattery is so over-the-top, so ornate, that I nearly laugh. And yet, for some, it appears effective. A few women nod their head in agreement; others mutter prayers for their king. Perhaps only those who have never met Artabanus and have no measure of his character – although I can't say for certain. I do not, as others do, keep a running tally of those who've been granted the honour of sharing his royal bed. There was a time when I kept score, when I was young and competitive and vain. Those days are behind me now, the victories as well.

Once he's finished, Himerus catches my eye and makes his way across the tent. Some women, anxious for more information or words of encouragement, step into his path or pull at his robes. The eunuch grants a soothing word or a sympathetic sigh, but never once breaks his stride.

When he reaches me, he whispers, 'The satrap would like a word.'

'Would he?' I raise an eyebrow. *Is that allowed?*

'He says it is of great importance.' Himerus's voice oozes with propriety. He is the Chief Eunuch of the King's Harem and would never suggest anything that lacked the proper decorum. 'I will chaperone.'

I nod, fasten my veil and discreetly follow the eunuch outside. Together we march across the camp, a sliver of white moon overhead, and into a different tent – one that's smaller than the harem's long, multi-peaked residence. Inside, it stinks of roasted game – ostrich perhaps – and the hint of incense, recently lit; an unsuccessful attempt to mask the smell of cooked flesh that I detest. It is a gesture – a gesture by an intractable old warrior who rarely makes them.

He misses me.

Or he needs me.

The tent flap opens and Darius, the satrap of Bactria, steps inside.

His frame is unchanged since our wedding night: short but powerful, the shoulders of a bull. His smile is the same as well: crooked, exposing a thin line of teeth, full of mischief or menace, depending on where you stand with him. Only his beard is different. It was black once; now it's mostly grey.

'Zenobia,' he says. 'My loving wife.'

'I am *not* your wife,' I say.

Darius stares at Himerus and twirls his finger. The eunuch obediently spins on the spot, turning his back to us. Save the king, the satrap is the only man Himerus would obey like that.

'Are you not?' Darius feigns surprise. 'Strange, I recall our wedding very well, even after all these years.'

He steps toward me and boldly lifts my veil.

His smile softens. The change is genuine, I think, a sign of affection – though I'm not sure what he sees. I'm past my prime, wrinkled, with a touch of grey. I'm not an old woman – I wouldn't go that far. But I am no longer the young beauty he married.

'No,' I say, 'I am not your wife. Not anymore. You cast me aside.'

He takes my hands in his and pulls them up to his chest. 'Never.'

He did. He tossed me out like used bath water, his wife of twenty-four years. I may have failed to give him a child – at least one that survived beyond pregnancy or the precarious first years of life. But I was otherwise loyal, respectful, loving, a confidant, a voice of reason – everything one could ask for in a wife.

In a time of peace, at least.

Then the war came and everything changed. After Vologases, the king of kings, became ill and nearly died, he named Pacorus his successor, the youngest of his thirty-eight sons. When two of his thirty-seven brothers refused to accept their father's decision, this brutal war began. Nobles across the empire were forced to choose a side. Darius chose Artabanus. Then, to find favour with his new king, Darius gave away three of his daughters and me, his favourite wife. It was a good plan at first. I quickly became indispensable in the harem, adopting the role of matron, instructing the king's young and inexperienced wives and concubines in the complexities of harem life – on its politics and etiquette, on one's personal toilette, on the art of pleasing their notoriously difficult to please husband. But Darius may have miscalculated: in the race for the throne, my former husband – the distinguished general, the brilliant tactician – may have picked the wrong horse.

'Do you regret it?' I ask.

'Every day.'

'And what will happen if our king loses? It will all be for nothing.'

'He cannot lose. I am advising him.'

'You may have forgotten, my dear, but I am not stupid. Persepolis was a terrible blow. And now we are forced to hide in the forests like animals, as Pacorus, the boy you didn't think would last a day, holds the west.'

Darius shakes his head. 'It's not the boy who impresses. It's the treasonous men who support him. They have proven more formidable than I anticipated.'

'But we can agree the war is not going well.'

Darius grins. 'You see! This is what I miss. Your fire. All my wives are so dull.'

'Slow-witted is what you mean. And so are you for giving me up.'

Darius sighs and dramatically drops my hands; he paces.

'Yes,' he says, 'that may be true. I gave you up, and that makes me a fool. But there is no going back, is there?'

'Then why, my dear, have you brought me here?'

Darius broods for a moment, staring at the tent wall. He says, 'It's the men who came tonight. The foreigners. What have you heard?'

'Silly things. We do not get the truth in the harem, only exaggerations the eunuchs and maids tell us.'

Darius shakes his head and says, more to himself than to me, 'Maybe not so silly.'

'Are they Roman?' I ask. 'We heard they are Roman soldiers.'

'Mainly. But there are Greeks, Jews, Syrians, brigands. All sorts have flocked to him.'

Darius pauses. He is taking his time, unsure or unwilling to get to the point. I have never seen him like this. The satrap of Bactria is not usually one to drag his feet.

'I should get back,' I say, 'before my absence is noted. Tell me, my dear. What do you need?'

Darius takes a deep breath, then nods, as if he's finally come to a decision.

'Our fortunes are tied to Artabanus. I am not asking you to do anything that will harm him or bring you dishonour. You are, after all, his wife now. But I fear others are working to improve their standing with our king. They are doing this to the king's detriment.'

He means this, I've no doubt, but with Darius there is always more to the story. If I had to guess, I'd say what he leaves unsaid is that these men are working against *his* interests. Darius is concerned about losing his rightful place at the king's side.

'Tomorrow,' he says, 'there is a meeting with the foreigners. Your Greek is better than mine. And you speak Latin, a skill very few in our camp have. I need you there, listening, making sure I know everything that's said.'

I do my best not to laugh at the absurdity of the request. 'I would like to help you, my dear. I would. But please explain how a member of the king's harem could attend a meeting between two armies?'

'Other than me and Himerus,' Darius says, pointing at my veil, 'only the women of the harem know your face. None of the king's wives will be in attendance tomorrow. I want you to attend disguised as my maid. Himerus will provide the appropriate attire. You will stand by my side and translate.'

The plan is one only Darius could devise: simple yet daring. But what he proposes would put me at great risk. If I were caught gallivanting about the camp dressed as a maid, my reputation would be ruined. At best, I would be thrown out of the harem, ostracised and left to survive on my own, the gods alone know how. At worst . . .

The king is unpredictable. Women have returned from his tent with swollen eyes or cut lips. Disproportionate replies to a harmless comment or innocent giggle. And then there is what he did on our march east, after Persepolis, after another noble family abandoned his cause. Furious, wanting someone to blame – someone other than the traitorous nobleman who was already halfway across the desert and out of reach – Artabanus blamed one of his secretaries, a distant relative of the fleeing nobleman. On the king's command, a hole was dug in the desert and, under the threat of death, the secretary was forced to sit in the hole and wait as the king's men shovelled dirt back in, burying the man up to his neck. He was left alone in the desert, sobbing, crying out for mercy, as our caravan resumed its march east. In the days since, I have dreamt of him, alone in the desert, carrions pecking at his eyes, peeling back the flesh from his sunburnt face.

It was a reminder of a rule one should never forget: it is wise to avoid the anger of kings.

And yet I find I am not content to sit on my hands and wait for the war to finish and hope my new husband is the victor. I may be married to a king, but that does not mean I cannot plan for a world in which he is king no longer.

To Darius, I say, 'I will do this for you, but on one condition.'

'Anything,' Darius says.

'I am loyal to our king, as are you.' I leave it unsaid that Darius had the luxury of choosing who deserved his loyalty, whereas I had no such luxury. 'But we are at war. If the tide changes, I want you to promise you will look out for me.'

He smiles. 'Of course. You needn't have asked. You are my loving wife.'

'I am not your wife and I need more assurances than that smile of yours.'

'You have my word.'

I shake my head. 'No, that is not enough.'

I look around his tent, searching for an idea. One strikes me as I stare at the satrap's chest.

'Your family's amulet,' I say. 'Let me have it until the war is done.'

Hidden under his Median robe and silk tunic, hanging on a golden chain around his neck, Darius has an amulet, a massive stone of ruby set in solid gold, which has been passed down in his family, from father to son, generation after generation, for hundreds of years. Darius claims it was a gift from Alexander to his Bactrian bride. It is the satrap's most prized possession. Our king may not survive this war, but Darius will. If I have Darius's amulet, he will find me, and he will take care of me.

The satrap is annoyed; his smile darkens. He cannot believe anyone, let alone a woman and his former wife, is not content to take him at his word. He asks, 'You doubt my loyalty?'

'Yes,' I say. 'You gave me away. I'd be a fool not to.'

Darius pretends to consider my proposal, but we both know he needs me.

He nods, opens his robe and pulls out the amulet from underneath his tunic. He admires its golden radiance in the lamp light before dropping it into my hands.

'Doubt no longer.'

The next morning, Himerus enters the harem, clears his throat, and – loud enough for every woman to hear – requests my assistance. He is the king's eunuch and no one will question my absence so long as I'm with him.

He takes me to his tent and hands me a long, sleeveless tunic and headdress a maid would wear. The material is cheap and irritates my skin.

After I've changed, the eunuch holds up a cracked mirror. My arms and face will be exposed in public for the first time since I was a girl in Seleucia. It feels equally thrilling and improper. I pinch loose skin below my shoulder and, for a moment, long for the arms of my youth. But that girl – the daughter of a Seleucian nobleman, spoilt and silly – would never have had the resolve to do what I am about to.

'Ready?' Himerus asks.

'Yes.'

The council is held in a clearing, a long rectangular table is placed in the middle of it. Poplars cast shadows under the mid-day sun. Somewhere, hidden from view, a mountain stream trickles downhill.

The foreigners arrive first. An acknowledgement, the eunuch whispers, that they are in the weaker position. Most are wearing dented armour, rusted mail, and faded rags that were probably once red capes. Some look like soldiers, at home in their armour; others like criminals, as comfortable as I would be in a cuirass. All of them have bad teeth and a worse smell that's evident the moment we enter the clearing. I'm struck with how brutal they appear, dim-witted and mean. Father always said Romans were thugs, but it's strange to see them in the flesh, living up to their reputations.

A parade of Artabanus's soldiers, generals, noblemen, satraps, secretaries and trusted advisors enters the clearing to the rhythm of a kettledrum. While the foreigners look wild and unkempt, our king's courtiers are immaculate: manicured beards of black, brown or silver, with matching hair, curled into swinging ringlets; some wear flowing Median robes over silk tunics; others wear armour of silver scales that rattles with each step.

The westerners are silent, their eyes wide.

They are impressed.

Darius does not, as I expected, take the seat in the middle of the table. This honour is given to the Toad. To Meherdates. He sits across from the commanding Roman, who, like so many of his comrades, has the nose of a drunkard, a massive crag that is a darker shade of red than his faded cloak.

It's a surprise the Toad has been given command today. For as long as I can remember, he has always been an outcast, a grotesque shadow that stalked the halls of the royal court. Bald, gaunt, and earless as a fish, his deformities are a living reminder of the cruelty of the Butcher, King Gotarez. The Toad may have royal blood, but he is no better than a foreigner.

For centuries, our kings have sent hostages to Rome under the pretence of fostering peace when their true aim was to rid themselves of their rivals. This is what happened to Meherdates's father. Seen as a rival to the throne, he was sent to Rome by King Phraates. And so Meherdates was born on Italian soil, and raised under the Italian sun. Years later, when the Butcher was king, his cruelty sent the nobility looking for a suitable rival with royal blood. Secret emissaries were sent to Rome. They returned with Meherdates at the head of an army. But the Butcher defeated him easily. And when the usurper was dragged before the king – true to his name – the Butcher ordered Meherdates's ears cut off, believing that with such deformities he would never rule. From that day forward, Meherdates was known as the Toad, a name he has grown into, with his grey skin, bulbous eyes, and earless head – a man so ugly that one could not bear to look at him, let alone follow him.

Yet he has command today. Further evidence the war is not going well and our king is in desperate need of friends.

After introductions are made in Greek, the Toad asks if they would prefer to speak in Latin. The Roman commander seems relieved.

This is what Darius was worried about. He knew the Toad would lead today and speak Latin, fluent after spending so many years at Rome.

Once he has the comfort of his native language, the Roman leader grows more confident and adopts a rougher demeanour. 'Where's your king?' he demands.

I grew up in Seleucia, a city equal parts Greek and Persian, one of the last bastions of the Seleucian empire. I learned Latin at the insistence of my father, who thought his daughter, a princess, should know, at a minimum, eleven languages. My tutor was a philosopher, banished from Rome. He taught me the Latin of the poets, as he called it, the Latin of the Senate, the Latin of the rich. But from time to time, when drunk or angry, he spoke differently. Afterwards, when he had sobered up or calmed down, he would apologize for speaking vulgar Latin, the Latin of the poor, which was unsuitable for the ears of a princess. There was a baseness to it, I recall, a lack of sophistication. It was so distinctive in character that I am able to recognize it now, after all these years, as it spews out of the Roman drunkard's mouth.

It's good our king is not speaking directly with the Romans. These barbarians have no sense of shame, sending a man like this to bargain with the king of kings.

'Where is *your* king?' the Toad demands.

'We have no king,' the red-nosed Roman says. 'We've something better than that. A god among mortals.'

I whisper into Darius's ear, translating everything I can.

'What is it you want?' the Toad asks. 'What use do we have for a worn-out army a long way from home?'

'Our interests are aligned,' the Roman commander says. 'We know Rome refused to acknowledge your king. We know your army needs soldiers.'

'Get to the point,' the Toad says. 'What do you want? What do you propose?'

'Kill the Flavians, restore the emperor, take back his throne.'

'Restore who to the throne?' the Toad asks. 'What are you talking about?'

The Roman commander smiles. He turns and whispers in the ear of a boy behind him. The boy runs off.

'Restore the emperor to the throne,' the drunkard says. 'The *rightful* emperor.' He nods at a man walking into the clearing, flanked by soldiers.

The man's face is hidden under a cloak. He approaches, slowly.

Once he's behind the seated Romans, he stops, then drags the hood of his cloak back to his shoulders.

Red hair. Black eyes. Copper beard. And a crown of laurels.

'I am Nero Claudius Caesar,' he says. 'Emperor of Rome.'

He speaks in Greek, so nothing is lost on his audience.

There are gasps on our side of the table.

The Roman commander smiles with pride.

'Together,' the man with the copper beard says, 'we will destroy our enemies and retake our thrones.'

Gaius

18 August

The foothills of Vesuvius, Campania, Italy

Dogs howl in the distance. On the heels of a wild, dangerous and probably petrified boar darting through the trees.

At least I think that's what we're chasing up and down Vesuvius's treacherous slope. This morning Uncle Pliny said, 'you're hunting boar today because that's what young men do.'

Didn't he? Or did he say deer? There's not much difference as far as I'm concerned. I'd rather be back in Misenum, reading, practising my declamations, studying Livy – anything but running through the woods with a spear in my hands.

'Gaius.'

I wonder what breed they are. The dogs that is. There's a good chance Uncle Pliny will ask because he asks about nearly everything. He'll be disappointed if I don't know.

'Gaius!'

I could ask someone in our party. But this is, perhaps, something I should know by now. They might laugh. I wonder—

'*GAIUS!*'

A storm cloud of black shoulders and rough, prickly hide bursts through the undergrowth and, by a distance of maybe two spear lengths, barrels past me.

I watch the beast pass, my eyes wide and mouth agape. It's close enough that I can feel a slight breeze spawned by its gait, and I'm vaguely aware that I've not made any attempt to stick it with my spear, the entire point of this sweaty, early-morning endeavour.

And then it's gone, snarling dogs trailing in its wake.

Hidden cicadas, which had gone silent in the tumult, resume their incessant screeching.

'Didn't you know, Gaius?' Domitian is standing to my left; he brushes his long black bangs from his eyes. 'Statues make poor hunters.'

There is laughter behind me. Domitian's hangers-on, no doubt, eager to please Caesar's younger brother.

Marcus Ulpius emerges from the hole in the brush made by the boar. He stops to catch his breath, bending at the waist, like a runner at the end of a race. Unlike Domitian and myself, who were straggling until the boar doubled back the way it came, Marcus was leading the charge through the forest. It's difficult to tell from my angle, but I think he's smiling. Later today he'll laugh about this with his friends. *Little Gaius Caecilius had the boar right in front of him but couldn't be bothered to throw his spear.*

Gods, I hate hunting. I'm not sure what's worse: running through a forest in the blistering heat or spending the day with the entitled sons of Rome's elite.

Zosimus hands me a skin of water. 'Not your fault, master. No man could have turned and thrown his spear that quickly. I was impressed you kept your cool, being so close.'

'Thank you, Zosimus.'

My tunic is cemented to my back with sweat. I pour water over my shoulder, hoping to dissolve the coagulate.

Sinnaces, the younger of the two Parthian hostages, steps into the clearing, bow in hand. He makes a comment about the bow being mightier than the spear, implying first-hand knowledge of warfare. But as the son of a Parthian hostage, born in Rome, he's likely never left Italy, let alone fought in any war.

Our guide – a freedman everyone calls Nine Fingers, on account of his missing little finger on his right hand – is next into the clearing. He walks to Domitian's side. 'My Lord, was that you making fun of young Gaius? I see *your* spear is as spotless as the one he's carrying.'

Domitian glares at Nine Fingers but says nothing. Caesar's younger brother is quick to criticise, but cannot stomach a word of it from anyone else.

The older Parthian hostage, Barlaas, and the centurion, Manlius, are the last to step into the clearing.

Barlaas has the look of a barbarian hero gone to seed. He is tall, with wonderful blue eyes, and a thick manicured beard, equal parts black and grey. But his belly is wider than his imposing shoulders, and his breathing labours with each step.

Manlius, the centurion, is Barlaas's physical opposite: short and stocky, he looks as though he were made entirely of stone, with cheek bones that could sharpen a blade. The centurion is charged with watching both Parthian hostages. But he has been with Barlaas so long, that they interact like a husband and wife, rather than a prisoner and guard.

'You're too slow, Barlaas,' Manlius says, smiling. 'The beast is long gone.'

'I was waiting for you,' Barlaas says. 'Are all Roman soldiers this slow at marching? It's a wonder Rome has ever been east of the Euphrates.'

Barlaas is old – too old, I'd have thought, to be chasing a boar through the woods. But he is, like all of his countrymen, fanatical about hunting. And when he is not panting or holding his back in discomfort, one can see the young man he once was;

the fluid grace with which he notches an arrow to the string of his bow and pulls it back to meet his ear; the way his bow seems an extension of his arm. Uncle Pliny says he was once a feared warrior in Parthia. But now, a Roman hostage for nearly thirty years, he can only use those skills hunting.

The men start to talk to each other as they sip water and catch their breath.

Marcus stands slightly apart from the crowd. Remembering Uncle Pliny's instructions – not wanting to disappoint him – I approach Marcus and do my best to engage in a conversation.

'Did you get close?' I ask. 'To the boar?'

With the charisma of a marble façade, Marcus says, 'no,' and nothing more. I continue for no other reason than I can tell Uncle Pliny I did my best.

'That is a shame,' I say. 'Have you ever killed a boar before?'

'Yes,' Marcus says and walks away as though I were a leper.

Nine Fingers hushes the group and listens for the dogs. 'Right,' he says, 'let's resume before we lose the beast altogether.'

Hours later – exhausted, sore, down to my last drop of water – I'm the last to emerge into the clearing.

And only just in time to watch Marcus thrust his spear into the shoulder of a black boar the size of a small horse. It must be twice the size of the beast we saw earlier this morning.

I watch with the rest of our hunting party from a distance.

The dogs are ravenous, barking as though they're possessed by the furies. The boar rears and its hooves stab the air. Marcus loses his balance. The boar whips its head around and its tusks collide with the shaft of Marcus's spear, snapping it in two.

Marcus falls backward. Somehow – miraculously – he narrowly avoids being gored.

The boar rears once more before charging the rest of our hunting party. It goes from standing still to a furious sprint before I can draw a breath.

Frozen, unable to move, I am overcome with one thought: a goring would be an exceptionally painful way to die.

I shut my eyes.

I curse Fortuna and the twists of life that brought me here. The pestilent summer that sent all of Rome's elite south to the Bay of Naples; Uncle Pliny's direction that I hunt this morning and make friends with Marcus Ulpius; Mother failing to intervene like she usually does.

And then I hear the release of an arrow and a dull *thwap* as it buries into hide and flesh.

I open my eyes and see the boar dive snout-first into the dirt and slide to a stop at Barlaas's feet. The old man's bow is empty.

After a moment of breathless silence, the men begin to laugh.

I look down at my crotch, hoping the urine that I'm quite certain escaped isn't visible. Thankfully, whatever crept out has blended into my sweat and dirt-polluted tunic.

Sinnaces is excited. He all but says the shot was a victory for Parthia.

'It was luck, boy,' Barlaas says, with obvious disgust for Sinnaces. 'Fight a war and you'll see. You can't fell anything that big with one arrow, not without the help of the gods.'

Nine Fingers inspects the dead creature. 'I think you're being modest, Barlaas.' He wiggles the arrow, which is buried deep into the animal's hide. 'This seems more skill than luck. It was quite the shot.'

Barlaas refuses the compliment with a snarl and a string of Parthian curses.

'Do you know the rule, Gaius?' Domitian asks me with a smug smile. He pushes his black bangs from his eyes. 'Last one to the kill has to drag the corpse back to camp.'

The men laugh.

Gods, I hate hunting.

Uncle Pliny – admiral Secundus, master of the Misenum fleet, author, scientist, historian, advisor and confidant to two emperors – is asleep at his desk. With the sun up, his back straight and a book open in front of him, he has the appearance of a man hard at work. Except that his eyes are closed and he's snoring.

Uncle Pliny's office is overrun with books. They are strewn across the desk, on top of tables and chairs, on the floor, on top of other books; a few have even crept out onto the balcony. When he is called away to Rome, as he often is, the household staff will spend an entire day mining papyrus, cataloguing and returning it to the Roman knight or senator who'd given up hope that the text lent to admiral Secundus would ever be returned. The staff have a long-standing joke that while it takes them a month to remove books from his office, Uncle Pliny, upon his return, can fill it again in less than an hour.

Across the room, half-hidden by curtains of translucent cream-white silk, there is a long balcony looking out onto the Imperial harbour and, beyond the jetty, the Bay of Naples. On the pier below, the admiral's fleet busies itself under the afternoon sun. Saws buzz; marines laugh; a ship's rigging tightens and slackens with the roll of the waves.

I take a seat in front of the sleeping admiral. He is a bear of a man, all chest and shoulders, belly and white whiskers, ruddy cheeks and two paws laid flat on the desk. His fingers are empty save a carnelian ring on his left ring finger. In the afternoon light, the red stone looks purple, nearly black.

Uncle Pliny's secretary clears his throat. On cue, Uncle Pliny opens his eyes. He's startled at first – his eyes widen like a lunatic's – but he quickly recovers. He takes a deep breath and calmly says, 'Thank you, Spartacus. That will be all.'

His secretary bows and leaves.

Uncle Pliny's work ethic outpaces his physical stamina. He wakes before sunrise, works into the evening, and sleeps less than four hours a night. He does this with strict regularity, no matter how much wine he's had or how far he's travelled that day. The pace is impossible to maintain, especially in one's fifty-sixth year. Out of necessity, he often pauses for short, apparently satisfying naps throughout the day. It's a strange routine, but after performing it for so many years, Uncle Pliny and his secretary have become oblivious to its strangeness.

'And how was the hunt?' Uncle Pliny asks.

'Awful.'

'You didn't catch a boar?'

'No, we caught a boar,' I say. 'A remarkably large one according to our guide.'

Uncle Pliny strokes his foam-white beard, a signal he is about to engage an adversary in a debate, like a gladiator raising his sword.

'You don't measure success by the very task you set out to do?'

'Chasing down and murdering some lonesome beast was not why you forced me to leave this morning. Was it?'

Uncle Pliny smiles. 'Quite so.'

'You said that hunting was good training for the soldiering I'll soon need to complete, and that it would help foster my connections. And you specifically instructed that I *cosy up* with

Marcus Ulpius Traianus, which I understood to be a euphemism for forming a friendship with him.'

'Ah,' Uncle Pliny says, 'I see. I take it you are no better prepared for the life of a soldier?'

'Not in the slightest.'

Uncle Pliny laughs. He knows my strengths and weaknesses. While he tries to improve the latter when and where he can, he knows I won't have the career as a soldier that he did. One wouldn't know it to look at the aging, heavyset admiral, but Uncle Pliny was an excellent soldier, an accomplished rider, and could throw a javelin as far and straight as anyone. Unfortunately, I do not possess his physical traits. I have always been slight of figure, on the shortish side, and as coordinated as a new-born foal. I've no proficiency with weapons – spears, swords, shields. I'm hopeless, no matter how much I train. I'm meant for study, not the life of a soldier, though custom will require I spend at least a year in the legions.

'And what of the other objectives we set for today? Did you foster better social connections?'

'I have the same connections that I did when I left this morning,' I say. 'I wouldn't know how to measure their improvement.'

'I see.' Uncle Pliny's smile is waning. 'I take it, then, that you're no closer to forming a bond of friendship with young Marcus Ulpius?'

'No, I am not,' I say. 'And I think you should extinguish any hope this will happen.'

'And why is that?'

'Firstly, he does not like me. He may even despise me. I've no idea why or what I've done to offend him, but his dislike for me is palpable, with no chance of diminishing. Secondly, I do not like him. He's a bully and a brute. The only thing worse than an arrogant patrician, is a *provincial* arrogant patrician. They're just as rude and condescending, but with a greater tendency to violence. Thirdly, he's mad.' I describe the scene with the boar. 'The gods alone know what Marcus was trying to prove. He seems intent on killing himself.'

'Is there something wrong with emulating the Romans of legend?' Uncle Pliny asks. 'Perhaps he's a young Romulus.'

'Perhaps. I wouldn't be surprised if he murdered his own brother.'

Uncle Pliny's smile is gone. He is about to scold me, but – thankfully – something occurs to him. He grabs his stylus and wax tablet. 'Before I forget, what breed of dog did you use today?'

Uncle Pliny's insatiable quest for knowledge requires that he record and understand everything. It is only a matter of time before he publishes a five-book treatise on hunting dogs.

'I'm not sure,' I say.

'Well, were the dogs swift and used for cornering the beast? Or were they larger, with strong jaws, used to bring the beast down?'

I try to recall what exactly the dogs did. 'Both I think.'

'Can you describe the colour and pattern of their coats?'

'Um. Brown?'

He sets his stylus aside and straightens his carnelian ring. His frown of frustration is fleeting, yet difficult to stomach. I hate to disappoint him. I worry he thinks: *well, if you're no soldier, if all you have is your wits, shouldn't you be smarter than this? More observant? More learned?*

He circles back to the Ulpii.

'You understand why I want you to forge a relationship with Marcus Ulpius?'

'Because you are obsessed with his uncle, Lucius Ulpius, who has seen a swift and dramatic rise. In less than eight months he

rose from an obscure provincial, newly arrived to Rome, to argu-
ably the emperor's closest advisor.' I wince, immediately regret-
ting the description. Hastily, I add, 'after admiral Secundus, of
course.'

Uncle Pliny swats at my comment with his bear paw. '*Pah!* I
wouldn't be so sure of that. I have always been close to Caesar.
But this Ulpius seems to have surpassed me. He helped expose
the plot hatched by Marcellus and his ilk – I will grant him that.
But he has his own agenda. Mark my words. And I am going to
find out what it is.'

Earlier this year, a group of senators and soldiers led by
Senators Marcellus and Caecina tried to overthrow Vespasian
Caesar and seize the Principate. Most of the conspirators were
arrested or killed. Marcellus is currently on trial in Rome.
Lucius Ulpius, Marcus's uncle – a blind, eccentric senator from
Spain – was instrumental in exposing the plot. He has grown
considerably closer to Caesar as a result. Uncle Pliny says he
is only concerned that Ulpius may have ulterior motives. But,
though he will never admit it, I think Uncle Pliny is also concerned that his own importance is diminishing next to Ulpius's
rising sun.

'Anyway,' Uncle Pliny continues, 'Ulpius may have helped save
Vespasian's life, but little good it did. Poor bastard. Though' –
Uncle Pliny tilts his head, offering, as he often does, a counter
argument to his original thought – 'I suppose it's better to die of
natural causes, by the will of Fortuna, rather than by poison at
the hands of your enemies. It certainly allowed a smooth transi-
tion of power, from father to son.'

Vespasian Caesar held the Principate for ten years. He passed
away two months ago. His son, Titus, succeeded him. Uncle
Pliny breathed a sigh of relief that the throne passed to Titus

without violence, without a civil war. Plans had been put in place for Vespasian's death and Titus's ascension. But in politics nothing is certain.

'And,' Uncle Pliny continues, 'you are wrong about Ulpius. I'm not obsessed with him. I am merely curious about his past.'

'Curious? You have a book on him, in which you record every detail that you uncover.'

'I have a book on a good number of men. I may even have one on you,' he says with a smile. 'But "book" is the wrong word. It is a list of facts that I do not want to forget.'

'Yes,' I say, 'but how many spies have you sent to Spain to investigate?'

'Spies? What spies? I sent a *friend* to Spain for a variety of reasons, one of which was to make inquiries about Ulpius. The answers he provided did not make sense so I sent someone else. But this is nothing new. I am in the service of Caesar. And it is my job to ensure Ulpius is friend rather than foe.'

'But hasn't Ulpius proved his loyalty to Caesar?'

'No.' Uncle Pliny shakes his head. 'In order to demonstrate one's loyalty, one must be honest. And Lucius Ulpius is not honest. He tells stories rather than the truth – stories that do not add up. And he is hiding something. I just don't know what.'

'I see. Hence your direction to cosy up to his nephew, Marcus?'

'Precisely. I am focused on the elder Ulpii, and you the younger. Together we will unearth the truth.' Uncle Pliny starts to rummage around the papers on his desk. 'Now that we are clear on the impetus of our endeavour, let us return to the substance. Are you certain you have the measure of young Marcus?'

'Quite certain.'

'Is that so? One's first impression is rarely the correct one.'

'I suppose this is one of those rare occasions then.'

The admiral stares at me a moment. How many soldiers have buckled under that gaze? I brace myself, waiting for him to commence another debate, but he doesn't. There was a time I would have considered his silence a victory. But I've seen Uncle Pliny pull this manoeuvre before. He hasn't retreated. He is only gathering his forces and searching out more favourable ground.

He changes the subject. 'Who else joined the hunt?' he asks. 'Were the Parthian hostages there?'

'Yes, Barlaas and Sinnaces.'

'Old Barlaas is never one to miss a hunt, is he? Did they discuss the Parthian envoy?'

'Not that I heard. The others were more interested in the civil war.'

'Oh? And what did old Barlaas have to say about that?'

'You know what he's like. He said it was a stupid question. That he knew as much about the civil war in Parthia as we did.'

'Yes, that sounds like Barlaas.'

'Will he play a role when the Parthian envoys arrive?'

'A role? He will certainly play *a* role, but not to the extent the emperor would like. Normally, Rome's hostages would be paraded in front of Parthian emissaries to demonstrate our power. Barlaas, however, is too stubborn and has too much pride to control. He will ultimately buck if Titus shows him too much whip.'

'And how many Parthians will there be?'

Uncle Pliny can see my excitement. 'Calm yourself, young Gaius. The Parthian envoy will not be like the ones you've read about. This is not Prince Tiridates, marching across Italy with five thousand archers on five thousand Nisean steeds, swallowing up the countryside as they go. We are expecting a small party representing their king.'

'And which king is that again?'

'The one who will ultimately win,' Uncle Pliny says. 'Pacorus. The boy. Younger than you, I'm told. He holds the west, Mesopotamia and Seleucia. His position is strongest.'

Parthia is in the midst of a civil war, with three brothers vying for the throne. King Vologases I had ruled Parthia for nearly thirty years. Two years ago, as his health was failing, he named his youngest son Pacorus his heir. The two brothers, Vologases II and Artabanus, wouldn't accept their father's decision. Each raised an army and the civil war began. On Uncle Pliny's advice, Vespasian Caesar refused to recognize any of the three until the winner was all but certain. We have had word from our contacts in the east that Pacorus is likely to win any day now.

After Titus was named Caesar, he invited Pacorus to send emissaries to Rome. Titus wants to ensure Rome's main rival is friendly. A newly proclaimed emperor does not need a border skirmish or a war with a foreign power while consolidating authority at home. The meeting is also an opportunity for both leaders to fortify their position at home by recognizing the other.

Uncle Pliny looks at his waterclock on his desk, which is usually a sign he is ready for me to leave. As I stand to go, he says, 'I will see you at the pier around the tenth hour or so?'

'The pier? Why?' I ask, unable to hide the look of terror on my face.

'We have a dinner party this evening. Obviously.'

'No. There can't possibly be another one tonight. Can there?'

Uncle Pliny smiles. 'You've forgotten where we are, nephew. On the Bay of Naples the socializing never ends.'

He's right, sadly. In a matter of days, I've already been dragged to more dinner parties than the rest of the year combined.

'Who is it tonight?'

'The Augusta herself. And we are not about to decline an invitation from the emperor's sister.'

All I can do is drop my head in dejection. Another evening lost.

'Our ship will leave before the eleventh hour,' Uncle Pliny says, enjoying my misery. 'Please come of your own free will. I'd hate to have my sailors drag you to the pier.'

I've missed the baths, so Zosimus comes to my room with a cloth and bucket of fresh water. After peeling off my soiled tunic, he devotes a good quarter of an hour scrubbing away the bits of forest I brought home with me. He douses his hands in crocus oil, vigorously rubs them together, as though trying to start a fire, and pats my cheeks, my neck, and wipes the excess on his sides. When I'm presentable, I've only a short time to speak to Mother.

I find her sitting on the balcony, staring at the harbour, which, under the flagging light, is a cobalt blue. She's watching a dinghy, manned by one sailor, slowly row from the pier to one of the two dozen anchored ships.

She gives me a passing glance and turns her eyes back to the dinghy.

'Your uncle sent you off hunting today?'

'Yes.' Rather than sit and signal a long conversation, I continue to stand, leaning against the railing.

'You needn't have gone if you didn't want to,' she says. 'I'm sure it was dangerous.'

'It wasn't dangerous,' I say. 'It was fine. Uncle Pliny was right. It was a good opportunity. A chance to learn skills I lack.'

'You're no hunter, though, are you?'

She keeps looking at the dinghy.

'No,' I say, 'I suppose I'm not.'

'And I don't approve of you spending as much time as you do with the sons of senators. Your Uncle oversteps his class too often. It is not something you should emulate. We are equestrians, after all.'

I nod, half-heartedly, without formally committing to the proposition. It is an outdated view I don't share.

'We must be careful, Gaius. Titus Caesar sought the advice of the Sibyl. And she predicted great disaster for Rome.'

Mother is, in many ways, Uncle Pliny's opposite. While the admiral is fearless, she is afraid of everything. Today it is hunting, the senatorial class, and a virgin priestess with oracular visions. But she is often a weathervane for gossip. I suppose this will be the new story circulating, that the Sibyl warned Caesar of a looming disaster.

'Have you spoken to Uncle Pliny about this?' I say. 'I do not think he puts much stock in the Sibyl. The idea that a woman could accurately predict the future, by speaking with Apollo himself . . .'

Mother clucks her tongue. 'Your Uncle laughs at the gods. One day it will catch up with him.'

I disagree, but there is no point arguing.

'Will you be accompanying us tonight?' I say, trying to change the subject.

'No,' she says. 'The sea is quite rough.'

I glance at the sea, which is as calm as it has been all day.

'I should go, Mother.'

She waves her hand, dismissing me, without taking her eyes off the dinghy.

The eleventh hour. Our ship casts off under a waning sun. Black-headed gulls cry overhead. Our captain marches back and forth across the deck issuing instructions. Below deck, drums begin their constant, undulating beat. The marines take up their oars – thirty or so on either side of the ship – and power us forward, one stroke at a time. Uncle Pliny, never idle, is near the bow dictating a letter. Spartacus furiously marks his wax tablet trying to record every word.

We clear the jetty of the Imperial harbour and enter the Bay of Naples. The sea is calm, the wind non-existent.

Misenum sits at the westernmost point of the bay. I lean against the ship's railing and watch it slowly diminish, until it begins to resemble the other cities along the coast, clusters of red-tiled roofs and white-stone walls, separated by green forests and vineyards cut into the steep coastline, like the seats of an amphitheatre. Baiae, our destination tonight, is the next city along the coast. Further east is Puteoli; then Naples, Herculaneum, Pompeii, and Stabiae. Vesuvius looms over the bay. In this light, it resembles a black spearhead aimed at the sky.

I approach Uncle Pliny at the bow and tell him what Mother told me about Caesar visiting the Sibyl. 'Did you know?'

'Of course. But he wasn't Caesar yet. Vespasian was still alive.'

'Are you concerned?'

'Concerned? About the predictions of an impressionable girl, manipulated by charlatans? No, I'm not worried. And you shouldn't worry either. I haven't spoken with Caesar about it, but he is not one to get conned by such nonsense. He has a strong mind.'

'Why would he bother to visit the Sibyl then?'

'Tradition demanded it,' Uncle Pliny says with a sigh. 'As you know, the Oracles are kept in Rome.' He puts up his hands in protest. 'And please do not ask me to explain why our great empire still consults a thousand-year-old book of verse to determine our nation's fate. It is pure nonsense, let us leave it at that. Anyway, as you *also* know, those famed Oracles predicted great misfortune for the empire if or when "the last of the Trojans crosses the Euphrates". The phrase was written by swindlers a thousand years ago. Men who knew that if you made a prediction vague enough, it will inevitably come true – to a weak mind, that is. Thus, when the False Nero was spotted near and possibly across the Euphrates . . . weak minds, or devious minds looking to undermine our newly proclaimed emperor, pointed to that one line in the Oracles and said, "By Jupiter! We are doomed!" The priests charged with interpreting the text did what any sensible man in their shoes would have done. They said the Oracles were "inconclusive" and suggested consulting the Sibyl herself. And by that they meant, "Please make this someone else's problem". And so, to placate Rome's superstitious soul, Caesar went. As I understand it, she gave imprecise warnings in verse on how to avoid disaster, which Caesar conveyed to the Senate. And that should be the end of it.'

'Nevertheless,' I say, 'the predictions sound . . . troubling. Even if we do not put stock in them, others might.'

'Yes,' Uncle Pliny says, 'that is the true problem.' He fiddles with his carnelian ring. 'If your mother is gossiping about it, you can bet the whole of Italy will soon be.' He shrugs. 'But there is always some disaster on the horizon. The people will gossip, whether they have cause or not. I am not concerned, so long as Caesar is not taken in by such lies.'

Our captain bellows. Oars slice into a tranquil sea. The sun continues to set and the sky turns from pink to a dark purple. Fires are being lit in the homes and colossal villas that populate the bay, and soon little pinpricks of light begin to dot the coast.

We draw closer to Baiae. The luxury and wealth that sets it apart from its neighbours gradually comes into view. There is the dome of the baths, a solid piece of concrete unlike anything in Rome, let alone in Campania; and the villas – white-walls and red-tiled roofs, like any other on the bay – but larger, more pristine, organized adeptly, row after row, as the coastline rises steeply, with each arch of the colonnades aimed at the sea.

And then there is the city's design itself. Baiae is situated on the Bay of Baiae – a bay within a bay. The coastline curves naturally, into a half-circle, culminating in Punta Epitaffio, a finger of mountainous rock that juts out into the sea. Through the ingeniousness of Roman engineering, this natural half-circle is completed artificially, by a cement pier and what might technically meet the definition of a break wall, but is thicker than any break wall – thick enough that built upon it are more villas. The coastline, together with the break wall, creates a man-made lake that, no matter the state of the sea, is perfectly tranquil. The only entrance to the lake is a long, narrow jetty, just wide enough for our ship's hull and churning oars to pass through. Two fires are lit on each arm of the jetty, to aid visibility after sunset.

The flames roar as our ship glides past.

Once we are inside the break wall, our ship slides along the water, as smooth as a barge upon Lake Coma.

The Flavians have three Imperial villas at their disposal in Baiae. Tonight, we are headed to the Villa Piso, named for the family that once owned it, which sits below the Punta Epitaffio, on the eastern end of the city. A purple canopy marks where guests are meant to disembark. It's flanked by two burning tripods. As our ship waits its turn, the crew crane their necks hoping to see if they can spot anyone famous stepping onto the pier. They exchange excited murmurs about the Batavian, the legend of the beast hunts. *Is it him? Can't be. He's not tall enough.* I find myself craning my neck to spot the living legend of the arena.

The crew turns their attention to the ship that floats into line behind us. It's manned by gladiators, dressed for the games, as though they were to enter the arena at any moment: loincloths, or short tunics, sword belts, bronze greaves over heavy padding; manacles from wrist to shoulders. Some are even wearing the helmets of the Myrmillo or Thracian class.

I ask Uncle Pliny who would arrive with such a guard? 'I'm not sure,' he says, frowning. 'Someone who feels the need to intimidate. Or a showman, trying to raise excitement in advance of the upcoming matches.'

When the pier is free, our oars power us to shore with three quick churns. A dull thud marks the end of our journey, as the ship nudges against the pier. An Imperial valet takes my hand and helps me step ashore and escorts us along a colonnade lit by torches. We enter a peristyle surrounding a tiny grove of lemon trees. The sun has set, and the sky's purple hue is nearly drowned out by torchlight. The garden is buzzing with men and women, dressed in their finest silk and weighed down by gold wrapped around their wrists and fingers, and dangling from their necks.

Uncle Pliny accepts two cups of wine from a slave and hands one to me.

'Remember,' he says. 'We lack the pedigree and wealth to become intoxicated at a dinner like this. We are mere knights working in the service of the emperor. You may drink two cups. Make them last.'

I can see most of my hunting party from this morning, mingling amongst the guests. The Parthian hostages, Barlaas and Sinnaces, are here. Domitian as well. He is across the room, surrounded by his entourage of patrician young men. They are laughing in the way young men drinking wine will laugh, loudly, and with a certain arrogance. Individually, some of them are tolerable. But together they are unbearable. Besides Domitian, Valerius and Catullus are the worst of the lot. Both are from rich families that, because of their close association with the Flavians, wield considerable power and influence in Rome.

'Admiral!'

We turn to see Virgilius, the newly appointed Prefect of the Praetorian Guard. He greets Uncle Pliny with an embrace. The old soldier is thin and bony, with a thick mop of white hair and matching beard.

'I hear young Gaius did well today,' Virgilius says.

Uncle Pliny gives a knowing smile. 'I've no doubt,' he says, 'no doubt at all, though I hear old Barlaas was the true hero of the day.'

We turn and stare at the Parthian hostages across the room.

'True,' Virgilius says. 'He is quite the shot. Thank the gods that bow will never again be aimed at Roman necks.'

'It's strange how the boy is dressed,' Uncle Pliny remarks. 'Like a Roman.'

I noticed this as well. Whereas old Barlaas is wearing a traditional Parthian dress – a long Median robe, trousers tucked into riding boots, and a dagger at his side – the younger Parthian is dressed like a Roman. He is wearing a short tunic and jacket, made from expensive silk, and he is clean shaven.

'A man dresses according to the task,' Virgilius says. 'He dons armour before going to war, a toga before addressing the senate.'

Uncle Pliny nods. 'Quite so.'

'And,' Virgilius continues, 'a young man, off to a dinner party, hell-bent on bedding a young Roman woman – he too must dress the part.'

Uncle Pliny holds his belly, chuckling. His laugh builds until it becomes a wheezing cough. His eyes begin to water from the strain.

I often marvel at Uncle Pliny's conversational range. He's as comfortable speaking with a priest in a temple as he is with a soldier in the barrack. He is like an actor, who can play any part, comedy or tragedy. And his range is best on display during a dinner party. He goes from conversation to conversation with ease. He seems genuinely engaged and happy to speak to whoever happens to grab the famous admiral's arm.

This is a skill one is born with, I think. Try as I might, I cannot replicate it. I am comfortable with my books and little else. Every moment of this party will feel like torture.

Virgilius's observation was humorous, but I wonder if it's off the mark. Despite his attire, something sets Sinnaces apart. He doesn't quite belong with the other young Roman men. He is neither Parthian nor Roman; he is lost somewhere in between.

When he's recovered, Uncle Pliny asks Virgilius: 'And where is Caesar? Surely he will be here in time to welcome the Parthian emissaries.'

'Not to worry, admiral,' Virgilius says. 'Caesar will be here soon.'

Uncle Pliny raises his eyebrows. 'And were you with Caesar when he met the Sibyl?'

Virgilius looks at the ground, not wanting to meet Uncle Pliny's eyes. 'I wasn't allowed in, but I spoke with him afterwards.'

'And?'

Virgilius shakes his head. 'Caesar was ... The Sibyl's words disturbed him, though he won't admit it.'

'Caesar wouldn't fall prey to those charlatans, would he? The priests in Cumae are notorious frauds.'

'I wasn't in the cave,' Virgilius says, 'so I don't know precisely what happened. But if you saw Caesar's face when he came out ... Anyway, it can't be a coincidence, can it? The False Nero has crossed the Euphrates. Just as the Oracles predicted.'

Uncle Pliny laughs. 'Merely because a brigand with red hair crosses the Euphrates doesn't make him Nero. Riddles can predict anything, so long as the man reading them ignores his reason. What happened in Cumae was smoke and mirrors. I will convince you of this, my friend,' Uncle Pliny says. 'Maybe not today, but I will.'

Virgilius nods. 'I am of no consequence. It is Caesar you will need to convince.'

'I intend to.'

Their conversation shifts to less compelling issues: taxes and provincial administration.

My eyes wander.

I watch our host, Caesar's sister, Domitilla, across the crowd. Her distinctive nutmeg curls are pinned up, away from her shoulders, exposing her long neck, as smooth and unblemished as Egyptian marble. She is wearing black, still mourning the death of her father. Most say her sister Vespasia is the beauty of the family, but I would disagree. I have to consciously peel my eyes away, so I do not stare too long.

Behind her, on the far side of the garden, is Marcus Ulpius. He's speaking to a slave. She's pretty, I suppose. Tall, with black hair and blue eyes. Marcus is gesturing angrily. She's staring at him with an icy glare. Unbelievable. He's yelling at a slave in the middle of a dinner party. I knew my first impression was correct: the boy is a brute.

Later, after a quarter of a cup of wine, a woman greets Uncle Pliny with a hug. Her cheeks are painted a chalky pink and her hair is curled and pinned above her head into a teetering beehive.

'My dear Rectina!' Uncle Pliny says.

'When are you going to visit my new villa?' she asks, batting her eyelashes in a manner that, if it were anyone other than my uncle, I would think she were flirting.

'You've a new villa?' Uncle Pliny asks.

She swats his arm. 'Oh, you wicked man. I wrote to you earlier this summer. It is on the sea, near Oplontis.'

A man rumbles over and interrupts the conversation. He grabs Uncle Pliny by the shoulders.

'Admiral Secundus!'

He is large and heavyset, with broad shoulders and a wider belly; cheeks perforated with old scars; and blue, nearly white eyes.

Rectina rolls her eyes and says, 'Pliny, you will remember Senator Sulpicius Peticus.'

'Of course,' Uncle Pliny replies. 'Recently returned from Syria, isn't that so?'

'Indeed,' Sulpicius says. 'Indeed.'

'Ah,' Uncle Pliny nods his head with sudden recognition, 'that was your ship filled with gladiators, wasn't it?'

Sulpicius nods. 'Yes, those were my fighters. I'm trying to whet the people's appetite in advance of the games. Was your interest sufficiently piqued?'

Uncle Pliny shrugs. Rectina smiles at the admiral's indifference.

'When did you return from Syria?' Uncle Pliny asks.

'I've been in Italy since the Kalens. Just in time, I'd say.'

'Oh?' Uncle Pliny does not provide the look of shock Sulpicius had been searching for.

'Yes. The emperor's body is still warm and already his son is falling under the influence of disreputable provincials.'

'And by that you mean?'

'The cripple. Ulpius. The man is a liar. An imposter.'

This is nothing new. Senators are a jealous lot. They're always vying to bring down their colleagues. I've seen this happen too many times to count, particularly with men like Ulpius, whose fortunes are rising. Uncle Pliny may have his own suspicions, but he is always fair, always judicious, and never abuses his relationship with Caesar. He responds as he normally does when a complaint like this is made: he takes Sulpicius by the arm and, in a tone that tells him, *What you are about to tell me is the most important news I have heard all day*, says, 'tell me all about it.'

I excuse myself as Sulpicius begins to air his grievances. I decide to take a tour of the infamous Villa Piso. Uncle Pliny will forgive a short absence from the party.

I leave the peristyle and enter a long, wide hallway. The floor is a mosaic of little white and black stones. Niches hold statues of gods and busts of men long dead. I stop to admire the marble façade of Piso, the villa's last owner before Nero acquired it, following Piso's execution. Sunken cheeks are cut into the marble, dead eyes and a nose pointed at the ceiling. The paint is faded and peeling, revealing the marble underneath. No one has touched it up in many years. The neglect I understand, but it's strange this bust was never removed. Piso plotted to kill Nero and take the throne for himself. I would have thought one of Nero's first acts after acquiring Piso's villa would be to remove the bust of the man who tried to kill him. Maybe it was removed and only restored when the villa passed from Nero to the Flavians. Or maybe Nero preferred to keep Piso's bust as a reminder, a warning that Caesar must stay vigilant.

Rising above the hum of conversation in the garden nearby, I can hear the distinctive sound of two people arguing. It seems to be coming from down the hallway, around the corner. Curiosity gets the better of me. Convinced I will turn and go once I've had a look, I quietly walk forward and then peer around the corner. Once again, I see Marcus and the poor slave girl arguing. The exchange is heated. The girl is about to storm off but Marcus grabs her arm and holds her put.

Before I know what I'm doing, before I've had time to consider my actions – a disregard for repercussions that is *very* unlike me – I step around the corner, clear my throat and say,

'Ex-ex-excuse me, Marcus. But I don't think you should be man-handling the young lady like that.'

Marcus drops the girl's arm and glares at me.

To the girl, I ask, 'are you alright?'

Rather than thank me for intervening, the girl spits in my general direction and storms off. As she's walking away, she says something to Marcus in a language I've never heard before.

Marcus watches her walk away.

Momentarily forgetting that I rudely intervened – motivated by genuine curiosity – I ask Marcus, 'what language was that?'

Marcus stares at the empty hallway. He looks upset. Absent-mindedly, he answers, 'Aramaic.'

'You speak Aramaic?' I ask, surprised that Marcus is capable of speaking with anything other than with his fists.

His focus is no longer on the girl. 'I do,' he says with a sneer.

By the look of him, he might assault me right here, in the middle of a dinner party.

I try to placate him.

'Listen, Marcus. Maybe it wasn't my place to interfere, but it looked like you were being quite rough with her, slave or not.'

He shakes his head. 'You patrician brats are all the same.' With that, he storms off.

After a moment of stunned silence, I say aloud, though no one is around to hear it, '*You* are the patrician brat.'

When I return to the garden, Uncle Pliny takes me by the arm. 'And how goes your cosying up to the younger Ulpius?'

I grimace and Uncle Pliny shakes his head. 'What about the other boys here your age? The connections you make at this age will serve you well for the rest of your life.'

'Please don't make me talk with Domitian or any of his friends. I can't stomach it. Not tonight.'

Uncle Pliny slaps me on the back. 'Don't force my hand, Gaius,' he says ominously.

'What does that mean?'

Uncle Pliny winks and strikes up a conversation with a passing senator.

At the end of the evening, the gods alone know what hour, Uncle Pliny and I exit the villa to the street rather than our waiting barge along the pier.

'Where are we going, Uncle?'

He hands me a skin of wine. 'Drink.'

As I'm taking a small sip, Uncle Pliny puts his hand under the skin and lifts it up. I'm immediately overwhelmed with wine, stronger than anything I normally drink, lemon-tart. I throw my head forward coughing.

'I thought I wasn't to drink more than two cups,' I say once I've finished coughing.

'That was at the party. Now you need some courage. You've more learning to do tonight.'

His smile is more ominous than his words.

Prefect Virgilius joins us on the street. 'Is he drunk yet?'

'Not yet,' Uncle Pliny says.

'Why do I need to be drunk?' I ask, frustrated that I'm the only one not in on the joke. I yearn for my bedroom, to be alone reading Cicero or Livy.

Young men empty out of the villa. A few I recognize as Domitian's hangers-on. They move with the swaggering confidence that comes with wine, coin and patrician lineage. Several howl like wolves before heading off into the night.

'Come along,' Virgilius says.

I issue a barrage of questions as we follow the howling young men through the dark streets of Baiae, but I receive stoic silence in reply. My worst fears are realized when we come to a stop outside a brothel.

The group we followed press between two large men and through the front door.

'Uncle,' I say, my eyes on the brothel, 'you can't be serious.'

'Think of tonight as an extension of the task you were given this morning. This is another thing young men do. You need to befriend these patrician scions.'

I want to fight this but I also do not want to let Uncle Pliny down.

'Are you coming in?' I ask.

'Certainly not,' he says. 'I'm going to dictate letters to Spartacus here' – he points at his secretary – 'until you're finished.' Spartacus produces his wax tablet, which he is never without. Uncle Pliny slaps me over the shoulder. 'Go. But don't rush. I have more than enough to do while I wait.'

Virgilius takes me under his arm and drags me into the brothel.

Inside, there is a middle-aged woman sitting on a chair in front of a closed door. She is holding a wax tablet in one hand, a silver stylus in the other. A man is standing beside her, occasionally looking over her shoulder. They look like two merchants going over their inventory. The walls are decorated with mosaics of satyrs exposing large phalluses, and sexual acts, between men and women, men and men, women and women, in a variety of poses that look more like a wrestling match than what I understand to be intercourse. There are three couches. One is occupied by a man who is snoring loudly. A skin of wine is strewn on the floor beneath his open, drooling mouth. I recognize him as a senator who often calls on Uncle Pliny, a zealot for Stoic ideals.

Most of the young men we followed inside have disappeared. Valerius and Catullus are on a couch, each with a woman on their lap. While I do not give a fig what either of them thinks of me, I had expected surprise that I joined them, and to gain a bit of respect for the effort. But neither notices me.

Without looking up from her tablet, the woman asks, 'Preferences?'

Virgilius answers, 'Eastern. Dark. Tall.'

The woman uses a stylus to mark the wax. 'Room fifteen.'

Virgilius follows the man through the door.

With her eyes still on the wax tablet, the woman says, 'And you?'

I don't say a word because – well – I've no idea what to say.

She looks up. She is confused, but then seems to recognize something in my appearance. Something humorous. She smiles. In a softer tone, she says, 'Don't worry, young Lord. You are in good hands here at The Satyr's Cock.' She escorts me through the door and down a long dark hallway. Strange noises emanate from beyond closed doors: laughing, moaning, a fleshy slap. She stops at a closed door. She knocks three times before swinging the door open. Inside, there is a woman, standing in front of a side table, pouring a cup of wine. She is wearing her robe in a scandalously loose manner.

'A virgin,' my guide says. 'Be kind.'

The half-naked woman considers me a moment. She sips her wine. 'Maybe send Achilles in as well. Just in case.'

'Good idea.'

Speechless, I watch as my guide pushes me fully into the room and shuts the door behind me.

While I am unsure of what to do or say, the half-naked woman is preternaturally calm. She moves to the bed. The lamp-light flickers golden hues across her plunging neckline. She is not young, but neither is she old. Beautiful, certainly. She has a warm confidence that I find comforting yet thrilling.

She pats a spot on the bed beside her.

Meekly, I obey and take a seat. She hands me her wine. I gulp down two mouthfuls.

'And what is your name, young man?'

'Gaius Caecilius,' I say, croaking like a frog.

'A pleasure.' She holds the cup of wine and takes a small, seductive sip. 'You can call me Red.'

Uncle Pliny, Virgilius and Spartacus are waiting for me on the street.

'Well?' Virgilius asks.

My cheeks burn like a funeral pyre. I stare at the street.

'Leave him be,' Uncle Pliny says. He puts his arm around my shoulder. 'Talk of it only if you want, nephew. Come. We should be getting back.'

'What about the others?' I ask.

'I'd prefer a quieter walk to the pier,' Uncle Pliny says. 'Wouldn't you?'

We make our way down the dark, narrow streets of Baiae. All we can hear is the crackle of our torches and Uncle Pliny's laboured breathing.

Suddenly we hear shouts ahead. The voices are muffled at first, but quickly grow loud and violent.

Uncle Pliny and Virgilius exchange a look and hurry their pace. I try to keep up.

A man shouts: 'Roman dog.'

Another cries out in pain.

We round the corner and see shadows twenty paces away. Dark shapes surrounding a figure on his knees. Blades glint in the moonlight.

Prefect Virgilius yells, 'Stop!'

The black shadows freeze and then disappear into the night.

They leave behind a man lying on the street.

Virgilius rushes to the man's side.

It's Barlaas, the Parthian hostage. He has been stabbed, close to his hip; blood stains his green Median robe. He appears to be wearing armour under his robe, yet the blade still made it through. He is moaning and his face is contorted in pain.

Virgilius is pressing down on Barlaas's wound, to slow the bleeding.

We notice another shape, ten paces away, splayed out on the ground. Uncle Pliny hurries over. 'It's the centurion,' he says. 'Manlius.' Uncle Pliny puts his ear to the centurion's chest. 'He's alive.' Then Uncle Pliny touches the centurion's scalp and holds up his blood-stained hand. The centurion's blood looks black in the moonlight. 'Barely.'

I can see a look of relief cross the old Parthian's face.

'What happened?' Virgilius asks.

Barlaas shakes his head. 'Nothing.'

'There's too much blood to say it was nothing,' Virgilius says.

Barlaas pushes Virgilius's hands away. He tries to stand, though he is too weak and staggers; he falls back to the road. 'It was nothing,' Barlaas pants. 'Thieves looking for coin.'

Uncle Pliny sends me back to the Imperial villa for help. I run off without a word.

A quarter of an hour later, I return with four Praetorians, half a dozen slaves, and two doctors. Barlaas and Manlius's wounds are dressed, then they are put onto litters and carried back to their villa.

Barlaas won't say anything more of what occurred, no matter how hard Virgilius presses. The doctors insist on letting Barlaas sleep, and Uncle Pliny and Virgilius eventually relent.

Virgilius walks us back to our ship. I do my best to match their stride and listen.

'Thieves after coin?' Virgilius says, incredulous.

'It doesn't seem likely.'

'He was wearing armour. Did you see? What man wears armour to a dinner party.'

'Someone expecting an attack on a dark street,' Uncle Pliny says.

'He's hiding something.'

'Yes, obviously. But what?' Uncle Pliny says. 'He's been a hostage here in Italy for nearly thirty years. Aside from his stubbornness and constant complaining, he's never caused a problem.'

'Manlius may have more to say when he wakes up.'

'*If* he wakes up.'

'Manlius is a good soldier,' Virgilius says. 'Better than good. There must have been a small army to bring him down like that.' Virgilius's lip curls in frustration. 'This has to relate to the Parthian emissaries. The timing . . . it can't be a coincidence.'

'That seems likely,' Uncle Pliny says, 'but we cannot know for certain. Even if it does, if a few Parthians arrived early, under the cover of dark, and attacked Barlaas – this could be some tribal dispute that is no concern of ours.'

'What are you suggesting, admiral?' Virgilius asks. 'Barlaas killed some other barbarian thirty years ago and his kin are getting their revenge now, on Roman soil.'

'Perhaps. We know nothing for certain.'

Virgilius shakes his head. 'This is not a dispute between men. It's between empires.'

'Likely,' Uncle Pliny says. 'In any event, we must be on guard while they are here.'

Uncle Pliny stops walking and grabs me by the shoulders. 'Gaius,' he says, 'I have a new task for you, another to add to this summer's growing list. I need you to learn as much as you can from the Parthians. Sinnaces, especially. He's young and impetuous. He could give you valuable information. He'll certainly tell us more than Barlaas. I don't need to remind you that we owe everything to Titus and his family. And our fates are tied to theirs. We will investigate this attack and ensure the Imperial family is not in any danger.'

I nod my head in agreement. 'Yes, Uncle.'

'Damned barbarians,' Virgilius says. 'Lying cheats, every last one.'

Barlaas

19 August
Baiae, the Bay of Naples

I hate the fucking Romans. I hate their short hair and bald faces; I hate their crassness, their lechery, their bottomless appetite for sex, commerce and drink. I hate their accents – northern, southern, patrician, pleb – each is an assault on the ears, a dagger to one's peace of mind. I hate the way they dress, the bright colours and exposed skin – arms, shoulders, hairless calves, five-eighths of thigh.

I hate Italy, every inch of it. I hate the oppressive heat of its summers, the sticky tentacles of humidity that clogs the lungs and suffocates the chest. I hate the filthy streets overflowing with even filthier poor. I hate the people: painters, bakers, soldiers, barkeeps, maids, chamberlains, cooks, butchers, fullers – crooks every last one.

Even this doctor – standing over me now, inspecting my wound – he stinks of wine and, no doubt, if I take my eye off him for a moment, he'll rifle through my room and snatch anything of value that I haven't nailed down.

After nearly thirty years, I've grown to hate the basic constituent parts that make a Roman Roman, the bricks and mortar of Roman-ness. I hate their hypocrisy, their façade of morality, while, underneath, at their core, they are as debauched as they come. I hate their scorn for harems, while they fuck whatever hole happens to be in front of them; or their disdain for kings, while they grovel at the feet of whoever happens to be named 'Caesar'.

Most of all, I hate the Romans' sense of superiority, the way every citizen – from baker's boy to senator's wife – spits out the word '*barbarian*', with a curled lip and a queasy expression, whenever I enter the room. I hate how they are ignorant of my royal lineage; that I am a descendant of Mithradates himself, the Great Unifier; that I come from a nation as refined as theirs is vulgar, as cultured as theirs is pitiless.

I hate the fucking Romans.

And yet – when put to it, when my countrymen came knocking at my door, under the cover of darkness, offering me an opportunity, the chance to diminish that Roman pride I hate so much, to bring the kingdom of the Aryans glory at the expense of the Flavians – I hesitated.

Why?

Would Carenes, my old friend and fellow hostage, consider this a betrayal if he were still alive? He warned against growing too close to our captors. He saw the danger immediately, during our first month in Italy, after my brother labelled us traitors and banished us from the home of our birth.

It was nearly thirty years ago, after our coup had failed. Gotarez was king. His subjects called him the Butcher on account of his cruelty. The nobility had had enough. Carenes and I travelled in secret to Rome to find a suitable challenger for the throne. We returned with Meherdates, King Phraates's grandson. We thought it was a master stroke. We believed that because Phraates's kin had a better claim to the throne than Gotarez, the nobility would flock to his banner and victory would be inevitable. We were wrong. We were too preoccupied with pedigree rather than the qualities of a king. Meherdates was indecisive and stupid and unaccomplished in battle. Some joined his cause but most eventually abandoned him. Our forces were small by the time we met the Butcher in the field. He defeated us easily. Carenes and I were imprisoned. But the Butcher died before he could deliver his punishment.

My younger brother, Vologases, was named king. If I was hoping for forgiveness from my kin, I was sorely mistaken. He had Carenes and I brought before him.

'Brother,' he said, as his men kicked the back of our legs and we fell to our knees. 'You are a traitor, a slave to foreign power, and you are no longer welcome in this country. My advisors say I should kill you and Carenes for your support for the Toad. But I am sparing your life. I am sending you to Rome, where you will live out your days.'

I spat in reply and cursed his name. He was ten years my junior and the son of a concubine. I had more right to the throne than he did. But now, with the benefit of hindsight, I must admit, my brother acted the king that day. He could have killed me. His soldiers were ready, their hands touching the hilts of their daggers – eager to show loyalty to their new king. It was a magnanimous act to spare his brother and send him to live in Rome. It was also a show of strength. *Look! Kings are not afraid of their older brothers.*

We were kept under lock and key until terms were reached with Rome. Then an armed group of twenty men escorted us by land to Syria, then Asia, and then Greece, where we crossed the Adriatic. The winter winds came early that year, cold and terrifying. The waves tossed the ship like a toy until we landed in Ariminum, on the northeast coast of Italy. There we learned that Rome's emperor, Claudius Caesar, was dead. He perished from natural causes, or he was poisoned by his treacherous wife, depending on who you asked. I remember thinking: good, if Caesar is dead, send us back. But my brother's soldiers were undeterred. We waited in Ariminum, as negotiations were revived with Claudius's successor, Nero, a boy of sixteen.

We waited for five months. Our chains were eventually removed (where would we run to?) and we were allowed to move about the city. Carenes and I would eat the strange Italian fare every night, complaining bitterly of our new home. One day a handsome slave delivered a bottle of wine. A gift, he said, from our new master, the Emperor Nero. He stayed to uncork the bottle and serve us dinner. I recall my first sip even now. We make palm wine in Parthia. We import wine made from grapes, from Italy or Greece. For the most part, whatever crosses the Euphrates is foreign swill. This was something different. It was complex, but also light and airy, sunlight in a sip.

A smile enveloped my face. I said, 'maybe it will not be so bad here.'

Carenes scrutinized me with his one good eye. He was old, even then, frail and insubstantial. Yet that piercing blue, nearly white, eye could level a legion. 'We made a grievous error backing the Toad,' he said. 'He was not an Aryan, despite being the grandson of Phraates. He was born here, in Italy. He was Roman, a foreigner. We were blinded by our hatred for the Butcher, our desire to see him fall. We shamed our families and our ancestors thinking the Toad worthy of the throne. We can never undo what we did. But we can live with dignity until we die.'

He poured his cup of wine onto the floor.

He waited.

Without taking the second sip I desperately desired, I followed his example, pouring my cup out and then the bottle itself.

The slave was aghast. He quoted the price of the bottle and said he had no choice but to report what had happened to his master. Nero brought it up the first time we met. He was angry, demanding to know why we wasted his generosity. We were defiant. We did not like Roman wine, we exclaimed. We did not like anything about his damned country.

Rather than have us executed, as we expected, Nero laughed. 'Well,' he said with a shrug, 'I thought *I* had expensive taste.'

Last night, my assailants asked the question: am I Roman or Aryan? But the question is poorly conceived. One's lineage changes depending on where he stands. Snatch up a Roman and drop him in Dacia or Egypt, and he'll say: I'm a Roman, through and through. But in Italy, ask a man where he's from and he'll name the city he hails from, maybe even the street. And if he's from Rome itself, he'll tell you the ward. He'll genuinely believe Ward 16 is superior to Wards 2, or 5, or any other of the two hundred in the city. It's the same in Parthia. Before my exile, I would never call myself Arsacid, or Parthian, as the Romans call us. I was Mesopotamian. God help you if you claimed I was from Persis or a backwater like Hyrcania.

But since my exile began, I have defined myself by what I am not. I am not Roman.

This begs the question: if I am not Roman, why did I resist joining against the Romans?

Why indeed.

The doctor returns in the second hour to re-dress my wound. 'The bleeding has lessened,' he says. 'You will live.'

I ask about Manlius. 'Will he live?'

'Perhaps,' the doctor says.

I hate the Romans as a rule. But every rule has exceptions.

Manlius was assigned to watch Carenes and me twelve years ago. He replaced an old, toothless veteran from Germania, who had watched us since we first arrived in Italy. Manlius was a decorated centurion, fresh from some hard-fought war in the east, and bitter about the appointment. He thought it was beneath him – though this was only apparent from the occasional roll of his eyes. He would constantly pace with his hand on the hilt of his sword, ready to murder his barbarian hostages should the need arise. My Latin was terrible then, his Aramaic – the *lingua franca* in Parthia – non-existent. He knew some Greek – enough to grunt instructions when he deemed it necessary. And we communicated like this – like animals, grunting and pointing – for years.

It wasn't until Carenes died that this changed. It happened gradually. After losing my companion, I begged Manlius to play Tables with me. He turned me down for two years. Two! Once he finally relented, and after I'd taught him the rules of the game, his competitive spirit took over. He became a man obsessed. Now we play every night. He improved, slowly, and so did our relationship. He used to supervise my afternoon walks from a distance, walking several paces behind me. Now we practically walk together, equals conversing in Latin (which I learned reluctantly). We speak of developments abroad, of Roman politics, which never cease to fascinate. We gossip about who is visiting whom after sunset.

I hate the Romans. Maybe Manlius is an exception to the rule. But he isn't a *Roman* Roman. Not really. His father was an Egyptian slave, freed at the age of fifty. Manlius was born and raised in Alexandria. He joined the legions at the age of seventeen. He'd served in Germania and Dacia, but had never been to Italy until he was assigned the undemanding task of watching the emperor's Parthian hostages. In substance, he is as Roman as I am.

To think of the wars he fought, the battlefields he's seen, only to fall in the streets of Baiae. He deserves better.

I am sorry, my friend, for dragging you into this.

It's not until the sixth hour when Sinnaces returns home. He bursts into the room and runs to the side of my bed. I can tell by his lethargic eyes and red cheeks he is still feeling the effects of last night's drink.

'You're alive,' he says. 'Thank the gods. I only just heard.'

'Stabbed but alive,' I say.

The boy tries to take my hand. 'What happened? Who stabbed you?'

I push his hand away. 'Shut up, boy. I'll not confide in a drunk.' I think of his father, Carenes, how he poured out Nero's wine.

I failed you, Carenes. I failed to keep your son true to his kin, to the land of his birth.

But the rot was there before Carenes passed.

'It's good your father isn't around to see the Roman you're turning into.'

Sinnaces stands; he has tears in his eyes.

This is an argument we have had before, usually after he spends a night drinking with the other Roman boys. He reacts as he always does, like a child.

'I am *not* a Roman.'

'Answer me this, boy,' I say. 'If an animal looks like an elephant, lumbers like an elephant, and trumpets like an elephant. If it has tusks and thick grey hide and a swishing tail. Isn't it fair to say that the animal is an elephant?'

The elephant gapes. He has no reply.

He leaves. The smell of stale wine lingers.

Good riddance.

I could have confided in Sinnaces. I could have asked for help. But I do not trust the boy. He would run to his Roman masters at the first sign of trouble. I do not need him. My assailants will fail. Their plan is too complicated, too over-wrought with contingencies. And without me they won't be bold enough to try.

Domitilla

19 August
The Villa Piso, Baiae

The last of our guests board their ships as the sun is rising. I watch from the balcony, waving at anyone who cares to look back. I force myself to smile as Titus would want. Father as well. The Flavians don't have a care in the world. Show them.

Our newly anointed emperor insisted on a party. A lavish one. *The time for grieving is over*, Titus wrote from Rome. *We need to show the world that we are moving on.* I understood the logic. Even so, I am still grieving. I miss Father. I miss his bad jokes and endless complaining, his tongue always firmly in cheek. I miss the way he would pat my hand when I was upset, ever since I was a little girl. 'We will fix it,' he would say. And he usually would.

I wasn't ready for a party. But Caesar insisted.

It's strange having a brother for an emperor. It wasn't the same when Father took the purple. Father had always been the head of our household, the paterfamilias, the emperor of our family. His ascension merely meant that his dominion grew. And I was used to Father's constant rise, from soldier to general, from civil official to senator. His rise to the Principate was stunning, but also understandable.

It's different with Titus. We were never equals – he is the first-born son after all. But Titus always loved and respected me. He valued my opinion. He would listen to me and take my counsel. He was my older brother, not a king.

Everything changed when Father died. I realized this too late and Titus is still punishing me for it.

It happened in Rome. I called on Titus in the throne room, while he was meeting with Ulpius and admiral Pliny, as they were discussing how to handle my sister Vespasia. This was before her sudden, fervent devotion to the Cult of Isis, during her vigil at the deathbed of Caecina, her former lover and accomplice in Marcellus's plot to take the throne. Vespasia and Caecina had been having an affair for months. She cared for him. She loved him – or so she said. After the plot was exposed and Titus nearly cut Caecina in two, she refused to leave Caecina's bedside as he slowly died. This was a problem, according to Titus. It undermined the Principate. Titus wanted to send her away, to a remote island, such as Pandateria, as Augustus did his daughter. A similar punishment for a similar crime: promiscuity.

Or so Titus said.

What he really meant was they both were guilty of embarrassing Caesar. I spoke up. I told Titus that he couldn't send Vespasia away. Or, as Titus later put it, I had the *temerity* to tell the emperor that there was something he – Caesar, master of all – could not do. Titus was furious. He ordered the room cleared. Once we were alone, he explained, through gritted teeth, the perception of Caesar being scolded by his younger sister – by a *woman* – was damaging. Possibly irreparable. 'I looked like Nero cowering before his mother.'

The next day Titus 'suggested' I visit Baiae for the remainder of the summer. The message was clear: stay away from politics. You are Caesar's sister, not his advisor. It's infuriating, how quickly he forgot my role in exposing Marcellus's plot. He would be dead if it weren't for me.

'Domitilla.'

Lost in thought, I had missed Senator Cocceius Nerva passing below the balcony. He has stopped and is staring up at me.

'The consummate hostess,' he says, 'saying goodbye to every last guest, no matter the hour.'

I force a smile. One does not smile naturally in conversation with Cocceius Nerva.

Nerva's face is dominated by a large, imposing nose. He has cold, black eyes and a tiny, non-existent chin.

Towering over Nerva is the Batavian, the legend of the wild beast hunts. His Tyrrhenian-blue eyes are aimed at the pier.

There was a time when I couldn't stop the Batavian from lavishing attention on me. Earlier this year, an assassin broke into the Imperial palace. He was sent to kill me; and he would have, I think, if not for the Batavian. Somehow the Batavian heard my screams and intervened just in time. My shawl was torn in the attack. The Batavian stole a piece of it and, out of the green silk, fashioned a mask that he wore in the arena. After each of his victories, he would bow in my direction and kiss the mask. All of Rome was gossiping about the love affair between the emperor's daughter and the slave in the hunts. I sent word that I wanted this to stop.

And he did.

There are times I feel a pang of disappointment. His attention was flattering; and it felt different from the senators who saw me as a means to a political end. But it's for the best. If Vespasia was nearly sent away for an affair with a patrician, I cannot imagine Titus's response if I were caught with a famous slave.

'I had meant to talk to you during the party,' Nerva says. 'But I could never track you down.'

That was by design, not chance. I have decided that I do not like Nerva, and have no interest in talking with him. But, as Caesar's sister, I am expected to be polite, especially to senators.

'Well,' I say, 'here I am.'

'I was hoping to ask you about Julius Calenus. Have you had any luck in locating him?'

Julius Calenus is a down-on-his-luck ex-soldier; a tough, capable, no-nonsense sort of man, who was adept at carrying out tasks that require such qualities. Nerva and I both relied on him. For protection, for information, to send a message. Unfortunately, he went missing in May. I felt responsible for Calenus. I wanted to know what became of him. So I have been searching for him, in Rome at first, and now across all of Italy. Nerva was dismissive when I first asked about Calenus. 'Look for him in a canteen,' he said. What, I wonder, has prompted the change of heart?

'No,' I say. 'Julius Calenus remains missing.'

'I understand you have sent your maid across half of Italy asking for him.'

'You are never short of information, are you?'

Nerva's smile is cold. 'Never. But I am willing to share information with you and Caesar, should you ask. Your father relied on me for a time, before he turned to other men. It's of no benefit to your family to cast me aside.'

Nerva was once a close advisor to Father when he first rose to power. But his importance diminished over the years. And now Titus has no use for Nerva. Did Nerva bring up Calenus merely to brag about his spies? Nerva may have spies everywhere, but he clearly has not heard I've been relegated to Imperial hostess. If his aim is to use me to get closer to Titus, he will be disappointed.

I ignore his offer and nod my head at the sea. 'I hope your journey home is smooth.'

Nerva bows. If he's frustrated with my response, he does not show it.

He and the Batavian continue down the pier.

The Batavian does not look back.

My maid Jacasta takes me by the arm. 'That is the last of your guests, Mistress. Let us get you to bed. You need to rest.'

'No,' I say. 'Not yet. I will pray first.'

Our family's shrine is a dark, private room on the eastern wing of the Imperial villa. At this hour, it's empty and silent, save for the muffled cries of gulls that leak through the stone. The main wall is decorated with a painting, centred around a man dressed in a toga, with folds of fabric over his head, like a priest before a sacrifice. The man represents our family's guardian spirit but looks remarkably like Father – by design, I suppose, as painters are wont to please their patron. The figure has Father's stout neck and shoulders, his full cheeks and half-knowing smile. He is holding a knife, red with sacrificial blood. He is surrounded by four Lares, the gods charged with protecting our household. They resemble boys, in short tunics, dancing, smiling, waving a horn overflowing with wine. The paint is fading and streaked with smoke. Beneath there is a shelf of bronze statues of the gods, Hercules, Minerva, and Isis, flanked by two burning oil lamps.

Jacasta and I cover our heads with our shawls before entering. She hands me a cake of spelt to offer up to the gods. I kneel before the altar and reach forward, to place my hand on Minerva –

Then the room – the entire earth – is shaking.

My hand misses its mark and I fall forward. My forearms slam against the floor.

Somewhere in the villa glass shatters; a man screams out in pain.

The earth continues to shake. It feels like a horse-drawn cart traversing a road riddled with pot-holes.

The bronze statues begin to topple.

The oil lamps tip over and smash on the floor; their flames extinguish.

I can feel Jacasta's weight on my shoulders, shielding me, keeping me safe.

And it's over. The earth is quiet again.

The silence is as menacing as the earthquake.

'Are you alright, mistress?' Jacasta asks.

'Fine,' I say, my heart racing. I run my hands over each limb. 'And you?'

'Yes,' she says. 'Unharmed.'

'Check on the staff. Make sure no one was hurt.'

Jacasta, muttering to herself, adds today's earthquake to this year's growing list of evil prodigies.

I grab her wrist. 'We can debate omens another time. Go.'

She nods, then leaves.

I stare up at the painting, at the man that looks like Father but isn't Father. His knowing half-smile remains unchanged.

For the second time today, I wish he were here.

Gaius

19 August

The office of admiral Pliny Secundus, Misenum

Uncle Pliny's office is a mess, though I'm not sure it's any worse than before the earthquake. In the corner, beside an overturned table, Spartacus is cleaning up a bowl of cuttlefish juice, which they use as ink. A black pool has spilled across the floor. Uncle Pliny is standing over Spartacus's shoulder, pointing, giving advice on how best to clean it. Spartacus is waving Uncle Pliny away.

'Tell me, Gaius,' he says as I walk in, without looking up. 'What did you observe before the earth shook?'

'Very little, Uncle,' I say. 'I was in my room, reading.'

'You have no observations about the wind? Or the state of the sea?'

I shake my head.

He scratches his beard. 'The Babylonians believed earthquakes are produced by the influence of the stars. But the evidence is not there. I have theorized that the wind will become pent up in fissures in the earth, and the earth trembling is the wind trying to escape. That is why before an earthquake, the sea and heavens are quiet. Usually. But this morning . . .'

Spartacus looks up and completes his master's thought. 'The sea was choppy. The wind moderate.'

Uncle Pliny shakes his head. 'Thus, my theory remains only that.' He sighs; but, as it often does, his disappointment quickly dissolves. 'Have you checked on your mother?'

'Yes.'

'And?'

'She is fine. Physically.'

Uncle Pliny smiles, knowingly. 'I'm sure she had quite the fright. But her nerves will recover.' He turns his gaze to the floor. 'Ah, bravo, Spartacus. Bravo.'

Spartacus has scooped up and rescued half the spilled ink using two wax tablets, pushing them together to capture the black liquid.

Uncle Pliny asks: 'And what about you, young Gaius? What do you have planned today?'

'I will continue with Livy,' I say, 'taking notes. Now that I know you and Mother are alright.'

Uncle Pliny frowns; he moves towards me. When he's close, within arm's reach, he towers over me, not only vertically, but horizontally, with his burly shoulders and foam white whiskers. 'Every young man should know Livy,' he says. 'A noble endeavour, certainly. But that is a task to better yourself. What do you plan to do for your country? For your emperor?'

'You mean *today*?'

I look past Uncle Pliny at Spartacus, who knows my uncle better than anyone. Spartacus understands my predicament, but he merely shrugs.

To Uncle Pliny, I say, 'Is this about what happened last night?'

Uncle Pliny continues to stare at me. His expression doesn't change.

'I could call on Sinnaces,' I say, reluctantly. This is the last thing I want to do, but there is no point delaying the inevitable. 'I could see what he knows about the attack on Barlaas. Or the expected emissaries from King Pacorus.'

Uncle Pliny smiles. 'A fine idea. Sinnaces is a fiend for the baths, I understand.'

I've seen Sinnaces at the baths before, in the exercise room, trying but never quite succeeding in befriending Domitian and his friends, as they wrestle and fight and carry on.

'Uncle,' I say, timidly, not wanting to disappoint him, but equally dreading the baths. 'You know what the baths are like, with Domitian and his ilk. Maybe I could try a different tack?'

Uncle Pliny points his fat finger at me. 'You think you know hardship? When I was your age, Nero was Princeps. Compared to Nero, Domitian is a philosopher king. You have to deal with a bully. I had to deal with a tyrant.'

What does one say to that?

With a sigh, I say, 'I will do my best.'

'I do not doubt it.'

Since the days of Augustus, all Parthian hostages have had their household provided for by the emperor. A house in Rome, another in Baiae, and a fleet of slaves as befits the station of foreign royalty. They may be barbarian hostages, Uncle Pliny says, but their presence is a great honour for Caesar, a demonstration of his power.

An Imperial slave answers the door. She is an old woman, with a bent back and stringy black hair. Zosimus and I step into the atrium and she leaves to fetch Sinnaces.

I can hear Barlaas's voice somewhere deep in the house, hollering insults at someone.

'Gaius.' Sinnaces looks confused as he walks into the atrium. 'This is unexpected.'

Unexpected and unwelcome, judging by his expression. I suppose Sinnaces and I are more acquaintances than friends.

'I came to see how Barlaas is faring.'

Barlaas's hollering culminates in the sound of glass smashing. I picture some poor soul – his doctor, or maybe a slave – narrowly avoiding a missile-like vase before it smashes against the wall.

'As you can hear,' Sinnaces says, 'Barlaas is . . . himself.'

'And Manlius?'

'He is awake, but a fever has taken hold. He knows not where he is.'

'Will he live?'

Sinnaces shrugs. He does not seem to care for the centurion like Barlaas does. 'The doctors are tending to him. You would have to ask them.'

'And how are you faring?'

'I was not attacked.'

'No, I suppose not.'

We stand awkwardly in silence. Finally, after a regretful gulp, I say, 'Are you going to the baths this afternoon?'

His brow furrows. 'Yes. Why?'

'Well . . . we could walk together.'

'You are going to the baths? In Baiae?' Sinnaces's confusion grows. 'I'm not sure I've ever seen you there before.'

'I normally attend my uncle's personal baths in Misenum, but . . . not today.'

Sinnaces looks horrified. Is arriving with me such an embarrassing proposition? Surely, I have higher social status than a Parthian hostage. Don't I?

I can feel Zosimus shifting his weight from foot to foot; he's wishing he were anywhere but here. It's a sad day when your slave is embarrassed for you.

I think of Uncle Pliny, the bear of a man who is rarely insulted or deterred.

'Well, Sinnaces,' I say, with a smile, 'shall we walk together?'

*

Sinnaces is not as forthcoming as I'd hoped. As we walk to the baths, I press him about the visiting Parthian emissaries. But if he knows anything, he does not give it away.

'And do you know when the emissaries are expected?'

'Your uncle is admiral of the Imperial fleet and a close advisor to the emperor. Shouldn't you know more than I?'

From a neighbouring apartment, liquid of some kind is thrown from the window and it splatters on the street. We glance up to see where it came from, but the windows are all empty.

We step around the puddle and continue along the road. We are not even past the puddle before it starts to evaporate in August's brutal heat.

'I was only curious if you'd heard anything different than I had.'

Sinnaces stares at me as though *I* were the foreigner. 'How would I have heard anything different? Because they are Parthian?'

His incredulity seems genuine. Either he doesn't know anything or the Parthian emissaries weren't involved in the attack on Barlaas.

I press on, not wanting to disappoint Uncle Pliny. 'Do you know who attacked Barlaas?'

Rather than look secretive, Sinnaces looks hurt. 'He would not tell me.'

'I wouldn't take it to heart,' I say. 'He seems a private man.'

Sinnaces changes the subject. 'Who did you have last night?'

'Pardon me?' I can feel my cheeks reddening.

'Your whore. What was her name?'

'I ... Umm ... I didn't realize you attended that establishment as well?'

'I arrived after you. All anyone could talk about was young Gaius, the little lawyer in training, attending the whore house. Out with it. Who was she? Or was it a he?'

I think of Red sitting beside me on the bed, her robe revealing her shoulder.

My cheeks are an inferno.

'I'd prefer not to say.'

Sinnaces shakes his head in frustration. 'Fine. We're almost there anyway.'

After a brief sojourn in the hot room, Sinnaces and I enter the gymnasium. It's as I feared. Domitian and his hangers-on are all here, including Valerius and Catullus. The young men are taking turns wrestling, with a slave acting as referee. A semicircle of spectators has formed. Domitian has somehow procured a seat, like a king holding court.

Sinnaces does not feel as I do. He sees the group of young men, smiles and makes his way over. He speeds ahead of me, as though to distance himself, so it is not obvious we arrived together.

Marcus is here as well. I can feel his eyes on me as I walk across the gymnasium. I was afraid of this. He's going to fixate on me after our encounter last night, when I interrupted him manhandling that poor slave girl.

A match has just ended. Two young men pick themselves off the floor. One looks discouraged, the other as though he's captured Gaul. The referee holds up the latter's hand and half the crowd cheers, the other hollers abuse.

Catullus notices my arrival. 'By Jupiter! Look who has his nose out of a book. Gaius Caecilius, as I live and breathe.' He looks at Domitian to ensure he's got the reaction he is looking for.

I blush. I can feel the tide shifting, as the group recognize an opportunity to follow up on Catullus's gibe.

My heart starts to race. I think of Uncle Pliny. He'll be disappointed. Rather than finding the information he needs, his hapless nephew turned into the butt of a joke. What would the great admiral do? He wouldn't have blushed for a start, and he would have had a quick reply for Catullus, to shut him up, and the smell of blood wouldn't be in the air.

The crowd looks to Domitian to see what their prince will do. Domitian opens his mouth and is about to speak, when something catches his eye. His lips twist into a menacing grin.

I turn to see what saved me. Walking across the gymnasium, fresh from the hot room, is our guide from yesterday, Nine Fingers. He is wearing a loincloth, with a towel casually thrown over his shoulder.

'Oh, Nine Fingers,' Domitian calls out. His voice is sweet as honey.

I remember the joke Nine Fingers made at Domitian's expense yesterday. But our former guide is not alive to his peril: he smiles and makes his way over.

'My Lord,' he says, with a slight bow. 'How is your afternoon faring? Are you wrestling?'

'We are indeed,' Domitian says. 'I wonder, though: are you ready?'

Nine Fingers looks confused. 'Ready for what?'

'For your match, of course.'

Nine Fingers' easy demeanour begins to crack. 'Oh, no thank you, my Lord. I am too old to wrestle.'

'Nonsense, a man like you – a hunter whose spear is never clean – you are a force to reckon with. But, in order to be fair, there must be odds.'

'Odds?' Nine Fingers now looks concerned.

'Yes. Odds. You are after all the great hunter. The man whose spear is never clean. We need to make the fight fair,' Domitian says. 'Three against your one should do it, I think.'

Without warning, Catullus surprises Nine Fingers and tries to get him in a hold. The crowd of boys erupts in cheers. Valerius and another young man grab Nine Fingers's arms and hold them behind his back. Catullus hits Nine Fingers in the belly. It sounds like a wet slap.

'My Lord,' Nine Fingers calls to Domitian, 'what offence did I cause?'

Catullus is now holding a knife. The handle and scabbard are encrusted with rubies. It's a rich man's showpiece, not a soldier's weapon. Still, the blade is made of steel.

I am appalled at this – the violence, the meanness of it all. But what can I do to stop it?

Catullus tests the blade with his thumb. The gesture is meant to intimidate.

'My Lord, please!' Nine Fingers cries out.

'Oh, stop whining,' Valerius says. 'We are only having a bit of fun.'

'Catullus . . .'

The voice comes from somewhere in the crowd. It is calm yet loud and commanding.

'. . . If you take one step closer with that little knife of yours, then I will cut off your hands . . .'

Everyone in the crowd looks about, trying to find who has spoken.

'. . . and feed them to the dogs.'

The crowd slowly parts around Marcus.

Domitian's entourage is suddenly quiet; the gymnasium has become a temple.

The threat is hyperbole. Yet coming from Marcus it feels entirely credible.

The change in Catullus is obvious. He was invincible a moment ago; now he's uncertain. He doesn't move and his mouth is slightly agape. Meekly, trying to save face, he says, 'This is none of your business, Marcus.'

I help Nine Fingers to his feet.

Domitian sighs like an actor in a play. 'And who are you again?'

He knows who Marcus is. It was only yesterday that we were hunting together. He does this sometimes: to show his pre-eminence, he implies everyone else is forgettable.

'Marcus Ulpius Traianus,' Marcus says.

'Ah yes. The Spaniard,' Domitian says. 'What is your interest here, Marcus? This man is only a freedman. A former slave.'

Marcus stands between the man and Domitian. His face is impassive.

'And that leaves him open to your abuse?'

'Yes,' Domitian says, blandly.

'The next time you intend to treat someone like this,' Marcus says, 'because they are a slave, or a former slave, you come tell me. Send your errand boy.' Marcus points at Catullus.

Domitian leans back in his chair. 'Marcus Ulpius.' He smiles. 'Trajan. A name I won't forget. You can be sure of it.'

'I hope not.'

Back in Misenum. Uncle Pliny is at his desk, behind a stack of papyrus. I wasn't able to learn anything from Sinnaces, so the day was a failure. I was certain Uncle Pliny would be disappointed, but he's not. 'Don't expect the world in a day, my boy. It will take time. Keep at it.'

I describe the scene in the gymnasium, still shaken by Domitian's cruelty.

Uncle Pliny shakes his head. 'The gods help us if Domitian is ever emperor.'

'What can be done?' I ask.

'Done? I'm not sure I understand the question. What is it you want, Gaius?'

'Justice.'

'Justice? And what form of justice would you suggest for the emperor's younger brother? Imprisonment? Labour in the mines?'

'Yes.'

Uncle Pliny snorts, derisively. 'I think it imperative you understand how this world works. Poor character and immoral acts do not necessarily lead to punishment. If you expect just punishment for every wrong committed you will live a long and miserable life. Domitian is the emperor's brother. And our emperor cannot see his brother's bad character. Actually, no' – Uncle Pliny twists his carnelian ring – 'that is not correct. Titus blames himself for Domitian's bad character. While Titus was off with their father, waging war in Germany and Palestine, Domitian lived in a hovel in Rome, poor and alone. While Titus learned at his father's feet, and earned his father's love and admiration, Domitian only earned his father's disappointment and scorn. Titus feels responsible for the man his brother became. I doubt he will ever punish Domitian or hold him to account.'

'So Domitian has licence to do as he pleases?'

'Of course! Any man can do as he pleases. Fortune decides what happens to him, not you or me. You need to look at the problem differently. You must understand that victory is not how you conceive it. Domitian's poor character and immoral acts mean he has lost. This is true of any man. And those who act morally, according to their principles, they have won.'

I shake my head. 'That is philosophy, and not the satisfying sort.'

'Domitian is one man,' Uncle Pliny says. 'His time will come. What does it matter if he lives a day or a hundred years? What matters are your principles and whether you follow them.'

'Is that how you lived under Nero?'

'Principles and wine.' Uncle Pliny starts to chuckle. 'Maybe more wine than principles.'

I laugh as well.

'And what do you make of Marcus Ulpius's actions?' Uncle Pliny asks. 'Has your opinion of him changed?'

'Not at all. He is brute.'

'Oh,' Uncle Pliny leans back in his chair. He scratches his beard. I sense that he may have found the favourable ground he was looking for. 'Didn't he rescue the hunter from humiliation or much worse?'

'By coincidence only,' I say. 'He is always looking for a fight. If anything, the incident showed Marcus's pride. His arrogance.'

Uncle Pliny is smiling.

'What?' I say. 'What is so funny?'

'You're jealous, my boy. Green with envy.'

My throat thickens with anger. 'I am not. That's ridiculous.'

Uncle Pliny, still smiling, reaches for my hand across the desk but I pull it away. 'My dear nephew,' he says, 'you have many strengths, not the least of which is an intellect that Zeno himself would envy. But there are areas where you' – he pauses, searching for the right words; words that will not offend – 'fall short. In your mind's eye, at least. Is it possible that you envy Marcus's daring?'

'Never. Marcus is a brute.'

'A brute? Really? I think, if you were to examine your conscience, you would agree that you are exhibiting a lack of empathy, an inability to see the heart of your fellow man.'

I shake my head. I can't believe this. Uncle Pliny is taking Marcus's side.

'Empathy,' Uncle Pliny continues, 'is a vital weapon. Don't forget that. Without it, you'll be no better than Domitian.'

My face is boiling with anger. I stand to go, but Uncle Pliny points at the chair. 'Sit, nephew.' He speaks with authority, but softens his tone. 'Please. Please sit. I did not mean to offend. We will not end our day on this note. Tell me where you are with Livy.'

I take a deep breath; I sit.

Uncle Pliny continues. 'Where are you this time around? Is Hannibal still running wild in Italy?'

Half of an hour later, Spartacus floats into the room. 'Master,' he says, 'Scipio is here to see you.'

Uncle Pliny furrows his brow. 'Scipio the philosopher or Scipio the Spaniard?'

'The Spaniard. A merchant, I believe. I noted the hour, but he says you asked him to call on you the moment he arrived in Baiae.'

'Yes, of course. Bring him in.'

Spartacus leaves and returns with a man that waddles, rather than walks. His head resembles a sea urchin, small and round, with prickly black hair.

'Scipio,' Uncle Pliny says, warmly. He stands and they embrace. Uncle Pliny motions for him to sit.

'I'm days ahead of schedule,' Scipio says. 'Are you impressed?'

'Well, that depends. Do you have useful information?

Scipio nods. 'I do.'

'Then I am impressed.'

'But you may be disappointed. With Ulpius, there remain more questions than answers.'

Uncle Pliny nods. 'One needs the question first before the answer.'

'You are a benevolent patron, as always.'

Scipio looks around the room, expectantly. Reading the Spaniard's mind, Uncle Pliny bellows, 'Wine! Wine for our weary traveller.'

Two slaves rush into the room, one is carrying cups, the other a pitcher of wine. It's only after Scipio has taken a sip that Uncle Pliny prods him to begin. Leaning back in his chair, Uncle Pliny raises his hands, as though he is welcoming the information with a warm embrace. 'Well?'

'The Ulpii are merchants,' Scipio says. 'Olive oil.'

'Are you sure?' Uncle Pliny asks. 'I've heard that before. But I've also heard silk, spices, slaves. One man swore to Apollo the Ulpii made a fortune on cats. Such is the state of disinformation about Lucius Ulpius.'

'I'm certain it was olive oil,' Scipio says. 'I saw their warehouse myself. Lucius – the blind one, your mysterious senator – his father had a respectable business. Small, though. Local. When he died, the two eldest took it over. They expanded. It continues to be based in Spain, in Hispalis, but the family's tentacles have reached across the empire and beyond.'

'And that's where you learned this? In Hispalis?'

'Yes,' Scipio nods, 'I spent nearly three weeks there. Asking questions. Interviewing whomever I could. But the Ulpii are respected.' Scipio rubs his thumb against his index finger together. 'They spend money, you see. On games, gladiators, on public works. Hard to find anyone to say a bad word about them.'

'I see,' Uncle Pliny says. His disappointment is obvious.

'Hard, but not impossible,' Scipio says with a wink. 'There are three brothers, all handsome, the envy of the town. The youngest went to join the legions and the older two, as I said, went to work in the family business. After their father died, they travelled across the empire for years, only rarely returning to Spain, and never for long. So, the Ulpii are as much of a mystery to the people of Hispalis as they are to us.'

Uncle Pliny twists his carnelian ring. 'Interesting.'

'And that was before the pirates,' Scipio adds.

Uncle Pliny snorts in reply. 'You already have my attention, Scipio. No need to work so hard.'

'You'll not rob me of my fun, admiral. Six weeks at sea or on the road, rain or shine, from Hispalis to Misenum. I intend to tell the story the right way.'

Uncle Pliny raises his cup of wine in the air. 'Very well. Please continue. Tell it as you wish.'

'About fifteen years ago, the two eldest brothers were at sea. Some say it happened in the Adriatic, some the Tyrrhenian. But all agree pirates were spotted in the distance. They tried to outrun them. But, inevitably, their slow merchant ship was caught. The two brothers were taken hostage. The pirates intended to ransom them for gold.'

'And did they?'

'Stories differ. Some say the brothers escaped. Others say the ransom was paid. One man claimed Lucius was a sorcerer and, after casting a spell, the pirates sailed the brothers home.'

'I see.' Uncle Pliny is frowning. He does not see much value in fiction. 'And is this how they say Lucius Ulpius lost his eyes? The pirates took them?'

Scipio nods. 'The pirates cut out Lucius's eyes and sent them to the younger brother, to show they were serious.'

'A story I have heard myself,' Uncle Pliny says. 'Here in Italy. Were you able to learn anything new?'

'Most of the people I spoke to told the same story,' Scipio says. 'Olive oil, pirates, ransom. And, like I said, the people of Hispalis admire the family. They don't want all those games and public works the Ulpii pay for to stop.'

Scipio leans forward.

'But not everyone?' Uncle Pliny asks.

'Not everyone. Not if you look hard enough. There is an old man the locals call Vermillion.'

'Vermillion?'

Scipio nods. 'On account of a birth mark, a red splotch across his face. I'd been asking questions for two weeks, up and down Hispalis, paying for information when I needed to. A few times, people said, "You want the real story? Find Vermillion." So I went looking for him. He'd been a slave with the Ulpii for years, and continued on in the house once he was freed. But after the brothers escaped from the pirates, or their ransom was paid, and they returned to Hispalis, Vermillion was dismissed. A misunderstanding, he said. They thought he'd been stealing from the family while the brothers had been missing. But he swears to Jupiter it wasn't true.' Scipio shrugs. 'He's angry about his dismissal. I would be too, if I was living hand to mouth by the river because of a misunderstanding.' He shrugs again. 'He was happy to talk. He said the wool had been pulled over everyone's eyes.'

'And what did this freedman, Vermillion, have to say?' Uncle Pliny asks.

'He said Lucius Ulpius isn't Lucius Ulpius.'

'What does that mean?'

'He says the man who was his master, Lucius Ulpius Traianus, isn't the man who returned five years later.'

'I'm still not following,' Uncle Pliny is frustrated.

'Vermillion said his former master, Lucius Ulpius, left and never returned. A different man came back. He says that with all of the scars the new man had, and his bandaged eyes, and because the real Lucius had been gone for so many years, no one in the Ulpii's house could tell the man claiming to be Lucius wasn't actually Lucius. Or they didn't want to notice. It was probably a great relief to have their patron, or a man claiming to be their patron, home.'

'Let me understand this: the freedman's contention is Lucius Ulpius is an imposter?'

Scipio nods.

'And what? The other brothers are in on it as well?'

'Yes. And likely the nephew too,' Scipio says. 'Vermillion claimed the boy is a fabrication. No one had heard of the younger Marcus Ulpius until the brothers returned.'

'What did the Ulpii have to gain by letting an imposter join their family?'

'The family was rich before, but nothing like they are now. Vermillion says before he was dismissed, he saw chests filled with gold and jewels. He says Lucius Ulpius could buy and sell the emperor himself.'

Uncle Pliny frowns. 'Let's not get carried away. I'm not sure a freedman living by the river is a sound economist.' Uncle Pliny – who cannot stand a mystery – shakes his head. 'But why? Why would one man pretend to be another?'

'Debts is what I figure,' Scipio says.

'Your contention,' Uncle Pliny asks, 'is that Lucius Ulpius had debts that made him pretend to be another man? But didn't you also say he's so wealthy that he could buy and sell the emperor? If he has coffers like that, then why didn't he just pay his debts?'

'I didn't say his debt was one that could be paid with coin, did I? Maybe he got the wrong girl pregnant. Maybe he killed a man. Or two.' Scipio sips his wine. 'Like I said before: with the Ulpii, there are more questions than answers.'

Uncle Pliny leans back in his chair and strokes his beard. 'Who is this man?' he mutters to himself. 'Who is Lucius Ulpius?'

Domitilla

♦

19 August
The Villa Piso, Baiae

A Praetorian announces that Senator Ulpius is here and would like to speak with me.

'Lucius Ulpius?' I ask. Given his blank stare, I add, 'The blind one?'

'Yes, Mistress.'

'Very well.'

I receive Ulpius on the eastern terrace, a half circle of tufa bricks, the colour of a goose egg, with a view of Baiae's man-made lake and, beyond the jetty, the bay itself. It's bordered by a wall, about three-quarters my height. On the other side is a massive saltwater pond, stocked with red mullet and other saltwater delicacies. Dark shadows dart beneath the green murk.

Ulpius is waiting for me, sitting on a bench, leaning onto his staff. His back is bent, his eyes covered by a rag tied around his head. His hair and beard, originally copper-red, seem to grow whiter each time I see him. There is scarring around his eyes – burned skin that is bulging and mottled pink in colour. Senator Ulpius has a strange timeless quality to him. He could, up to a point, claim to be nearly any age. He could be forty or sixty-five. The injuries he's suffered, combined with his many eccentricities and mysterious background – all of this gives Ulpius a sense of mystery. If you ask him about his injuries or his past, the answer, told with an ironic smile, is always shifting, like the ocean breeze.

Lucius Ulpius is an enigma.

Standing beside him are his two freedmen, the Parthian, Cyrus, who is constantly whispering in his patron's ear, and the one-eyed behemoth, Theseus. Theseus is not particularly tall, but is built like the Servian Wall. A patch covers his bad eye. Today he is muddy from the knees down. A faint trail of footprints shows his route across the colonnade.

'Lucius,' I say, walking across the terrace into the cool of the colonnade. 'This is a surprise. I thought you were waiting until Marcellus's trial was finished before quitting Rome.'

'The trial' – Ulpius briefly lifts his bum, as a sign of respect, before flopping back onto his chair – 'or Marcellus himself. And I kept my word. Marcellus is dead.'

His voice is flat. One wonders how much death this man has experienced to describe it so.

'I see,' I say. 'How?'

Slaves swarm the balcony. A chair is placed by Ulpius and, as I take a seat, a table is placed between us; a bowl of plump, fresh olives is dropped on top.

'The trial was going very well,' Ulpius says, 'for the prosecution, that is. Not for Marcellus. Indeed, the outcome was all but certain. But old Marcellus was not one to let others dictate his fate. After the prosecution delivered its closing remarks and court was adjourned for the day, Marcellus went home and took his own life.'

'I'm surprised you are not more' – I pause, looking for the right word – '*pleased*. Didn't you have a grudge against Marcellus? Didn't he try to kill your nephew, Marcus, many years ago?'

Ulpius considers the question and I'm once again struck by how different he is from anyone I have ever met. He lies to me often, I think, particularly about his past. Yet, in other ways, he is an open book. The more time I spend with him, the more

skilled I am at determining what pages of that book he is showing me, and what he is holding back.

'You have it right, my dear. I had a grudge against Marcellus.
But after his death, with my victory finally realized, I feel . . .
indifferent.' He shrugs. 'Have you ever wished a man dead?'

'No. When I was young, I would often curse my sister's name,'
I say with a smile. 'But I have never truly desired another dead.'

He nods. 'Your father was a good man. He kept you away
from Rome for most of your life, away from the tragedies and
intrigue. My father died when I was young. Of dropsy, they say.'

Such insight into Ulpius's own past is unprecedented. The
sense of irony that usually hangs over his every word is momentarily absent. I proceed cautiously. Any wrong move and Ulpius
the sparrow will startle and fly away.

'Fortuna is fickle,' I say. 'My mother, like your father, died
when I was very young.' I reach for an olive. I keep my eyes on
the bowl. 'What was your mother like? Did she keep you safe
like my father kept me safe?'

'My mother inflicted tragedies rather than avoided them.'

'She sounds a formidable woman.'

'She was indeed.' He smiles. 'She ate Caesars whole.'

'Oh,' I say, though I don't understand the point. What interaction could a Spanish provincial have with the Imperial court?

The one-eyed freedman Theseus – who, up until this point, has
stood as still as a statue – clears his throat. Cyrus, the Parthian
freedman, whispers in Ulpius's ear.

Ulpius laughs. 'A figure of speech, of course. I'm not aware
of her eating any emperor alive, though I cannot vouch for her
actions before I was born.'

The sparrow twitches nervously. More questions about his
mother and he'll take to the air. I try a different tack. 'Did
Marcellus take your eyes?'

'No,' Ulpius says, seriously. 'Three men took my eyes. Two are dead. The third has escaped me for many years.'

'Who was he?'

'A soldier.'

'Does he have a name?'

He smiles. 'The Fox.'

I wait for him to say more, to give the man a proper name, but he leaves it at that.

'And you continue to look for him?'

'I do.'

'To kill him?'

He shrugs.

'Why? Marcellus's death has not brought you any peace. Why would this Fox be any different?'

'I promised the gods.' Ulpius pops an olive in his mouth. He chews slowly. 'And habit, I suppose. I've been doing this for so long. What else would I do? Anyway, my revenge has lined up nicely with your family's interests. Has it not?'

'I suppose it has. And now you and Titus are thick as thieves, aren't you?'

'Your brother can recognize a man's talent.'

'Oh? And what is your talent, Senator Ulpius?'

'Scheming.'

I smile. 'Yes, I must admit, you seem quite adept at that. And speaking of my brother, do you know when he is expected in Baiae?'

'Soon,' Ulpius says. 'In time for your wedding.'

I am struck dumb, but only for a moment; then I can't help but laugh. I have been engaged so many times that I have lost count. The only mystery is why Ulpius is telling me and not my own brother. Is this further punishment from Titus? Or is the will of Caesar best revealed through proxy, like the gods reveal theirs through prodigies?

'Another engagement?' I say. 'Is that a good idea? You know what happened with my last engagement?'

'Ah, yes, I had forgotten. I agree, old Marcellus was a poor match. This one is much better.'

'It would have to be. It is easy to improve on calamitous.'

Ulpius laughs. 'Such wit! General Cerialis is a lucky man.'

'Oh, is it Cerialis this time? At least he is closer to my age than Marcellus.'

Ulpius pats my hand. 'It must be difficult,' he says, 'to be imbued, as you are, with the power of the state, to be an extension of the empire itself. At least your new husband is a general. He will be off on campaign more often than not. If you don't like him, you won't have to see him very often.'

'My husband's best quality is that I will not have to see him very often?'

'It could be worse.'

Before I decide whether this is true or not, we are interrupted by the heavy footsteps of a Praetorian entering the terrace.

'Mistress,' he says, 'admiral Secundus is here. He has asked to see you.'

'Of course. See him in.'

Ulpius cannot hide his jealousy. 'Does the admiral call on you often?'

Caesar's closest advisors are always measuring themselves against each other. This quest to outdo the other often extends to Caesar's family.

The admiral sweeps onto the balcony and his massive frame bounds towards us. His secretary and young nephew Gaius Caecilius trail in his wake. Although they are related, Gaius is the physical opposite of his uncle. Gaius is soft-spoken, slight of figure and I'm certain a stiff breeze could knock him over. Pliny, however, is never quiet – even at rest his breathing sounds like a storm at sea – and I'm not sure anything could knock him over. Breeze, man, earthquake, act of god.

'Ah, Ulpius,' Pliny says. He has the same jealous unease Ulpius had a moment ago. 'I thought you were in Rome.'

'An incorrect assumption. Clearly.'

Pliny's smile is disingenuous. 'Do you know, senator, I recently have had men telling me of your wicked ways.'

'Oh? And who was that?'

'Senator Sulpicius for a start,' Pliny says.

There is a visible change in Ulpius: he grows tense, like a cat when a dog enters the room. Sulpicius Peticus is a senator whose brother was put to death under Nero. He ran east after his brother was killed and I haven't heard much of him since.

'Has Sulpicius returned from Syria already?' Ulpius asks. 'A pity for Rome.'

'Syria? You have travelled far, haven't you?' I say. 'And what, Pliny, was Senator Sulpicius's complaint of our dear friend Lucius Ulpius.'

Whatever Sulpicius said, Pliny will not repeat it. That is not Pliny's style. He shakes his head and only says, 'Nothing good. Some of it I almost believed.'

Looking to regain the upper hand, Ulpius says, 'Did you hear that Domitilla here is engaged?'

Pliny's look of surprise is fleeting but unmistakable. He isn't surprised that I'm engaged – this happens as often as the seasons change. Rather, he is surprised – hurt, even – that Ulpius knew before him.

The admiral has countless questions. To whom? When? Is there a dowry? Ulpius answers with obvious glee. Pliny has always been close with Titus, and he has always worked tire-lessly for our family's interests. He is right to feel aggrieved.

But there is only so much bickering between grown men that I can take.

With my right hand, I twirl the earring dangling from my left earlobe – a signal only Jacasta knows. On cue, she swoops in and tells my guests that my presence is required inside.

They both bow as I leave.

Evening, after the sun has set, one of my maids delivers a message. She has been with our family for a few months, I think, though I've forgotten her name. She is young and pretty, except for her one eyebrow – two thick, fuzzy arches that connect above her nose, like the wings of a bird on the horizon.

'There is a man at the north door who requests an audience.'

'Who is it?' I ask.

'His name is Plinius Pinarius. He says that he hails from your father's home town of Reate. He says that he has important information for you. But he says he can only tell you this information, face-to-face. He says that he has been turned away twice before.'

'Pinarius?' I say. 'I don't recall a Pinarius requesting an audience.'

Jacasta growls with frustration. She prefers to have all requests filter through her. 'The Augusta cannot be expected to meet with anyone who calls on her.'

'Yes, of course,' the maid says. 'I only brought it to your attention, Augusta, because of what he said. I thought you should decide whether to speak with him.'

She hesitates, wishing to say more.

'What is it, dear?' I say.

'He appears to be an undertaker.'

Jacasta gasps. 'He shouldn't be in the city walls, let alone meeting with the Augusta. He could pollute our Mistress with the contamination of death.'

I put my hand on Jacasta's arm. She's right, of course, but she is being dramatic. The man is not a leper.

'What is your name?'

'Livia, Mistress,' the maid says.

'Thank you for bringing this to my attention, Livia. But I don't think it would be a good idea for me to meet with this man. This is a trick people often use to meet with me – one I've grown too shrewd to fall for. They say only I can hear what they have to say, but ultimately their information is never of any use.'

Livia bows and is about to leave when something occurs to her. 'Mistress, I should also let you know I believe your brother has arrived.'

'Has he? Strange he hasn't asked to see me.'

Jacasta is glaring at Livia. She is, no doubt, furious that this information was brought to me directly. 'Thank you, Livia. I will not forget what a good servant you are.'

She bows and leaves.

'Let us call on Caesar,' I say to Jacasta. 'Whether he wants me to or not.'

Father rarely came to Baiae. What it has to offer – thermal baths, a beautiful view, leisure, relaxation, debauchery – did not appeal to him. He was at home among his letters, ledgers, official dispatches and proclamations. When he had to be here, he would hole up in the east end of the villa with a legion of clerks and secretaries and freedmen, counting and weighing coins, opening and sealing letters – the machinery of empire working all hours of the night.

This is where we find Titus.

The receiving room is empty save for two Praetorians guarding the entrance to Father's—

No, this is Titus's study now.

I tell the guards to move aside, but they do not obey. One opens the door a crack, slides through and returns with Virgilius, Titus's right-hand man. He has replaced Titus as Prefect of the Praetorian Guard and – possibly – Caesar's attack dog, though he is smiling when he pokes his head through the door.

'Domitilla. How are you?'

'I would like to see my brother.'

'Caesar is quite busy.'

'I am his sister.'

'The burdens of office,' he says, as though that should settle the matter. He adds, 'Caesar has work that he must finish tonight. He knows you will understand.'

Is Titus still angry with me?

Whatever the motivation, I won't stand for this. If I am to spend my days assuaging the hurt feelings of Caesar's advisors and my nights hosting dinner parties, if I am asked to marry a man of Titus's choosing – then I will be damned if I will be sent away like some household servant.

I smile at Virgilius, lean forward and whisper in his ear, 'Tell my brother that I will wait. And tell him that for every quarter of an hour I am left waiting, I will divulge one of his secrets. To these soldiers or to anyone who cares to listen. I will start by listing his mistresses and the names of their clueless husbands.'

Virgilius's eyes widen in alarm, but he otherwise maintains his composure. 'I will convey the message, Mistress.'

When he returns, Virgilius opens the doors wide and extends his arm. 'This way, Mistress.'

The office is nearly as Father left it: a massive desk, inlaid with porphyry, overrun with papyrus; couches arranged in front; a floor of black and white ceramic stones, depicting a massive black one-eyed fish.

Titus is sitting behind the desk, dressed in a purple tunic, like a king. Like Nero. His dog Cleopatra hurries to greet me, her tail swinging back and forth. The room is filled with a dozen freedmen and soldiers.

I crouch and scratch the underside of Cleopatra's chin.

'May we have the room,' Titus says and the army of Imperial administrators files out of the office.

'Congratulations, Sister,' Titus says, when we are alone. 'You have the honour of being the first to blackmail me as Caesar.'

Once seated, I spot something new: a statue of Father. It has the old general's thick neck and receding hairline. The marble of his cuirass and cape are painted red and blue. The paint is fresh, with a sticky sheen. Perhaps Titus misses Father after all, in his own way.

'It is not blackmail,' I say, 'if our interests are aligned.'

'How would my interests be served if you tried to ruin my reputation?'

'There would be no need to,' I say, confidently. 'I knew you would see me once my message was delivered.'

'So it was a bluff?'

'No,' I say. 'A bluff involves a certain level of guessing, of closing one's eyes and hoping a certain outcome is achieved. I knew what you would do.'

Ptolemy, Titus's young secretary, scurries into the room. He pours us each a cup of wine from a decanter. He dilutes mine with seawater, a ratio of nearly one-to-one. To Titus's cup he adds only a drop. As a boy, Titus thought strong men drink strong wine. I'm not sure he ever grew out of the notion.

'You are the one who should apologize,' I continue. 'You refused to speak with me in some silly attempt to appear important. You used your sister as an example. It was arrogant, unnecessary . . . '

Titus puts his hands up in defeat. 'Alright. I'm sorry. But it wasn't meant to send a message. I'm overwhelmed with work. And I thought you were coming to complain about your engagement. But I have learned my lesson. The Augusta will not be deterred. You are Father's daughter, and I should not forget that.'

'Thank you.' I swirl my wine, savouring my brother's mea culpa. 'I am glad to hear it. But you don't give me enough credit, Titus. I am pleased with the match.'

'You are?' Titus looks dubious. He thinks I'm laying a trap.

'Why wouldn't I be? Cerialis is relatively young – he's a child compared to the last man Father paired me with. He's had success as a general, so he must have *some* intelligence. He has his hair. Or most of it, anyway. Is Cerialis pleased with the match?'

Titus laughs. 'Yes. He's no idea he's marrying a blackmailer and bully.'

'Don't warn him,' I say with a smile. 'I want it to be a surprise.'

It is a relief to laugh with Titus, to once again be on the same side.

'I'm glad you approve of the match. Because I haven't left you much time to get used to it. The wedding will take place in two days.'

'So soon?'

'It was part of the agreement with Cerialis. Other men had been embarrassed by the long engagements Father set up, only to have him back out at the last moment, once Father had the concession he was looking for. I promised Cerialis this time it would be different.'

'You're right,' I say, thinking of all that must be done in the meantime. 'That is not much time. Who should I speak with about the arrangements?'

Titus looks confused. He picked the date and the man. What else is there?

'I can see I have some work to do. Will all of our family be in attendance?'

Titus grimaces, as if he's just picked at an open wound; his face hardens. 'Vespasia is not to attend.'

'Titus, she is my sister.'

'She made her choice. Her duty is to the gods now.'

Ptolemy pokes his head through the door and says. 'Admiral Secundus is here, Caesar. He insists on speaking with you.'

'Of course,' Titus says. 'Send him in.'

'Shall I escort your sister back to her room?' Ptolemy asks.

I stare at Titus defiantly.

To avoid any further arguments, or – possibly – because our rift has started to heal, Caesar says, 'No, she may stay.'

Secundus arrives painted with sweat – on his brow, his back, the underside of his belly – and he is breathing heavily. He looks as though he's run to Misenum and back. Virgilius is with him.

Titus stands and hugs Pliny. 'Old friend!' After they have exchanged pleasantries, Titus asks, 'So what is so pressing?'

'I wish to speak to you about the attack on the Parthian hostage Barlaas.'

'Ah, that,' Titus says dismissively. 'Do we need to? Virgilius has already described the incident in detail. It's a strange tale, certainly. But I'm not sure why you are so concerned about it?'

Most would be discouraged by Titus's response. The admiral, however, is not most men. He finds it interesting. 'Strange,' he says, stroking his beard. 'Earlier this year, as Prefect, when charged with keeping your father safe and in power, you would have taken this type of news on the edge of your seat. You'd have gone straight to your father to warn him. You'd have questioned Barlaas yourself. Men would be rounded up. Interrogations would follow. Blood would be spilt. But now that you are emperor . . . You take the news as your father would have. You dismiss it.'

Titus smiles. 'I'm happy to give the admiral new puzzles to solve. But we have more pressing issues than a botched robbery, don't we?'

Pliny and Virgilius look at each other – the exchange is brief but obvious.

'Are you referring to the Sibyl's . . . predictions?' Pliny says, choking on the last word.

Titus ignores Pliny's reference to the Sibyl. 'The False Nero is becoming an embarrassment and possibly dangerous. I have held the Principate for less than two months. My position remains tenuous. Having a man in Parthia, claiming to be Nero – it undermines my position as emperor. It's worse than it was with Father. Father won the civil war; he took the Principate by force. I was handed the throne.' Titus holds up a piece of paper. 'Have you heard the latest? The governor of Bithynia says there are now rumours the False Nero has been welcomed by King Artabanus. Apparently this king has a man in his service, a former hostage here in Rome, who knew Nero. He has confirmed the False Nero's legitimacy.'

Pliny must have heard this already: rather than gape, as I am, he is composed.

'Mere rumours,' Pliny says. 'And Artabanus will not win the war. The boy Pacorus will. And it is Pacorus's emissaries we are to meet tomorrow. Through his emissaries, King Pacorus will recognize you as the legitimate emperor of Rome. In a few months' time, no one will care what a ragtag army in the wilds of Hyrcania said or did.'

'We should send an army east,' Titus says.

Pliny and Virgilius look at each other again. Titus sees it this time.

'What is it?' he says. 'What are you two on about? Do you think I put too much credence in the Sibyl?' He stares at me, to see what my reaction is. Is he embarrassed? This is very unlike my brother the general. 'Out with it,' he says to Pliny. 'Tell me your concerns.'

Pliny is reluctant to speak his mind; he sighs.

Finally, Pliny says, 'It is . . . unwise to act on the ravings of a starved girl in a cave. What you witnessed was a show. A persuasive show, yes; one that has persuaded many Roman leaders for a thousand years. But a show nonetheless. The attack on Barlaas, however, could constitute a real threat to the empire and the Imperial family.'

'Ulpius agrees that we should send an army east,' Titus says.

Virgilius swears under his breath.

'The Spaniard is not to be trusted,' Pliny says. 'He has his own agenda.'

'I disagree,' Titus says. He points at the paper on his desk. 'If you gentlemen will excuse me, I have much to get through.'

'But we need to discuss the reception of the Parthian emissaries tomorrow,' Pliny says.

'Do we?' Titus says. 'Ulpius says I should not receive them on the road. Caesar can meet a king. But to receive the king's subjects – the Parthians will view it as weakness.'

'Ulpius is not shy giving Caesar advice, is he?' Pliny says, under his breath. Then, in a louder voice, he says, 'Who then will receive our guests tomorrow?'

Titus points at me. 'Take Domitilla and Domitian. I will meet the emissaries in the evening, in Puetoli, at the reception.'

The admiral smiles. 'A fine idea.' He stands. 'Until tomorrow evening, Caesar.'

I stand with Pliny and Virgilius but linger after they leave. 'I didn't know you visited the Sibyl?'

Caesar scowls.

'What did she say, Titus?' I ask. 'This is not like you, Titus. To be . . . devout.'

'It was nothing, sister. My aims would be the same, with or without the Sibyl's visions.'

Pliny is waiting for me in the receiving room. Together we walk down the dark hallway, toward the pier. 'You're concerned for my brother?'

Pliny smiles. 'Always.'

'You don't trust Ulpius?'

Pliny shakes his head. 'The man is a liar.'

'Yes,' I say, 'but that doesn't necessarily mean that he can't be trusted. He was instrumental in exposing Marcellus.'

'I disagree.'

We continue down the hallway.

I ask, 'You think Titus has taken the Sibyl's words to heart?'

Pliny shrugs. 'It's odd, isn't it? He cares little about the attack on Barlaas. Yet the False Nero, on the other side of the world, is a threat he cannot countenance. Your brother was never a superstitious man. But perhaps the Sibyl has seduced him.'

At the pier, Pliny's ship is ready to depart. When the captain spots the admiral, he bellows orders.

We stop at the gangplank.

'I wonder,' Pliny says, 'if, as emperor, acknowledging every threat to the Principate would lead one to go mad. Indeed, one could say that happened to Nero, dealing with the hint of a threat as if it were a knife to his throat – he became more violent, the threats more real.'

'Perhaps,' I say.

'Nevertheless,' Pliny says. 'Threats to the Principate cannot be ignored.'

I put my hand on Pliny's shoulder. 'That is why Caesar is lucky to have you. Together we will keep our eyes on the visiting Parthians.'

Pliny nods.

'Get some sleep, admiral,' I say. 'We need you sharp tomorrow.'

'Sleep?' Pliny looks confused.

'Yes, sleep. Or write, exercise by the light of the moon. Whatever it is that you do to stay vital – go do that. There is nothing more to be done in Baiae tonight.'

II

The Emissaries
A.D. 79

Gaius

◆

20 August

A clearing, north of Neapolis

The Parthians enter the field on horseback. The beat of a kettle-drum drowns out the screaming cicadas. There are three emissaries, riding the famous Nisean breed, as beautiful and elegant as their legend claims. Two dark bay and one midnight black. They are accompanied by a dozen soldiers and slaves. Riding in the rear of the column are four Roman soldiers, the Parthian escorts since landing on Italian soil.

This morning, Uncle Pliny and I left Misenum at an ungodly hour. We rendezvoused with Prefect Virgilius, Domitilla, Domitian, and four dozen Praetorians in Baiae. Ulpius was there as well, along with Marcus, and their two freedmen, the one-eyed Theseus and the man always whispering in Ulpius's ear, Cyrus. Senators and knights of varying importance were also invited, and both Parthian hostages. Uncle Pliny and I watched as Barlaas mounted his horse, his doctor pulling at his robes and ranting that Barlaas was too ill to be out of bed, let alone ride a horse. Barlaas looked exhausted, his complexion ashen, but he would not be deterred. He scared the doctor away with a swift kick to the ribs.

As we marched to Neapolis, Uncle Pliny reminded me of the task at hand. 'Remember, Gaius,' he whispered, 'we must watch the Parthians closely.'

We rendezvoused with the emissaries of King Pacorus two miles north of Neapolis.

Now four mounted Parthians are riding out to the middle of the field. They are followed at a distance by the four Roman soldiers who escorted them across Italy. Uncle Pliny, Virgilius, Spartacus and four Praetorians ride to meet the emissaries. Trumpets drown out the dull sound of their horses' hooves on the sun-baked field.

The parties converse. Spartacus waves his hands as he translates.

The sun seems to grow stronger as we wait. My exposed arms and the back of my neck sizzle in the heat. Globs of sweat drip down my back.

'Jupiter's cock!' Domitian whines. 'How much longer is this going to take?'

Domitilla shushes her brother. The young prince brushes his black bangs from his eyes.

The party in the field finally gallops toward us.

Of the four Parthians on horseback, two are tall, bearded and noble in appearance. Brothers, if I had to guess. Twins possibly. The third is shorter than his countrymen, his beard wild and unkempt, with mismatched eyes: one green and one brown. The twins and the man with the strange eyes are wearing the traditional Parthian armour, chain mail, with trousers tucked into riding boots. The fourth Parthian is obviously less important than the other three. He is not wearing armour, but a weathered Median robe that is too large for his small, bony frame. He is quite ugly, with an unhealthy pallor and severe expression – although most of him is hidden under his oversized robes and his green Scythian cap, a pointed hat that covers his head, the back of his neck and ears.

Uncle Pliny introduces the short, dishevelled Parthian first, a sign that he is the one in charge. Arshad is his name. The brothers are Farbod and Farhad. The ugly old man is their translator, Atropates.

Arshad speaks in a strange dialect and Atropates translates it into Latin. 'We are honoured to meet the Augusta and the emperor's brother. Pacorus, the second of his name, our king of kings, sends his greetings.'

'Yes, well. Good,' Domitian says. The young prince is out of his element.

His sister takes naturally to the role. 'I hope your journey was not a difficult one,' she says.

Arshad, via his translator, says, 'may we converse in Greek?'

Domitian shrugs.

'Of course,' Domitilla says.

Arshad's Greek is surprisingly good, though they say the influence of Alexander still lingers in Parthia. He describes their journey to Italy, across land to Syria, through Asia to Thrace, where they proceeded by boat. He complains of the heat, wiping sweat from his brow. 'I do not know how Romans live in this heat. It is like a forge.'

'The only way to escape the heat,' Domitian says, 'is through distraction. Tomorrow there will be an array of games to welcome you to Italy. You will have the true Roman experience.'

Arshad nods. 'Excellent. Will there be gladiators? We cannot leave Rome without seeing gladiators.'

Domitian nods. 'Oh yes. We have planned a spectacle like no other.'

'We have brought a famed fighter from Sogdiana,' Arshad says. He claps his hands and a giant of a man emerges from the emissaries' cortege. He is not any taller than the Parthian twins, but he is wide and muscular. 'This is the Sogdian Spear. One of Parthia's greatest warriors. He wishes to test his skills against a Roman gladiator.'

Domitian is amused. 'You brought your own champion? Bravo.'

'What of this Bat-av-ian?' Arshad asks. He stumbles over the name, spitting out each syllable. 'We have heard his name many times since landing in Italy. He is all the countryside speaks of.'

I can tell Uncle Pliny is frustrated with the frivolous turn the conversation has taken. 'The Batavian's exploits have been in the hunt,' he says, 'not the gladiatorial fights. And we cannot speak for his owner, Senator Nerva.'

'He will not fight our champion?' Arshad asks. He whispers to the brothers and all three of them laugh.

'Oh, I'm sure we could arrange something,' Domitian says.

'Splendid,' Arshad says.

On the march back to Naples, Uncle Pliny and Virgilius talk quietly. I ride beside them, trying to listen over the sound of hooves thumping the well-trodden path.

'I spoke to the Roman soldiers who escorted the Parthians across Italy,' Virgilius says. 'I asked whether any of the Parthians could have been in Baiae two nights ago. Their officer said it wasn't possible. He said they made camp five miles away, and they have had eyes on the Parthians the entire time.'

'Do you believe him?' Uncle Pliny asks.

'I'm not sure,' Virgilius says. 'Something was off about those men.'

'What do you mean *off*?'

'The legate in Ravenna was under orders to send his best men with the emissaries. If those men are his best and brightest . . .' Virgilius shakes his head. 'I will write to their commander to see what I can find out.'

Uncle Pliny nods, then asks me, 'what about you, nephew? Did you notice anything peculiar?'

In all the of the excitement, I'd forgotten to watch Barlaas and Sinnaces. Uncle Pliny sees I'm embarrassed.

'You didn't watch them at all?'

'No,' I say. 'I'm sorry, Uncle.'

'No matter,' he says. 'We will have more opportunities.'

'Did you watch them?' I ask.

'When I could. Barlaas was agitated. He knows these emissaries. I'm certain of it.'

'What do we do now?' I ask.

'We keep our eyes open. And we watch these men like hawks.'

Domitilla

◆

20 August
The subterranean tunnels beneath
the amphitheatre, Puteoli

'Apart from the elephant,' admiral Pliny says, his voice rising above the crackle of torches, 'the lion is the noblest of creatures. Indeed, the lion is the only wild beast to show mercy to its victims.'

His demeanour is that of a philosopher, lecturing for his audience – not just the Parthian emissaries, but also the half-dozen Romans who have come to see the beasts in advance of tomorrow's games, caged beneath the amphitheatre in Puteoli. Behind him, an impatient lion stalks the corners of its cage. Its half-hearted growl echoes along the cavernous web of subterranean tunnels.

Terracotta bricks, stacked like pancakes, pulse in the flickering torchlight. Beyond the nearest arches, to our left and right, the tunnel is a bottomless black.

'Indeed,' Pliny continues, 'the lion will rarely attack women or children.'

Ulpius is bent over his walking staff. 'What do you say, Augusta?' he asks, smiling. 'Do you care to test the admiral's theories? Can we put you in the cage for the night and fetch you in the morning?'

The crowd laughs.

If Pliny is frustrated by Ulpius's joke, he doesn't show it. He waits for me to answer.

'I'm sorry, admiral,' I say, with a smile, 'I would not agree to spend the night with this beast, noble or not.'

'I understand,' Pliny says amiably, 'a reasonable response.' He turns to Ulpius and his tone becomes more combative. 'You doubt the lion's nobility, Senator Ulpius? You deny the unique nature of it's character?'

From further down the black tunnel comes the blare of an elephant's trumpet. The sound is magnified by the narrow tunnels. The noise pushes its way past us, like a heavy wind.

'I doubt everything,' Ulpius says. 'It's a good way to avoid being bitten.'

Pliny remains sanguine. The man could talk of lions the entire evening, with or without Ulpius's heckling. 'When the lion is dying,' Pliny continues, as though Ulpius hadn't interrupted, 'should it have time for reflection, it will often bite the earth and shed a tear at the misery of her fate.'

'No creature likes to die,' Ulpius says. 'We can agree on that at least.'

The Roman world can be divided into those who love the games and those who do not; those who see drama, courage and physical feats, and those who only see a riot of blood, torn flesh and death.

I count myself in the latter group. I cannot stand the games. Tonight, when all we talk of is the gladiatorial fights and beast hunts, and tomorrow, during the games itself, I will bite my tongue and stomach it. Because that is what is expected of me. Because I am Caesar's sister. But it will be a chore.

Tomorrow will begin with the butchering of beautiful, often exotic animals, dragged from the far corners of the empire, to die as entertainment; at midday, convicted criminals will be torn apart by starved animals; and the day will conclude with armoured gladiators fighting – cutting, stabbing, beating, and sometimes murdering each other. All three events are tied together by suffering: a torrent of blood that will flood the sand of the arena floor. The audience will drink until they can barely see the violence they are cheering on.

Those that appreciate the games have a certain giddiness to them the night before. Titus is a good example. The tour of the animal cages is complete and he is engaged in conversation with Arshad, the head Parthian emissary. Titus is smiling. Not a half-smile, or even the hint of a smile, which is normally all he's capable of. But a full grin, ear-to-ear. He is explaining to his Parthian guest the fights, though his audience cannot quite follow its intricacies.

'I don't understand,' Arshad says in Greek. 'The man you cheer for is from Thrace?'

Titus waves his finger. 'No, no. He is a Thracian fighter. It is a *class* of fighter.'

We are staring at one of the gladiators that Senator Sulpicius has brought to the banquet. The gladiators are dressed as they would be for the fights: armour, manacles, swords and shields. The heavily armed fighters are wearing crested helmets made of bronze, with metal grates covering their faces.

Senator Sulpicius looks at his doctore, an older man, with long grey hair, carrying a whip. The doctore calls over a Myrmillo to stand beside the Thracian.

'Generally,' Titus continues, 'the rule is that one combatant is heavily armed, like this Myrmillo and the other is not, like this Thracian. You'll note that the Thracian has a small shield, a short curved sword, or scimitar, greaves and manacles that cover his hands and forearms. In comparison, the Myrmillo has a much larger shield and sword, and a large bronze helmet. Thracians and Myrmillos are often pitted against each other in the arena. The contrast makes for excellent fights.'

Three young elephants, connected by tail and trunk, are led through the party by a boy. Their trainer, an Alexandrian brandishing a stick, brings up the rear. The smiling crowd parts to let them pass.

'The Thracian class requires the greatest skill as a fighter,' Titus continues. 'Thugs are chosen to be the heavily armed fighters. Myrmillos, Gallic and the like. Lanistas pick giant men to hide behind their armour. But to be a Thracian, one must have skill and cunning; he must be strategic. To see a Thracian outlast and out-think a heavily armed and armoured opponent – it is to see humanity at its finest.'

'Wrong, wrong, wrong. Don't listen to him, Arshad.' Domitian is drunk and pronounces the Parthian's name incorrectly. It sounds like Ar-*shit*. He says, 'Myrmillo is the finest class there is.'

'This is who you like,' Arshad asks Domitian, pointing at the heavily armoured gladiator. We are speaking in Greek, but he pronounces the class of gladiator in Latin, as Domitian did, but carefully. 'The Mir-*mill*-oh.'

Domitian nods vigorously. He fails to mention that, in his constant quest to escape his older brother's shadow, he chooses to cheer against whatever class Titus cheers for.

'And how do they see anything with those helmets?' Arshad asks.

'They make due,' Sulpicius says dismissively. 'Some better than others.'

'Perhaps we can let Arshad try on a Myrmillo's helmet?' Titus asks. 'So he can see the world through the eyes of a fighter.' This is the most carefree I have seen Titus since taking the purple. He is enjoying himself.

'Of course, Caesar.' Sulpicius claps his hands together and the Myrmillo removes his helmet. He has a thick brown beard and his long hair is tied into a knot at the back of his head.

'What is your name, gladiator?' Titus asks.

'They call me Minnow,' the gladiator says.

Titus smiles. 'Oh, and how did a large man like you get such a name?'

'Because I'm fast.'

Titus laughs. I can tell he likes the gladiator's bravado. 'Good,' he says, 'I look forward to seeing it.'

Arshad asks, 'And how does one end up as a Mir-*mill*-oh?'

Minnow shrugs. 'I was taken as a slave when I was young. I don't remember how.'

'And do you like being a Mir-*mill*-oh?' Arshad asks.

Minnow is taken aback by the question. I wonder if he's ever even asked himself this before. 'It's better than the mines.'

Ulpius is escorted over to our conversation by the one-eyed Theseus. Sulpicius's lip curls in disgust; his eyes dart back and forth, trying to judge how Caesar reacts to Ulpius. I recall Pliny had said Sulpicius does not care for Ulpius. But surely he's been in Italy long enough to know Ulpius is on the rise.

Sulpicius isn't the only one to react to Ulpius and Theseus's appearance. The gladiator Minnow does as well. But rather than snarl, he grins and possibly winks – though it's so subtle and quick that, after it's done, I'm not sure it even happened.

'Now Caesar,' Ulpius says, 'I must warn you. Don't grow too attached to Sulpicius's gladiators. He has a poor record when it comes to the health of his slaves.'

'Lies,' Sulpicius says. 'This man is a born liar, Caesar. Don't believe a word that comes out of his mouth.'

Titus ignores the exchange. He has no patience for senators bickering, especially in front of foreign emissaries.

Prefect Virgilius stops the conflict from escalating further. He emerges from the crowd, puts his hand on Sulpicius's arm, and gives the senator a steely look.

Titus puts his arm around Arshad's shoulders and steers him away from the arguing senators. 'The next type of gladiator you need to see is the Retarius. They are villains to a man, but their skill – to use only a net and trident – is spellbinding.'

As Titus escorts Arshad away, Virgilius's hand stays on Sulpicius's arm. The senator narrows his wolf-like eyes. 'Take your hand off me, pleb.'

Virgilius's free hand goes to the hilt of his sword.

'Now, gentlemen,' I say, stepping in between them, 'how would it look to our Parthian guests if two of Rome's distinguished citizens drew blood the night before the gladiatorial games? Can't we wait until tomorrow to see a fight?'

Virgilius smiles. 'Of course, Augusta.' His smile fades when he looks at Sulpicius. 'Senator,' he says cordially, before turning to leave.

Sulpicius bows slightly. 'Mistress,' he says and then storms off.

Later in the evening, Titus grabs my arm. 'Come,' he says quietly, 'we both have business to see to before dinner is served.'

For a moment, I had thought Titus meant we were going somewhere alone, discreetly. But Caesar is never wanting for company. Lictors, dressed all in white, Virgilius and a dozen Praetorians follow us out of the party. We walk a short distance to an empty warehouse not far from the docks.

There is a man waiting for us. His face is cloaked in shadow.

'Cerialis,' Titus says.

General Cerialis steps out of the shadow and the two veterans embrace. Titus signals for me to come closer.

'Sister,' Titus says, 'you remember general Cerialis.'

Cerialis bows, respectfully.

'Of course,' I say.

Staring at my fiancé for the first time in many months, I have to admit: Titus could have done worse. While Cerialis does not make my knees weak, he does not repulse me either. He is in his late forties, with a full head of hair, brown with a streak of grey – not from age, but a mark he has borne since he was a child. His face and neck have the look most men his age cannot fight – puffy jowls like a bullfrog – but he is otherwise handsome.

'I have spoken with my sister,' Titus says. 'She is more than agreeable to marriage.'

Cerialis smiles. 'Excellent. And has Caesar chosen a date?'

'Two days from now.'

Cerialis looks like a man about to purchase a slave well below market price.

But maybe that is unfair. There is nothing to be gained by waiting.

We sit and talk about Cerialis's journey to the Bay. We are interrupted by Ptolemy, Caesar's secretary. 'Caesar,' he says, 'Senator Nerva requests an audience.'

'Nerva?' Titus says. 'How did he know we were here?'

'Not much is missed by Nerva,' I say. 'He has spies everywhere.'

Cerialis and I begin to stand, but Titus waves his hand. 'Please stay, Cerialis. I could use your counsel.'

My future husband cannot hide his smile.

Nerva walks into the warehouse with his prow of a nose leading the way. He is accompanied by his secretary and the Batavian.

'Caesar,' Nerva says, 'I trust that I am not disturbing you.'

Nerva's eyes pass over Cerialis. One can feel him calculating the different reasons Caesar, his sister and Cerialis would be meeting like this. I can't think of a second.

'Not at all,' Titus says. 'What do you wish to discuss?'

'I've heard of the promise your brother made to the Parthians, that the Batavian will fight their champion tomorrow. I know Caesar would never force one of his senators to put their property at risk against his will. But I also know Caesar wishes to be a man of his word, even if it was his brother who made the promise.'

Titus nods. 'Go on.'

'I thought that I could sell the Batavian to the Imperial family. And you would be free to put him into the gladiatorial flights, should you choose.'

'You don't mind giving up such a prize?' Titus asks.

Nerva stares at the Batavian. 'He is harder to control than you think. In truth, I would be pleased to be rid of the headache.'

The Batavian shows no sign of understanding what is being discussed.

'And maybe,' Nerva continues, 'such a gesture could help bridge the divide between us? Between Caesar and his loyal subject. And, anyway, I expect Caesar will pay his worth?'

Titus stands and walks to the Batavian. He inspects the Batavian's arms, his chest, his thighs. He slaps the slave's long calves.

He looks the Batavian in the eye and says, 'You've impressed in the hunts. But can you fight?'

The Batavian stares at him blankly.

To Nerva, Titus says, 'Who was the man you used to translate?'

'Calenus,' I say. 'Julius Calenus.'

'That's right,' Titus says. 'Calenus. Where is he?'

Nerva looks at me with his small, dark eyes. 'Gone,' he says.

There is something about the way Nerva says this, the absolute certainty in his voice, that I find unnerving. But the moment is short lived. To Titus, in a lighter tone, he says, 'Missing. He is a troubled veteran. He uses drink to escape that trouble.'

Titus hasn't taken his eyes off the Batavian. 'Then how do you communicate with him?'

'I don't,' Nerva says. 'Not any more. I point in the direction I want him to walk. He knows how the hunts work. The more animals he kills, the more women and drink I give him in return. He is not fluent in Latin or Greek, but he understands more than he lets on.' Nerva shakes his head. 'As I said, the man is stubborn. Whipping will not remedy the problem. It's in his bones.'

'It isn't good to whip a prize chariot horse,' Titus says, still eyeing the Batavian. 'Their love of the fight is what makes them a prize.' He turns to his entourage. 'Is Caesar's estate so paltry he has no one who speaks . . . whatever language this slave speaks.'

Caesar's cortege exchange uncertain glances.

After a frustrated shake of his head, Titus says, 'Where is admiral Secundus? Between the admiral and his secretary, they know nearly every language there is.'

Ptolemy rushes off and returns with Pliny and his secretary. Pliny's forehead is dappled with sweat; he is out of breath, even from such a short journey from the market. The situation is explained. After he exchanges whispers with his secretary, Pliny says, 'Say what you need, Caesar. Spartacus and I should be able to translate.'

Now that Caesar's demands have been met, his frustration ebbs. He says to the Batavian, 'I may buy you from your master.

If I do, I intend to put you in the gladiatorial fights. What do you have to say to that?'

Pliny and his secretary debate how to translate what Titus has said. Once they settle on the right words, Pliny speaks to the Batavian. The Batavian responds in a similar dialect and Pliny laughs. His secretary's eyes are wide with shock.

'He says,' Pliny translates, 'anyone would be a better master than Big Nose.'

Titus smiles. Nerva looks indifferent, but that is nothing new: Nerva would look indifferent with a knife in his belly.

'Can you fight?' Titus asks.

Pliny translates. As the Batavian is responding in his own tongue, he nods his head at the Praetorians.

Pliny smiles. 'He said, "Better than this lot." This lot, I believe, is in reference to your Praetorians.'

'See what I mean,' Nerva says. 'Stubborn.'

Titus bites his lip, thinking. 'Virgilius,' he says to the prefect, 'who is your best man?'

Virgilius looks at his men. 'That would be Goose.'

'Alright,' Titus says to the Batavian, 'let's see if you're right.'

Ptolemy is sent for wooden practice swords and shields. Space is cleared. Titus claps his hands and the men begin to fight. The Praetorian is obviously skilled. He goes on the attack immediately, thrashing at the Batavian's shield. Eventually the Praetorian's wooden blade connects with the Batavian's shoulder. He grimaces.

Despite myself, I emit a sympathetic yelp.

The Batavian glances in my direction. Something crosses his face. Is it embarrassment?

The Batavian changes tactics. He throws his shield to the side. The Praetorian Goose smiles. 'That won't help you, barbarian.'

Goose takes two quick steps forward and thrashes his sword. The Batavian takes two steps, one backward, and one to the side. Goose's wooden blade swipes harmlessly through the air.

The two fighters repeat this sequence again and again. Goose swings his wooden blade and the Batavian dodges them, calmly, elegantly.

Soon – sooner than I'd have thought – Goose is out of breath. He's exhausted. Each swipe of his sword is slower. The Batavian is unfazed, as quick and precise as when the fight began.

Finally, after dodging a harmless swipe by the Praetorian, the Batavian unleashes a torrent of hits with his wooden sword, bringing the blade down onto the Praetorian's shoulders and helmet and arms.

The first seven or so hit the soldier's cuirass and helmet. The final three connect with flesh.

Blood splashes through the air.

The soldier falls backwards. His helmet has fallen off and his head is about to smash against the stone floor, but the Batavian reaches forward and grabs the soldier's sword belt and slowly lowers him to the floor.

A violent flurry followed by a merciful act: the Batavian constantly surprises. It's as though he gets pleasure out of being unpredictable.

The fight is over. I realize I've been gripping the arm of my chair as though my life were in jeopardy.

'Bravo. Bravo,' Titus says clapping his hands together. Two lictors pull the Praetorian to his feet and help him out of the warehouse. 'We have a deal, Nerva. Ptolemy will see to the price.'

I walk arm-in-arm with Titus back to the party. He whispers, 'Dear Sister, I'm never one to believe rumours, especially scandalous rumours aimed at my sister and a famous slave. But you are not helping by sighing whenever said slave's physical well-being is put in jeopardy. Yes?'

My cheeks burn with embarrassment and anger. I know better than to act like that. Titus is right. I can't bring myself to admit what happened. Not aloud. 'I don't know what you're talking about.'

'It's fine,' Titus says. 'Other than me, I don't think anyone saw. Tomorrow, when the Batavian fights, perhaps you should take a walk.'

Gaius

♦

20 August

The Puetoli market

A stage has been set up at one end of the market. A poet stands on at its edge, reciting bawdy poetry. A crowd has gathered to watch. Zosimus and I stand on the periphery. When the crowd laughs uproariously at a punchline that ends with the words, 'Me arse,' we roll our eyes.

Near the edge of the market, I spot the blue-eyed, dark-haired slave that Marcus had been talking to the other night. The girl who spat at me. She's walking toward the warehouses. I feel compelled to catch up to her, to explain myself, to tell her I am sorry that I interfered, that I only meant to help.

'Come along, Zosimus,' I say, pointing at the girl.

I can tell Zosimus disapproves of chasing a slave girl across a party, but he does as I ask.

We hurry after the girl. Rather than head toward the city centre or the pier, as I had expected, she takes a turn into a dark alleyway.

We reach the mouth of the alleyway and I hesitate.

'What's wrong, Master?' Zosimus asks.

Why would the girl head down this dark alleyway? Am I only going to repeat my blunder from before?

My caution has unnerved Zosimus. 'Maybe we should head back to the party?' he says.

I peer around the corner.

Walking towards us is the girl. She is with Senator Sulpicius and his doctore. They are moving quickly. I'm not sure why, but I feel compelled to hide.

'Quick, Zosimus,' I whisper, 'over here.'

I drag Zosimus from the mouth of the alleyway and down behind a crate.

Sulpicius, his doctore, the girl and another slave carrying a torch walk past.

Zosimus is about to say something, but he stops himself. He feels the same urge I do to remain unnoticed.

Sulpicius is grumbling at his doctore. 'Everything is arranged.'

'What do we do in the meantime?'

I can't hear Sulpicius's response.

The three of them walk to the market.

'Should we go back, Master?' Zosimus asks.

Before I can reply, I hear a noise down the alleyway. I am again taken with the instinct not to move. I put my hand on Zosimus's shoulder and put a finger to my lips. 'Shhhh.'

Three more figures emerge from the alleyway. Their distinctive trousers and Median robes give them away, even before I see their faces.

Parthians.

It is Arshad, the leading emissary, and his translator, the man who wears a Scythian cap. They are accompanied by one of their slaves carrying a torch.

Were the Parthians meeting with Sulpicius? The idea seems so strange that I immediately doubt it. I must be wrong. Maybe the Parthians were passing through the alleyway, as Sulpicius had, from some other location.

After I'm certain no one else is going to emerge from the alleyway, I stand and drag Zosimus down the alleyway to investigate. It ends after thirty paces.

'A dead-end,' Zosimus says.

'Yes,' I say, 'which means Sulpicius was meeting with the Parthian emissaries. And it appears that meeting was done in secret.'

I find Uncle Pliny admiring a giraffe, which is being led through the market. He whispers in my ear, 'You missed quite the show, nephew.' He sees my inquisitive expression and adds, 'I will tell you later.'

'I have something to tell you as well.'

'Do you?' He puts his beefy arm around me. 'That's my boy. Never a moment wasted.'

I describe what I saw.

Uncle Pliny frowns. 'The mystery thickens by the day, doesn't it? A Parthian hostage attacked in the streets of Baiae, days before the Parthians' emissaries are expected. And those same emissaries are meeting in secret with Senator Sulpicius, who recently returned from the east. Meanwhile, Senator Ulpius, an imposter, has Caesar's ear, and is pleading for an army to march east, to Parthia. And Sulpicius hates Ulpius.' He shakes his head. 'There are three elements – Ulpius, Parthia and Sulpicius. They seem connected until you look at it closely, and then it all falls apart.'

My head spins trying to make sense of it all. 'What now, Uncle?'

'Every problem has a solution, nephew. We press on until we have the answer.'

Domitilla

21 August
The Villa Piso, Baiae

Morning, the crack of dawn. Pink skies and August's oppressive heat, even at this hour. My flamingo-pink silk stola sticks to my ribs like a wet cloth.

I leave Baiae in a litter, on the shoulders of slaves, hidden behind sheets of translucent white silk. Jacasta sits beside me. We head east, first along the coast, and then across the Herculaneum road, a narrow bridge over the sea, and into the heart of Puteoli. We hear the screech of black-headed gulls and the gentle lapping of waves against the cement pier. Then, once inside the city, we hear the clamour of the crowd, pulsing with the sense of excitement only the games can inspire. Bets are placed. Wine is sold. Near the arena we hear the unmistakable sound of someone being slapped and a fight breaks out.

Soldiers clear space and my litter is lowered to the ground. The silk sheets part; I present my hand and a Praetorian helps me to my feet.

The crowd has been watching the litter expectantly.

'Look, the Augusta!'

'The emperor's sister! Here!'

Soldiers hold their spears perpendicular to the ground and push the throng backward.

As I'm making my way to the gates of the amphitheatre there is a commotion behind me.

Someone calls out my name.

I turn to see two soldiers holding a man by the arms. He is poor, fifty or so, dressed in black, save a bright green cap. His beard is thin and matted.

'Who is he?'

I had asked Jacasta, but it is the maid with the one eyebrow who answers. She emerges from the entourage of servants that followed my litter on foot. 'Mistress,' she says, 'that is the undertaker who begged to speak to you. Plinius Pinarius.'

The undertaker's expression is sad and expectant. It would only take a moment to speak with him. But what kind of precedent would that set?

'Mistress,' Jacasta says, 'we must get you inside.'

'I can speak with him, Mistress,' the maid says.

Jacasta – instantly territorial – is about to take on the task herself, but I wave my hand. *Let her do this.*

The maid goes to the undertaker. Because they are a distance away, with a raucous crowd in between us, I can't hear what is said. The man speaks; the maid nods, says something in reply, and then hands him something. He smiles and nods his head vigorously. He rushes off, disappearing into the crowd.

'That was well done,' I say when the girl comes back. 'What did you say to him?'

'It was nothing, Mistress. He was only after money. I promised him a gold coin if he stayed away. He won't bother you again.'

'Excellent. Well done indeed,' I say. 'What was your name again?'

'Livia, Mistress.'

'Yes, that's right. Livia. I shall not forget it this time.'

Jacasta, still frowning at Livia's success, takes my arm and together we walk under the arched entryway of the arena.

'I'm not sure about her, Mistress,' she says.

'Oh, honestly, Jacasta. You have nothing to worry about. No one will ever replace you.'

Gaius

♦

21 August
The amphitheatre, Puteoli

The amphitheatre is an oval of sand, surrounded by cement seats. Today it will be full, nearly thirty thousand people, cheering and drinking and carrying on as if this is the best day of their lives. And maybe for some it is. Games thrown by Caesar himself, in the flesh, do not happen every day, not for those who live outside the capital.

Uncle Pliny and I make our way to our seats. Overhead rectangular strips of purple canvas – the crowd's protection from August's unforgiving sun – catch and lose the breeze like the sail of a ship.

Uncle Pliny points at Domitian and his entourage. They are not sitting in Caesar's box, but in their own separate section. Sinnaces and Marcus are there as well.

'See what you can find out,' Uncle Pliny says. 'Make sure the Parthian drinks his fill. Loosen his tongue.'

I take a deep breath.

'You'll do fine,' he says, slapping me on the back. 'Soon they will be drunk and ready to brag if asked. But remember: don't drink too much yourself. You need your wits today.'

I nod in agreement and descend the stairs to Domitian's box. At the entrance, two guards put their hands on my shoulders, barring my entry.

Catullus, yells: 'Look! The philosopher Gaius Caecilius is descending from the heavens to join us mortals.'

Nearly to a man, the group smiles; some – those already drunk – laugh.

'You have it wrong, Catullus,' Domitian says, 'young Gaius isn't a philosopher. He is a lawyer. A young Cicero. He's obviously here hunting for a juicy brief.'

Catullus nearly falls off of his chair laughing at a very poor joke. He seems to be the drunkest out of everyone.

'I'm here to watch the fights,' I say. My voice sounds as anaemic as I feel.

'Never,' Catullus says, still doubled over.

'Prove it,' Domitian says. He tosses a skin of wine. 'Drink!'

I stare at Domitian a moment. Surely, he's joking? Domitian, who is several years my senior, is too old to act like this. But no, he and his friends wait for me to drink the skin of wine. Uncle Pliny warned me not to drink. But, equally, he would be disappointed if I couldn't even make it into Domitian's section, let alone get valuable information from Sinnaces.

I pop the cork and squeeze a draught of wine into the back of my mouth.

Domitian and his friends begin to sing; some cheer. And despite not liking a single one of them, their cheers are welcome; they push me past the point I would normally stop, and I keep drinking until the skin is empty. When I'm done I double over, coughing; I nearly retch.

Uncle Pliny will be disappointed. He'll say, 'well, what about the tricks I've shown you?' He's always said: 'Handle your drink or pour it out.' And he means it. Not wanting to alienate his friends or superiors by refusing wine, Uncle Pliny will dispose of it secretly. It doesn't matter where he is – at dinner parties, in the presence of the emperor. He'll pour it out, back into the carafe or into the garden. Sometimes he'll hand it to Spartacus who has to take it down in one clandestine swig. I've left several events where Uncle Pliny is dead sober and Spartacus is nearly unconscious.

But I couldn't do that today, could I? Not with more than a dozen pairs of eyes on me.

Anyway, drinking the entire skin of wine has made me popular – or at least less ridiculed. As I make my way to sit beside Sinnaces, young men slap me on the back. One boy slides out of the way so I can sit beside Sinnaces. The Parthian hostage hands me another skin of wine. He's smiling, and so am I.

It feels good that I am welcome here – this is not a feeling I am accustomed to with my peers.

But this victorious feeling is quashed, or at least diminished, when I see Marcus sitting behind me. He's glaring at me, disapprovingly. Without thinking it through, aided by the wine and the sense of daring it provides, I look back at Marcus and wink. *I don't care what you think.*

I try not to waste any time. As Sinnaces and I sip wine, I barrage him with questions. *Do you know the Parthian emissaries? Their families? Will you speak with them directly? What do you make of the King Pacorus?* But Sinnaces isn't interested in my questions. He, like the other young men around us, points at women in the stands and describes them lewdly, or revels in the blood being spilt in front of us, as the animals we had admired last night are cut down on the arena floor.

These young men seem to have an endless lust for women and blood – though I'm convinced this is only when they are together. If you were to watch them at home, secretly, hiding in their closet or under their bed, they'd be different people: respectful, considerate, less lewd, less violent. But they have an idea of what a man is: dominant, strong, violent; and they all fight to show they are the embodiment of this ideal. That's part of it at least. Domitian also encourages it. He is not a good man.

But because his brother is Caesar, his hangers-on not only forgive his poor qualities, they emulate them.

The morning continues; I keep drinking wine.

I should slow down. But how?

Anyway, I'm handling my wine well enough.

The last animal to be slain is a panther. A hunter – wobbly legs, streaked with blood – sticks his spear into the beast one final time and collapses to the arena's sandy floor.

The crowd roars.

An army of slaves enters the arena. They clear the carcasses, help the bloodied hunter hobble off, and sprinkle sand onto the various lakes and snaking rivulets of blood.

I decide to give Sinnaces one last try before we retire for lunch.

'More wine?' I say, brandishing a skin of wine.

Sinnaces peels his eyes away from the arena. 'Yes, why not.'

I take a sip first. As I'm handing the skin to Sinnaces I say, 'Did you mention you were kin of any of the emissaries?'

Sinnaces drinks; his sip transforms into a glug. When he's finished, he wipes his mouth with the back of his hand.

'Honestly, Gaius. How many questions will you ask me? Sitting beside you feels like a chore.'

A trumpet marks the end of the hunts.

We are halfway through the day and I've accomplished nothing.

What's worse: as I stand to leave, I see that Marcus is watching me. He has a look on his face – an amused, patronizing smile – as though he knows what I was trying to do, and knows I failed.

Failing Uncle Pliny is bad enough. But having Marcus witness the whole affair . . .

Salt in the wound.

Barlaas

21 August

The amphitheatre, Puteoli

The executions start in the sixth hour. Criminals are chained to stakes hammered deep into the sand. They are all afraid, but it manifests in different ways. A few are quietly crying; others are muttering prayers. The largest of the lot urinates and warm piss cascades down his leg, staining the sand.

The Romans are cruel. Truly. In Media, I witnessed men killed in a variety of ways, many I'd like to forget. But never for sport. Even the Butcher, when he maimed or killed – it was for political ends. It had a purpose.

The lower sections of the stadium – where the rich sit – empties during the executions, as the well-to-do lunch outside the stadium. I am invited to lunch with Caesar, but I am in too much pain to move. The wound in my side is healing slowly – if at all – and pain radiates along my flank whenever I move.

I'd hoped to sit in peace, but peace may be something I never have again.

The translator, the one who is calling himself Atropates, sits beside me.

I do not acknowledge him. I keep my eyes focused on the shivering convicts.

'Do you enjoy the executions?' he croaks. He looks older than the last time I saw him, and gaunter – though it's hard to say for certain. Much of him is hidden under his oversized robe and Scythian cap.

'Not particularly,' I say.

He shakes his head. 'No, that's not the Barlaas I remember. The man I knew enjoys the sight of blood. When did you last kill a man?'

'You should know,' I say. 'You were there.'

'Ah,' he says, 'a long time indeed. Is that why you refused us? You're old and out of practice?'

'I didn't refuse you.'

'That's true. But you didn't agree either.'

'And for that you tried to kill me?'

He is unapologetic; he shrugs. 'If you are not with us, then you are against us.'

'I could have given you up,' I say. 'But I didn't.'

'So far,' he says. 'So far.'

A panther, starving and furious, is released. It creeps along the arena floor toward the chained criminals.

'We were surprised to see you when Caesar's men greeted us upon our arrival,' he says. 'We thought you were dead. Farhad swore he opened your belly.'

'He doesn't have much skill with a blade,' I say. 'He's too slow.'

The translator smiles. 'Did you have armour on? Of course you did. You were always careful.'

The panther bounds across the arena and throws itself at a criminal. Its jaws sink into the poor man's shoulder. Warm blood spits into the air. A shrill, deafening scream drowns out the cheers of drunken plebs above us.

I keep my eyes on the arena.

'So,' he says, 'tell me: why didn't you give us up? Why didn't you run to your Roman masters and tell them what happened?'

'I'm not a traitor. I'm not Roman.'

The man being mauled has stopped screaming. The other convicts are watching the animal feast on their former colleague. The sound of flesh tearing is occasionally interrupted by the sound of a bone snapping like a twig.

One criminal cries out for mercy.

'Maybe that's true. But what then? You'll just let us do what we want?'

I nod. 'Manlius is to be left alive.'

He cackles. 'You've grown fond of your centurion. It happens, I suppose.'

'And,' I say, 'keep Sinnaces out of it. It's in your interests as well. He'd only screw up whatever you would ask him to do.'

I pull my eyes away from the carnage in the arena. 'Well?'

He nods. 'If Manlius survives, we will leave him be.'

'And Sinnaces?'

'We will stay away from Sinnaces. But, if you betray us, the centurion and Sinnaces are as good as dead.'

'When will it happen?'

The one who now calls himself Atropates stands. 'Do not attend the wedding. Say you are ill.'

He walks away as another convict screams out in pain.

Domitilla

21 August

Outside the amphitheatre, Puteoli

'You have nothing further to offer?' Ulpius asks.

Slaves mill about with platters of food. Those who had the honour of being invited to Caesar's box are seated around a table, under a purple awning.

We are conversing in Greek.

'There is little to tell,' Arshad says. He is prying open a clam with his knife. He pauses to suck out its juices.

'A man falsely claiming to be the deposed emperor, Nero,' Ulipus says, 'enters your country with an army, joins forces with your king's enemy, and you've no other information to offer?'

'Artabanus is in Hyrcania, on the other side of the desert,' Arshad says. 'We know as much as you.'

'Earlier this year,' Ulpius says, 'Roman forces captured a man serving the False Nero. In Thrace, before he crossed the Euphrates. He said the False Nero's true name is Terentius. He said the man is an ex-Roman soldier.'

'I have heard no such thing,' Arshad says. 'How do you know the man's claims are not true?'

'Wait,' Pliny interjects. 'You aren't suggesting the man *is* Nero?'

Arshad's silence is non-committal.

'Preposterous!' Pliny says. 'The man who cut Caesar's throat is right there.' He points across the square to Epaphroditus, the Imperial Exchequer and one of Nero's former-freedman. Epaphroditus is said to have helped Nero kill himself, after the

Praetorian Guard and the Senate had declared him an enemy of the state.

One of the Parthian brothers says something in a Parthian dialect.

'What was that?' Pliny asks.

Ulpius says, 'He said, "Romans lie."'

Pliny is about to say something, but, before he can, Titus interrupts. 'I have a surprise for you, Arshad.' Titus is peeling a pistachio. He is looking to change the subject – there is nothing to be gained from convincing the Parthian emissaries that Nero is dead. 'The last fight today,' Titus says, 'will be the Batavian.'

Arshad smiles. 'Excellent. And he will fight our champion, the Sogdian Spear?'

'Yes,' Titus says, 'so long as you will agree to have your man adopt a correct role.'

'Oh,' Arshad says, 'I see. He must be a Mir-*mill*-oh?'

'A Myrmillo, or any other heavily armed fighter. The Batavian will enter the fights as a lightly armed fighter. A Thracian.'

Arshad says something to the Parthian brothers in their own language. It sounds different to the language Ulpius deciphered a moment ago. They laugh. Then, to Titus, in Greek, he says, 'Very well. He will be a Mir-*mill*-oh.'

'And shall we bet,' Titus says.

'A bet?' Arshad asks. 'You Romans cannot go an hour without gambling, can you?'

'Don't tell me you're afraid of a friendly bet. It is nothing. If the Batavian wins,' Titus says, 'when you leave, to head back to Parthia, your Nisean horse stays here.'

'You like my horse, do you?' Arshad says. 'You've a good eye. And if I win?'

'What do you want?' Titus asks.

Arshad thinks about the question. His eyes linger on Ptolemy, Titus's secretary, who is standing at Titus's side. 'The boy.'

Arshad seems to enjoy the concern that crosses Titus's face. 'I also have a good eye.'

The colour drains from Ptolemy's cheeks, even in the heat.

'Not the boy,' Titus says. 'Name something else.'

Arshad repeats Titus's words back to him with relish: 'Don't tell me you are afraid of a friendly bet. Anyway, the boy is probably a fraction of the value of my horse.'

Outmanoeuvred, unwilling to show weakness – not to Rome's greatest rival – Titus says, 'Fine. The boy goes to you if your man wins. If the Batavian wins, your horse is mine.'

They shake hands to seal the bet.

On the walk back to the arena after lunch, I ask Ulpius what Arshad said to the Parthian brothers that caused them to laugh, after Titus said their warrior would need to be a heavily armed fighter.

'Did you understand what was said?'

'Yes,' Ulpius says. 'They had been speaking in Aramaic. But when they saw I knew the language, they switched to a Median dialect. But, of course, I know that language as well. Not well, but enough to understand it.'

'And what did they say?'

'He said, "Light or heavily armed, our man can do it all."'

'What does that mean?'

'I think,' Ulpius says, 'their man has more experience in gladiatorial fights than they let on. I think it means your brother has been had.'

The crowd is uniformly drunk by the time the gladiators take to the sand. They are on their feet, cheering euphorically, booing rancorously. Even Pliny's timid nephew is on his feet, booing at the top of his lungs.

I notice something odd while staring at Domitian's section of the arena. Nerva is there, talking with Domitian. He is whispering in his ear. It is difficult to tell from this angle, but it looks like Domitian is smiling. Why would Nerva want to talk with my younger brother? After I refused Nerva's overtures, has he moved on to Domitian? I'm not sure he'll have much luck using Domitian to ingratiate himself to Caesar. Domitian dabbled with politics when Father first took the purple, but Father eventually pushed him to the periphery and Domitian's interests grew more superficial. Now he prefers wine and the games more than the Senate.

The fights are bloody but no one dies. At least not in the arena. One man, a Gallic fighter, is cut in the neck and the wound is terrible. As he was being dragged off, Virgilius said his chances are not good. When he fell, there was a scream from Sulpicius's section of the stadium and a slave girl, with dark hair and brilliant blue eyes, ran down the stadium steps. Virgilius says the fighter was one of Sulpicius's, so the injured gladiator was probably the girl's relation.

The fighter Minnow, whom Titus took a liking to, is the last fight before the Batavian. Titus, for the first time, bets on a Myrmillo. Virgilius takes the bet – though he complains bitterly he cannot afford the amount should he lose.

Minnow has moments where he looks beaten, but Theseus, Ulpius's one-eyed freedman, whispers in my ear, 'he's only working the crowd. He's a good fighter. He has this match.'

'You know the gladiatorial games well?' I ask.

'Theseus is a veteran of the matches,' Ulpius says. 'He won his freedom.'

I look at Theseus. He does have the build of a gladiator. Did he lose his eye in the arena? I wonder what kind of blow could make it through the iron screen of a gladiator's helmet and ruin an eye.

As Theseus predicted, Minnow goes from ostensibly running scared to taking full control of the fight. He knocks his man down with the end of his shield. The defeated fighter's helmet flies off and skitters across the sandy floor of the arena. The crowd loves the drama of it all. Minnow removes his helmet and basks in the crowd's adoration.

Virgilius curses. Titus pats his shoulder. 'You can work off your debt, old man. I need loyal men in my service.'

The defeated gladiator is helped to his feet. He is alive, but shaken. He and Minnow walk to the tunnel. Slaves run into the arena and dump buckets of sand onto pools of blood.

The last fight of the day is the Batavian's. Despite myself, I am nervous. My knuckles are white from gripping my stola bunched at my knees.

'Tell me, Theseus,' I say, 'what chance do you give the Batavian today?'

He shakes his head. 'His chances? Not good. He has never fought as a gladiator. Most men train for months before entering their first match. The Batavian is capable, that is obvious, but the gladiator fights are different from the hunts or fighting a war. You are alone in the arena. The weapons are foreign. The crowd is difficult to ignore or use to your advantage. If the arena was as foreign to his opponent as it is to him, then I'd think the Batavian had a chance.' He shakes his head. 'But the Parthians' man is more experienced, I think.'

Trumpets announce the next fight.

The crowd begins to chant: *Bat*-avian, *Bat*-avian, *Bat*-avian.

The Batavian enters the arena as a Thracian. He is carrying a short, curved sword and a small shield. His right arm is hidden, from shoulder to knuckle, under a silver manacle. Although he is wearing a large, crested helmet, the crowd knows it's the Batavian by the two long strips of green silk from the mask he wore in the beast hunts, which are dangling down his back.

The gates open at the other end of the arena, revealing the Sogdian warrior. He is armoured like a Myrmillo, with a long sword and square shield three-quarters his size. He is not any taller than the Batavian; but where the Batavian is lean, with long muscles, the Parthian champion is thick as a mountain.

The Sogdian doesn't waste any time. He steps forward quickly and methodically. When he is within range he swipes his sword; the Batavian moves quickly, parrying the attack with his shorter blade. Before the Batavian can recover the Sogdian rams his massive shield into the Batavian's face and chest, sending the Batavian backward. But he keeps his footing, stepping backward quickly, to put distance between him and the Sogdian's blade.

The crowd boos.

This engagement is repeated three or four times. The Batavian's movements get slower each time; he seems to be stumbling.

Ptolemy is on his feet, watching over Caesar's shoulder.

'He's tired,' Theseus says. 'And those hits from the shield – he'll be woozy. It will be difficult to concentrate. He will need to go on the offensive or he will lose.'

As if on cue, the Batavian lunges at the Sogdian. He stabs his sword low, near his enemy's belly, and then swings his shield high, at the Sogdian's head. He does this repeatedly and, eventually, lands two solid hits against the Sogdian's helmet.

For a moment, it seems the Batavian could win the fight. The crowd is roaring its approval, chanting for him to kill the Sogdian. Titus is leaning forward, smiling.

And then the tide turns.

While the Batavian's sword arm is outstretched, the Sogdian steps to the side and, using the edge of his shield, hammers the Batavian twice in the head.

The Batavian goes down; his helmet jars loose and skips along the sand.

I gasp and jump to my feet.

The Batavian is face down in the dirt. He is still wearing his green mask.

The crowd is nearly silent, save for a few people muttering, 'No.'

I rush to the balcony's railing.

The Sogdian kicks the Batavian in the ribs and Titus's champion cries out in pain. The Batavian rolls over.

'Mercy,' someone in the crowd calls out.

Behind me, Arshad is laughing.

The Sogdian – knowing the protocol – looks to Caesar's box to see whether the Batavian lives or dies.

Before I can give the signal that the Batavian is to live, Titus – who knows what I am about to do – is at my side; he subtly puts his hand on my arm, to stop me.

Titus signals to let the Batavian live. The crowd cheers; the Sogdian shrugs and throws his sword into the dirt.

The Batavian slowly gets to his feet. He is dizzy and nearly topples over. The two warriors walk closer to Caesar's box and salute. The Sogdian lifts his arm in the air, victorious.

The crowd is quiet.

The Batavian is ashamed; he stares at the arena floor.

I look around Caesar's box but see no sign of Ptolemy.

Arshad says, 'and where did my prize run off to?'

Gaius

◆

21 August

The streets of Puteoli

I feel funny, like I'm not myself. My head is swimming, my legs are soggy overcooked leeks, my bladder – despite my best efforts – is painfully full, and I'm swearing like a centurion.

Also, I'm not sure where I am.

The streets of Puteoli, obviously. But other than that, I've no idea.

We left the arena after the Batavian lost and we were headed . . .

Where again?

Sinnaces and some of the others were ahead of me. Where did they go?

I try calling out, but I'm hoarse from booing all afternoon.

The crowd seethes around me. Shoulders push me one way, then the next.

My head continues to swim.

Did they abandon me on purpose? Are they laughing about it at this very moment, little Gaius having to walk home on his own? I'd thought maybe – just maybe – I'd made friends today. Perhaps not.

I walk down an alleyway and bump into a man who has the look of a soldier, though he is in a civilian's tunic. He barely moves an inch, whereas I stumble backwards three steps. Yet he acts like the aggrieved party.

'Watch it, boy,' he says. He is with two other men. They have the look of off-duty soldiers. Their cheeks are flush from drinking all day.

'Sorry,' I say, bowing my head. 'I didn't see you there.'

'Oh,' he says, 'am I not worthy of your attention?' He steps forward and gives me a push.

'I don't want any trouble,' I say.

'Do you hear that, boys?' one of them says. 'This little shit doesn't want to talk to us. Thinks he's better than us.'

One of them grabs me by the shoulder and delivers a blow to my stomach.

The air flies from my lungs and I'm winded. My knees buckle and I fall to the ground. The pain is immense. I keep gasping, trying to catch my breath. But it feels like I will never breathe again.

'That will teach you.'

One of them looks around and says, 'the boy'd be cheaper than the whore house.'

'He would indeed.'

My heart begins to stroke with fury, like a blacksmith's hammer. From the ground, I say, 'my uncle is Plinius Secundus,' I say, 'admiral of the Misenum fleet.'

'Sure he is, boy.'

They grab me by the feet and drag me deeper into the alleyway.

I'm too terrified to scream. I begin to cry.

Then I hear his voice.

'If all of you run away right now, you might survive today.'

I twist on my back to look behind me. There is someone at the mouth of the alleyway. The sun is behind him so he is cast in shadow.

He steps forward.

I never thought I'd be as happy to see Marcus Ulpius as I am right now.

The three men laugh; their soldierly arrogance heightened by wine.

The two holding me let go and all three men run at Marcus.

I crawl along the ground to the wall of the alleyway and sit up, with my back against the wall. I watch Marcus duck the first soldier's punch, rise and, with a two-foot-long wooden beam that he'd hidden behind his back, crack it against the soldier's ear. The man falls to the ground. Before Marcus can do anything more, the second soldier punches him below the eye. Marcus crumples. The second soldier straddles Marcus and begins to tear at Marcus's tunic.

'You little shit!' the man screams. 'You'll have the same as your friend.'

Marcus flails his arms like a wild animal, trying to protect himself. His tunic rips and is nearly torn off.

I stand and – I can hardly believe it – charge at the man. I land on his back and try to corral his arms.

Once, when I was a boy, a classmate gave me a severe beating at school. Afterwards, as Uncle Pliny held a cold cloth to the various goose eggs on my head, he gave me advice on how to avoid fights and, if it came to it, how to win them. Ever since, I'd excelled at the former, never having to use the latter. Although Uncle Pliny's advice is ten years old, I can hear his voice clear as day. 'If the boy is bigger than you, go for the eyes, Gaius. Poke, claw, scratch, rip, stab. You may find yourself up against thick skulls or granite torsos. But every man's eyes are vulnerable.'

Heeding the admiral's advice, with both hands, I bunch my fingers into fleshy claws and rip at the man's eyes.

He screams in agony and momentarily stops his assault on Marcus.

My victory is short-lived. My scalp burns as another man picks me up by my hair.

I holler in pain.

'Drop the boy.'

The voice doesn't belong to Marcus. It comes from behind me. I cannot turn to see who has said it.

Chaos ensues.

I fall to the ground. I hear blow after blow, and by the time I look up, the only man standing is Marcus's one-eyed freedman, Theseus. At his feet are the three off-duty soldiers. One is unconscious. The other two are wailing in pain. I help Marcus to his feet. He looks like I feel, with the start of a black eye and a bleeding lip. His tunic is torn and a scar on his left shoulder blade catches my eye. It looks like a portion of flesh was ripped off. But the wound is old. The injury happened years ago.

Marcus sees me staring. He turns, so that I can no longer see his old wound.

'Thank you,' I say. 'Thank you both.'

'Thank Marcus's hatred for soldiers,' Theseus says. 'He hates them like Juno hates Aeneas.'

Marcus looks down at the ailing soldiers. 'It's best we leave.'

I wake the next morning to the greatest pain imaginable. It is as though a spear has been pushed through one temple and out the other. My body aches, from head to toe, especially my stomach, where the soldier first struck me.

Zosimus is on a stool muddling a mixture of herbs in a mortar and pestle. I have the sense he has been here all evening, caring for me.

'Your healing time is over.'

The voice belongs to Uncle Pliny.

I turn my head – delicately, because any movement only brings more pain – and see the admiral standing over me. 'I have given you the morning to lick your wounds. Now we talk about what happened yesterday.'

Memories of the afternoon come back, but only in fragments. I recall the fight with the soldiers, and Marcus coming to my rescue, and Theseus coming to both of our rescue. And I recall the terrible scar on Marcus's left shoulder blade. But I've no recollection of what happened after that or how I made it to Misenum.

I sit up and a rush of blood swirls between my temples.

'Uncle,' I say, as I grip my skull, trying to hold the pain at bay. 'Can this possibly wait for later in the day?'

'It cannot,' he says. 'If you're too hungover, it's your own fault. Not mine.'

I grab Zosimus's arm and, with imploring eyes, say, 'Water, Zosimus. Water *please*.'

'First drink this,' he says and hands me a black-ish bubbling concoction. I down the gritty liquid in one gulp.

'Ugh. *Please*, Zosimus. Water.'

My dutiful slave rushes out of the room.

'Let's start with how much you drank yesterday,' Uncle Pliny says.

'I had no choice, Uncle. Domitian wouldn't let me sit with him *unless* I drank a whole skin of wine.'

Uncle Pliny shakes his head. 'This is my fault. I have kept you too sheltered. You've no idea how to handle a bully like Domitian.' He frowns and stares at me for a moment, thinking. 'And how did you fare getting information from Sinnaces?'

I shake my head.

'So this self-harm was for nothing?'

'Not entirely,' I say. I explain what happened after the gladiatorial fights, how I was attacked by soldiers and Marcus came to my aid.

Uncle Pliny twists his carnelian ring. 'Hmmm. That is something, isn't it? Friendships are formed in conflict.' He smiles. 'And it sounds like you handled yourself well, my boy.'

The guilt I feel at having no success with Sinnaces eases. I can't help but smile. 'Thank you, Uncle.'

'And do you now have a different view of Marcus Ulpius?'

Reluctant to concede our earlier debate so easily, I merely shrug. 'Possibly. He did rescue me from a terrible fate.'

Uncle Pliny nods but does not gloat. He is only glad someone else can see the truth of the matter.

'Get dressed,' he says.

'Where are we going?'

'Baiae. To call on the Ulpii.'

An old woman answers the door. She is a little thing, with wispy grey hair tied in a bun on the top of her head.

'Tell your master admiral Secundus is here to see him,' Uncle Pliny says.

The old woman is clearly a house slave. Yet she is bold enough to ignore Uncle Pliny. Instead, she obsesses over me. She stares at my face; she leans in, like a doctor. She opens my right eye with two hands and examines it, as though she were trying to see inside my head. 'On what day were you born?' she asks.

I tell her and she nods gravely.

'And the year?'

'The consulship of Petronius Turpilianus and Caesennius Paetus.'

She is impressed by this. 'Come in, my Lord. Come in.'

She takes us to the tablinum and points at a couch. We sit and she sits beside me.

There is no sign of Ulpius or Marcus, and she hasn't sent any other staff to alert them that we are here. It is as though she thinks we are here for her.

'May I?' she asks, pointing at my hand. I nod and she takes my hand in hers, turns the palm up, and inspects it. 'Ah,' she says, as if something were obvious, 'as I thought.'

Uncle Pliny whispers in my ear. 'A witch, nephew. Pay her no mind.' To the woman, he says, 'Is your master home?'

The old woman keeps staring at my palm. 'My Lord Ulpius is here. As is young Marcus. I will fetch Master Ulpius for you. Maybe the young Lord would like to visit master Marcus in his room?'

Prior to yesterday, I couldn't think of anything more terrifying than surprising Marcus Ulpius in his bedroom. But we are friends now. I think.

Uncle Pliny answers for me. 'Yes, that is a fine idea.'

The old woman bows. 'My Lord. Should you need anything more, my name is Elsie.'

Elsie guides me through the villa. Marcus's room is large, with a bed on one side and a desk in the corner. On one wall, there is a painting of a young man, carrying an older man over his shoulder. It's a dark night, lit by a momentary bolt of lightning. Behind the figures, in the distance, are the fortified walls of a city, surrounded by an army. Aeneas carrying his father away from the walls of Troy.

Marcus is reading. Elsie announces my presence and Marcus looks up.

I had thought I would receive a smile after what we had both been through the day before, but his face is impassive. Our relationship has progressed far less than I'd hoped: we've gone from antagonistic to cold, possibly lukewarm.

'What are you doing here?' he asks.

Elsie interjects. 'Marcus! Master Gaius is a guest in your home. Yes? That is no way to talk to a guest.'

I have never heard anyone talk to Marcus Ulpius like that. Not even his uncle. For a slave to speak so boldly to her master . . . .

It is astonishing. And rather than take offence at her tone, Marcus acknowledges she is correct. He smiles at her; he nods. 'Welcome, Gaius,' he says.

This woman Elsie is truly a force of nature.

She nods, satisfied Marcus has made amends for his poor manners, and leaves.

'What are you reading?' I ask.

'Homer,' he says. '*The Iliad*.'

'Oh,' I say. 'I am surprised. I did not think you were one for the poets.'

A misstep. He is offended. 'Do you have a monopoly on reading?'

'I – um – of course not. I . . .' Inspired by the mural on the wall, I say, 'I prefer Virgil.'

'You would,' he says, bluntly.

'What does that mean?'

'Rich boys like Virgil.'

I want to say: *What are you then*? *You're twice as rich as we are. Three times.*

But Uncle Pliny wouldn't say anything of the kind. He never takes offence. He would only make a note: *Young Marcus Ulpius doesn't see himself as rich*. He would consider that interesting and aim to find out why.

I change the subject: 'Why did your slave want to know my birthday?'

Marcus smiles. 'She is a Chaldean priest in training. Careful, she will tell you your future and life will no longer be a surprise.'

I have found the one topic of conversation Marcus likes to discuss: an old slave named Elsie.

'She said the date was very auspicious.'

Marcus is impressed. 'Did she?' He looks at me as though he is seeing me for the first time. He says, 'she was concerned that I was rude to you. Maybe you'll be a powerful man one day – one I shouldn't be on the wrong side of. Consul, perhaps. Or the emperor.'

I laugh nervously at the absurd suggestion. It's dangerous to speak of anyone other than Titus as the Princeps. 'I have no such desire. I can assure you.'

'Are you sure?' he asks. 'You could have any book you want.'

He is smiling. Was that meant to be a joke?

'That would be an advantage,' I say. 'Is she a witch?'

'She'd like to think so.'

'My uncle is dubious of magic, but I think she unnerved him.' I smile. 'It was a sight to see, my uncle unnerved.'

'Is the admiral here now?'

'Yes, I think he's meeting with your uncle.'

Marcus stands. 'We should go. They may need a referee.'

'Because I don't trust you! I never have.' The voice is Uncle Pliny's. He is nearly yelling, which, for the admiral, is unusual. Uncle Pliny is rarely angry. But Ulpius can get under his skin like no other. 'Despite my distrust for you, your nephew came to the aide of mine yesterday. That counts for something. So, I am giving you a chance to explain yourself.'

Marcus and I enter the tablinum. Uncle Pliny is on the edge of the couch. Ulpius is bent over his walking staff. He is as calm as Uncle Pliny is agitated.

'What is it you want, admiral?' Ulpius says.

'What is your relationship to Sulpicius? What happened between you two?'

'What do you care of Sulpicius?' Ulpius says. 'You've told Caesar the greatest threat to the empire at the moment is the Parthian emissaries – as though three ambassadors were an invading army.'

'You are certain the emissaries are benign? Did you know Gaius saw Sulpicius meeting with two of the Parthian emissaries,' Uncle Pliny says, 'in secret.'

Ulpius frowns; he leans back and whispers with Cyrus, his Parthian freedman.

'My dispute with Sulpicius had nothing to do with Parthia,' Ulpius says. 'I do not know why Sulpicius would meet with the emissaries in secret.'

'Come now, Ulpius,' Uncle Pliny says. 'Tell me what happened between you two. It could help us get to the bottom of whatever it is Sulpicius and the Parthians have planned.'

'Are you proposing we work together?' Ulpius asks.

Uncle Pliny shakes his head. 'No. We will not work together until you tell me the truth.'

'The truth?'

'Yes. The truth. Not just about Sulpicius. I want to know who you are. Who you *really* are.'

Ulpius smiles. 'Truth. Identity. Sticky subjects, are they not?'

'In my experience,' Uncle Pliny says, 'only liars have trouble telling the truth, and only imposters cannot say who they are.'

'You don't think I was born Lucius Ulpius?' Ulpius's smile grows. He is enjoying this.

'I do not.'

'But you don't know. Do you? You only have a suspicion.'

Uncle Pliny's silence confirms Ulpius's theory.

Ulpius's smile grows. 'How many questions has the great admiral left unanswered? Not many I'd wager. How it must nag. But it shouldn't bother you, Pliny. Think of it as a gift, an intellectual challenge worthy of the great admiral.'

Uncle Pliny is furious; his face reddens. He goes on the offensive: 'Why have you been trying to convince Caesar to send an army east, to the False Nero?'

Ulpius shrugs. 'I do not wish to say.'

'You are an imposter.' Uncle Pliny points an accusatory finger at Ulpius. 'One I will unearth.' He stands suddenly. 'Come, Gaius. We are leaving.'

Without waiting for me, he departs, like a boulder rolling down a hill.

'It seems we did a poor job refereeing,' Marcus says. 'Come. I will show you out.'

As we follow Uncle Pliny, curiosity gets the better of me. 'I saw your wound. The one on your shoulder.'

Marcus frowns at my question. Does he think I am prying? He is going to ignore the question, but Elsie, who is walking behind us, clears her throat.

Chastised once again, Marcus sighs and asks, 'and?'

'It looked terribly painful.'

'It was.'

'What happened?'

'A knife,' he says, and leaves it at that.

His scar is clearly not something he wants to discuss. I wonder who would take a knife to Marcus. I would hate to see the man who did it.

III

New to Town
A.D. 75

III

New to Town

A.D. 75

Captain Verecundus

17 October

The Middle Sea, near Selecuia Pieria

I nearly sent them away. They didn't look like they could afford the cost. There were four of them without a single slave. That alone is a sign of poverty. Plus, the eldest is as blind as Polyphemus, once Ulysses is done with him, and looked like a beggar, rags and all. Because it is winter, the sea and winds are treacherous. I thought: wherever they want to go, the price is double. How could a beggar and three hangers-on afford such a price?

But when they handed me a bag of gold coins that was triple the price, I thought: their money is as good as any others'. Isn't it?

'Where to?' I asked.

'Syria,' the blind man said. 'And we leave within the hour.'

We left Pergamum, sailing east. From the start, it was obvious they were a strange group. I thought they were father and son, or possibly uncle and nephew, with two slaves. But they disregarded any sense of hierarchy. The slaves addressed the other two as though they were equals. And all four slept in the rented cabin, rather than the slaves making due on the deck, as any respectable patrician would insist. And they always at, ate together, sometimes laughing but usually bickering over stale bread and fish sauce.

Stranger still: about halfway through our journey, I learned they are chasing a eunuch. A powerful one, with powerful friends. I heard them talking about it. *The eunuch this, the eunuch that. The eunuch would have gone here, he would have gone there.*

I've captained this ship for fifteen years, and I've had all sorts aboard for all sorts of reasons. Four men chasing a powerful eunuch across the empire is, hands down, the oddest yet.

Despite their comradery, they seem on edge. Tempers are short, voices quick to rise. It's as though they've recently escaped some great threat to their lives. They remind me of my crew after narrowly escaping a storm. Not the immediate aftermath, when everyone is happy to be alive. But the next day, when they're exhausted and all they want is to set their feet on solid ground.

It's near the end of our journey that I begin to feel sorry for the boy. His uncle – I eventually learned the blind man is his uncle – expects a great deal of him. I hear the blind man talk about his plans for the boy, as though he were a marble bust an artist was looking to chisel. *My plans. Your future.* The sentiment sends a chill down my spine because it sounds all too familiar.

It was an overbearing father that sent me running from my home before my fourteenth birthday. Father was a freedman. He'd made a fortune in business after earning his freedom. But his servile past barred him from politics. It was a bargain that never set well with Father. He could earn all the money he wanted, but he was precluded from holding any of the power that should come with it. He focused on my political career. My earliest memories are of Father pushing me, nagging me, bullying me to learn the skills he thought I needed to succeed in politics. By fourteen, I'd had enough.

I ran. I left by sea, earning passage on a ship by taking up the oar.

It was my first time aboard a ship and I fell in love with it. Over the course of forty years, I worked my way up, from lowly oarsman to captain.

I watch the boy bicker with his uncle and think: how long until this boy runs? I give it a year.

I caught the boy crying once. It was the middle of the night, and he was alone at the bow. I left him be. I asked one of the freedmen about it. He said the boy lost a friend in Rhodes not too long ago. He left it at that.

Despite myself, I eventually fall victim to the cripple's charm. He makes jokes and they are often funny. Plus, he is knowledge-able about a great deal and can tell a good story. He is, in short, a perfect drinking partner.

At sea you do not shun a drinking partner.

We are near the end of our journey now. Tomorrow, in the morning, we will arrive in the port of Seleucia Pieria. As my blind passenger and I enjoy wine near the stern, my curiosity propels me to ask the questions I've been asking myself for weeks.

'What is your name?'

The blind man smiles. 'I've never told you?'

'No.'

'How strange you waited until now to ask.'

'I thought you'd lie. Why ask for a lie?'

The cripple nods. 'These days I go by the name Ulpius.'

'These days?' I mutter. 'Alright, Ulpius, now that I've gotten you to open up, tell me this: why are you for heading to Syria?'

'Have you not asked this already?'

'You told me you wanted to see the Euphrates before you die, which was obviously a lie.'

'Why? Because I am blind?'

'For a start.' I clasp my hands together, praying for relief. 'Come now, Ulpius. What do you have to lose? There's no harm in telling an old captain sailing the seas the truth. Tell me who you *really* are.'

The blind man ruminates over his cup of wine. He swirls it.

'You want to know the truth?' he asks. 'You want to know who I am?'

'Yes.'

The blind man smiles, mischievously.

'I am Nero Claudius Caesar. Seven years ago I was deposed, betrayed by a cabal of ambitious senators and soldiers. Ever since, I have been chasing the men who did this to me – the men who took my eyes and my throne. I swore an oath to Apollo I would have my revenge.'

I am half-drunk – maybe three-quarters – and slow to react. Finally, I sigh. 'Fine. Don't tell me.'

I fill our cups and we drink until dawn.

Nero

◆

15 December

Antioch, Syria

Marcus screams. The sound is primordial.

The pain must be excruciating.

My stomach turns.

Even though Marcus has drunk enough wine to fell an elephant, and he's biting down on a leather belt to muzzle his screams, as Theseus hacks off a strip of skin the size of my hand, tearing it from Marcus's shoulder blade, the pain is too much.

'Hold him still,' Theseus yells.

'I am,' Doryphorus yells back. 'You need to *hurry*. When Sulpicius's gladiators return, if we don't have this tattoo gone, we're all dead.'

Blind as I am, I can't see what's happening.

I can't see Marcus face down on the table. I can't see Doryphorus, my freedman and actor, holding Marcus in place. I can't see Theseus, my one-eyed freedman and former gladiator, grasping a knife. I can't see the bloody ribbons of flesh being peeled away from Marcus's back.

But I can hear it, in between Marcus's screams, while he pants, gaining the energy to scream again. I can hear the wet, elastic pull of flesh. It sounds like a ram being torn up after the sacrifice – after its throat is cut and its belly is sliced open.

And this is a sacrifice of a kind. In exchange for Marcus's blood and pain, the gods will grant him his freedom.

This is not manumission, though. This is not a slave who has been granted his freedom by his master. This is not a public act, overseen by a magistrate, permissible under the law. Marcus will not be known as a freedman and always bear the mark of his master, and thus never fully escape his servile past.

This is something different entirely. This is Marcus's final step to becoming free – not only of a life of servitude, but free of his past itself.

Today Marcus is born again.

I met Marcus on a blisteringly hot June morning, the night after I had been deposed by my own soldiers, my eyes cut out, and my empire stolen from me. Marcus was a slave in the jail that held me. He was beaten and terrorized by his master. He was a quivering bird about to take flight at the slightest hint of conflict.

But that's not fair, is it? I am trying to tell a good story rather than the truth. Marcus was timid, but he was also brave, in his own way, which, considering his circumstances, made his bravery all the more remarkable.

Three soldiers dragged me to the prison. Their leader, a centurion named Terentius, who Marcus called the Fox because of his red hair and dark beady eyes, ordered Marcus to let me lie on the floor of the prison cell, cold, starving and thirsty. But Marcus's compassion overruled his fear. After the Fox left, Marcus took care of me, nursed me back to health. He brought me water and blankets and whatever else I needed to survive. He brought me hope.

I eventually sent him to find and enlist Doryphorus, my former freedman who was making his living as an actor. The three of us orchestrated my escape. Doryphorus helped me flee, no doubt. But it was Marcus who saved me. Without him, I would be dead.

This is what inspired my decision to raise Marcus up, from slave to something more. Not only because he saved my life, but because I knew – even then, when he was a frightened bird – that there was something beneath his timid exterior.

This was not entirely new for me. I had taken an interest in slaves before. I had taken many under my wing, raised them up from nothing to something. Theseus was once called Spiculus. A gladiator in the arena, owned by a brute who thought Theseus was best used as fodder for other fighters. But I saw potential. He was the size of a mountain, yet moved quickly, and with a certain grace. I purchased Theseus for a song, had him trained, and after he mastered the arena and won his freedom, I made him head of my personal bodyguard.

But Theseus will always be a freedman. I didn't try to do what I am doing with Marcus. It never occurred to me that I could snap my fingers and erase his life of servitude. It wasn't until the opposite happened to me – when, in an evening, I fell from emperor to prisoner – that I understood how utterly unremarkable one's identity is, how malleable it can be.

Rome's hierarchy is as unjust as it is inflexible. At the bottom, there are slaves, the lowest of the low; above the slave, is the freedmen, former slaves; then merchants and tradesmen; then knights; and then the senatorial class. Actors, prostitutes and the like are near the bottom as well, maybe a tick above slave, but definitely below freedmen. Each rung is further divided by wealth and lineage – though *how* these factors are applied differs according to the class in question. Senators consider pedigree – the number of former consuls in one's family, the number of former praetors – more important than wealth. Freedmen, in comparison, couldn't give a fig about who your parents were. The size of one's coffers is how you judge a man's worth.

This system was in place for nearly a thousand years. And then Augustus came, proclaimed himself the pre-eminent citizen – the Princeps – and put himself at the top.

Rome's hierarchy has an ingenious way of perpetuating itself. Each person on a rung does his best to get to the rung above, rather than to topple the whole system. If a slave is unhappy, rather than deciding he will be a senator, snapping his fingers and making it so, he looks to the station above him and does what he can to get there. The goal of a freedman is not to free more slaves, but to own as many slaves as they can afford. Knights work tirelessly so their sons can become senators, senators aspire to become the next emperor, and the emperor works like mad to stay where he is, at the very top.

For much of my life I thumbed my nose at all this. I socialized with slaves and actors and prostitutes. I gave important ministerial posts to a freedman or knight, so long as they were capable or if I enjoyed their company. It was only after I fell – after I was deposed and blinded – that I saw the system for what it is. Power is everything. Political power, financial, physical, sexual. And power only exists if you use it. A slave is a slave – not because it is the will of the gods – but because one man had the opportunity to conquer another.

Once I understood this, it's easy to move beyond it. Why not snap my fingers and make a slave a freeborn citizen?

And my plan was working. One day the little slave who saved my life was Marcus, slave to Creon. The next, he wasn't. He was Marcus Ulpius, heir to an olive oil fortune.

After we escaped Rome, we went looking for Theseus on the island of Sardinia. There I had the good fortune to meet Marcus Ulpius Traianus, a prisoner in the camp. He was a Spanish merchant who had been kidnapped years before. He told us how his brother had died after their merchant ship had been overrun by pirates. His brother, Lucius, had the approximate features that I had: height; weight; hair colour. They had been missing for years. No one knew their fate, that one was alive and being held captive, while the other was dead. The deceased brother offered me an opportunity – a name, a family, a background – to reintegrate into the empire. To be born again, a new man. When we left Sardinia, I was Lucius Ulpius Traianus. Marcus was my nephew, Marcus Ulpius Traianus. The elder Marcus had travelled so broadly, and for so many years, he said people would be surprised if he *didn't* return to Spain with a son.

The plan was perfect.

Or so I thought.

Theseus warned me. He said erasing Marcus's past, rather than manumit him like any other slave, was against nature and the gods would punish us. He raised these concerns constantly during our travels, at night mainly, after Marcus had gone to sleep. I'd pat my old friend on the hand and say, 'Don't forget,Theseus, I was a god. I know what I'm doing.'

I had thought Marcus's transformation was complete.

I was wrong.

It happened a few months ago, when we were in Pergamum. We were on the trail of one of the conspirators in the coup that brought me down, the eunuch Halotus. We learned that we had only missed Halotus by a day or two. He was headed east, to Syria. The night before we were to set out on the road again, Theseus was once more raising his concerns about erasing Marcus's past. He mentioned it for the first time.

The tattoo.

He said, 'And, of course, there is the mark of his master.'

It was night, after a fair bit of wine. I had been reclining on a couch, but Theseus's words made me sit up with a start. 'What?'

'The mark of his master. On his left shoulder blade.'

'What are you talking about?' I demanded. 'I asked Marcus if he bore his master's mark and he said no.'

'Well, it's there. It says CREON, clear as day.'

Often slaves are tattooed with the name of their master, so there is never any doubt about whether a man or woman is chattel or freeborn citizen. I had thought Marcus did not bear any such mark.

'When did you ask him?' Theseus asks.

'Years ago.'

'He was a boy,' Theseus said, 'and the mark is on his back. He probably didn't know or he forgot.'

I was furious – at myself more than anything. 'Why didn't you tell me?'

'I assumed you knew. You're always bragging about having the power of the gods. I thought you considered it within your providence.'

After I'd ranted and raved for a time, I said, 'The tattoo comes off tonight. We'll cut the flesh right off his back.'

But none of us could bring ourselves to do it. We let him sleep, and then we never raised it with Marcus.

Not until today, our first day in Antioch, when it became necessary to cut it off or risk losing everything.

We had left Pergamum and sailed to the port town of Selecuia Pieria, and made our way inland, to Antioch. On the road into the city, under the brutal desert sun, just before the city gates, we came upon two slaves being crucified.

Marcus lingered, staring at the dead slaves.

At the city gates, there were gladiators searching carts and harassing people, but only as they were leaving the city, not entering, so we were left unmolested.

'I wonder what this is all about?' Theseus asked.

'A bad omen,' Doryphorus said.

We made inquiries about accommodations in the forum. While there, Marcus couldn't help himself: he had to know what the poor devils outside the city gates did to deserve crucifixion.

He asked a merchant, but the man did not share Marcus's empathy. 'Their own damned fault,' he said. 'A family of slaves escaped from the home of Senator Sulpicius Peticus. The mother and father were the ones you saw on the crosses.'

It takes me a moment to remember the name. One Sulpicius committed some sort of treason when I was Princeps (I can't recall what, now), and he was put to death. His brother ran to the east, for fear of drawing my ire for being the relation of a traitor. He must have run here, to Syria.

'Why did they run?' Theseus asked.

'Sulpicius was going to make the boy a gladiator. The parents were worried he'd die, so the whole family ran. The city alarm was sounded before they'd gotten very far. The parents were discovered trying to scale the city walls.'

'And the daughter and son are still on the run?' Marcus asked.

'So they say. Senator Sulpicius's gladiators have been searching day and night for his missing slaves.'

'Who is this Senator Sulpicius?' Marcus asked.

'He's one of those Romans who couldn't make it in Rome,' the merchant says, 'so he came to Antioch to be a big fish in a small pond. But he's the richest man in Asia with as many gladiators as the emperor has soldiers. Antioch is *his* town.'

The merchant was clearly wrong: there was little chance Sulpicius had that many gladiators. I knew Sulpicius from my days as emperor. In Rome, he wasn't influential. He was a bully when the opportunity presented itself, uncivilized, and not particularly bright. But he must have power and influence in Antioch if a man in the street is talking about him like this.

'What about the governor?'

'You mean Ceionius Commodus?' the merchant said. 'That man doesn't give a damn about Antioch or Syria. The governor has been here since January and – believe me – he's counting the days until he can go back to Rome. It's not that he's scared of Sulpicius, mind you. He just doesn't give a damn, so long as Sulpicius doesn't give him extra work. He's happy to let Sulpicius do as he pleases.'

Marcus was more concerned about the murdered slaves than the local politics. He said, 'a cruel way to punish a mother and father for trying to protect their children.'

The merchant was indifferent. 'The law is the law. Slaves know what they get if they escape.'

'He's right,' Theseus said – more to me, than the merchant. 'The law is the law.'

'Are you new in town?' the merchant asked. 'Well, I'd expect a visit from Sulpicius's gladiators. They're watching everyone who comes and goes. Just because you made it through the gate, doesn't mean they're done with you.'

That afternoon, after we found an apartment to rent, we all agreed: Marcus's, tattoo had to come off immediately. It was too dangerous to keep it – not with Sulpicius's gladiators going door to door, looking for missing slaves.

Marcus agreed. 'Get that damned man's name off of me.'

And here we are: Marcus screaming; Theseus playing surgeon; and Doryphorus struggling to hold Marcus down.

Then all of a sudden the screaming stops.

'He's passed out,' Theseus says.

'Hurry and finish,' Doryphorus says.

When the tattoo is removed, Theseus treats and dresses the wound.

Marcus is still unconscious when, hours later, we hear a violent knock on the door.

Theseus leaves and, when he returns, I can hear the heavy footsteps of a dozen men and the chaos of our apartment being searched. Cupboards are opened, furniture overturned.

'How many slaves in this house?' a gruff voice asks.

'I am the wrong person to ask,' I say, pointing at my missing eyes. 'We could have one, we could have a hundred.'

There is only angry silence in reply.

Theseus says, 'We have three slaves. All purchased this afternoon. We only arrived in Antioch this morning.'

'Three?' the voice is incredulous. 'For an apartment like this?'

It is a large apartment. He thinks there should be more.

'As I said,' Theseus says, 'we only just arrived.'

Theseus is telling the truth. We freed all of our slaves when we left Rhodes. We have a rule: we do not keep slaves longer than three months. In our experience, three months is about the time it takes before slaves begin to ask questions. Marcus insists we free rather than sell the slaves. It's an expensive habit, but we can afford it.

'What are you looking for?' I ask.

'Escaped slaves,' the one in charge says. 'A boy and a girl. Young. The boy about fourteen, the girl sixteen.'

'You will see that our slaves are all old,' Theseus says.

'What about him?'

'He's pointing at Marcus,' Doryphorus whispers in my ear, 'asleep on a couch.'

'He is not a slave,' Theseus says.

'What happened to him?'

'Wine,' I say. 'It fells man or child. The great equalizer.'

'Wake him up,' the gladiator says.

I hear Theseus rousing Marcus with a light slap on his cheek. Marcus mumbles, half-awake, still drunk.

'Stand up,' the gladiator says.

'What kind of city is this,' I say, 'where a gladiator can accost a freeborn Roman citizen?'

'Just making sure we're not being had, alright old man?'

'I am not old,' I mutter, 'only haggard.'

'Strip him down,' the one in charge says. 'Make sure he doesn't bear Master Sulpicius's mark.'

Fabric tears.

Doryphorus whispers: 'They are inspecting Marcus's arms, his neck.'

'What happened here,' another gladiator says, 'to your back?'

'He fell from a horse today,' I say. 'Treacherous roads into this damned city, aren't there?'

'You're a gladiator?' Theseus asks.

'Yes,' the gladiator in charge says.

'What class?' Theseus asks. He is trying to draw attention away from Marcus, raising the only point of conversation gladiators care about: fighting.

'A Myrmillo,' the gladiator says.

Theseus lets out a derisive snort. 'Myrmillos are all shit.'

I can feel the man's attention shift away from Marcus.

'What do you know of it?'

'I was a gladiator,' Theseus says.

A pause as the man considers Theseus. But no one could look at the one-eyed, wide-shouldered Theseus and picture him doing anything other than fighting.

'What class?'

'Thracian.'

'*Pff*,' the man mocks disgust. 'Thracians are all cheats. And you're too big to be a Thracian.'

I don't need my eyes to know Theseus is smiling. He loves nothing more than surprising his opponent. 'It's all about speed, my friend.'

'You're fast?'

'As an eel.'

'Where'd you fight?'

'Rome.'

The man whistles.

'You don't fight anymore?'

'Retired. Won my freedom.'

'Is that right?' The gladiator is impressed. His tone lightens. 'So you're scared,' he says, teasing Theseus.

'Maybe.' I can hear the smile in Theseus's voice.

There is a sense of community among gladiators, so long as they are not in the arena; a sense of belonging, of knowing your hardships are shared.

'If you fought in Rome,' the gladiator says, 'you must have seen some things.'

'Yes,' Theseus says, 'I'd say so.'

'Maybe you can come to Master Sulpicius's school. I'd like to hear the tricks you learned in Rome.'

'Buy me a cup and we've got a deal.'

'They call me Minnow.'

'Theseus.'

I can hear the two shake hands. It's odd, but the deadliest man I know is also the most personable, the man everyone wants to be friends with.

'Will you be much longer?' Theseus asks.

'Nah,' the gladiator in charge says. 'We're all done here.' He claps his hands and says loudly, 'On to the next house, you fat bastards. We want to finish before sunrise.'

They leave.

Marcus is snoring.

'Fuck me in the ear,' Doryphorus says. 'That was close.'

Yes. Yes it was.

Two days later we celebrate the Saturnalia. The one day a year when Rome's silly hierarchy is inverted; when master serves slave, and slaves have freedom to do as they please. To gamble, to drink.

I refrained from the festivities for most of the day. I do not feel like celebrating. Not with so much left unaccomplished. But in the evening, when it is time to make dinner for our slaves – the three women we purchased when we arrived – Doryphorus drags me from my room.

'Come,' he says. 'You will help with dinner. The gods will be angry if you don't participate.'

'And how will I cook without any eyes?'

'I have it worked out. You will not use your blindness as an excuse.'

Doryphorus guides me into the kitchen. Theseus, who knows how to cook, is directing Marcus, and soon directs me. They have me peel prawns, and I'm soon covered in slime and smell of the sea.

'Marcus,' Theseus says, 'take these pistachios to the tablinum.'

'Finished,' I say, proudly, after I've peeled the last of the prawns. 'Can someone help me wash up?'

'Come,' Doryphorus says, 'the towels are in the next room.' He takes me by the arm and walks me into the adjoining room. 'Wait here,' he says, and I can hear him opening and closing cupboards.

The smell of burning comes from the next room.

'Doryphorus,' Theseus calls from the kitchen. 'I need you. Now.'

Doryphorus puts my hands on the door handles of a cupboard. 'Stay put. I will be back,' he says and rushes off to help Theseus.

Not content to wait, I open the cupboard and start groping for a towel.

'Stop!' Marcus yells from the next room – at who I'm not entirely sure.

I keep searching the cupboard.

'Wait!' Marcus yells – louder this time.

I have been with my companions so many years that I know how each of them walks. I know by the length of their strides and the force with which they place their feet on the floor, whether we are inside or out, in the rain or on sun-baked trails in the woods. Thus, I know the person running toward me is Marcus.

My hand touches the unmistakable curve of a shoulder – a slender, bony shoulder. Unmistakable, but so unexpected – so strange to find a human shoulder in a cupboard – that, with my other free hand, I reach out to find what the shoulder is attached to. My other hand touches flesh – a cheek, the corner of a lip.

Marcus is behind me. He sighs in defeat.

Theseus and Doryphorus barrel into the room.

'And who might you be?' I ask the person hiding in our pantry.

'It's a girl,' Theseus says. 'About sixteen years old.'

'Sulpicius's missing slave girl,' I say. It is not a question, so no one feels the need to answer.

We lock the girl in a bedroom and Marcus tries to explain himself.

The day after we ripped the tattoo off his shoulder blade, hungover and thirsty, he dragged himself to the crossroads for fresh water. He filled a carafe, but was too exhausted to walk back right away. He waited to restore his energy. As he was sipping his water, gathering his strength, he heard a sneeze. There was an overturned amphora nearby, the massive ones used to cart wine and olive oil across the empire. There was a large hole in its side. Marcus poked his head into it and saw the girl, clutching her knees. He knew who she was right away.

'She'll be crucified if she's caught,' he says. 'You saw what they did to her parents.'

'We cannot afford to draw the ire of the most powerful Senator in Asia,' Doryphorus says. 'Every moment she is under our roof, we put ourselves in danger. We haven't come this far to be undone by a slave girl. We must return her to Sulpicius.'

'Coward,' Marcus roars at Doryphorus.

The lightness we felt from the Saturnalia is gone. We are once again on edge – as we've been since we nearly lost Marcus in Rhodes. And that's what this is about, Marcus surviving when his friend Orestes did not. We had tracked the eunuch Halotus to Asia and laid a trap for him in Rhodes, but he was on to us. While we successfully surprised Halotus, members of his cult, Torcus, kidnapped Marcus and his friend. We saved Marcus, but were too late to save his friend from being butchered to some dark German god.

Marcus couldn't save Orestes, but he can save this girl.

'Theseus,' I ask, 'what do you think?'

'I agree with Doryphorus that we must be careful,' he says. 'If this girl's presence in our home is a significant danger to us, we should return her to Sulpicius. But I think the danger has passed. Our home has already been searched. They are unlikely to do so again. And I am now friends with Minnow. We have a man on the inside, so to speak, if they decide to search our home again.'

'What are you proposing?' I say.

'I can only speak for myself,' Theseus says, 'but I do not want to cause the death of a young girl, particularly after Marcus has given his word to protect her. I propose she stays here, so long as she follows certain rules. The most important being that she cannot leave this house. Not ever.'

Is this what I've become? A rooming house for slaves and freedmen, outcasts and runaways?

I nod my head in agreement, but cut Marcus off before he can say thank you. 'This is a tenuous compact,' I say. 'We are agreeing to keep her safe so long as the danger to us is not great. This could change. Do you understand?'

'I understand.'

We unlock the girl.

I explain that we will keep her hidden for the time being, but that could change. She thanks me, though not as ebulliently as I would have expected. Then again, she lost two parents and spent two nights sleeping in an empty amphorae. She must be exhausted and devastated. I'd be in a pissy mood myself.

'What's your name?' I ask.

'Olympias.'

In a matter of days, Olympias has made herself a member of our tribe. Her presence has shown us what we have been lacking. For five years my world smelled of leather, sharpened steel and poorly concealed body odour. Now, seven days after taking her in, walking through our home is like walking through a spring meadow. There are bouquets of flowers in every room – a feat in itself, considering she is not allowed to leave our home. And the incense she burns is fresher, less medicinal than whatever it was we burned before. Twice I have caught Theseus inhaling and then sighing like a lovesick youth. Yesterday, she volunteered to comb my hair and trim my beard – not because she is a slave, but because she has a maternal instinct. She felt sorry for the dishevelled, blind man stalking the halls of our home.

I asked her, 'am I so disgusting?' as she picked something large and sticky from below my chin.

'Not disgusting,' she said, 'but there is room for improvement.'

Doryphorus was sceptical at first, but he is now her greatest advocate. All it took was her to laugh at his jokes, to marvel at his impressions, to clap at his disguises. He is an actor, after all. She even appreciates his most recent creation – a Persian named

Cyrus – and gave him pointers on how to make the disguise more believable.

The greatest impact, though, has been on Marcus. He is happy again, for the first time since Rhodes. We can hear him talking with Olympias – talking! – rather than brooding in silence. I even heard him laugh the other day. She is, I would guess, two years his senior. He tries to impress her with stories of where he's been and what he's seen. But, thankfully, she does not fawn over the rich boy who took her in.

'I lived in Alexandria,' I heard him say last night.

'Oh?'

'Yes. It's beautiful. The most beautiful city in the empire.'

'I heard there are too many snakes. I don't like snakes.'

Marcus conceded the point. 'I don't like snakes either.'

This evening, after Marcus and Olympias have gone to bed, Theseus and I discuss the new woman in our lives. 'You raised Marcus to be a patrician and he falls in love with a slave. He takes after you.'

I nod. 'I suppose so. My first love was a slave. Her name was Acte. Olympias reminds me of her.'

'Because she knew how to handle a lusty teenager?'

I smile. 'In part. Yes.'

Olympias is bright and wonderfully observant. I can feel her eyes on me, trying to figure out the eccentric Senator from Spain. She asks questions, subtly trying to learn more. She must know there is more to us than we care to admit.

Today she watches me cross the room without Doryphorus, using only my staff.

Tap tap tap.

She cannot help herself. 'Master Ulpius . . .'

'I'm not your master, Olympias. You are my guest. Call me Lucius.'

'Sorry, Mas – Sorry, Lucius,' she says, awkwardly. 'Normally, you have your freedman helping you walk. But just now you walked without him, as though you could see.'

'Yes.'

'Well, how did you do it?'

'This is what we have been lacking in our household. Someone who appreciates me. Do you think Theseus or Marcus would admire a blind man walking across the room? No, they are immune to my daily Herculean efforts.'

She laughs. Gods, it is nice to hear a woman laugh.

'Since you asked so nicely, I will tell you.' I motion for her to come sit beside me. I hold my staff in the air. 'You see, my dear, I have become quite proficient with my staff. I can tap it, like this' – I tap it three times on the floor, then sweep it side to side – 'and move it side-to-side. By doing this I can get a sense of my terrain, and I can spot objects blocking my path. It's not only whether the staff hits an object or a rut in the road. It's the sound the staff makes that can give me confidence to move forward or lead me to proceed with caution. When the territory is new, I must move slowly. But I've covered the ground in this apartment so many times already that I have a crude mental map.'

'How impressive,' she says.

'Oh, I'm not sure how impressive it is. You would not congratulate a bird for flapping its wings, rather than it plummeting to its death, would you?'

Olympias is a joy in our household. Yet she is worried about her brother, Alexander. Constantly, unbearably worried. She is grateful for our generosity in taking her in, so she consciously works to ensure we do not share her emotional toll. But her pain is obvious. She cries, nearly every day. She does so in private, but we can hear her through the paper-thin walls.

The best she can hope for is no news at all. If her brother is able to avoid Sulpicius's gladiators and escape the city – this will only be confirmed through endless silence. And if he's successful in escaping Antioch, there is little chance she will ever see him again. If he is discovered, however, judging from Sulpicius's treatment of their parents, the boy has little hope of surviving.

These are the two fates open to her: Alexander lives but she never sees him again; or he is discovered and crucified. Quite the dilemma for a girl of sixteen to deal with, particularly after losing her parents earlier this month.

In the evening, I receive a letter.

'Who is it from?' I ask.

I can hear Doryphorus unspool the papyrus. 'Senator Sulpicius.'

Doryphorus reads the letter. It is an invitation to visit his home.

'What, by Jupiter, does that man hope to gain by inviting me to his home?'

'The invitation is not only for you, but Theseus as well,' Doryphorus says.

'Ah, I see. His gladiator Minnow must have told him about Theseus. He wants the retired Roman gladiator to come teach his provincial hacks how to win.'

'I can go,' Theseus says, 'but is there a risk in you going? Why give him the chance to figure out who you really are?'

'I don't know what you mean, Theseus. I am Lucius Ulpius. Spaniard. King of the olive tree. Besides, I am bored. Don't deny me the chance to escape this small apartment.'

Sulpicius's compound is less than a mile north of the city limits. We arrive at midday.

We are greeted by a slave who takes us to his master. I can hear the empty slap of our shoes on the atrium floor before we traverse a set of stairs; then the sound of wood cracking against wood, and men, growling, shouting, whistling and laughing.

'We are on a balcony,' Doryphorus says, 'overlooking the training ground. Two gladiators are fighting.'

The doctore's whip cracks below.

'You're a cripple?'

The voice is deep and gritty, like pebbles under a wagon's wheel. Sulpicius.

Sulpicius would have met me in Rome. But I am not worried he will recognise me. It was many years ago and I am a shell of my former self. The bits torn of a prawn before Theseus throws it in the pan. People only notice what is missing: my eyes.

'I am blind,' I say to Sulpicius, 'but not a cripple. Lucius Ulpius,' I say and hold out my hand.

He doesn't take it.

'Why would you come to see my fighters if you can't *see* my fighters?'

'I can hear everything you can see,' I say.

'Oh?'

'Try me.'

'Alright,' Sulpicius says. He roars at his doctore below, who in turn barks out instructions to his men.

I can hear feet shuffling on the sandy floor of the training ground as two fighters take their position. Doryphorus stands behind me as we planned. He touches my left elbow and right hip. According to the system we have worked out in advance, left elbow means Gallic class of fighter. Right hip means Hoplomachus class, a rarely used denomination of fighter.

'A Gallic and Hoplomachus,' I say to Sulpicius. 'A strange pairing.'

'How did you know that?' Sulpicius is unable to hide his surprise.

'I told you,' I say, pointing at my right ear. 'I can hear it.'

'A lucky guess.'

'If it were a guess,' I say, 'it would be very lucky indeed.'

A fight begins. Feet slide across sand; idle gladiators whistle and hiss; occasionally there is a tumult of wood cracking against wood.

Doryphorus touches my left elbow, and then taps my right shoulder blade three times.

'An effective defence from your Gallic fighter.'

Someone other than Sulpicius – one of his slaves, perhaps – mumbles, 'Wow,' at my ability to follow the fight.

Doryphorus and I continue this routine. He signals to me every attack and defence, and I describe it to Sulpicius. It's a good trick. But, in truth, not very difficult. There isn't much to gladiatorial fights: attack and defence, attack and defence, until one man is victorious.

'Enough,' Sulpicius says, and the doctore stops the fight.

Sulpicius takes my hand and shakes it. 'Hell of a set of ears you have.'

And like that, Sulpicius and I are friends. He takes us for a tour of his facility. He has gone from one extreme to the other. Before he thought my lack of eyes prevented me from knowing anything about the physical world. Now he thinks – despite my handicap – I see and understand everything. He asks my opinion on mosaics and sculptures, whether the bust of his grandfather looks anything like him. (He even gives me time to run my hands along the marble.) And he asks for my thoughts on gladiatorial diets or how to treat his favourite Myrmillo's wound. Rather than demur, I play the part. 'Yes, I see a likeness, in the chin and the eyes.' 'Oh, it does not look good, but you'll have to ask my man, Theseus, on how to treat it.'

Theseus and Minnow are reunited. We leave them to talk while Sulpicius and I enjoy lunch on the portico looking down on the training ground.

Near the end of our meal, there is a commotion below. Doryphorus leans in and whispers that four visitors are entering the training ground through a set of double doors. Tradesmen, Doryphorus says, by the look of their rough clothing and lack of gold. They have one horse between them. Sitting on top is a boy, about fourteen or so, with his hands tied behind his back and a rag tied across his mouth. 'He looks scared,' Doryphorus whispers.

'Master,' a slave yells from below, 'these men found Alexander.'

'Excellent,' Sulpicius roars as he stands up from our table. 'Where was the damned boy hiding?'

'In our warehouse, senator. We caught him trying to hide in a carriage headed for the port.'

'And his sister? Any sign of her?'

'None. We found only the boy.'

'Bring the little prick forward,' Sulpicius yells.

I hear Alexander's muffled cries of resistance as he's dragged through the sand.

'Let him speak. Remove the rag,' Sulpicius says. 'Where's your sister, boy?'

'I don't know.' Alexander's voice quivers with fear.

'You will tell me, boy,' Sulpicius says. 'I have ways of making people talk.'

I can hear the boy begin to sob.

'He could be telling the truth,' I say to Sulpicius. 'If they were separated, he'd not know where she ran to.'

'Maybe,' Sulpicius says, quietly. Then, louder, to the men below, he says, 'You. What's your name?'

The tradesman below gives his name.

'You'll get your reward today, but your work isn't done. You're to go back to Antioch and let it be known that this boy, Alexander, the runaway slave, will be crucified in the market tomorrow. Unless his sister comes forward. If she does, they both may live.'

After the tradesmen have left, I ask Sulpicius, 'Do you think such a plan will work?'

'You've never seen a brother and sister closer than those two. She'll not want to let any harm come to her brother – not if she can stop it.'

'But why does it matter,' I say, 'one slave girl? I'm sure you have your share of slaves.'

'If one slave escapes successfully, it gives the others hope. They reckon: maybe I could get away as well. Any slave thinks that, it's bad enough. But if you own gladiators, it can be deadly. No slave of mine escapes. No exceptions.'

'Will you kill the boy if his sister doesn't come forward?' I ask. 'I'd heard you planned on training him as a gladiator. He must have some talent. It would be a waste to simply kill him.'

'Like I said: it's policy. I'll have to make an example out of him.'

'You can't trust him!' Marcus grabs my arm, looking for me to support his cause. 'Tell her. Sulpicius can't be trusted.'

Marcus has grown close to Olympias and does not want to lose her. Truth be told: neither do I.

The girl is crying and furious. 'I've already lost my parents. I can't lose Alexander as well.'

'But Sulpicius could kill you,' Marcus says. 'Despite his promise.'

'If he kills Alexander,' Olympias says, 'I might as well be dead.'

'We can rescue your brother,' Marcus says. 'We can break into Sulpicius's compound tonight.'

'You haven't seen it, Marcus,' Theseus says. 'Breaking in would be impossible.'

'This is cowardice.'

'Damn it, Marcus!' I say. 'Enough. You can't always use your fists. You need to think. Haven't you learned this by now?'

Marcus storms off in a fury.

'Please, Master Lucius.' Olympias grabs my arm. 'You have to let me do this. I cannot let my brother die.'

Olympias is a slave. She seeks permission for everything – even when to end her escape.

'It is foolish to make a decision now,' I say. 'What I propose is this: we will escort you to the market tomorrow. We shall keep you in disguise and leave it for you to make the decision whether to come forward or not.'

'Thank you,' Olympias says, and kisses me on the cheek. 'Thank you.'

All of Antioch has turned out for the chance to see a boy crucified. The forum, according to Doryphorus, is overflowing with people. I can feel their numbers, the pulse of the crowd around us, as we push our way into the market. The mood is sombre, but there is a sense of expectation one feels with mobs, of violence bubbling below the surface, like a pot about to boil over.

All four of us have come with Olympias. We are armed, a sword or dagger tucked into our belts – though I would probably cause as much harm to myself as I would to an opponent. Olympias is hidden under a hooded cloak. She intends to come forward, but with her face hidden, she could change her mind until the very last moment.

'There is a platform at the other end of the market,' Doryphorus says. 'Sulpicius is on it, with the boy. And his gladiators. There are dozens of them.'

'And the governor?' I ask.

'He's here as well. He's on a separate dais, with his soldiers.'

'Good. Maybe there will be some semblance of order. How does the governor look?'

'Bored. Like he thinks the sun is too bright and wants to go inside.'

We push our way closer to the platform. Sulpicius's deep baritone carries across the forum. 'It is the sixth hour,' he yells. 'If you are here, Olympias, speak now. Otherwise, true to my word, your brother dies.'

'He's holding a blade to the boy's throat,' Doryphorus whispers.

'Please don't,' Marcus whispers behind me. 'You cannot trust him.'

I can feel Olympias push her way past me.

She calls out, 'Stop! I'm here.'

'She's pulled back her hood,' Doryphorus says. 'Sulpicius has lowered his blade.'

There is a commotion all around us – not just the normal ebb and flow of a crowd. This is something different.

I hear swords being drawn. A man cries out in pain. Someone grabs me by the arms, throws me to the ground and drags me towards the stage. I'm dropped onto the wooden planks of the stage, and I feel cold steel touch my neck.

Another man cries out in pain.

It sounds as though Theseus was not as easily coerced as I was.

Sulpicius yells, 'put down your weapons or your patron dies.'

Silence.

The crowd waits to see whether Theseus will give up his sword.

Sulpicius must have had gladiators hidden in the crowd. He must have known Olympias had help to keep hidden for so long.

'Stop!'

A new voice. One that is annoyed and dripping with authority. Has our governor decided to do more than watch? He may be our only hope to survive Sulpicius's brutality.

A body drops beside me. A distinctive moan tells me it's Doryphorus. 'The governor has come down from his dais,' he says. 'His soldiers have their blades drawn. I'd say there are as many gladiators as there are soldiers. If there's going to be a fight, it will be a bloodbath.'

'Sulpicius,' the governor says, 'what is the meaning of this? I thought you were after one slave, not aiming to start a riot.'

'These men,' Sulpicius says, his voice quaking with rage, 'have made a fool of me. They hid my slave – my *property* – while enjoying my hospitality.'

'Governor Commodus,' I say, still on my knees. 'It is a pleasure to make your acquaintance.' I stand up, slowly. 'I am Senator Lucius Ulpius Traianus. Regretfully, I have not had the chance to meet you prior to these unfortunate developments.'

'A senator? I have never heard of you.'

'No? A shame. We must hold a dear friend of mine in common, given your illustrious posting.' The governor does not appear to have understood my point, so I add, 'I mean the emperor, of course.'

'I see. You count Vespasian Caesar as a friend of yours, do you?'

'Yes, indeed. Our family backed him early in his bid for the Principate. I would invite you to write to Rome to confirm this. Hopefully,' I add, 'my throat is not cut by a wayward gladiator in the meantime.'

More silence as our governor tries to make sense of the blind, talkative senator before him.

'I wonder, governor,' I say, 'as you can see, I do not have the benefit of my eyes, but I have the sense half of Antioch is watching Roman business, which I think we can agree is of no concern to a provincial.'

'Quite,' the governor says.

'And this sun has me terribly parched. Maybe we could find shade and a cup of wine to discuss this like civilized Romans, rather than barbarians, with blades at each other's throat?'

'Yes,' he says again. 'I agree. On all counts. Sulpicius, have your men put their arms away.'

'Two of my gladiators were injured, governor. It looks like one could die. This man's freedman is to blame.'

'When it comes to dead slaves,' the governor says, 'it seems you are in surplus this month. But that is no concern of mine. We will discuss this like gentlemen. Have your gladiators return to your compound. Now.'

There is an uncomfortable moment as Sulpicius weighs his options. If Sulpicius were smart, he would have immediately followed the governor's orders. There is nothing to be gained by going to war with Roman soldiers. But Sulpicius is not smart. Ego drives him, rather than reason. For a moment, I think he will order his gladiators to attack. If he does, there will be an awful amount of blood spilled today.

But Sulpicius proves not altogether a creature of ego and vice.

'You heard the governor,' he says to his men. 'Stand down.'

We reconvene at the governor's residence. We sit in the shade, around a table. The breeze off the river is cool and pleasant. But it does nothing to soothe Sulpicius's anger.

The governor speaks first. 'Well, Sulpicius, why don't you outline what your grievance is. I am not sure I followed it before. Not with so much steel on display.'

'I knew my slave couldn't have stayed hidden for as long as she did without someone's help,' Sulpicius growls. 'I had gladiators in the audience, waiting to see who Olympias arrived with. When she revealed herself, they pounced on the men who'd brought her. Not only did this man, Ulpius' – he spits the word – 'steal my slave for his own, he visited my home, enjoyed my hospitality. The gods know what other humiliations he had planned.'

'Is this true?' the governor asks. He is now mildly interested.

'It is,' I say.

Sulpicius slams his hand on the table.

'But,' I add, 'you cannot fault me for not returning the girl. You see my nephew discovered her and brought her home. But she was not talkative. It was after her parents' death, you see, and she was terribly distraught. And we were new to town and didn't know the particulars of Sulpicius's missing slaves. We thought, *Ah what luck, a new slave*, and put her to work.'

'Liar!'

'Please, Sulpicius,' the governor says, already tired of the conversation, 'let's not argue like children.'

I continue, my voice as innocent as a child's. 'And you cannot fault me, governor, for not seeing the mark naming her as Sulpicius's property – if there is one.' I point at my missing eyes.

The governor laughs. 'Very true. You must agree with that, Sulpicius.'

'Once we realized the girl belonged to Sulpicius, we brought her to the forum this morning. And, governor, let's not forget, we are discussing property – not the constitution! What problem cannot be remedied?'

'Quite right,' the governor says. 'Well, Sulpicius, you have your slave returned to you. What price will compensate you for your trouble?'

'This man and his freedman should be arrested.'

The governor makes a *tsk-tsk* sound, chastising Sulpicius. 'Let's move forward, not backward, shall we. These are Roman citizens and they will not be arrested for a scuffle that ended with a few nicks to your gladiators. Isn't that what gladiators are for? Receiving a few nicks?'

'His gladiators are marvellous, governor,' I say. 'I've had the pleasure of hearing them practise. I am truly sorry for the misunderstanding and the damage caused. To make reparations, I would be prepared to offer one hundred thousand sesterces.'

The governor is impressed. Now he has a sense of my wealth, and he is the sort of man who is impressed by wealth. 'A more than fair offer.'

'Two hundred thousand,' Sulpicius demands.

'For two cut gladiators?' I say.

The price is ludicrous but what do I care? I have a fortune I couldn't spend in one lifetime.

'Fine,' I say. 'An overpayment, but I wish to make amends.'

'Good,' the governor says. He mutters, 'Well done, Sulpicius.'

'And,' I say, 'while we are at it, as I'm making you richer by the hour, how much for the girl and her brother? They've cost you too much trouble to want to hold on to them.' To the governor, I say, 'the girl makes a sort of cinnamon tea I cannot live without.'

The governor chuckles.

'She's not for sale,' Sulpicius says, fuming. 'Neither is her brother.'

'Don't be silly. Everything is for sale,' I say, 'name a price.'

Sulpicius's chair slides back.

I forgot who I was dealing with. Logic and reason are not Sulpicius's allies. I should have appealed to his ego, rather than call him silly.

'If I want more of your money,' Sulpicius says, 'I will take it. You will regret crossing me, Ulpius.'

We listen to Sulpicius's shoes slide along the colonnade.

'Thank you, governor,' I say, trying to hide my frustration at letting Olympias remain in Sulpicius's clutches. 'Your intervention today is most appreciated.'

'Yes,' the governor says, 'we were able to keep it civil in the end, I suppose. But I think you should take Sulpicius's parting remarks as a threat.'

'Oh, I'm sure it was. Nothing I can't handle.'

'I think you will need to leave Antioch and very likely all of Syria for now.'

'Is that really necessary?'

I bite my tongue. The governor is lazy and weak, and rather than disarm Sulpicius for his insubordination and threats, and strip him of his gladiators, he prefers the easier course, to send me away.

'I'm afraid so, Ulpius. I do not do it without regret. I can see I am saying goodbye to one of the few real Romans this side of the Adriatic. But I cannot afford more unrest in the area. I need to focus on the rumours coming in from Thrace.'

'Oh,' I say. 'What rumours?'

The governor leans in. He reeks of garlic and rosemary. 'Rumours of a man claiming to be Nero himself,' he says softly.

My heart stops.

'Another False Nero?'

The governor laughs. 'You are a true friend of Vespasian, emphasising the *false-ness* of the imposter. But it's an intriguing rumour, is it not? Nero alive and well, plotting to take back the throne.'

'You think Nero is alive?'

'Whether or not the last of the Trojans is alive, I don't know. But this most recent imposter is certainly not Nero.' The governor's voice softens to a whisper. 'We have a man who deserted from the False Nero's fledgling army. He arrived here, in Antioch, three days ago. He was wounded, on the verge of death, begging to speak with me. He said the man posing as Nero was a fraud. A former soldier, apparently.'

'Oh.' I cannot help but lean forward myself, waiting impatiently for more information.

The governor continues: 'This deserter . . . he had believed the man claiming to be Nero was *actually* Nero.' He chuckles. 'He followed the imposter for months, blindly. When he discovered the truth, that the man claiming to be Nero was only an imposter, he tried to flee the camp. But he was stabbed and nearly killed.'

'Did he give the name of the imposter – his real name?'

'He did.' The governor's voice is no longer a whisper. 'I've written it down somewhere. But believe me: you've never heard the name before.'

'I would like to speak to this deserter,' I say. 'I would be interested in what he has to say.'

'I'm not sure that would be a good idea,' the governor says. 'The emperor is quite sensitive when it comes to the False Neros. You know what he was like with the last one. I probably shouldn't have told you anything at all. You'll keep what I told you to yourself. Yes?'

'Of course,' I say. 'What will you do with this information?'

'Very little for now,' the governor says. 'I'm not sure what I *could* do. I will need to confirm this information before informing Rome. And I don't even know where this False Nero is. I'm sure it will all sort itself out.' He claps his hands for more wine. 'Shall we have dinner tonight before you get on the road tomorrow?'

Marcus is upset. He cannot accept that Olympias belongs to Sulpicius.

'There is nothing we can do,' I say.

Marcus is fighting back tears. Did he love this girl after so little time? How long did it take me to fall in love with Acte? An hour, maybe. Two at most.

'You are a coward,' Marcus says, reviving our argument from yesterday. But his voice is dejected rather than angry.

'I know you are angry – angry at being born a slave, angry at losing your friend in Rhodes, angry at losing Olympias. You are furious at the cruelty of this world. But unless one has an army, brute strength gets you little in this world. You need to use this.' I point at my right temple. 'You need to apply reason. That is the only way you will distinguish yourself.'

'Do not lose hope,' Theseus says. 'This is not over. The outcome is only delayed. I'll tell you a story. When I first started as a gladiator, there was another slave, a Gallic everyone called Roach, who trained with me. He was a foot taller and twice as strong. My master at the time, he favoured Roach – with food, women, wine. Meanwhile, I was beaten and starved. I was meant as fodder for Roach's blade. When we trained Roach would pummel me. He would disarm me and hit me again and again with his wooden sword. I would have cried at night, but I was too sore and exhausted to spare the energy. My first match in Rome was against Roach. He nearly killed me. If the crowd had had its way, I would have died that day. Roach was about to cut me down, and the crowd was cheering him on, but the gods – *a* god – intervened. You should have seen Nero with the mob. He was a force to behold. They would follow him over a cliff. Caesar signalled that I should live. The crowd shifted and cried for clemency. I lived. Nero bought me that very day. He trained me, fed me, educated me. It was more than a year before I fought in the arena again. I was stronger, faster, better trained. Years later, after I had made a name for myself, I was pitted against Roach for a second time.'

'Did you win?' Marcus asks.

'Of course, he won,' I say.

'Did you kill him?' Doryphorus asks.

'Better than that,' Theseus says. 'I humiliated him. I toyed with him, like a cat with a mouse, and he begged me to spare his life. You see, I won in the end. It only took time. And patience. Real victories aren't won in a day. You must swallow your pride and anger, and wait.'

'You'll help me get her back?' Marcus asks.

'You've my word,' Theseus says.

'All of us will,' I say.

I kick Doryphorus and he says, 'yes, all of us.'

'And what about this False Nero?' Theseus asks. His voice is suddenly tired. He is sick of chasing my enemies across the empire.

'I want to speak to the deserter. I want the False Nero's real name.'

The moon is full – or so Theseus tells me. He guides us to the prison gate. By the sounds of it, there are two guards.

'Who goes there?'

'Friends,' Theseus says. 'Friends with coin.'

'Is that so?'

'There are two guards,' Theseus whispers. They are likely slaves. Possibly soldiers. Either way, they could use extra coin.

'We'd like to see the prisoner,' I say, 'the injured one.'

'No one is allowed in to see that prisoner. Especially at this hour.'

'We are prepared to pay,' I say.

'Yeah?' one guard says.

'What's that?' the second guard asks. 'One coin? You've got to be joking. It will cost more than that.'

Theseus is holding up a coin. In the moonlight, they can't see its colour.

'Not any coin,' Theseus says. 'Here.'

He tosses the coin.

One of them catches it and whistles. 'Gold.'

'Give it here,' his colleague says.

'How many will it take for us to get inside?' I ask.

There is a long pause as these men try to guess the highest number we would go.

'Three?'

'We will make it five a man,' I say, 'but you let us have some privacy with the prisoner. Agreed?'

The two guards start to laugh. This is the best day of their lives.

The only sound inside is a man snoring.

'They've brought a pallet into the cell,' Theseus says. 'There's a man lying on it. He looks injured.'

Theseus guides me to a nearby stool. I hear him rouse the sleeping prisoner.

The man is startled. He starts to cry out, but the noise is muffled by Theseus's massive hand.

'We will need you to be quiet,' I say. 'If you promise to keep your voice down, my friend here will take his hand off of your mouth. If you are not . . . I'm not sure what he will do.'

'He's nodding,' Theseus says, and I hear him release the prisoner's jaw.

'What do you want?' he asks.

'A name.'

The man snorts with disgust. He knows who I mean.

'He's an imposter. But I suppose you know that. If you thought he was Nero, you wouldn't want his name.'

'That is true. Very astute.' I decide to make friends with the deserter. I want more than just a name. 'I hear you were a true believer. You thought the man was Nero himself?'

'Nero is a god,' he says. 'He is alive. I know it.'

'Is that so?'

'You're laughing at me,' he says, 'but I know Nero. Or I *knew* him.'

'I am not laughing, my friend. I also think he is alive. When did you meet the last of the Trojans?'

'He touched me once, on the hand.'

'An auspicious event.'

'It was.'

'Where? When?'

'During his tour of Greece.'

'Ah, I see. And how did you come to join the False Nero's army?'

'I wanted to serve my emperor. I knew he was still alive. I *knew* it. Nero would never abandon us. When I heard he was alive, in Thrace, with an army, I left Greece – I left my wife and my children – I gave up everything. I found them in Thrace . . . It was not as I'd imagined. There were only two hundred men or so. Only a handful had tents, the rest slept under the stars. Their arms were old and rusted. And the man claiming to be Nero was kept hidden most of the time. But I didn't lose faith.' He laughs, derisively. 'Like I said, we barely saw the imposter. Every so often we would stand on top of a massive rock in the middle of the camp, and we would gather before him.'

'And he would what? Give a speech?'

'More like a sermon. He would tell us we had been chosen by the gods, to right a great injustice, and he would tell us the great deeds we were destined for. We would chant his name and curse the usurper who had taken his crown. One of his closest advisors was a priest of Apollo. The priest would sacrifice a dozen animals on top of that same rock, and he would read the entrails for hours. The rock was painted red with blood.'

'How did you discover he was an imposter?'

'Aside from these sermons, I never got close to him. When he'd mount the rock, he wore a crown of laurels and a purple robe. He had a thick red beard. He looked the part. But these sermons were never enough for me. I needed to get close to him. I *had* to. If you'd ever met Nero, you'd understand. You'd know the pull he has. One night, I crept through the camp to the imposter's tent. The canvas was lit from the inside, by torch light. He was meeting with his consilium. I knew it wasn't my place to spy, but I wanted to see him once, up close, to hear him speak. I laid on the ground and lifted the tent wall up an inch or two and looked inside.

'And?'

His voice grows angry. 'It was all a lie. Once he was out of his purple robe and crown of laurels – he didn't look like a senator, let alone a god. And he and his men talked about their plans like thieves rather than an emperor and his consilium.'

'What do you mean?' I ask.

'They talked about the sermons, how to improve them, how to make them seem more believable. They talked about what cities to take and loot, or how to trick more people into joining them.'

'And you heard a name?'

'Yes.'

'What name did you hear? Who is the imposter?'

'They were all former soldiers. They'd all served together. They'd call each other by their former rank. His men mainly called him centurion.' He snorts. 'A common centurion.'

'But you heard a name?'

'Yes. Terentius. His men called him Terentius.'

Terentius. The man Marcus calls the Fox. The centurion who five years ago dragged me from my bed and ordered his men to cut out my eyes with white-hot blades. Perhaps I had suspected this, though I never said it aloud. We have been following the men who had betrayed me across the empire for five years. All of them left a trail, except for Terentius. He was bold enough to cut out Caesar's eyes. Why not claim to be Caesar himself?

'What is his plan?' I ask. 'What does the False Nero intend to do?'

'Kill his enemies and retake his throne.'

IV

I, Gaius
A.D. 79

Domitilla

22 August
The Villa Piso, Baiae

The undertaker's body is discovered the day of my wedding. Jacasta brings me the news in the morning, after her daily visit to the market.

'He was floating in the lake,' Jacasta says, 'inside the break wall.'

We are in the shade of the colonnade, by the fish pond. Red mullet tails break the surface, with a splash of water.

'You're sure it was the same man who tried so desperately to speak with me?'

I think of the skinny man standing outside the stadium in Puteoli, held at bay by Praetorians, holding his green cap. He'd looked earnest and hopeful.

'Yes, Mistress,' she says. 'I happened upon the Praetorians dragging him out of the water. His face was bloated and sickly, but I recognized him from the day of the gladiatorial matches. He wore the same black robe, and he had the same balding head and black beard.'

I had refused to see him because Caesar's sister should not make it a habit to meet with undertakers. But now that he is gone, the decision seems cruel.

'He was from Reate? Was he not?'

Reate was the city of Father's birth. We still have a family home there.

Jacasta shrugs. She doesn't remember where he was from.

'I would like to see him,' I say.

Livia, the maid who dealt with the undertaker, is within earshot of the conversation. She says, 'There is no need, Mistress. You shouldn't be close to an undertaker, even one who is dead.'

Jacasta reluctantly agrees. 'She's right. And we are short on Praetorians to escort you,' she says. 'They have been called out to help drag the undertaker out of the lake.'

Beyond the colonnade, walking through the garden under the unforgiving summer sun is the Batavian. Since his defeat, Titus has put him to work as an Imperial Guard. 'We can bring him,' I say, pointing at the Batavian.

At the Praetorian barracks, we are escorted to the stables. We find Virgilius and three Praetorians standing over a naked body.

'Mistress,' Virgilius says. 'This is unexpected.' He motions for his soldiers to give us space and, with his hand on my arm, turns me away from the corpse. 'What are you doing here?'

'I came to see him,' I say turning to the lifeless body.

'Oh?' Virgilius looks confused. 'Do you know him?'

'I think so,' I say. 'May I look closer?'

He nods reluctantly and we move toward the corpse.

The man's skin looks reptilian, nearly green, and bloated. Patches of black hair stick out of his armpits and cover his crotch and shrivelled cock. His feet are pointing in opposite directions. He looks more eel than man.

Still, his beard and balding head are distinctive.

'I know him.'

'Who is he?'

'He tried to meet with me, twice. He is – he *was* an undertaker. He told my maid that he had important information for me. But' – my voice begins to sound defensive – 'I can't count the number of times I've heard such a claim. I thought him opportunistic, and declined to meet with him.'

Virgilius nods.

'Was he killed?' I ask.

'I don't know,' Virgilius says. 'There is a cut on his forehead, but we only found the one. I think it likely that he was walking along the break wall, slipped, hit his head and drowned.'

Virgilius stares at me, sympathetically. Do I look sad? Guilty?

Perhaps I do feel guilty. I'm not sure that if I *had* spoken with the undertaker, I could have prevented his death. But I could have done more than I did.

Virgilius says, 'I wouldn't worry about this, Mistress. Odds are he was what you expected: opportunistic. And his death had nothing to do with you. He was only a man who couldn't keep his balance.'

'Come, Mistress,' Jacasta says, taking my arm, 'We have much planning to do today.'

'Ah yes,' Virgilius says, raising his white eyebrows. 'The wedding. I am looking forward to it.'

Nerva calls in the afternoon, during my final fitting for my wedding stola. Livia is holding a mirror and two seamstresses are on their knees measuring and pinching fabric.

'What does he want?' I ask.

'He claims to have news of the missing soldier,' Jacasta says, 'Julius Calenus.'

Did I lose an undertaker only to reclaim my missing veteran?

'See him in.'

Nerva enters the tablinum with purpose, taking strides as long as his little legs can manage. His slave follows at his heels. He stops and bows.

'You have news of Julius Calenus?'

'Yes, Mistress,' he says. 'Only a titbit, but it is encouraging.'

'Well?'

'I had word from a creditor in Beneventum. He said a man was asking for a loan on my account. He gave the name Calenus, and he matches our mutual friend's description.'

Calenus is our mutual friend now?

'I thought you were of the opinion that Calenus was in a tavern somewhere, getting drunk?'

Nerva bows slightly. 'At first, Mistress. But as his absence continued, I began to worry. I've had my eyes and ears searching for him. Right now, we only have a hint of his whereabouts, but it's a start.'

'Thank you, Nerva. I look forward to hearing more news.'

'My pleasure, Mistress.' His smile doesn't reach his cold eyes. 'As I've said, I am here, at the Principate's disposal, should you ask. My eyes and ears could be put to good use. And they have seen much these last few days.'

This is meant to entice. Nerva wants me to ask, *And what have you seen, Dear Nerva*? And he wants to be rewarded for the answers he gives. Consulships, governorships, priesthoods. This worked for him in the past, under Nero. And then early on during Father's reign. He would help expose a traitorous senator or knight and reap the rewards.

But I wonder how much of Nerva's information is real? And how much is manufactured? Why did Nerva come today? Did he really have news of Calenus? Or was it contrived to get in the door?

'Thank you for the offer,' I say, blandly.

He bows and turns to go.

'Nerva,' I say, and he turns back to face me. 'Did I see you speaking with Domitian at the games?'

He smiles. 'I – yes. I spoke with Domitian.'

'Why, I wonder? What could you and Domitian have in common? You are a politician. And Domitian is not.'

Nerva is still smiling. He seems – for perhaps the first time – lost for words.

Suddenly Livia drops the mirror. She cries out and immediately apologizes. The room stares as she picks it up. A large crack runs from one corner to the next.

'I'm so sorry, Mistress.'

'Not to worry, Livia,' I say. 'We have more, I'm sure.'

Livia bows and rushes off to find another mirror.

I turn to Nerva. 'Where was I?'

'You were wondering why I was speaking with your brother. Actually, Mistress, I was seeking out your brother's advice. He is quite knowledgeable about the gladiatorial fights, and I am quite ignorant.'

'I see,' I say. 'Well, you had the right man. The fights are one of the few things my brother knows well.'

As Nerva is turning to leave, I ask, 'Will we see you at the wedding?'

Nerva grimaces. 'I do not believe I was invited.'

Barlaas

22 August
Baiae, the Bay of Naples

Admiral Secundus barrels through the door. He barely acknowledges the doctor, sitting on the edge of my bed, dressing my wound in fresh bandages.

'I have been informed you are too ill to attend the wedding,' the admiral says.

He starts to pace my bedroom, scrutinizing every item, as though he'll find a dagger labelled 'For Caesar's belly' sitting on a shelf.

I wince as the doctor peels away a bandage. 'Yes,' I say, 'as you can see, I am not well.'

'Yet you could attend the gladiatorial games?'

'I have regressed.'

'And how is Manlius, your centurion?'

'Alive,' I say, 'but still consumed by fever. He mutters a girl's name. A lost love from his youth in Alexandria, perhaps.'

The admiral looks at the doctor, who nods, agreeing with my account. He sits on the chair beside my bed and stares into my eyes. 'Now is the time,' he says, sternly.

'The time for what?'

'To tell me what you know. Tell me who attacked you and why.'

Unable to look the admiral in the eye, I stare at the doctor, watching him work. 'I don't know what you are talking about. I was attacked by thieves.'

'You are in a difficult situation,' the admiral says. 'I see that. You have loyalties to your homeland, to your kin. Yet you have friends here in Italy.'

I keep staring at the doctor.

'What about Senator Sulpicius?' the admiral asks.

'Which one is Senator Sulpicius?' I ask. 'All you Romans look the same to me.'

The admiral leans back in his chair and scratches his white whiskers.

'You have lived here, in Italy, for how long?' he asks. 'Thirty years?'

'Twenty-nine come October,' I say.

The admiral smiles. 'Twenty-nine years. A reluctant twenty-nine if you know the number off the top of your head. And I cannot blame you for counting the years. I would too, if I were held in Parthia against my will. But have you ever wanted for anything over those twenty-eight years? Have you not had slaves and beautiful homes? Were you not treated like a man with royal blood, like you deserve?'

'Bugger your slaves and beautiful homes,' I say through gritted teeth. 'I am a hostage, no better than a slave.'

The doctor finishes and quietly scurries from the room.

'Did any Roman put you in chains?' the admiral asks, feigning confusion. 'No, I thought not. If you have a complaint about being a hostage, I think it lies with King Volgases, your brother.'

I think of that damned tent, all those years ago. On my knees, before my half-brother, his chest puffed out. The smell of crocus oil and burnt meat. A lamp that creaked as it swayed.

'The Flavians have been good to you, Barlaas. Yet you keep back important information.'

'Not all twenty-eight years,' I say.

'What?'

'I came here under Nero's reign.'

The admiral's face hardens at the mention of Nero's name. This an opportunity to turn the tables. To distract.

'Why does every Roman look as though they've seen a ghost when Nero's name is mentioned? I know the poor in the street think Nero is coming back to take the throne, but I didn't think *you*, the great admiral, put any stock in the Sibyl.'

The admiral frowns. He says, 'Nero is gone. The Flavians will rule for a generation.'

'There is a man on the other side of the Euphrates, at the head of an army, who would disagree with you.'

The admiral breathes angrily.

'Is that the plan? Help the False Nero retake the throne?'

I laugh. 'It's a sad day when the famous admiral is raving like a lunatic.'

The admiral stabs my breast with a fat finger. 'Why aren't you going to the wedding, Barlaas?'

'I told you. I'm unwell.'

'Who attacked you?'

'Thieves.'

We are at an impasse.

The admiral changes course. He stands and walks to the far wall. On a shelf there is a sculpture of a crocodile carved out of amber. A trinket – the origin of which I can't recall.

'Do you know,' he asks, 'that the crocodile, after feasting on fish, will have traces of its dinner caught in his teeth? And there is a bird that will walk among the rows of deadly sharp teeth, picking out portions of food. A dangerous way to earn one's dinner. But the bird grows used to the danger. He doesn't see it.'

The admiral picks up the carving and admires it.

'It occurs to me the precarious situation of a hostage in Rome is akin to the bird who walks inside the jaws of the crocodile. He forgets that his life could very easily be lost should the crocodile choose.'

'And are you the crocodile?'

The admiral puts the sculpture back on the shelf.

'Rome is the crocodile. I am merely one of its many sharp teeth. Try not to forget it.'

After the admiral is gone, I call for Sinnaces.

'You're not going to the wedding tomorrow,' I say.

'Yes I am.'

'No, you're not.'

'I need to go.'

I look at the boy, trying to read his expression. Is this merely a desire not to miss a social occasion or something more? They promised to leave Sinnaces out of it. Was I wrong to trust them?

'Why?' I demand. 'Why must you go?'

He pauses, longer than he should.

'Why do you need to go, Sinnaces?'

'I will prove you wrong yet, Barlaas,' he says before running away.

Gaius

♦

22 August

The home of General Cerialis, Naples

The wedding takes place in the home of General Cerialis, a villa on the water, on the outskirts of Naples. The groom is on the pier, greeting guests as they arrive. He is dressed in a fine silk tunic, dark red in colour; gold adorns his neck and wrists and glints in the torchlight like a fish darting through the sea. He is shaking each man's hand vigorously, his grin ear-to-ear.

There are about two hundred guests; only those closest to the emperor were invited. Uncle Pliny successfully lobbied Titus not to invite the Parthian emissaries. There had been a fight between Ulpius and Uncle Pliny about it. Ulpius said it would be rude not to invite the Parthians. Uncle Pliny, however, thought it was dangerous. He thought Barlaas declining to attend meant something. 'He's hiding something, Caesar,' he told the emperor. It was a testament to their long friendship that Caesar relented. Anyway, he was happy to insult the Parthians after they had duped him into giving up his favourite secretary, Ptolemy. Titus delayed delivering Ptolemy until this morning, but his pride overruled his love for the boy. He didn't want to seem weak by backing out of the bet he'd made.

Sinnaces is the only Parthian in attendance. Normally, you wouldn't know it to look at him because he is usually dressed and shaved like a Roman. But tonight he seems to have discovered his heritage. He is dressed like a Parthian, wearing trousers, a Median robe, and a dagger is fixed to his belt.

The bride and her family arrive by water; two ships in all, filled with family, friends and attendants; they glide into the harbour after dark, each deck awash in yellow lamplight. The ships have been stripped of any remnants of their original use, warfare, and converted into pleasure crafts, with plush seating, and well stocked with wine and tanks of seawater, filled with oysters and other local fare. Tonight, after the ceremony, the ships will take all of the guests out into the bay for a cruise – to drink and relax until dawn.

Uncle Pliny and I follow the line of guests from the pier, up to the house, and into the garden. A priest stands at the far end and a dozen armoured Praetorians are stationed throughout.

Uncle Pliny finds Virgilius in the crowd. 'Is this all the men you brought?'

'It's a wedding, admiral,' Virgilius says, smiling. 'I thought I might have brought too many.'

Uncle Pliny scowls. 'Virgilius you know my—'

Virgilius puts his hand on Uncle Pliny's shoulders. 'Calm yourself, admiral. Do not let me get under your skin. There are twice as many soldiers outside, ready to move if necessary.'

Appeased, Uncle Pliny nods.

The garden continues to fill with guests. Quiet, easy conversations fill the night.

I find Sinnaces leaving the garden and rush to catch him. 'Sinnaces,' I say as I grab him by the arm.

Sinnaces stops but does not look me in the eye.

'What do you want, Gaius?'

'Where are you off to? The ceremony is about to begin.'

'Goodbye, Gaius,' he says and walks off.

'Strange,' I mutter to myself.

I find Uncle Pliny and pull at his sleeve. 'I had an odd conversation with Sinnaces,' I whisper. I begin to explain the exchange, but the ceremony commences before I can finish.

At one end of the garden, opposite the priest, the bride appears, arm-in-arm with the emperor. A hush falls over the crowd.

She looks stunning. Her almond hair is crimped and twisted into a weightless cloud above her head. She is wearing a white stola, with a belt of rope tied at her waist.

Caesar and his sister come to a stop in front of the priest. Praetorians and Imperial body guards stand on either side. The Batavian, who has been put to use as an Imperial guard since his loss in the arena, is there as well.

The priest takes the couple through their vows. He brandishes a rope, which he will use to tie the couple's hands together for their vows. The priest is old, though, and clumsy. He drops the rope.

The audience laughs in a mild, good-natured way. The priest smiles; as do the bride and groom.

The old priest starts to bend down to pick it up, but Domitilla stops him with a light touch to his arm; she crouches to retrieve the rope herself.

There is a sound – something whizzing through the air.

And then there is an arrow in the priest's chest.

The arrow must have passed directly above the Augusta's head.

The audience stands in stunned silence.

The priest looks down at the arrow; his eyes wide with terror.

A rim of blood forms around the shaft of the arrow.

The priest cries out in pain.

The Batavian is the first to move, throwing his body on top of the bride. He uses the shield, which is strapped to his left arm, to protect her, aiming it in the direction the arrow came from. He moves quickly and, in his haste, knocks the priest and Cerialis off balance. Both men fall to the floor.

Caesar – his instincts as a general taking over – pulls a sword from the scabbard of one of the Praetorians standing beside him and he starts to scream instructions to his soldiers.

A second arrow hits the Batavian's shield with a heavy thud.

Prefect Virgilius – concerned only with Caesar's safety – tackles the emperor to the ground. Three lictors pile on top, shielding Caesar from harm.

A third arrow misses the Batavian's shield and buries into his flesh. He cries out in pain.

The stunned audience finally realizes what is happening. Guests start to scream.

Every soldier draws their sword and looks about wildly.

Uncle Pliny calls out to Virgilius and points to where the arrow came from. There is an open window from Cerialis's home, looking down into the garden.

But it's empty now, its drapes blowing in the sea breeze.

Domitilla

22 August

The home of General Cerialis, Naples

I bend down to pick up the rope the priest dropped. Before I can stand, I hear a strange sound, a dull slap, and then I feel the weight of someone draped over the top of me, a black shadow of warmth and sweat, covering me like a blanket.

My heart races.

Titus screams at his soldiers.

I hear that sound again and the man on top of me cries out in pain. I can sense his body clench when he screams.

He stands and helps me to my feet.

It's the Batavian. Pain has leached the colour from his face.

I look around the garden, trying to understand what has happened. Guests are now shrieking. Titus is beside me. He grabs the Batavian by the arm and says, 'Get her to the ship, back to Baiae. Don't let anything happen to her.'

'Titus, what are you—'

Before I can finish, the Batavian is dragging me through the garden, through the atrium and out of the house. Praetorians are on either side of us, swords drawn, shields up.

The Batavian pulls me along the pier to the ships. We swing our heads back and forth, looking for an attack that never comes.

Three soldiers are lying dead on the pier, their throats slit. We don't have time to mourn them. The Batavian drags me onto one of the ships.

Panicked wedding guests are streaming out of Cerialis's home. Some follow us onto the ships – more than we arrived with.

Prefect Virgilius is on our ship. He is shouting orders, demanding we leave immediately or he'll 'skin them alive'.

I can see Titus being dragged onto the ship behind us, surrounded by his lictors and Praetorians. Another cluster of soldiers surrounds a figure that must be Domitian.

Our boat casts off. Oars power us into the bay.

Titus's ship is slower to leave the pier. The general is reluctant to retreat.

Jacasta is nearby, calling for me, but I cannot see her.

The Batavian pushes me to the deck and, with arms like the branches of a tree, stands over the top of me.

My face is next to the deck. It smells strange – different than it did hours before when we sailed here from Baiae. It smells medicinal, or like strong wine.

'The smell . . .' I say.

The Batavian looks at me and I point at the deck, then my nose. He bends and smells the wooden planks.

Virgilius is watching us. His gaze narrows, he also bends and smells the deck. From his knees, he yells, 'back to shore! Back to shore NOW!'

There is a crackling whiz, like a torch flying through the air, and I watch as three blazing arrows land on the deck of Titus's ship.

It ignites in flames.

The Batavian drags me to the gunwales.

'No, no, no,' I say, 'I can't swim.'

He throws me over the side. I hit the water face first.

As I'm sliding down, below the surface, under the weight of my dress, I can feel the heat of our ship go up in flames.

Gaius

23 August
The home of General Cerialis, Naples

'She did *not* drown!'

Caesar is sopping wet; his purple tunic a second skin.

The smell of fire – of burning wood, resin and flesh – wafts off of the sea. Dinghies continue to ferry in survivors. Along the pier, those who survived drowning but not the fires cry out in pain.

Uncle Pliny is calm. 'Did anyone see the Augusta? Gaius and I saw her fall into the water, but her ship was far from shore when it was set on fire. It appeared to have headed east in the chaos. And she was not among those we helped bring to shore.'

'She is alive,' Caesar growls.

Uncle Pliny and I – thank Fortuna – did not board the ships headed back to Baiae. We stood on the pier, helping direct those who were escaping, when flaming arrows were shot from somewhere on shore and the three ships carrying Caesar and his family went up in flames.

Uncle Pliny acted quickly. He ordered the remaining soldiers and Imperial slaves – anyone with a pulse – to commandeer any available ships and rescue those who had abandoned the burning ships in time. Thanks to him, many lives were saved. Caesar didn't need Uncle Pliny's help, however. I watched Caesar grab Domitian and dive into the water as flames were consuming their ship. He tucked Domitian under his arm and swam to shore while the dinghies were still pulling survivors from the sea.

'Does she know how to swim?' Virgilius asks.

Titus shakes his head. 'No. But she was with the Batavian. They are the greatest swimmers in the empire. They swim with their armour on. I'm sure he can swim with a ten-stone woman.'

'I'm not indifferent to your sister's fate, Caesar,' Uncle Pliny says, 'but our ships are scouring the water. If she's not drowned, they will find her. We also need to act against those who tried to take not only your sister's life, but the entire Imperial family. We need to move quickly, to stop them before they can make another attempt.'

'The admiral is right,' Virgilius says, with one eye still on his troops along the shore.

'What are you proposing, admiral?' Caesar says. 'Do you know who did this?'

'It was the Parthian emissaries,' Uncle Pliny says. 'I have little doubt.'

'How did they get inside?' Caesar asks.

'Sinnaces,' Uncle Pliny says. He explains my strange interaction with him earlier this evening.

'I agree with the admiral,' Virgilius says. 'No Roman could have shot arrows like that.'

'The use of arrows is hardly conclusive,' Caesar says. 'But I agree they are the most likely suspects.' To Virgilius, he says, 'Take soldiers to the Parthians now, under the pretence of seeing that they are safe. If they were involved in tonight's attack – it may be obvious. Take enough men to protect yourself, but not enough that it looks as though you are going to war. And Virgilius,' he adds, 'bring me back Ptolemy.'

Virgilius nods and hurries off.

*

We travel to Baiae, to the Imperial villa. We convene in the throne room. Ulpius and Marcus join us during the second hour. They were at the wedding. Like Uncle Pliny and I, they had not boarded the ships in the chaos.

During the third hour, Virgilius arrives out of breath. He is bleeding from his arm. He looks fresh from battle.

'Well?' Caesar asks.

'We did as you asked,' Virgilius says. 'We went to the home you lent to the Parthian emissaries. I brought twenty men. We knocked on the door and said there had been violence at the wedding and wished to see that they were alright. The old interpreter, Atropates, answered the door. He invited me into the atrium. The three Parthian emissaries were there. The four Roman soldiers charged with watching the Parthians. Their presence put us at ease – not completely, but enough that they could surprise us.'

'What do you mean?' Caesar asks.

'I don't know how, or why, but the Roman escorts are with the Parthians. They attacked our men, stabbing their fellow soldiers without warning. And they had the assistance of gladiators. About a dozen of them came streaming into the atrium. We lost four Praetorians before we overwhelmed them. We killed one of the Roman turncoats and a few gladiators. We captured the Parthian Arshad, their translator, and a few of their slaves.'

'And the brothers?'

'They escaped, along with many of the Parthian soldiers.'

'Escaped?'

Caesar is furious.

'Sulpicius,' Ulpius says. 'Who else would have supplied gladiators?'

'Perhaps,' Virgilius says. 'But I didn't recognize any of the gladiators. The ones we killed didn't have any markings on them.'

'It *has* to be Sulpicius,' Ulpius says. 'Sulpicius was seen talking with the Parthians two nights prior. Isn't that right, Gaius?'

I had been watching this argument like a fly on the wall. But now I feel the weight of a dozen sets of eyes on me. I had forgotten that I told Uncle Pliny about Sulpicius's secret meeting with the Parthians and he'd told Ulpius.

'Is this true?' Caesar asks. This is the first time Caesar has acknowledged my existence since becoming emperor.

My cheeks flush, a mottled bright red.

Uncle Pliny nods at me to speak.

'I – um – yes,' I say. 'Sulpicius met with the Parthians the night before the gladiatorial matches, the day they arrived. In secret, I think. But I don't know what they said.'

Caesar curses.

A moment of angry silence follows.

Then Caesar asks: 'What about Ptolemy? Was he in their home? Where is he?'

Virgilius stares at the ground. 'We have Ptolemy. But . . .'

'Out with it, Virgilius.'

'He's not in good shape, Titus. They tortured him.'

'What? Why?' Caesar is visibly shaken.

'For information.'

'What information?'

'He was too weak to say.'

'Will he live?' Caesar asks.

Virgilius nods. 'I think so.'

'And what of Sinnaces?' Uncle Pliny asks. 'Was he with the Parthians?'

'I am not sure,' Virgilius says. 'He could have been. But if he was, he escaped with the brothers.'

'I don't understand,' Caesar says. 'What did emissaries of King Pocorus hope to gain by attacking the Imperial family like this?

I was acknowledging their leader as the rightful king of Parthia. *That* alone is a victory. What more could they hope to achieve?'

'And how did they turn Roman soldiers to their cause?' Virgilius adds. 'And possibly Sulpicius?'

The room is silent. No one knows the answers to these questions.

I look to Uncle Pliny. I'm certain he has a theory, but he is reluctant to voice it until he's certain.

'What next, Caesar?' Virgilius asks.

'How many men do we have?'

Virgilius and Uncle Pliny exchange a flurry of numbers, figuring out how many soldiers are stationed in Baiae, Puetoli and Misenum, and debating how best to deploy them.

'We don't know for certain Sulpicius is involved,' Uncle Pliny says. 'And we don't know the Parthians ran to him. We should send soldiers to Sulpicius's compound, but also on the roads that head north and east, in case the Parthians have tried to escape Italy. And my sailors should continue scouring the bay to find Domitilla.'

'Agreed,' Caesar says. 'I will lead the men going to Sulpicius's home.'

'You can't,' Uncle Pliny says, sternly. 'You are no longer Prefect, Titus. You are no longer a soldier. You are Caesar. You are the state itself. You must stay here, in Baiae, and the majority of our men should be here, protecting you.'

Caesar is about to argue, but Ulpius uncharacteristically comes to Uncle Pliny's aid. 'He's right, Caesar. Your safety is paramount. You must remain here.'

Caesar shakes his head in frustration, but he sees his advisors are right. It is the same advice he would have given his father, when Titus was Prefect.

'I will take men to Sulpicius's compound. It is only a short ride north of Misenum,' Virgilius says. 'Do we attack right away?'

Caesar shakes his head. 'No, he is a Roman citizen. We do not break down the door of Roman citizens on mere suspicion.'

We are surprised at Caesar's comment. As Prefect, Titus would kick in any door he pleased. It appears that Titus, emperor of Rome, is more judicious.

'Barlaas knows something,' Uncle Pliny says. 'The attack on him the night before the Parthian emissaries arrived cannot be a coincidence. They must have sent men ahead, secretly, to compel him to help.'

'And it's possible he was involved as well,' Virgilius says.

'Perhaps,' Uncle Pliny says. 'We cannot rule it out. But I think Barlaas would see it as dishonourable.'

'Can you make him talk?' Caesar asks.

'I don't know,' Uncle Pliny says. 'I have tried before and failed. But it is worth trying again.'

Caesar nods. 'Agreed.'

'Give me the captured Parthians,' Ulpius says. 'I will see what I can learn from them.'

'Do you have experience in interrogations?' Virgilius asks.

'Yes,' Ulpius says, ominously.

'Fine,' Virgilius says. 'But give me him' – he points at Ulpius's one-eyed freedman, Theseus – 'I've seen him fight and he's worth ten soldiers.'

'I'm coming with you,' Marcus says to Virgilius. He, like me, has been watching silently from the periphery. But now he seems impassioned. I had forgotten about the girl he tried to speak to at Domitilla's dinner party. She is Sulpicius's slave.

I'm surprised that Virgilius is happy to accept Marcus's help. He would probably laugh if I'd volunteered. Uncle Pliny said Marcus was impressive earlier this year, in battle, when Marcellus and his ex-soldiers were held up in the Temple of Jupiter.

'Find my sister. Find the missing Parthians,' Caesar says. He looks exhausted. 'Use whatever means you can.'

I walk with Marcus to the door. 'May I ask why you want to go with Virgilius? Is this about the girl – the slave I saw you talking with?'

He nods. 'Yes.'

'How do you know her?' I ask.

'Years ago we were in Antioch, when Sulpicius was there. She was a runaway. We tried to protect her. We failed. I don't want to fail her again.'

I am struck that, as always, Uncle Pliny is proven correct. My first impression of Marcus was wrong. He is not a brute. Far from it. He has the sensibilities of a poet, but this is only evident to those whom he chooses to show. He is a gentleman, but so long as you are on his good side.

The gods help you if you are not.

Domitilla

◆

23 August
The shore, near Oplontis

His arm is around me, holding me tight to the plank of wood. We have been floating for hours. The current has dragged us east. The world is grey and sombre; the sun imminent, but still hidden by the earth. We are exhausted. If I think about how close I came to dying, to burning alive, I want to retch. I worry my brothers and Jacasta were not so lucky.

Our attackers must have soaked each boat in something that made them burn and catch fire. Who would try to kill so many people? What were they trying to accomplish? It seemed the first arrow was aimed at me. But could it all have been a trick to cause our entire family to run to the ships?

After the Batavian threw me over the gunwale, he dove in after me, pulled me up to the surface, and we started swimming as fast as we could, away from the burning ships. We found a piece of wood in the water and we clung to it like wet rats.

We did not head straight to shore. Our ship had gone deep into the bay before it went up in flames. And it was so dark we had difficulty orienting ourselves. We let the strong current pull us away from the burning ships. It wasn't until the grey light of morning that it was obvious how far southeast we had travelled, toward Pompeii and Stabiae, rather than toward the safety of Baiae.

I point at a section of abandoned rocky beach. 'There,' I say. 'That is as good a place as any to go to shore.'

He looks over his shoulder. We kick our make shift raft to the shore.

Once we are close, we wade through the shallow water. My shoes were discarded hours ago; rocks stab my feet. When I'm clear of the water, my wedding stola looks like it is painted to my skin and feels five times as heavy.

We head towards the tree line. Cicadas erupt around us. It is only now that I see the Batavian's wound, a gory hole in his shoulder blade. He'd been hit with an arrow last night and, while we were floating east, he was able to snap off the shaft and then slowly and methodically remove the arrow head. He cried in pain and I thought he was going to pass out. But he's barely shown signs of the injury since.

I try to inspect it, but he pushes me away.

'Fine,' he says.

We head northeast and happen upon a farm. The Batavian helps me step over a derelict fence and we cross the field toward the house. There is a line with freshly washed clothes. The Batavian grabs a few items off it. I try to stop him – the emperor's sister should not steal clothes from some poor farmer – but the Batavian shakes his head and points at my soaking wet wedding dress and his loincloth and manacled arm.

'No good,' he says.

He's right. If we don't change, we will stand out wherever we go.

Of the jewellery I wore last night, two gold bangles and a hairpin survived our escape east. I remove one of the bangles and hook it into the remaining item of clothing hanging on the line. I've no idea how much the farmer's clothes are worth, but I'm quite certain the exchange, his two tunics for my bangle, is a windfall.

We head back to the forest, out of sight, to change.

The Batavian is lightheaded from the effort. He puts one knee on the forest floor and gathers his strength. I wonder how much blood he's lost.

We have stolen two tunics similar in size and colour, a dull light brown. The Batavian goes behind a tree to give me privacy. I peel off my wedding dress. The sun is out and the air warms my clammy skin.

Once changed, the Batavian and I compare our new costumes. The matching tunic looks too large on me – I am lost inside it – whereas his is too small, showing nearly all of his thighs. I use the belt from my wedding dress, which cinches the waist and gives the tunic more form.

'We should head back to Baiae,' I say, pointing west.

He shakes his head. 'Dangerous.'

'I need to see if my brothers are alive. I need to help, in whatever way I can.'

He shakes his head again. 'Too far by land,' he says. 'Too dangerous.'

The Batavian is right. The route to Baiae by land is arduous. And until Titus has had time to find and arrest the men who tried to kill us, it could be hazardous. Travelling by boat would be safer and far less difficult.

'Alright,' I say, pointing east, the direction the sun is rising. 'From the sea, it looked like the closest city was east of here. Pompeii, I think. Pompeii has a large port. We can purchase a ride back to Baiae there.'

The Batavian nods and we start walking toward Pompeii.

Gaius

23 August
The home of Barlaas, Baiae

The doctor answers the door. Uncle Pliny demands to see Barlaas, but the doctor says the Parthian hostage is missing.

'Where is he?' Uncle Pliny demands.

'He left the night of the wedding, my Lord. We haven't seen him since.'

'And what of Manlius?'

'He's finally awake, my Lord.'

'Take me to him,' Uncle Pliny says.

The doctor shakes his head and starts to explain Manlius needs to rest, but Uncle Pliny pushes past him.

The centurion is still in bed. A bandage is wrapped around his head and he looks frail, a shadow of the man I was hunting with only five days ago.

'Admiral Secundus,' he says, trying to stand.

'Please, don't rise,' Uncle Pliny says, waving his hand. 'There is no need. And we haven't the time. I am here on important business, Manlius. I need answers and I need them now.' Uncle Pliny explains the attack on the Imperial family. 'The Parthians have escaped and the Augusta is missing. I need you to tell me every detail you can about what happened the night you were attacked.'

Manlius grimaces as he concentrates. Casting his mind back requires considerable effort. 'I think it started the day before the attack. Two men called on Barlaas. One was Roman, a soldier. He wasn't in a uniform, but I could tell. A soldier can always spot another soldier. The other man . . . I'm not sure where he hailed from – but he wore a strange, eastern-style cap. He was slight, bent over, all bones.'

'A Scythian cap?' Uncle Pliny asks. 'Curved conical top, with flaps that hang over the neck and ears?'

Manlius nods. 'Yes, that sounds right.'

'The second man meets the description of the Parthians' translator. Was he named Atropates?'

Manlius shakes his head. 'I don't know. I had been training in the yard, and I only saw them when they left. Both nodded to me as they walked through the atrium. Barlaas seemed concerned afterwards. And angry.'

'Were these the same men who attacked you?'

Manlius concentrates; the effort is taxing. 'The soldier,' he says. He's hesitant at first but then grows more convinced. 'Yes, I'm certain it was the soldier who attacked us. It was the night of the Augusta's party. Barlaas and I were walking home from the Imperial villa. Out of nowhere I felt a blow to my head. I never saw it coming. I turned and saw the soldier. He was smiling. I drew my blade and readied myself for a fight. But a second blow again caught me from behind. After that, all was black.' Manlius shakes his head. 'Maybe these men are the same that tried to kill the emperor. But Barlaas would never do such a thing. I know it. Killing the family that has provided for him all these years . . . He would think it lacked honour.'

'Barlaas may not have shot the arrows himself,' Uncle Pliny says. 'But he could have stopped it and chose not to. That is treason. Where is he?'

'I don't know,' Manlius says.

'Yes, but you know him,' Uncle Pliny says. 'You're his closest friend. Where does he go to think or drink? Where would he go to bury his head in the sand?'

'I will take you,' Manlius says.

Barlaas

23 August
The Imperial harbour, Misenum

The Romans may be uncultured and thick as a slab of travertine, but they surpass all other nations in two skills: engineering and sailing.

Take Misenum. Home to the navy's eastern fleet.

I come here often, to a bluff above the harbour, to marvel at the sight of it. The harbour extends to the north and west; and it is so vast that it disappears from sight. On the opposite shore, there are docks filled with ships and warehouses and barracks. Beyond that is a mountain of rock, topped with green trees, the westernmost point of the Bay of Naples. This morning, the navy is busier than usual. Nearly every oared ship is churning its way out of the harbour; their deck master's hollering instructions – though, for me, it is softened by distance, and sounds more like gentle encouragement.

Manlius once asked why I like to come here. I forget the lie I told in reply. I didn't want to admit the truth: that looking at this harbour – at this feat of engineering – lessened the sting of being held hostage by the Romans. Who can lament being held, against one's will, by a nation that can do this? Who could resist this mastery of sea and land?

I have been coming to the Bay of Naples every summer for nearly thirty years. I found this vantage, a flat rock with a view of the harbour, while walking with Carenes. It was our fourth summer in Italy. We both silently marvelled at the size of the harbour, the visionary audacity that was required to conceive it, let alone build it. We returned to it often. We would sit and watch ships coming and going, sailors chanting, swearing, the buzz of saws cutting through wood as they continued the ceaseless task of repairing their weathered vessels.

Only Manlius knows that I come here. Thus, when I hear the crack of a twig snapping under a boot, I know it is my centurion. Awake, finally.

But he is not alone.

The admiral takes a seat beside me on the rock. Manlius stands at a distance, with the admiral's spindly nephew.

The admiral scratches his wild, white beard. 'You like my harbour?'

I nod. 'This is a good place to come and think.'

'Or hide?'

I say nothing.

'You knew it would happen at the wedding, didn't you?'

My sullen silence gives me away.

'What else do you know, Barlaas?' the admiral asks.

I keep my mouth shut.

He says, 'Have you heard how it was done? They burned two ships full of people. Dozens died or drowned. I personally pulled them from the water.' He holds up his hand. 'Smell. I still have the stink of burnt flesh on me.'

I bristle. 'What would you have me do? Betray my own countrymen?'

'Please!' the admiral scoffs. 'Your countrymen are killing each other in a civil war. One forgets about *countrymen* when it is convenient. We Romans do the same.'

I stare at the harbour.

The admiral asks, 'Which king of Parthia do you serve?'

I shift uncomfortably. How much does he know?

He turns the screw. 'It must have been hard, to see your younger brother become king instead of you. The son of a concubine no less. Don't worry, we Romans have also had sons of whores beat out better men to lead our empire.'

'He was a good king,' I say, despite myself.

'Yes,' the admiral says. 'Vologases was a noble creature – or so I've heard. His people loved him. And now he is sick or possibly dead. I wonder where your loyalty lies.'

'With my brother's rightful heir.'

'And who is that?'

'Pacorus.'

'I see. Now I understood that we were expecting emissaries from Pacorus. But that is not who came to Italy. Is it?'

Slowly, reluctantly, I shake my head. 'No.'

'Which king? Which king do the emissaries serve?'

I keep staring out at the harbour. A ship glides past, the closest yet. Sixty oars rotate through the water, like the legs of a centipede.

'Artabanus,' I say. 'The fourth of his name.'

The admiral nods. He has suspected as much. 'The brother faring the worst in the civil war has tried the most drastic measure.'

'You do not know the half of it,' I say.

'What don't I know?'

I am silent again. Does he not see the position he puts me in?

'The brothers escaped, but we have their leader, Arshad, and a few of their slaves.'

'He is not the one you need.'

'No? Who then?'

Artabanus's men are being held in the Praetorian stables beyond the city limits of Baiae. A senator, the strange one, who has no eyes and gets under the skin of everyone he speaks with – Lucius Ulpius – and several Praetorians are outside when we arrive. Ulpius is wiping sweat from his forehead. One soldier is cleaning his blade, drawing a soiled rag along the blood-stained steel.

Before the admiral speaks with Ulpius, he stops and grabs his nephew by the shoulders. 'Gaius, I need you to fetch Spartacus for me, in Misenum.'

The boy can see it all – what's happening in the stables and that his uncle doesn't want him to witness it. He's a good lad, the nephew. Delicate and bookish, but he respects his uncle, which is more than I can say for most Roman boys. He doesn't argue, just nods, turns and runs off.

'I have Barlaas,' the admiral says to Ulpius, explaining what would be obvious to anyone with eyes. 'What have you found out here?'

'Nothing.' Ulpius is still wiping sweat from his brow. 'Only that Parthians bleed like the rest of us.'

Ulpius takes us inside the stable. The room is dark, lit only with a flagging oil lamp. The horses have been removed from the pens and replaced with my captured countrymen. There is a man, dangling from the ceiling by his wrists. His chin is touching his chest. Blood drips from his mouth. He coughs three times, wet and weak. As I walk further into the room, I see that it is Arshad. In my day, he was not a warrior, but a man behind the scenes, pulling strings and doing the Butcher's bidding. He's been on the opposite side of something like this. Many times. The translator, the one who calls himself Atropates, is on his knees outside the pens, chained to the wall. He looks at me and his lip curls with disgust. Somehow, he still has his Scythian cap on.

I point at Arshad, dangling from the ceiling. 'Why did you start with this one?'

'We thought it best to start with their leader,' a soldier says.

'A good plan,' I say, 'but you have the wrong man.'

The soldiers exchange confused glances. They look to the admiral for guidance but he merely watches me, waiting for an explanation.

I walk over to the translator.

'You gave us up,' he says.

'I didn't need to,' I say. 'The arrows gave you away. Romans do not assassinate with arrows. Poison or the mob is how they kill their rivals.'

I stand beside the kneeling translator and put my hand on his Scythian cap. To the admiral and Ulpius, I say, 'you will recall a Parthian hostage held in Rome for decades, a son of a hostage, and a descendant of King Phraates himself. The Aryans were once ruled by King Gotarez. A king so violent and capricious he came to be known as the Butcher. A coup was planned. More than twenty nobles signed a pact. Carenes and I came to Rome, and we asked the emperor, Claudius Caesar, to let us take his royal hostage back to Parthia, so that we could put him forward as the true king of kings, challenging the Butcher's claim to the throne. An act that I would later pay for with my freedom. Claudius agreed. We brought Meherdates, the grandson of Phraates, back across the Euphrates. He proved to be a disaster of a commander. He'd grown fat on Roman living, and he was ignorant of warfare. He was indecisive, mean, cruel, cowardly. Initially, men flocked to him because they were desperate to overthrow the Butcher. But slowly, as his character revealed itself, those same men deserted the usurper. He was eventually defeated in the field and dragged before the Butcher, chained and pathetic. And the Butcher lived up to his name.'

In one flourish, I tear off the prisoner's Scythian cap, revealing the translator's bald, earless head.

'The Butcher cut off his ears, and Meherdates would forever be known as the Toad.'

The Toad spits at me.

'The Toad is now allied with Artabanus. And who better than a former Roman hostage to lead the mission to kill the Roman emperor on Italian soil.'

The admiral looks shocked, his eyes are wide.

Ulpius laughs.

'I can't believe it,' the admiral says. 'I knew Meherdates. It may be more than thirty years since I saw him last, but I *knew* him. How could I have been so blind?'

'It was a shrewd decision,' Ulpius says, 'to disguise himself as an interpreter. Who pays anything but a passing regard to an interpreter?'

'You were treated well here,' the admiral says. 'Why come back to murder Caesar and his family?'

Meherdates doesn't respond. He stares bitterly at the wall.

'Because,' I say, 'Rome ruined his life. Because of Rome, he would forever be a foreigner to the Aryans. His time here ensured he had no place in the world, that he was a foreigner on either side of the Euphrates. Not until he found Artabanus, a king who had a use for him; a king in the midst of the civil war and would take friendship from whomever was willing to give it.'

While Ulpius and the admiral are still at a distance, I kneel down and whisper to Meherdates, 'Did you keep your word? Did you keep Sinnaces out of this?'

The Toad raises his eyes from the floor to meet mine. He smiles. 'It seems neither of us kept our word.'

I feel a stab of regret in my stomach. I have never much cared for Sinnaces. But if what the Toad says is true, it is a death sentence for the boy.

I realize now that the Toad, unlike any other, knows what Sinnaces's life must be like. They were both born and raised in a foreign land. The Toad would have known what lies to tell Sinnaces to get him to help in their cause.

'Why kill the Flavians?' the admiral asks as he walks closer. 'What did you hope to achieve?'

'The man you call Caesar has no right to the name.'

'No?' the admiral asks. 'Why is that?'

'Nero is the rightful heir,' Meherdates says. 'He is alive. He and his army have joined forces with Artabanus. First they will take Parthia. Then Syria. Then all of the Roman empire.'

The Toad wants to show his worth. The admiral sees this as well and tries to use it to his advantage. He asks, 'And what happened to Pacorus's emissaries?'

'We intercepted them in Thrace,' the Toad brags. 'They are no more.'

'And what of the Roman soldiers who were supposed to escort you across Italy?'

'They are gone as well. We killed them a few miles outside of Ravenna.'

'Then who are the Roman soldiers you came with?'

The Toad smiles. 'They are Nero's soldiers, sworn to put the last of the Trojans back on his rightful throne.'

The admiral pauses, lost in thought.

Ulpius takes over. 'Where did your friends go? You must have had a fallback position. Somewhere to run to if you were found out. Did they run to Sulpicius?'

The Toad looks at me. He wants to incur more damage before all is said and done.

'Ask Barlaas. He and the boy, Sinnaces, were both involved. It was Barlaas who shot the arrows at Caesar's sister.'

I explode with anger. 'Lies!'

It is a lie, but a believable one. The admiral knows I am skilled with the bow. Thankfully the admiral has a strong mind and is not easily turned. 'Then why attack Barlaas in the streets four days before the attempt on the Imperial family?' the admiral asks. 'Why try to kill your co-conspirator?'

'To remind him of where his loyalties lie,' the Toad says.

'With a king he has never met?'

'With his countrymen,' the Toad says.

'Lies!' I scream, unable to control my anger.

Ulpius waves his hand. 'This debate is pointless. Shall we go outside?'

The admiral nods, but I can see he is thinking. He may not be convinced I was involved, but this will not be the end of it. I will need to prove I had no hand in the attempt on Caesar's life. If I can't . . .

I am as good as dead.

We reconvene outside. My eyes need a moment to adjust to the blinding summer sun.

'Meherdates believes that the False Nero is actually Nero,' the admiral says, shaking his head. 'This is troubling. He was in Rome when Claudius was emperor. Nero was at court then. They would have met. Meherdates' support of the False Nero will lend the rumour credence.'

Ulpius seems distracted. Absently, he says, 'They met once. Only in passing.'

The admiral is about to say something but thinks better of it. Instead, he scratches his beard and stares at Ulpius, as if trying to solve a puzzle.

'What now?' I ask.

'We wait,' the admiral says. 'We have men scouring the bay for the Parthians, and we have men camped outside Sulpicius's compound. We'll keep applying pressure to the men we've captured. The tide will turn eventually.'

'I would like to help, admiral,' I say, eager to prove I was not involved. 'Send me to Sulpicius's.'

The admiral frowns. He is still deciding whether I am friend or foe. 'And what will you do if you have to fight your kin?'

'I did not know it before – I did not know it until today – but I am for Pacorus. For my brother's rightful heir.'

'And what if Sinnaces is with them?' the admiral asks. 'I know there was no love lost between you and the boy. Still . . .'

'If he was involved, Sinnaces must be punished.'

'But you were close with his father.'

'Yes. But Carenes would agree Sinnaces should be punished. And he would want me to do it.'

The admiral nods. 'Very well,' he says.

The admiral lets me sit with him and Ulpius in the carriage that brings us back to Baiae. A good sign, I think. If even a small part of the admiral thought I had helped set the Imperial ships on fire, I would be walking back to Baiae alone. Possibly in chains. If the admiral is on my side – that is good. He whispers in Caesar's ear. But I will still need to prove myself.

'Caesar should go back to Rome,' Ulpius says.

The admiral nods. 'Yes, he should go back to Rome. But I doubt he will listen until his sister is safe.'

'You could convince him.'

The admiral smiles. 'I was about to say the same of you. Indeed, you seem to have a knack for advising emperors. Where, I wonder, did you develop this skill? Certainly not in Spain.'

Ulpius is holding something in his hand. It looks like a shard of terracotta brick, worn smooth. He's rubbing it with his thumb. He doesn't answer the admiral.

The wagon sways.

We listen to the sound of hooves on stone.

Domitilla

♦

23 August
The road into Pompeii

We enter Pompeii through the Salt Gate. It's the Festival of
Vulcan today – I had forgotten. People are streaming into
the city from the surrounding countryside. Open fires are lit
along the road and smiling, half-drunk peasants are throwing fish into the flames, an offering to the fire god. Trumpets
are playing on nearly every corner. All of it – the noise, the
bustling crowd, the activity – provides a welcome cover for
the Batavian and me. With our worn tunics and dust-streaked
faces, we look like any other couple hoping to enjoy the
festival.

Inside the city walls, the smell of frying fish and salty fish-
sauce draws the Batavian to a roadside canteen. The woman
working behind the counter sees the look in the Batavian's eye
and, as she's handing a customer their order, over the din of
the crowd behind us, yells out prices and recommendations.

I pull the Batavian by the arm. 'Come, we need to find a ship
first.'

'You need passage on a ship?' the proprietor asks. 'Impossible.
Not today. The city is on holiday and very drunk.'

The proprietor looks formidable. Stout shoulders, shrewd
and narrow eyes, and a confident smile. Her hair is crimped
and pinned into the shape of a beehive. It is fashionable and

reasonably well done considering she did not have, as I would, half a dozen maids to help her.

'We will have to take our chances,' I say.

'I could help.'

'You could sail us to Baiae?'

'Better than that. I have a room you can rent before you set sail tomorrow.'

She is probably right. The Festival of Vulcan is a holiday the people take seriously. And we do not know how safe it is to travel until we find out more about the attempt on my life. A room for the night is a good idea.

The proprietor sees me nodding. She adds, 'Yes, but it will not be cheap. It is the only room available in the city.' She stares at my worn tunic. 'I'm not sure you can afford it.'

She is well practised at bargaining and seems to be enjoying herself. Dealing with the senators of Rome as I often do, I am not unprepared for this.

'The problem is not that I can't afford it,' I say, as I reach into my pocket and produce my remaining gold bangle. 'But that what I have to pay with could probably buy the whole building.'

The woman grabs my hand and pulls the bangle in for a closer look. The craftsmanship is unmistakably expert. It's the jewellery of a rich woman and she is imagining herself wearing it, showing the world how successful she is.

She lets go of my hand. 'It is a nice item, certainly. But it could not buy you a building. Not even close. I could give you the room and passage to Baiae. I know a captain. He'll give me a good rate. I think that would be fair.'

'And all of our meals,' I say.

She feigns reluctance, but she knows this is a windfall. 'Fine. Only because I feel bad for you. I don't want you sleeping in the street.'

She reaches for the bangle and I pull it toward me. 'And,' I say, 'you will have someone send a message to Baiae for me. If they cannot travel by ship they can travel by land.'

She snaps her fingers and a boy of twelve appears. 'My nephew here, hates festivals, don't you, Statius? He'd be happy to deliver a message to Baiae for you.'

The boy looks distraught but knows better than to fight his aunt.

'And,' I say, 'I need medicine to treat a wound.'

'Yes, yes. Fine.'

'And,' the Batavian chimes in, 'a sword.'

The landlady, desperate for the bangle, looks about the canteen. She hands the Batavian a long knife. 'This will have to do.'

I hand her the bangle.

She admires it for a moment and then she snaps her fingers. The boy fetches ink and a roll of papyrus.

I want to let Titus know I am alive, but sending a message directly could be dangerous. Anyone looking for me could follow the boy back here. I would send it to Jacasta, but she was on my ship when it went up in flames. I don't know if she is injured or whether she's even alive.

Who then?

Livia. She wasn't on the ships the night we were attacked. She could get a message to Titus.

I write the note: *Titus, the blackmailer is alive and well. She will return when she knows it is safe.*

I give the message to the boy. 'You are to deliver this to the Villa Piso and hand it to Livia, a maid in the Imperial household. She is pretty, but with one thick eyebrow. Do not hand this letter to anyone else. Do you understand?'

He nods and then runs off.

The proprietor is at my side. She is already wearing the bangle. She stares at the Batavian and smiles. 'Shall I show you two to your room?' She thinks I am a rich, married woman who has run off with a slave, or something equally seedy. 'I'm sure you're eager to settle in.'

Hours later, after sunset, the Batavian is standing outside, arms crossed, back straight, staring into the endless black of night.

The celebrations for the fire god are winding down.

Somewhere a dog barks. An infant wails.

'Come inside, please.'

He looks at me, shakes his head. 'Not safe.'

The Batavian has been on guard since the proprietor let us in, breaking his vigil only once to fetch dinner. The effort seems pointless. No one knows we are here. I'm sure half the world thinks I'm dead.

I grab the Batavian by the hand and pull him towards the door. 'Come in. I'm not asking anymore. We need to put more balm on your wound.'

He comes inside. He is a slave after all and must obey.

The Batavian has to remove his tunic so I can apply the balm to his shoulder, where the arrow pierced his flesh. His flank and shoulders are littered with old scars. One is particularly gruesome: it is two fingers wide and goes from his breast to his collar bone.

He sits on the bed, and I sit beside him.

I feel a sensation in my stomach – a fluttering, slightly sickening feeling. This is new for me. I've never been alone with another man, without the weight of family and state on my shoulders. There was my wedding night, which I barely remember, and nothing more. I recall an old man – vinegar breath, bones that creaked, balding head, curved back, glassy eyes – and the impression of the gulf between my fifteen years and his half a century. The ceremony was short, the night together even shorter. He ordered me to undress and lie on the bed. He lay on top of me, hitched up his tunic and was dead before morning. From this dreadful night of marriage, I was given the nickname the Widow – one I could never shake. I was heartbroken when I first heard it. I thought it was true, that my touch meant death, and this was why I never remarried. It was years before I learned that father thought using his first-born daughter as bait to snare senators was more valuable than a proper union. There were plenty of engagements, but none that ended in marriage.

The fluttering in my stomach is overtaken by a more familiar stab of anger, directed at Father – not only for forcing me to marry an old man and the humiliation that came with it, but for the lack of experience I've had with love or men. The powerlessness is maddening.

I could have conducted affairs in secret, as Vespasia did. But I didn't. I'm not sure why. Maybe I was worried I'd give up something of myself in the bargain.

The Batavian looks over his shoulder. 'Thank you.'

I continue to rub the balm onto his wound.

'You understand Latin better than you let on. Don't you?'

'Understand some. Not all.'

'Does it make it easier as a slave? Pretending not to understand what is said to you by your master?'

'Not easier for me. Harder for him.'

'Ah, I see. It is out of spite.'

'Spite?'

'Anger. Pettiness. Hatred.'

He nods. 'Yes. For spite.'

'That I understand.'

When I am finished applying the balm and dressing the wound, the Batavian walks to his tunic, which is hanging on the wall.

I nearly laugh at the comparison between him and my deceased husband. Vinegar breath and bones that creaked, versus long muscles and patches of black hair. Death versus vitality.

'Stop,' I say.

He turns and looks at me.

Soon we will return to Baiae, then Rome. I will again be forced to marry a man I did not choose.

Not tonight.

'Take off your loincloth,' I say. 'And lie on the bed.'

Like a young girl on her wedding night, he does as he's told.

V

Fire and Ash
A.D. 79

V

Fire and Ash

A.D. 79

Gaius

24 August

The home of admiral Plinius Secundus, Misenum

The twenty-fourth of August begins with another earthquake.

It's the morning. One moment I am diligently reading Livy, taking notes. The next the world is moving beneath me.

I clutch my desk.

Terracotta tiles rattle on the roof above.

Then the black shadow of Zosimos is sheltering me.

A vase slides off my desk and smashes on the floor.

Suddenly it's over.

Zosimos looks me over. 'Are you alright, Master?'

I wave him away. 'Yes, thank you. I'm fine.'

He seems upset. 'So many earthquakes this summer,' he says. 'A bad omen.'

I take stock of the damage. Minus one vase, the room looks as it did when I went to bed.

'I would agree it's unusual,' I say. 'Whether it is the gods telling us something, I am not so sure. Let's see how Uncle Pliny fared, shall we?'

Domitilla

24 August

Pompeii

The Batavian and I are making love when the earthquake starts. I had been on top of him, my hands gripping the mat of black hair on his chest, my thighs pinching his waist. When the Batavian realizes the earth is shaking and the roof over our heads could come crashing down, he spins us around, so that he is on top of me, and he covers my head with his arms.

And then the earthquake is over.

Our eyes meet. We smile. We laugh, hesitantly at first, and then he drops his head into the space between my shoulder and neck, and we convulse with laughter.

He is still inside me. We kiss and start again, as though nothing had happened.

Barlaas

24 August

Two miles north of Naples

The dogs continue to bark, even after the earthquake. The sound is driving me mad.

'Will someone shut them up!' I yell.

The boy – Ulpius's nephew, Marcus – says, 'In my experience, yelling at a dog only makes it worse.'

'You're the dog expert, are you?'

'Yes,' says the arrogant prick.

Manlius puts his hand on my arm to calm me down.

'Just roll,' I say.

Marcus tosses the dice against the wall.

'Damn!' Manlius shakes his head. 'Venus again. You've the luck of Ulysses, boy.'

Marcus is on his knees. He leans forward and, with both hands, drags his winnings towards him. A boy his age would normally gloat after a few good rolls. But he seems to have enough experience to know better.

'When should we start to worry about your man Theseus?' I ask.

'He'll be fine,' Marcus says. 'The world could be ending and Theseus would be fine.'

'And what if he's wrong. What if his friend – Sulpicius's gladiator – what if he isn't his friend at all?'

'Theseus isn't wrong.'

We are in a home that neighbours Sulpicius's compound. Virgilius and his Praetorians confiscated it yesterday. There are two dozen soldiers spread across the atrium, dicing, drinking, and napping to pass the time. Another half-dozen are outside, their eyes on Sulpicius's compound, looking for any sign of Artabanus's men. At the far end of the room is the young military tribune, Catullus, who Virgilius put in charge when he returned to Baiae. He is one of the rich fools that follow Domitian around all day, laughing at his jokes. No doubt, he was only named legate because he's friends with Caesar's brother.

'Say your man Theseus confirms the Parthians are inside.' I point at the young tribune. 'What are the chances that boy orders his soldiers into the compound?'

The three of us stare at the boy in charge.

'The Prefect's orders were to wait and watch,' Manlius says. 'So that is what we will do.'

Manlius is a good soldier. It isn't in his nature to question authority.

'I've had colds older than that boy,' I say. 'Look at him. He's overwhelmed already, and all we're doing is playing dice and killing time. He's not got the balls to order us over Sulpicius's walls.'

Marcus snorts. 'Agreed.'

'He's in command,' Manlius says. 'Let's give him the benefit of the doubt. Even if the Parthians are in there, they're not getting away.' He picks up the dice. 'Another game?'

The boy and I nod our heads.

I watch the boy grab the dice and roll. His technique, the way he rolls the dice, the jibes he makes at his adversaries – he plays like a man on the docks rather than a patrician's coiffed and pampered son.

'What's your story, young Marcus?'

'What do you mean?'

'Where'd you learn to play dice?'

'Spain.'

'Spanish crooks?'

He laughs. 'Maybe.'

'And what's your stake in this? Why do you care so much about what happens to Sulpicius?'

The boy thinks about his answer. 'There's a girl. In his household.'

Manlius, always the gentleman, says, 'Ah, a girl. Say no more.'

I keep pressing. 'Sulpicius has been in Syria for more than a decade. When did you meet this girl of his?'

Marcus ignores me and rolls the dice. This annoys me. Is it because he considers me a barbarian? He looks comfortable and that is something I want to change.

'Alright,' I say, 'keep your little romance a secret. But tell me this: what is it you're trying to prove?'

This gets the boy's attention. 'What do you mean?'

'Take the hunt we were on together. You were a man possessed trying to prove yourself, being the first into the fray. You weren't doing it for the spoilt shits we were hunting with. You hate those boys more than I do. Don't shake your head. You're an outsider like me, despite your best efforts. Which begs the question: what are you trying to prove? Who are you measuring yourself against?'

The boy ignores me and rolls.

'Is it that strange uncle of yours? Or are your origins so pathetic that you hope to wipe it out entirely through what you do now?'

The boy doesn't rise to the bait. He stares at the dice. 'I win again.'

A soldier by the window calls out: 'The freedman's back.'

Theseus, flanked by two soldiers, enters through the front door. He heads for the tribune. The men coalesce around them.

'My friend inside, the gladiator, he confirmed the Parthians are there.'

Catullus frowns. 'But you didn't see the Parthians yourself?'

Theseus, an honest man, says, 'No. But I trust him.'

'Has he explained why a Roman senator would provide shelter to Parthian assassins?' Catullus asks.

'Why does that matter?' Marcus asks. 'The Parthians are inside.'

The little tribune scowls. He's not going to take orders from a provincial like Marcus, especially one who is a few years his junior.

'If the Parthians *are* inside,' Catullus says, 'which we do not know for certain, and I very much doubt they are, then they are not going anywhere. Are they? When Prefect Virgilius returns, he will decide whether we storm Sulpicius's walls.'

Marcus is incredulous. He curses under his breath.

'There is more,' Theseus says. 'While I was waiting for Minnow, I saw a woman go into the compound. Not long afterwards, she left with three men. All four wore cloaks, covering their heads, so it was impossible to know who they were. But Minnow said they were Parthians. Our soldiers didn't stop them. They let them walk right past.'

Theseus leaves the most damning fact unsaid: in order for four people to leave Sulpicius's and walk away unmolested, Catullus must have given the order to allow it. One of them could have been Sinnaces.

I round on the tribune before Marcus can. 'Stupid boy! You let them escape?'

'Our orders are to engage Parthians,' the tribune says. 'I hardly see how three men dressed in Roman cloaks could be Parthians.'

I throw my hands up in disgust. 'Who left this boy in charge!'

A loyal soldier grabs me by the collar. 'Barbarian! Who are you to talk to a Roman soldier like that?'

Manlius steps in between us. 'Calm yourself, friend. We cannot afford to fight like this.'

Marcus points his finger at the tribune. 'Catullus. Discipline your troops or Sulpicius's entire compound will hear us.'

A soldier shoves Marcus from behind and Theseus is on the man like the plague.

The soldier holding my collar throws me to the ground, face first.

With my eyes on a beautiful mosaic of Neptune under the sea, I hear the first punch.

A fight, long brewing, follows.

Gaius

24 August

The office of admiral Secundus, Misenum

Uncle Pliny is reading in his office as though the earthquake had never happened. The books scattered across his desk and office floor may look more disorganized than they normally do, but I'm not sure.

Without looking up from his book, he says, 'Nephew.'

'Is there any word yet?' I ask.

He looks up. 'From whom?'

'From anyone? From Virgilius? From Domitilla? From Barlaas?'

'No news yet, young Gaius. I would tell you if there were.'

I flop down into the seat across from him.

'Domitilla must have drowned,' I say.

'On the contrary,' Uncle Pliny says. 'No news is good news, I'd say. Bodies do not sink. If she had drowned or was terribly burned the night of her wedding, her body would have washed to shore somewhere. I've had the navy searching for her day and night. If they've not found her floating in the bay, it likely means she has walked away on her own two feet.'

'You think so?'

'Yes, I do.'

'And what about the missing Parthians? You're not concerned they may try to kill Caesar and his family again? Or sneak back to Parthia?'

'Patience, young Gaius. The odds are stacked against them. They took their shot and missed. Now they are hiding somewhere, waiting for the right time to sneak out of Italy.'

'What are they waiting for?'

Uncle Pliny shrugs. 'For our attention to be elsewhere. But you needn't worry about that.'

Something catches my eye in the open book on Uncle Pliny's desk. I see names of emperors past. Claudius and Nero.

'What are you reading, Uncle?'

'Oh, nothing.'

It is a rare occasion when Uncle Pliny does not want to discuss what he is reading. I angle my head to get a better look at the upside-down book. 'Are you reading Fabius Rusticus's histories? And Corbulo's memoirs? Why the interest in Claudius's court?'

Uncle Pliny looks – embarrassed, maybe. He leans back in his chair and sighs. 'Ulpius made a strange comment yesterday.'

'Oh?'

'You know the Parthian that we captured. Meherdates?'

'The Toad?'

'Yes, the *Toad*.' Uncle Pliny nearly chokes on the epithet. 'Yesterday, after Barlaas helped us uncover his true identity, Meherdates claimed the False Nero is *actually* Nero, the deposed emperor. Meherdates and Nero were in Rome at the same time, when Claudius was emperor. They would have met. In theory, Meherdates should be well placed to judge the veracity of the False Nero's claims. Naturally, I found this revelation concerning. Ulpius, however, disagreed. He said Nero only met Meherdates once. "In passing".'

'You think that a strange observation?'

'It is oddly specific, isn't it? How would a Spanish provincial, who isn't supposed to have set foot in Rome until this year, know something only Nero's inner circle should know?'

'So, you have been studying Rusticus to see – what? To see if Ulpius was quoting a historian?'

'Precisely,' Uncle Pliny says. 'Rusticus and Corbulo had first-hand knowledge of Nero's court. I hoped to find that Ulpius, whether knowingly or unknowingly, was quoting a historian from memory.'

'And?'

Uncle Pliny shakes his head. 'Nothing. The comment remains a mystery.'

'What do you think the explanation is?'

Uncle Pliny fiddles with his carnelian ring. He seems tired. 'I can only think of one explanation,' he says, 'but I'm too embarrassed to say.'

'You should take a cold dip, Uncle, and relax in the sun with lunch and a good book.'

'Sound advice, nephew.'

'But,' I say, as I stand to leave, 'I'm not sure how you can read with the dogs barking? They've not stopped since the earthquake.'

'Are they still?' Uncle Pliny asks. His eyes are now on the paper on his desk. 'I hadn't noticed.'

Domitilla

24 August

Pompeii

We lie in bed for hours, dozing, making love, laughing, trying our best to drown out the incessant barking of dogs. I am lying on my side, propped up by my elbow. He is on his back, staring at the ceiling. I'm running my hand through the hair on his chest.

'It's time,' I say.

'Time?'

'Yes – for you to tell me your real name.'

'Batavian.'

'No, the one your mother gave you.'

After a long pause, he says, 'Alwin.'

'Alwin,' I say, smiling. 'A good name.'

'Romans once called me, Alban. Before.'

'Before you were taken slave?'

He nods.

'You were given a Romanized name? Why? Did you fight for the Roman legions?'

He nods. 'Auxiliary. Not long.'

'What happened to you during the revolt?'

He shakes his head, unwilling or unable to tell me more of what happened when his countrymen revolted against Roman rule. I put my hand on the terrible scar on his chest.

The mystery that is the Batavian thickens. I want to know everything. How did he come to fight as an auxiliary? What happened to him during the Batavian revolt? Why was he taken prisoner and sold as a slave? Did he fight to escape Rome's yoke, only to be robbed of his liberty?

I can see he is reluctant to talk about the revolt. It can wait. There is something more pressing.

'That night you saved my life, earlier this year, at the Palace,' I say, 'why were you there?'

Jacasta and I had returned from a dinner party and found a man with a knife was waiting for us. He had killed two of my slaves and would have killed me as well. But the Batavian appeared, seemingly out of thin air. He killed the attacker and saved my life. I never had a proper explanation why he was in the Imperial palace in the middle of the night.

After a long pause, he says, 'To find you.'

'In the middle of the night? To what, declare your love? To force yourself on me? What?'

I pull at his chin, until he's looking me in the eyes.

'What did you plan to do that night?'

He shrugs. 'Don't know. But I had to see you.'

A quarter of an hour later there is a noise outside.

An explosion.

The sound is unlike anything I have heard before. Deafening and so strong it moves the earth.

The Batavian goes to the window. He puts on his loincloth, stands flush with the wall and peels back the curtain. He watches for a time, angling his head, trying to get a better view of the street.

His gaze hardens.

'Dress.' He grabs my tunic, strewn on the ground, and throws it at me. 'Now.'

Instinctively, my eyes bulge with anger. I am about to tell him that, despite what has transpired here in Pompeii, he cannot order me around or toss an article of clothing at me.

He puts his finger to his lips and whispers: *shhhh.*

There is a knock at the door.

The Batavian grabs the long knife the landlady gave him and again stands flush with the wall.

I quickly pull on my tunic.

Something slams against the door – once, twice – and the door splinters open. The first two men into the room I don't recognize. The third is the huge Parthian champion – the Sogdian Spear – who fought the Batavian a few days ago. All three are armed with a sword.

The first man is barely through the door before the Batavian grabs him by the shoulder, spins him away from the door, and repeatedly stabs him in the neck. The other two step inside the apartment before realizing there is a man with a knife behind them, stabbing their colleague. The huge Sogdian raises his sword and swings it down at the Batavian. The room is so small and cramped that the Batavian has virtually nowhere to move to dodge the blow. He dives forward, under the Parthian's arms, rolls on the ground, and, as he's rising from the floor, stabs the second man in the groin. He bends over in pain and I see the Sogdian already turned with his sword raised, about to take a second swipe at the Batavian.

'Look out!' I yell.

The Batavian sees the blade coming toward him. Still on his knees, the Batavian uses the wounded Parthian as a shield. The Sogdian's blade slashes at his comrade's back. The dying Parthian shrieks in pain.

The Sogdian Spear is off balance but the Batavian is on the ground, under the second attacker, and unable to take advantage.

I am still on the bed. Nearby is a large pitcher half-full of water. I grab it with both hands and bring it crashing down on the Sogdian's head. The Sogdian falls to one knee and his free hand instinctively goes to the cuts the pitcher made to his scalp.

Rather than finish him off, the Batavian's focus is on my safety. He grabs me by the wrist and pulls me off the bed, out the door, and down into the city's recessed street, a foot below the pavement.

The Batavian's arrow wound is open again and bleeding badly.

The street is crowded with people staring at the horizon, at something in the northwest. We don't have time to see what has captured the town's attention because there is a blood-letting scream behind us and we turn and see the Sogdian running out of the apartment door.

The Sogdian raises his sword above his head. The Batavian pushes me away and I fall violently to the unforgiving black stone street. He stumbles backwards, barely avoiding the Sogdian's blade.

The crowd creates space for the two fighters, but only seem half-interested in the life-and-death fight before them. Whatever they are watching on the horizon is more important.

I don't dare look up.

The Batavian and the Sogdian Spear stare at each other, panting, catching their breath. They both assume the pose of a gladiator; they begin to circle each other, like fighters in the arena.

The Sogdian mutters a curse in a language I don't know.

I pull myself onto the elevated pavement.

Behind the Batavian there is a store with tools on display. He grabs a long hoe and, with his eyes still on the Parthian, he snaps off the head of the hoe with his foot, turning the long wooden handle into a make shift spear. He walks quickly and methodically at the Sogdian, stabbing at him with the spear.

The Sogdian swipes at the spear and cuts a length off the wooden shaft. The Batavian keeps moving forward and thrusts it into the Sogdian's belly. Then he backpedals, anticipating the swing of the Sogdian's blade. The Sogdian's blade nicks the Batavian's chest, a scratch, long and bloody but not fatal.

The two fighters again stalk each other.

The Sogdian's attention is on the Batavian: he has lost track of me.

I pull from my hair my last remaining item of value: the hairpin, a golden butterfly with two long, sharp prongs. I move slowly, toward the Sogdian, as he continues to circle the Batavian.

When the Sogdian is only a few feet away I stab my hairpin into his neck. He shrieks in agony and reels, wildly swinging his arms. His elbow hits me and knocks me off balance. As I am falling I see the Batavian flying toward the Sogdian.

I hit the stone pavement hard.

Someone screams out in pain.

Groggily, I drag myself up.

The Batavian is standing over the lifeless Sogdian. I join him. 'How?' he asks.

'How did he find us?' I say. 'I don't know.'

I keep staring at the dead Sogdian. Who told the Parthians where to find us?

The Batavian pulls on my arm and points to the horizon.

I turn to look. For a moment, the sight is so strange that I am not sure what I am looking at.

On the horizon, from the peak of Mount Vesuvius, there is a cloud of smoke – greyish-white, endlessly pulsing upwards and filling the sky. It starts as the width of the mountain's peak, but as it rises into the air, it spreads out, like the branches of a tree, with throbbing veins of smoke, consuming the clouds and the sky itself. It is as though Vesuvius were on fire, a mighty, insatiable conflagration.

'What is that?' the Batavian asks.

'I don't know.'

Just then it inexplicably starts to snow. It is the hottest August in years and yet snow is falling from the sky.

I put out my hand.

White debris collects on my palm and my arm.

The snow is . . .

Warm.

I hold what has collected on my skin to my face. It's ash, not snow, like the residue on a hearth after a sacrifice.

'It's time we left,' I say. I pull my golden hairpin from the Sogdian's neck. 'To Baiae. To my brother.'

The Batavian nods. He takes my hand and we head toward the sea.

The pier. Chaos reigns. It is mid-afternoon, yet the sky is growing dark. Warm ash continues to fall; and stones of pumice – lightweight and porous, the size of pebbles – fall like hail. They are not deadly – not on their own – but they sting.

The wind is howling and the sea is a tumult of waves and foam, tossing ships against the jetty. The Batavian pushes us through the crowd. Sailors are forcing back the panicking crowd. We see a man – a beggar by the look of him – jump off the pier onto a ship. Two sailors grab him and toss him into the water. The man disappears below the foaming waves. I slow down – surely, we can do something to help the man – but the Batavian keeps dragging me down the pier.

We pass an old man with a little girl. They look lost and frightened.

'There,' I say, pointing at a ship. That one.' The captain is on the pier directing his crew to tie down the sail and add more bumpers between the ship and the shore. Like all of the ships we have seen, he is not intending to leave Pompeii. He looks calm.

'Are you this ship's captain?' I say.

I'm dressed in my stolen tunic and a worn cloak The captain glances at me and says, 'Bugger off. No free rides. Not today.'

'How much to sail to Baiae?' I ask.

He stares. My voice – clear, strong-willed, used to getting its way – gives him pause. I'd wager he rarely hears a voice like mine, and never from a woman. He considers me again. 'On a normal day, Pompeii to Baiae would cost you a thousand sesterces? But today' – he points at the smoke billowing from Vesuvius – 'you can't afford it.'

I show him my hairpin. It is a solid gold butterfly with two rubies for its eyes.

'What's that?' he says. He recognizes its value.

'Half your reward for taking us to Baiae?'

'Half?'

'I have a matching one at home. I will give it to you as well when you get us to Baiae.'

'You live in Baiae?'

Pumice stones continue to hit and scatter against the pier. The sky is nearly as dark as the night.

'I have a summer home there.'

'You're rich then?'

'Very.'

He nods, as if reaching a conclusion. He offers me his hand. 'Captain Verecundus at your service.'

In the distance, there is a loud noise like thunder.

The old man and the little girl are where we passed them, standing stunned on the pier. 'Captain,' I say, 'those two are with me. See that they are helped on board.'

'As you wish, Mistress,' he says, before hollering at his crew, 'We are leaving. For Baiae. Now.'

His crew is mortified.

'There will be all the wine you can drink in Baiae, boys.' He claps his hands. 'Let's go!'

The wind howls. Waves of white foam push our ship backward, away from the safety of Baiae. Captain Verecundus screams instructions at his rowers, but his words are barely heard over the violent winds. The sky is black and thick with falling ash collecting on the ship's deck like snow. Pumice stones and smouldering black stones hit the deck as though thrown from a sling. Fifty oars creak with each stroke through the water and sound on the verge of snapping in two.

It feels as though we have not moved for hours, that the waves and our oars have reached a standstill. It is impossible to tell, however. The shore is invisible.

The little girl we found on the pier is named Petra. She's huddled with her grandfather by the mast. I have gone to her often, to tell her that all will be fine. My words sound emptier by the hour, as my unease calcifies into terror.

'Mistress,' the captain cries. 'We cannot reach Baiae. The sea and wind won't allow it. Our ship will be torn apart if we continue. We must head to shore.'

'Fine,' I say. 'Do what you must, captain. But not Pompeii. Anywhere but where we came from.'

'Our path will be determined by the wind.'

He shouts instructions at his crew and the ship turns east.

We are moving with the waves now, rather than against them. Our ship moves so quickly that it hums.

We continue east. The shore cannot be seen until suddenly it is shockingly close. I see four ships of the Imperial fleet beached before a large villa.

'There, captain,' I say, pointing at the ships. 'Take us there.'

Near the shore the water is filled with floating ash and pumice stones. The ash is like cement, sealing the pumice stones together into large floating boulders. They thump against the hull as it surges on waves towards the shore.

The ship hits the shore with a jolt; sailors jump into the foaming sea and pull at lines, dragging the ship onto the shore.

The ash continues to fall – with greater frequency. The Imperial ships are black shadows on the beach. A marine runs up to us, one hand over his head to protect against falling pumice stones.

'Soldier,' I say, 'who is in command of your ships today?'

The marine does not recognise the poorly dressed woman before him. But my voice has the similar effect it had on our ship's captain. He replies, quickly: 'The admiral himself, Mistress.'

My heart lifts. Admiral Secundus. Pliny. I couldn't have asked for a better man to find.

'Where is he?'

'We had attempted to rescue the widow Rectina from Oplontis, but the winds forced us to shore here.' The marine points at the villa. 'We've taken shelter inside the home of Pomponianus.'

'Captain,' I say to Verecundus, 'you and your crew will find shelter here. But let me go first.'

'Thank you, Mistress. We will wait at the ship.'

The Batavian and I follow the soldier to the villa.

Suddenly the earth moves. The Batavian grabs my arm and we fall to the beach.

Once the earthquake is over, the Batavian helps me to my feet and we continue our dash to the villa.

The three of us burst into Pomponianus's villa. The atrium is lit by two weak oil lamps. There are more than a dozen people huddled around a long table. Dinner is being served. Household staff are in the midst of clearing the first course. Beneath the skylight, where once water collected in a pool, there is a heap of warm ash and pumice stone. Everyone is cowering, as though the ceiling were about to drop on their heads at any moment. The table is at an odd angle and sparsely set.

As I walk into the atrium, Pomponianus rises and starts wagging his finger. 'We do not have room to house the poor. Off with you!'

I pull back my hood.

'Now, Pomponianus,' I say, 'is that any way to treat a guest on a day like to today.'

There are gasps along the table.

Pliny, who I had not noticed at first, stands. He is beaming. 'Domitilla!' He is on me in an instant, pulling me close with his bear-like arms. Then he pushes me away and admires me, like a long-lost relative. His eyes go to the Batavian and then back to me. 'No doubt you have a story to tell.'

I look past Pliny to the table of cowering guests. 'As do you, I'm sure.'

He smiles. 'You may not be able to tell, but I am in the middle of a rescue mission.' Pliny and his nephew were in Misenum this morning. They had experienced the earthquake but hadn't thought it was serious. Until they spotted the cloud of smoke over Vesuvius. Pliny planned to investigate and had readied three quadriremes to take him close to the phenomenon. As he was leaving, he received a message from Rectina, who lives in Oplontis, which sits at the foot of Vesuvius. Rectina said that there was ash and stone falling from the sky, that it was as dark as night, and that she was prevented from escaping by an unfavourable wind. 'Thus, my scientific foray became a rescue mission. Good intentions that the wind and seas have stymied. We never made it to Oplontis. The winds sent us here. Poor Rectina. She might still be waiting for me.'

I tell Pliny parts of my story, referring to the Batavian as little as possible. 'We were headed to Baiae,' I say. 'but, in these conditions, the journey was nearly impossible.'

'Not *near* impossible,' Pliny says. 'The sea is truly impassable at the moment.'

I had always thought Pliny perpetually composed, too interested in the world to ever be troubled by it. But his excitement as the world is ending is truly remarkable.

And possibly mad.

He seems excited about the novelty of what is happening. It is only when Pliny stops talking, as he stands and listens to wait for my reply, that I notice his breathing is laboured – more than usual. Whatever is happening to the air – the heat and ash – it is not to his benefit.

'So, what happened, Pliny? You could not sail away, so you decided to have a feast?'

'Yes, why not?' he says. 'How else should we wait until the sea is navigable? Speaking of eating, are you hungry?' I am about to say no, but Pliny puts his arm around my shoulder. 'Who knows when we will have the opportunity to eat again, Mistress. We will all need the energy.'

No one speaks. We listen to the sound of Pliny chewing loudly and the hollow thud of pumice stones hitting the roof above. Occasionally one will ricochet through the skylight and everyone at the table jumps with fright.

Everyone except for Pliny.

Captain Verecundus is invited to join us. His crew takes shelter in a separate room with Pliny's sailors. The Batavian sits with the other slaves in the corner of the atrium. Our night in Pompeii is over and we are once again master and slave.

Pliny explains what happened the night of my wedding, after the ships went up in flames. How he helped people out of the sea, and the confrontation between Virgilius's Praetorians and the Parthians.

'How many people died?' I ask.

'A good many. Your brothers lived, thank the gods. But I've seen your brother escape far worse.'

I smile, thinking of my invincible older brother. I'm not sure I ever considered Titus being anything but alive and well. 'And what of my maid, Jacasta?' I ask.

'She was burned, on her hand and arm. Quite badly. But she lived.'

I sigh with relief. 'And the Parthians?'

'Missing. Your brother sent soldiers through the region to find them. But so far they have been unsuccessful.'

The slaves across the room begin to swap theories on what is happening outside. Our table grows quiet to listen.

'The Giants are rising up in revolt,' an old man says. 'They've clawed their way to the surface, from the depths of hell. You can hear their trumpets playing their war song. They're angry. Who wouldn't be? When they find us, they'll crush us with their hands. We're mad not to run. Mad.'

'The whole countryside is alight,' a grey-haired woman says. 'You can smell flesh burning.' She sniffs the air. 'We will all burn when the day is done.'

The scholar, Caecinnius Rufus, a guest of Pomponianus when this all began, is seated at the other end of the table. 'The world is being consumed,' he whispers, 'by chaos and fire. The gods are punishing us.'

Many at the table nod their heads.

Pliny, however, laughs.

'Rufus,' he says, 'you disappoint me. Haven't you read my book? What is happening today is nothing new.'

'Your book never described anything like this.' Rufus's voice has lost its scholarly detachment. It sounds like a twig about to snap in two.

'On the contrary,' Pliny says. 'I refer you to book two, chapter one hundred and ten. I describe mountains, always burning, in which Nature rages, threatening to consume the earth with fire. In the past, from such mountains, clouds of ash have been observed. There is Mount Etna, in Sicily; and the summit of Cophantus, in Bactria; and the White Tower in Susa. There is a mountain in Ethiopia . . .'

'I recall the passage, admiral,' Rufus interrupts, 'but what do those mountains have to do with the fires consuming the countryside.'

'Let's not let fear overwhelm our reason.'

Pliny is enjoying the debate. But then suddenly he is overtaken by a violent cough. When it's over, for a brief moment, he looks defeated; his eyes are glassy and he is out of breath.

Pliny clears his throat and continues, though not with the vigour he had before. 'I also described an event from the Social War, in which the island of Hiera, one of the Æolian isles, erupted in a fire that burned for several days, until the senate performed the proper sacrifices and the fire ceased. It's obvious, isn't it? What we are seeing is the same phenomenon. The difference between the fires of Hiera and the fires of Vesuvius is not in kind, but in degree.'

For Pliny, the world isn't ending; it has merely become more interesting.

We watch as he resumes dipping his bread in fishsauce.

Pliny sends his secretary Spartacus to see if the winds are more favourable. He returns with two men. Both faces are cast in shadow when they enter the atrium; one is bent over a staff.

They shuffle into the atrium.

'My god, Ulpius!' I say, realizing who it is. He is accompanied by his freedman Cyrus. 'What are you doing here?'

A dozen Praetorians and marines stream into the atrium.

'And where is here?' Ulpius asks.

'Stabiae.'

He laughs. 'See, Cyrus. We missed the mark. We'd been on Caesar's business, sailing back to Baiae. But the seas had a different plan for us. The winds and the sea pushed us here.'

Pliny's secretary adds: 'The seas are worse than ever, admiral. There is no hope of sailing today.'

Captain Verecundus appears to know Ulpius. He rises from the table and they embrace. 'Fitting I'd run into you on the strangest day of my life.'

They talk quietly for a moment, like long lost friends. I am too tired to guess how they know each other.

A space is cleared for Ulpius beside me. There is a noticeable change in Pliny. He stares at Ulpius with a look he rarely shows: distrust. Or possibly disgust. I had thought the coldness between them had thawed.

Ulpius cannot see Pliny's glare. He asks for bread, for fish-sauce, for wine.

'I've been thinking of you, Ulpius,' Pliny says.

'Have you?' Ulpius dips his bread.

A large stone collides with the roof. Everyone in the room crouches and looks up. We wait to see if the ceiling will come crashing down.

Pliny remains focused on Ulpius. 'Yes,' he says. 'I have been thinking about a comment you made.'

'You will have to be more specific, Secundus. I am a true wit.'

'You will recall that you recently stated to me – with absolute certainty – the number of times the Parthian hostage, Meherdates, met with the emperor Nero. It was a remarkable observation,' Pliny says. 'How could a Spanish provincial know such an event of the Imperial court?'

There is a shift in Ulpius. He drops his bread and aims his ruined eyes at the admiral.

'And so,' Pliny continues, 'finding this inexplicable, I went to the historians, to the authors who were in Rome at the time, during Claudius's reign, when Nero was an entitled prince running about the Palace. I read Rusticus and Corbulo and other historians. I thought, *now this must be how Ulpius knew what he did.*'

Ulpius's freedman whispers in his ear, but Ulpius waves him away.

'But I reviewed all of the histories and found not a word about the number of times Meherdates met with the Tyrant.'

'Pliny,' I say, trying to diffuse what seems a pointless argument, 'this is an odd time to speak about history. Can this wait for another time?'

Pliny ignores me. To Ulpius, he says, 'I could tell you the number of times that *I* met with Nero. But I was there, in Rome.

You won't find it in any history book. I'm sure Nero could tell you as well. Couldn't he?'

A sequence of large stones hit the roof and those around our table shudder. Our host Pomponianus – whose spirit is waning – squawks like a bird.

I am not sure what Pliny's complaint is with Ulpius, but this is neither the time nor the place.

'Now Pliny,' I say, 'I'm sure this can wait. Ulpius has just been through a great ordeal – as we all have.'

Pliny stares at Ulpius. 'Confess,' he says.

'Confess to what?' Ulpius says.

Pliny waits for what feels like an eternity, then he smiles, as though he's won a great victory. 'I can see I'm right.' He laughs. 'A coward cannot escape his nature.' He slides his chair back with the help of his secretary. 'I think I will close my eyes and get some rest, as we wait for the seas to clear.'

The admiral's breathing is ragged. He has trouble standing. His secretary has to help him.

'I'm sorry, Lucius,' I say to Ulpius, after Pliny has left. 'I'm not sure what has gotten into the admiral.'

'I do,' Ulpius says. 'But it's no fault of yours.'

'What business of Caesar's brought you here?'

Ulpius fills in the blanks of Pliny's story. Senator Sulpicius was suspected of helping the Parthians, so Titus ordered soldiers to watch his home, secretly. Prefect Virgilius left a young tribune in charge who didn't stop or question anyone seen leaving. A woman visited Sulpicius's, and then she left with three men. They headed east, towards the cities along the bay, rather than inland or north.

'Marcus and Theseus were there,' Ulpius says. 'They sent word to me about the three men leaving Sulpicius's. I wouldn't have been much help watching Sulpicius's home, or storming it, if it came to that. So, with the Prefect's blessing, I took two dozen soldiers to see if we could find the three men who'd left Sulpicius's.'

'And?'

'We never found them. We went to Putoeli first. My best guess was they had gone to the largest port to secure passage on a ship. It would be the safest way to escape Italy. We had no luck there, so we headed east. We went to Herculaneum and then we were heading to Pompeii when the wind and seas sent us here.'

'I might know what happened to those three men.' I tell Ulpius how three Parthians found the Batavian and me in Pompeii.

'There were three of them? You are sure? And the Batavian killed all three?'

'Yes.'

Ulpius shakes his head. 'How could they have known where you were? Did anyone know you were hiding in Pompeii?'

'I sent a boy to deliver a message to one of my maids. I wrote a letter to Titus, letting him know I was alive. The boy was to give it to my maid.'

'Which maid?' Ulpius asks. 'Jacasta?'

'No,' I say. 'A different girl.'

Ulpius frowns. 'Is she reliable?'

'Yes,' I say.

Ulpius is thinking, but with his blindfold and ruined eyes, he looks like a lifeless statue. 'It's possible that your message was intercepted. Or the boy who delivered it knew who you were and tried to profit from it. Word somehow got to the Parthians that you were in Pompeii.'

'It's possible,' I say. 'But the boy I hired – he did not seem to know me. And what would the Parthians hope to gain by killing me?'

'That was their mission. Kill the Flavians. And Titus was too well protected. And, I suspect, they needed a distraction to escape Italy. Something to draw attention away from the ports. They didn't know Fortuna was on their side?'

'It was?'

'Yes. Vesuvius has provided a better distraction than they could have ever hoped for.'

Another tremor shakes the earth.

Gaius

24 August

The home of admiral Secundus, Misenum

'Gaius,' Mother says, her voice trembling. 'How much longer must we stay outside?'

'As long as the tremors continue,' I say. 'The buildings have stayed standing so far. But there will come a point when they can't withstand it any longer.'

We are in the garden, under a lemon tree. Dozens of plump lemons lie on the ground, shaken loose by the earth's tremors. Uncle Pliny left on his rescue mission several hours ago. I had tried to stay busy inside, but the tremors became too great. I have been sending Zosimos to the pier to see if word has come from Uncle Pliny. He is coming back now, shaking his head. 'Nothing, Master. The sailors I spoke to doubt whether your uncle's ships could return, given the wind and the sea. They could be waiting for more favourable conditions.'

I picture Uncle Pliny at Rectina's home in Oplontis – or wherever he had to land – calm, confident, enjoying himself as the world unravelled before him. I try my best to emulate his example. I have Zosimos fetch Livy and, taking a seat beside my mother, resume taking notes.

The tremors continue.

Mother abandons her weaving and finds comfort in the arms of her maid. Huddled together, they rock each other, waiting for it all to end. I clench my stylus and close my eyes.

*

Uncle Pliny's Spanish client, Scipio the Spaniard, arrives in the eighth hour.

'Scipio,' I say. 'What are you doing here?'

'I came to see your uncle before I run north. To see if he needed me.'

He looks about the garden and sees mother and her maid under a lemon tree. He sees my books and wax tablet.

'But what are you doing?' he asks. 'Are you reading? The world is ending. You must find safety.'

'Uncle Pliny is on a rescue mission near Vesuvius. I am waiting for him to return.'

'You're mad.' Scipio grabs me by the shoulders. 'Come. I'm heading north, toward Rome. I've spoken to people fleeing the cities under Vesuvius. The closer to the mountain the greater the danger. Everyone is heading north, to safety. Your uncle may already be headed that way himself.'

I push him away. 'All is fine. Nature is nothing to fear,' I say, echoing Uncle Pliny.

Scipio shakes his head. 'Stubbornness runs in the family, doesn't it? If you survive, tell your uncle I was here.'

He turns and leaves.

Zosimos watches Scipio go. He says, 'Master Gaius, I know we must wait for the admiral, but there are many in the household who are scared. They fear for their lives. How much longer will we stay?'

There are two slaves standing behind Zosimos. They are shivering, pale faced, their shoulders stooped. They look defeated and terrified.

I want to wait for Uncle Pliny, to be brave – but would he do the same? I don't think so. His main concern would be those in his household. 'You're right, Zosimus. Gather everyone in the household. Tell them to bring only what they can carry. We'll leave a note for Uncle Pliny, so he knows where to find us.'

Domitilla

◆

25 August
The home of Pomponianus, Stabiae

It's nearly morning and I'm flanked by torches. Yet it is still darker than a moonless night. With my arm outstretched, I can see my hand and no further.

The courtyard is filled with ash and stones, piled up to my knees. The ash has changed. It was once grey, nearly white. Now it's a sinister black. Wading through it is like pushing through heavy snow after a blizzard. The rotting smell of sulphur is also new. It burns my nose; my eyes water. We pass Pomponianus's slaves who are trying to smother a beam of wood that has caught fire. Halfway across the courtyard, I can hear Pliny snoring.

Pomponianus knocks on the door. 'Admiral!' He sounds exhausted and shaken. 'Please wake up. Our lives hang in the balance.'

The admiral's secretary does not wait for his master to rise. He begins to pull on the door, but it is blocked by the ash and stones in the courtyard. Spartacus slams his hand on the door. 'Master!'

We hear the admiral on the other side of the door. 'What's wrong, Spartacus? Are you pushing on the door? Move.'

'No, Master,' Spartacus yells. 'It's the debris. It's up to our knees in the courtyard. You will need to push.'

'Is it? Curious,' Pliny says. 'Alright. On three. One. Two. Three.'

Spartacus and Pomponianus pull on the door's handle. We can hear Pliny grunting as he pushes from the other side. The door opens wide enough for the admiral to squeeze through.

Pliny stares at the ground, marvelling at the accumulated debris. He smells the air. 'Is that sulphur?'

'Yes, Master,' Spartacus says. 'The phenomena have grown more ominous. The ash is black now, and the earth tremors are more frequent.'

'Curious,' Pliny says.

The admiral's laboured breathing has grown worse. He sounds as though he has just finished sprinting across the courtyard.

'Admiral,' I say, 'we fear Pomponianus's home could fall down on our heads. We need a plan.'

'Yes,' he says. 'Let's gather everyone together.'

Inside the atrium, the air is thick with heat and the bitter taste of ash.

The murmuring crowd gathers before Pliny. 'As I see it, we have two, possibly three options,' he says. 'We can remain inside, we can go to the ships, or we can walk north.'

The crowd hollers their preference.

Pliny waves his arms and the crowd quiets. 'We must pick the least dangerous course, of course. Staying inside is possibly the *most* dangerous. Brick homes such as this can withstand tremors, but only up to a certain point. I think it only a matter of time before Pomponianus's home falls.'

'But if we leave,' someone interjects, 'it is too dark to walk. And the falling stones could kill a man.'

'I agree. The darkness is not ideal but lack of light will not kill a man,' Pliny says. 'As for the stones, we can use items from this house to protect ourselves.'

'Where to then?' a man yells.

'The safest course is to head back to the shore and wait for the sea to improve,' Pliny says. 'There are so many of us, going north, through difficult terrain – it would be slow and treacherous. And—'

Pliny coughs uncontrollably. He braces himself by putting his hand on his secretary's shoulder. When he's done, blood stains his lower lip. He continues, 'And we do not know if the conditions are worse inland. They very well could be.' He takes a deep breath. 'Well? Shall we head to the shore?'

The crowd agrees with the admiral's suggestion with reluctant silence.

The sea is a slurry of floating pumice stone and ash. The sky is so dark we cannot see past the breaking waves. We have no hope of leaving by ship. We will have to wait.

Many of us are wearing a pillow tied to the top of our head to protect us from the pumice stones that continue to fall. Others, like the Batavian, have made makeshift shields out of items from Pomponianus's home. Tables and chairs with the legs removed.

Captain Verecundus and his crew decide to take their chances inland. 'Good luck to you, Mistress,' he says. 'I hope to find you in Baiae, alive and well.'

'Good fortune, Captain.'

They march off into the darkness. Those of us who remain take shelter beside the hull of one of Pliny's ships. Sails are removed to create a canopy. We have to swat ash and pumice stone off of it, over and over again, and from ourselves, for fear of being buried alive.

Morning does not come. I wonder if it ever will, whether the sun has been extinguished. The air is dense with sulphur and ash. I feel as though I am going to choke on it. The sea remains mountainous and unnavigable; the wind unrelenting.

Suddenly, from the direction of Vesuvius, there is an explosion – so strong that it shakes the earth, followed by the sound of an inferno scorching the countryside.

A fire is visible in the distance.

We stare in the direction of Vesuvius. We wait for a fire to consume us all.

But it doesn't come. Only a stronger smell of sulphur.

People are crying and praying to the gods.

I go to Pliny and kneel beside him. 'The sea is not improving, admiral. We should leave. We should run.'

His eyes are slow to focus on me. 'Domitilla?' he says. He looks disoriented. His secretary is on his knees, holding a wet cloth on his master's forehead. I did not think it possible, but his breathing has grown worse.

'Water, Spartacus. Please.'

Spartacus leaves.

I grab Pliny by the arm. 'We need to get you to where the air is less oppressive,' I say, trying to help him stand. He raises a foot off the ground, before collapsing back to the sail he is using as a bed.

'I will remain here, I think.' His voice is solemn. 'Make sure your brother listens to you,' he says.

'Pliny, don't talk—'

He waves his hand, interrupting me.

'Listen to me, Mistress. Ensure the emperor heeds your advice. He trusts you. He relies on you.'

I feel tears forming.

'You must get everyone away from here. But first, before you go, get me Ulpius. I would like a word with him.'

With the help of his freedman, Ulpius is brought to Pliny's side. They speak in whispers. Ulpius nods, gravely.

Pliny removes a ring and hands it to Ulpius.

When they are finished, Pliny waves me over. 'I shall give it one final effort,' he says. 'But if I cannot make it, you must keep this group moving. Go north. Stay on this side of the Sorno river. Give Vesuvius a wide berth.'

I take Pliny's hand and kiss it. 'You are a credit to the empire.' I begin to cry. 'To our family.'

'As are you, my dear.'

The group is organised into double file. We have ten torches – which barely provides enough light to see a pace in any direction. One of Pomponianus's slaves, a local Campanian boy who knows the region well, is put at the head of the column. I make sure little Petra and her grandfather are close to me.

Pliny is the last to join the line. Spartacus helps his master stand and puts the admiral's arm on his shoulders.

They take two steps towards us and then Pliny collapses. His breathing quickens.

Spartacus is crying out, 'No, no, no.'

Pliny's breathing grows faster and shorter.

We are unable to do anything but watch.

Pliny's final breath seems to stick in his lungs: he breathes in but not out. He grabs his chest, his body spasms for a time, and then it finally relaxes, as life escapes him.

The admiral – the invincible, tireless Pliny – is gone.

Spartacus sobs.

All of us are paralyzed.

The Batavian walks to Pliny and glides his hand over the admiral's face, closing his eyes. He grabs Spartacus by the arm and drags him to his feet. 'Come,' the Batavian says. He pulls Spartacus toward us and he eventually relents. He joins the line, still sobbing.

We start to walk north.

Pliny's body is left on the shore, buried under warm black ash.

The hill is steep and densely populated with trees. Everyone grips the filthy tunic of the man or woman ahead of them, making a human chain. Our torches provide enough light that we do not trip on the earth, but little more. The local boy seems to know the way and for a time we move with purpose.

There is another explosion in the distance. We stop and wait for a fire to consume us. The earth trembles and a few people lose their balance and fall to the forest floor.

But no fires come.

We keep walking.

Our torches begin to run out of fuel. They extinguish one after the next. When the last one goes out, it is as though we are locked in a room in the middle of the night without a window.

There is a weight to the darkness. A presence.

We stand in silence, shaking with fear.

More than one person is crying.

I kneel beside little Petra, the girl we brought from Pompeii. I can't see her or she me. I grip her hand and whisper that everything will be okay.

'Why have we stopped?'

The voice belongs to Ulpius.

Cyrus, his freedman, must have explained that the torches have gone out because Ulpius then says, 'What does that matter?'

For the blind senator, every day is lost in darkness.

'Ulpius,' I say, trying to control the fear in my voice, 'can you lead us through this?'

'Of course,' he says. 'If someone puts me at the head of the line.'

Ulpius makes his way to the front of the line. The local boy who had been leading stands on my left, gripping my tunic.

Ulpius starts walking without warning. It's good to move again. The darkness is still overwhelming, but the sound of our feet on the forest floor, and Ulpius tapping trees and rocks with his staff keep the malevolence at bay.

We walk for hours, over the hill and out of the forest.

There is a grey dot on the horizon. It looks like a giant grey eye, watching us walk towards it.

We keep trudging uphill, toward the grey eye. Slowly the blackness lightens into a dense grey fog. Then the fog begins to dissipate. A quarter of an hour later we step into natural sunlight.

It is the middle of the day, the sun is overhead.

Some scream with pleasure. Others drop to their knees to thank their favourite god.

Behind us is a wall of grey smoke; it stretches north and west, as far as the eye can see.

Ulpius asks why everyone is reacting as they are.

'We have been delivered from the darkness,' Pomponianus says.

'Ah,' Ulpius says, 'how fortunate for you.'

Barlaas

25 August

Two miles north of Naples

Marcus returns with Prefect Virgilius and three Praetorians. Their faces are grim.

'The barracks in Baiae were empty,' Marcus says. He had left hours ago to find help. 'The entire bay is running north. Or hiding, waiting for this to be over.' He shakes his head. 'Some are saying giants have been spotted in the hills around Vesuvius.'

'Giants?'

Marcus nods. The boy is not one to scare easily, but whatever is happening out there, it has him shaken – all of us.

Prefect Virgilius looks around the empty villa – the one he left filled with soldiers. He is surprised to find only Theseus, Manlius and myself. 'How long ago did Catullus run off?'

'Three, maybe four hours ago,' Manlius says. 'Just before we sent Marcus for more help. The legate said he and his soldiers were needed elsewhere, to help with whatever is happening at Vesuvius.'

Without hiding my disgust, I say, 'The little Roman shit was scared. You could see it in his eyes.'

'So how many does that make us?' Virgilius asks. 'Eight. Eight against – how many? At least a dozen Parthians and an army of gladiators?'.

Theseus calls from the window where he has been watching Sulpicius's villa. He says, 'Sulpicius plans to leave before dawn. We need to move. Now.'

We abandon the villa. Outside, the air is warm and thick. We are on top of a hill and Sulpicius's compound is below, with a thin forest of trees in between. To the west, there is Vesuvius and the endless, billowing cloud of smoke.

'Eight against an army,' Virgilius says, staring at Vesuvius. 'But it could be worse. Apollo protect those caught under Vesuvius's shadow.'

We stand and watch the fire, mesmerized.

Theseus starts to move downhill and we follow, single file, toward Sulpicius's villa.

Halfway down the hill we hear an explosion – a roaring crack – and the ground sways. I put out my arms, trying to keep my balance. Two of the Praetorians fall to the forest floor.

'What was *that*?' the Prefect asks.

No one has the answer.

We reach a grove of lemon trees. A gladiator is waiting for us, Theseus's man on the inside. He likely fought in the games – the gladiatorial matches that seem a lifetime ago – but I cannot place him, not without his helmet.

'This is Minnow,' Theseus says. 'He's agreed to help.'

Minnow squints and counts our group. 'Is this all of you?'

'Afraid so,' Theseus says.

'How many are inside?' Manlius asks.

'Sulpicius has thirty gladiators,' Minnow says. 'There's another dozen Parthians and three Roman soldiers.'

'Shit,' the Prefect says.

'How is Olympias?' Marcus asks.

'She'll be happy to see you,' Minnow says.

Olympias must be the girl Marcus was talking about before.

'And what of the gladiators?' Virgilius asks. 'Are any with you?'

'Three for certain,' Minnow says. 'We've been with Sulpicius for years, and we've had enough of his cruelty. But one,' he looks at Marcus, 'Olympias's brother – he was badly injured in the games. So he won't be much help. The rest . . . I'm not sure. If this were any other day, I'd wager they'd fight to save their master's life. But today . . .' He looks in the direction of Vesuvius. 'We are a superstitious lot,' he says, 'Gladiators, I mean. The gods hold our fate in their hands. They decide whether we live or die in each fight. So, all this . . .' He pauses again, trying to describe the unravelling of the world. 'They're scared. They might jump at the chance to run.'

'What's Sulpicius's plan?' Virgilius asks. 'Is he expecting us?'

'He's had us ready for a fight ever since the Parthians came,' Minnow says. 'He knew you were watching his house – your men made it obvious. Red capes don't blend into a forest very well. We also saw most of your men pack up and leave a few hours ago, but Sulpicius won't relax until the Parthians are away.'

'Is that the plan?' Virgilius asks. 'For the Parthians to run?'

Minnow nods. 'They've got a boat in Puteoli ready to take them from Italy.'

'Is the Aryan boy inside,' I ask. 'Sinnaces?'

I picture Sinnaces escaping on a boat, staring at the Italian shore as it recedes into the distance.

'You mean a Parthian?' Minnow asks. 'I don't know his name, but there's a Parthian boy. Eighteen or so? He's not faring well. He paces nervously, day and night.'

I can feel every man's eyes on me. Do they see my shame?

'The boy is mine,' I say. 'He will die by my hand, not a Roman's.'

They wait for me to say more. But what more is there to say? Honour demands I kill the boy.

Manlius, knowing I have nothing more to say, breaks the silence. 'How will we get in?'

'Same way I got out,' Minnow says. He kneels and draws in the dirt two large squares, connected by a smaller rectangle. 'There's an old pipe, tall enough for a man to stand, which connects to the baths. It will bring us into this part of Sulpicius's villa.' He points at one of the squares. Then he points at the second large square. 'This is the Lanista. Other than a few gladiators patrolling the villa, most of the gladiators will be here.'

'Can we keep the gladiators locked inside the Lanista?' Virgilius asks.

'I don't think so,' Minnow says. 'The gate is open. And the moment Sulpicius or the Parthians see us, they will sound the alarm and all the gladiators will come running.'

'What do we do then?' Virgilius asks. 'We can't fight that many men at once.'

'I can handle them,' Marcus says.

A few eyebrows are raised.

'You?' Manlius asks. 'You are going to handle thirty gladiators on your own?'

Marcus looks up at the setting sun. 'Yes, but after dark. And I'll need a chicken and a translator.'

'A what?' I ask, with obvious annoyance. I had been coming around on Marcus. But I can't stomach arrogance. Particularly in battle. In my experience, it is what gets you killed.

The boy ignores me. 'Theseus,' he asks, 'how's your Etruscan?'

'Shit,' Theseus says.

'It doesn't matter,' Marcus says, then turns to Minnow. 'Can you get me into the Lanista, without the Parthians sounding the alarm?'

Minnow nods.

'Are we really going to put our lives into the hands of this boy?' I ask.

Prefect Virgilius looks at Marcus. 'What do you plan to do?'

'I'm going to tell them to leave,' Marcus says. He begins to admire my cloak, even though it is twice his size. 'Can I borrow this?'

Marcus's brief explanation is enough to convince Virgilius – maybe not that his plan will work but to let him try. I argue against it, but only up to a point. This is my one chance to get Sinnaces and clear my name. The odds are long – whether we use Marcus's plan or any other.

We follow Minnow through a ditch, water up to our knees. We move slowly, crouched as low as we are able, until we reach the pipe. It's tall enough for a boy to stand in, but I have to duck like a giant entering a peasant's hut. But it serves its purpose. After a hundred paces or so, we climb into Sulpicius's baths. Two people are waiting for us. A gladiator with his arm in a sling and a girl with stunning blue eyes.

When the girl sees Marcus she runs to him and they embrace.

Olympias, I suppose.

The gladiator with his arm in a sling watches us empty out of the sewer and says, 'This is it?'

'Not to worry,' Minnow says, nodding at Marcus. 'We have a plan.'

Marcus slides his finger along the rim of the sewer and uses the sludge he scavenged to paint a design on his face, lines under his eyes, along his nose, and two strikes across his chin.

'What sort of plan?' the injured gladiator asks.

Minnow takes us to the training ground, a rectangle of sand, surrounded by a two-storey colonnade.

The sky is grey and growing darker.

Marcus begins to carve a large square into the dirt, the size of three ox carts, side-by-side.

A bell rings. Our presence has been detected.

Gladiators stream into the training ground and along the balcony. They look exhausted and fragile and ready to kill to save their own skin.

There are dozens of them, surrounding us on all sides. They whack their steel swords against wooden shields; they are growling and whistling and chanting. All of it is meant to intimidate us.

It works.

We are all trained warriors but we have fought enough wars to know it is usually a numbers game. They have the numbers, we don't.

Did we make a mistake thinking this boy could somehow overcome these odds? There is something special about this boy, though. I saw it when we hunted together, what feels like an eternity ago; I saw it when we diced; I heard it in Sinnaces's voice when he talked about Marcus the Spaniard; and I see it now. He is smart, focused, determined, and slightly mad – all of which we'll need if we are going to walk out of here alive.

The girl, Olympias, pushes her way toward us. She's fetched the two chickens Marcus asked for. She's carrying them by the feet, their wings flapping.

The gladiators are reluctant to attack. I'm not sure why. There is something strange about Marcus – his incongruous pacing, his chanting in a foreign tongue; the markings on his face; my oversized cloak. I can understand their reluctance. He looks like a demented priest or a sorcerer.

Marcus mutters something in a foreign tongue and Theseus yells at Minnow, 'Tell them you have brought a priest of Vulcan.'

Minnow yells this and the gladiators' uproar – their growling and the clang of steel against wood – lessens.

There is a commotion on the balcony above. Sulpicius and the Roman soldiers – the three traitors – are at the railing. The Parthian brothers, Farhod and Farhad, and Sinnaces are there as well. Sinnaces is nervously biting his lip, though I'm not sure he sees me yet.

'What are you waiting for!' Sulpicius cries. 'Kill them!'

Marcus resumes his chanting, louder this time. Theseus translates. 'This is a priest of Vulcan. He is here to tell you how to survive the wrath of his patron god.'

The gladiators don't move.

Then there is an explosion in the distance, like the one we heard before, and the ground shakes violently.

When it's over the gladiators are silent.

Marcus takes one of the chickens from Olympias. He kneels and cuts it with his dagger. Blood pours onto the sand. He continues his strange chant.

Sulpicius yells, 'Kill them, kill them all.' But his gladiators are mesmerized.

Marcus inspects the chicken's small, bloody liver, pinched between his thumb and index finger.

He chants and Theseus translates. 'The god of fire is *angry* . . . '

Marcus points at Sulpicius.

'. . . at your master.'

Marcus sacrifices the second chicken.

'Soon,' Theseus says, translating Marcus's chanting, 'Sulpicius and all he holds dear will burn. If you wish to be spared, you only have one hope.'

Marcus points at the gate.

'Run,' Theseus says. '*Run!*'

The gladiators take a moment to absorb these words.

Sulpicius screams at his doctore to whip his gladiators out of their stupor. The doctore unfurls his whip, but Minnow grabs the doctore by the wrist and shakes his head.

The gladiators are exhausted, superstitious, terrified of whatever is happening near Vesuvius, and wanting nothing more than to run. But years of servitude make abandoning their master nearly impossible. A stalemate is reached. One that feels impossible to break.

But this day is not short of phenomenon.

Ash begins to fall around us, like snow, warm and smelling of fire.

The gladiators look horrified. We all are.

Marcus chants.

'Run,' Theseus says, 'or burn.'

One gladiator pushes his way through the crowd toward the gate. The herd follows. Soon they become a mob, shoving each other, barrelling their way to the gate.

Sulpicius is screaming at his men to stop, threatening their lives if they abandon him.

'Jupiter's fucking arse,' Virgilius says. 'It worked.'

The gladiators are streaming out one end of the training ground, running for their lives. A gate opens at the other end and Sulpicius, the turncoat Roman soldiers and my fellow countrymen enter the training ground.

Two battle lines are drawn. We are still outnumbered, but not like before. Now it is a fair fight.

Across from me are the two brothers, Farhad and Farbod, daggers in hand.

They charge, running as fast as they can.

I have time for one arrow. For one man to die. I notch an arrow in the string of my bow, draw it back, and aim it at the brother on the left.

I open my hand and the arrow is gone.

It hits the mark; the force is so strong it sends the brother backwards before he drops to the ground.

The second brother slows to watch his brother die.

Will this give me time to draw another arrow?

I reach for my quiver . . .

The brother is again running toward me.

I pull out an arrow . . .

And Farhad's dagger pierces my chest, near my shoulder. My left hand instinctively drops the bow and reaches up to stop the blade from going any deeper.

Farhad's force carries us backward, and we slam into the sand. He is on top of me, his hands on his dagger. He twists the blade and I scream in agony.

I've dropped the arrow, but see it lying beside me.

Farhad pulls his dagger out of my chest and I scream, a rush of blood fills the void left by the blade.

Farhad raises the blade to finish me.

I grab the arrow, along the shaft, near the tip, and swing it toward his neck. It pierces the flesh below his ear. His eyes go wide with surprise.

He drops his dagger.

Blood drips from his mouth.

I push the arrow deeper and his hands fall to his side; his eyes go dark and lifeless.

I push the corpse off me.

The battle continues throughout the training ground. Virgilius and his Praetorians are squared off against the turncoat Romans. Manlius and Theseus are surrounded by Parthian soldiers. I retrieve my bow and notch an arrow. I fell one, two, then three Parthians, quickly. Expertly. As I did when I was a young man.

Manlius kills a turncoat Roman soldier, then goes down onto one knee to catch his breath. He smiles at me from across the training ground.

Marcus is guiding the girl Olympias and her brother away from the fighting. He is getting them away, to safety.

On the other side of the training ground, peering around the gate, is Sinnaces. He is too scared to fight.

He sees me. We lock eyes.

He runs.

I sprint toward the villa. Inside the hallways are empty save for a few slaves. They scream when they see me running toward them and fall to the ground. I reach the atrium and glimpse the black of Sinnaces's cloak disappear around a corner.

I follow him down a set of stairs, and I see him across a hallway closing a caged door behind him.

'Stop,' I yell.

He looks up as he is fumbling with the lock.

I draw an arrow from my quiver, raise my bow, aim and shoot. The arrow flies between the iron bars and pierces his shoulder. He falls back, crying in agony. Surprisingly, he has enough fortitude to quickly stand and go for the lock. He knows locking that door is the only way to save his life.

The lock clicks.

'You betrayed me,' I say. 'And the memory of your father.'

'You are the turncoat,' he says. 'It was *you* who betrayed your country.'

I hear the lock click. I draw another arrow and let it fly. I'd been aiming for a spot between two iron bars, at the boy's chest, but I miss the mark by an inch, and it ricochets off of an iron bar and narrowly misses Sinnaces.

He smiles and runs for his life.

Back in the training ground, the battle is over. Of the three Praetorians we brought, two are dead. Another is injured but handling it like a man. Theseus is wiping his blade clean. He looks like he's been to the market, or on a hike, rather than a battle for his life. Manlius is cut and bruised, but alive. He still does not have his strength back so the fight tonight has exhausted him. He smiles when he sees me.

Virgilius is kneeling beside a soldier – one of the Roman turncoats. The soldier has a large red nose, the type a man gets from too much drink. He is badly injured: there is a gash across his belly, wide and bloody. He's on his back, panting and spitting blood.

'What was your plan?' Virgilius asks.

The man spits in Virgilius's direction.

The Prefect sticks his hand into the injured soldier's belly.

The traitor cries out.

'Make this easier on yourself,' Virgilius says. 'Tell us where your friends who escaped planned to go.'

'Fuck you.'

'Be sensible, soldier,' Virgilius says, 'this could be your chance.'

'My chance?'

'To make amends for being a traitor.'

The soldier laughs. Blood drips from the corners of his mouth.

'*You* are the traitor. You support a pretender to the throne. I serve the last of the Trojans. The legitimate emperor.'

Virgilius rolls his eyes. 'Don't tell me.'

The soldier is fervent; his voice rises. 'I serve Nero Claudius Caesar, emperor of Rome.'

Virgilius sticks his hand back into the man's guts and the soldier hollers in pain. Virgilius removes his hand and we listen to the soldier's pathetic panting.

And then he is gone.

'Fuck,' Virgilius says. He looks up. 'Are any more of them alive?'

Manlius shakes his head. 'They are all dead or they ran.'

'And what of Sulpicius?'

'Gone.'

'Fuck,' Virgilius says again.

We hear a noise and turn to see Marcus walking back into the training ground. He has Sulpicius with him. The senator's face is cut and his arms are tied behind his back. The girl, Olympias, and the injured gladiator are with them.

The boy never ceases to surprise.

'I thought you ran?' I say to Marcus.

'I took Olympias into the house to keep her safe. We were in Sulpicius's office when he came running in. He opened his safe and was filling a bag with gold.' Marcus kicks the back of Sulpicius's legs and the senator falls to his knees. 'The greedy bastard could have gotten away but wanted his money.'

Theseus walks up to Marcus and inspects the cuts on his face. 'Was he alone?'

'No, his doctore was with him,' Marcus says. He's exhausted but smiling. 'Nothing I couldn't handle.'

Domitilla

♦

26 August
Three miles north of Stabiae

There is a town in the hills above Stabiae. When the people who
live there saw us approaching – exhausted and filthy refugees –
they brought us water and bread. We spent the night camped by
a fire, listening to the stories of a local woman, who claims to
have lived long enough to see Hannibal marching through these
hills on elephants. We are happy for the distraction.

The cloud from Vesuvius is gone the next morning. The air is
less smoky, less grey. And the tremors have stopped.

For now.

We decide to go back the way we came. The terrain between
here and Baiae is treacherous and it would take us days to walk
what we could traverse by boat in a matter of hours. We retrace
the route we walked in darkness. By the light of the day, the forest is ominous. There is a thick coat of grey ash over everything,
and there are no animals. No birds chirping above us. No deer
disappearing into the brush.

But the sun – the glorious, warm, beautiful sun – is in the sky
once again. It seems proof the world did not end.

We reach the shore and find the sea is calm. There are pumice
stones floating in the water, but they are not nearly the large
islands of stone that they formed the night before.

Pliny's secretary finds the spot where he left his master. The
body is buried under several feet of ash. He kneels, paying his
respects.

Captain Verecundus's ship is gone. He and his crew have already sailed away, or their ship dislodged from the beach during the tremors and the gods alone know where they are.

Spartacus sees me staring off at the bay, looking for the ship that brought me here. 'Augusta,' he says, 'not to worry. Two of our three ships are ready to leave immediately. We can take you home.'

'And the third ship?'

'Beyond repair. Another victim to leave on the beach.'

Before departing, we go to the water to rinse the ash from our hair and skin, wading in up to our shoulders. The sea is warm and a cloudy grey, polluted with Vesuvius's waste. The sensation of water on my skin is welcome; it's a relief to scrub away the ash and grime that caked my skin for days.

The Batavian is beside me.

'Alwin,' I say, quietly, so no one can hear. He is scrubbing the pulse of black hair on his chest. 'We are going back to Baiae today. What happened in Pompeii . . . It can never happen again.'

His eyes shift from me to the horizon. Is he sad? It's difficult to say.

He nods.

Without warning, he dives under water. He appears a few paces away and swims away from shore, arm over arm, and then floats alone in the sea.

Our ship heads west. Vesuvius is off our starboard flank, visible for the first time in two days. The mountain is different. It looks shorter, with a less tapered peak, as though the top third of a pomegranate had been lopped off. The cities at the foot of the hills are gone. Pompeii, Herculaneum, Oplontis – all gone, as if they never existed. In their place is a grey emptiness, a desert of ash. There are no trees, no buildings. The fire must have burned it all or buried it under the falling ash. How many people perished? How many thousands?

The people on the ship are staring at the wasteland in silence. Even the rowers have paused from their task, to watch, to mutter prayers.

'Where is our home?' Petra whispers to her grandfather.

Her grandfather quietly weeps.

I convince Spartacus to go to Misenum first, so he can tell Pliny's nephew about the admiral's fate. He has a right to know as soon as we can tell him.

We pass through the break wall into Misenum's harbour. There is havoc but not devastation. The city's streets and red roofs are covered in grey ash, but the aggregate is not as deep as in Stabiae, and there are no pumice stones. A few buildings have collapsed, and a ship sits on the pier, with its hull cracked open like an egg. Nearby, a man and his slave are pulling a squid off a roof.

Pliny's nephew is on the pier when we arrive. He must have spotted the ships as they were approaching, recognizing them as two of the three his uncle left with.

Our ship slides against the pier; sailors throw lines to their colleagues on shore.

Gaius is waiting by the gangplank. He sees Spartacus, but not his uncle. He is uneasy. He studies Spartacus's face, then mine.

Before we take another step, Gaius collapses in tears.

Within the hour, our ship casts off again to take me to Baiae. We arrive as the sun is setting.

Praetorians on the pier recognize me. Before hurrying me into a waiting litter, I point at Petra and her grandfather. 'Those two are coming with me. They are guests of the Imperial family. Treat them accordingly.'

The soldiers nod and we make our way through the city.

Baiae has fared much as Misenum did. Ash blankets everything, and a few buildings have fallen. Otherwise, the city is still standing. The Praetorians tell me the city was abandoned early yesterday, and its populace has only started to return. Now there are owners standing outside their buildings, evaluating the damage; everywhere slaves are sweeping up the ash.

Livia is in the atrium when I arrive.

'Mistress,' she says, 'thank the gods you are alive.'

'You received my message?' I say. 'From Pompeii?'

'Yes, Mistress. And I did as you instructed. I gave it to your brother.'

'Did you tell anyone else?'

'No, Mistress,' she says. 'Of course not. I did only as you asked. Why?'

'Someone knew where I was.'

'What do you mean?'

I explain the attack by the Parthians, how they must have known where I was staying. Livia looks shocked. 'Perhaps someone spotted you coming into Pompeii. You are the most famous woman in the empire, after all.' She takes my hand. 'But you won't need to worry about the Parthians.'

She explains that the Parthians have all been captured or escaped from Italy.

'How is Jacasta?' I ask.

Livia bites her lip.

'Take me to her.'

Livia takes my hand and escorts me through the villa to Jacasta's room, which neighbours mine. Jacasta is lying down and half-awake when we arrive. She stumbles to her feet when she sees me.

'Mistress,' she says, with tears in her eyes. 'You're alive.'

Now that she is standing, I can see that she has bandages on her left arm and the left side of her neck. As Pliny had told me, she was badly burned when her ship was set alight, before she could jump into the water. She tells me how she clung to a shard of wood until the admiral pulled her out of the water.

She is in pain. She moves slowly, and there is a grimace on her face as she gets back into bed.

She sees me watching her and says, 'I'm fine, Mistress. Really, I am. A bit uncomfortable but that will pass.'

That night I dream of impenetrable black hills above Stabiae. I hear a child crying for help and the crackle of invisible flames. I look frantically for the child, but the darkness is unrelenting. The earth shakes and I fall to my knees.

I wake up with an intense nausea and a metallic taste in my mouth. The sickness persists until the sixth hour. Jacasta – who has, against her doctor's wishes, left her bed to see me – worries my nausea is from exposure to the ash and heat of Vesuvius. 'I should get the doctor,' she says.

'No need,' I say, as I force myself to eat some bread. 'The nausea is gone now.'

Jacasta studies me. Then she smiles. She checks to make sure we are alone.

'Tell me again what happened in Pompeii?'

Gaius

◆

1 September

Outside the home of Lucius Ulpius
Traianus, Rome

Back in Rome, amid the bedlam. The narrow alleyways teeming with people, the tenements towering overhead, casting long, cool shadows. The constant, chaotic symphony of noise: terracotta smashing, hellos in Latin, goodbyes in Hebrew, a Bactrian curse; laughing, crying, bartering; somewhere liquid – water? wine? urine? – splashes against a slab of travertine; dogs barking, children crying, a snake hissing; the steady scrape of a sharpening stone against an old rusty blade. And the smell. Medicinal unguents, fermented fishsauce, frying oil, freshly baked bread, stale urine, the fuller's ammonia, and always, in every corner of the city, something burning. Wood, incense, myrrh, rosemary, braziers.

This chaos used to require a reprieve, a trip south or north, to the hills or the sea, anywhere quiet and slow, to restore one's peace of mind. Now, after what happened on the bay, I find the bedlam comforting; and the quiet of Campania menacing.

I call on the Ulpii early, not long after sunrise. The old woman, Elsie, lets me in. I can tell by the way she smiles at me that she pities me. 'This way, my Lord.'

Marcus and his uncle are in the library, deep in conversation. In front of them is a map of Parthia. For a brief moment, I think this will be good intelligence to give Uncle Pliny. But then it hits me by surprise – as it has often since his death – the awful reality that I can never tell him anything again.

The black emptiness in my stomach grows; my legs feel heavy.

'Gaius,' Ulpius says, after Elsie announces my arrival. 'Welcome.' He waves me towards a chair.

'I can't stay long,' I say. 'Uncle Pliny's will is being unsealed this morning. I need to be at his ho—'

My voice cracks when I realize this is wrong. It's not *his* home anymore, by law. Later today I will learn who inherited it. It makes me sad to think of it being in the possession of someone else.

'I need to be there by the third hour,' I say.

'Of course,' Ulpius says.

I chance a look at Marcus. He has the same pitiful smile that Elsie had. He asks about my journey back to Rome, trying to distract me. The route, the timing. He asks about my mother.

'You're to meet with the emperor?' I ask, steering the conversation to a more serious subject. 'You're petitioning to go to Parthia? To deal with the False Nero?'

Marcus nods.

This begs two questions, both of which Uncle Pliny wanted to answer before he passed. Why is Ulpius obsessed with the False Nero? And who *is* Ulpius?

But I don't have the strength to pursue these questions, not with the vigour that Uncle Pliny would have.

'Do you know Parthia well?' Ulpius asks.

'Not at all.'

Marcus points at a tract of land near the Caspian Sea. 'The False Nero is rumoured to be here. In Hyrcania. With Artabanus. This is likely where Sinnaces and the missing Parthians escaped to as well.'

'I cannot fathom travelling so far,' I say, marvelling at the map.

'Do you want to come with us?' Ulpius asks. 'We could ask Caesar. I'm sure he would agree.'

'Oh, I couldn't possibly,' I say. 'I hope to hold a minor office next year, possibly preside in the Centumviral court. And I am not sure, with my uncle's death . . .' I try to fight it but there is emotion in my voice. 'What duties I will have here in Rome.'

'Marcus,' Ulpius says, holding up his hands, 'help me please.'

The younger Ulpii goes to the elder and helps him stand and walk to a chair beside mine. Ulpius sits and leans on his staff. He pats my knee.

'I barely knew my father,' he says. 'He died when I was still very young, but I recall two characteristics well. The man was a drunk and he was an embarrassment. And one must be a true embarrassment for a boy of three to see it. It is from this vantage that I offer you the following advice. You were given one of the greatest fortunes a man can have. You had a role model, an exemplary one. He died, but all men die. Before he breathed his last, you had many good years with the admiral. Be grateful. Mourn him because the admiral is deserving of mourning. But thank the gods you had the uncle you did.'

It takes all my strength not to weep at this advice.

'Thank you,' I say.

A throat is cleared.

I turn to see blue eyes. They belong to the girl, Olympias. Ulpius must have taken her into their home after Sulpicius was arrested.

'Master Gaius,' she says, bowing, 'I am so sorry for the loss of your uncle.'

She whispers in Marcus's ear and he says to me, 'I have to go, Gaius. I will write to you while we are in Parthia.' We embrace and he leaves with Olympias.

I am alone with Ulpius.

'Did you know that I was with your uncle when he died?' Ulpius says.

'Yes, I heard.'

'It is no secret he did not like me, but I think, in his last moments, we reached an accord of a kind.' He takes out a gold ring from his pocket with a large carnelian stone. Uncle Pliny's ring. 'Before he died, your uncle told me I was to offer you whatever assistance you required. And he gave me this ring, to give to you.'

I take the ring and admire the dark red stone. 'He told you to look after me? That does not sound like Uncle Pliny. He did not . . .'

'Your uncle did not trust me. Don't be afraid to say it, Gaius. He despised me. He did not ask me to look after you, but to assist you should you need me. That is an important distinction. Your uncle was as smart as they come. In his last moments, he articulated something to me that I knew in my heart but hadn't understood. He knew that I have a debt I am trying to repay. He did not trust me to look after you. But he said, as part of my atonement, I was to do whatever you request of me. I am not your mentor, but your humble serv-ant. I'm sure this makes no sense to you, and you do not need to take me up on the offer. I am only letting you know the bargain that was struck between your uncle and me. You have a friend in the Ulpii. Don't be afraid to call on us, should the need arise.'

Less than an hour later, I am at Uncle Pliny's home. Spartacus, Uncle Pliny's secretary, greets me at the door. He looks like I feel. Lost.

We embrace.

'Come,' he says, taking my arm. 'The praetor is here.'

Uncle Pliny's house is unchanged since I saw it last, yet it feels strange as I enter the atrium, unfamiliar and empty.

The praetor is in the study. He has brought a secretary to record what happens, several attendant slaves, and a Vestal Virgin, dressed in white, her head bowed. She is holding a sealed roll of papyrus.

Uncle Pliny's will.

The praetor is a serious man, short in stature and in temperament. He has taken the liberty of sitting at Uncle Pliny's desk.

'Come. Sit,' he says pointing at a chair. He does not look up from his wax tablet. 'Shall we begin?'

'Are we waiting for anyone else?' I ask.

'No,' the praetor says. He snaps his fingers. 'The will.'

The Vestal Virgin frowns at the lack of decorum.

'I have been handed the will of the deceased, Gaius Plinius Secundus,' the praetor says as he takes the papyrus from his secretary. 'I confirm the seal is unbroken.'

The praetor's secretary, standing over his shoulder, inspects the seal. 'I, as witness, confirm the seal is unbroken.' He makes a note.

The praetor cracks open the wax seal and unfurls the papyrus.

'Good,' he says. 'A short one.'

The secretary, looking over the praetor's shoulder, nods.

'The will reads as follows. *I, Gaius Plinius Secundus, manumit my secretary, Spartacus, to take effect the date my will is read. He shall take the name Spartacus Plinius. And I gift to Spartacus Plinius the sum of fifty thousand sesterces. I would commend him to the service of my nephew, Gaius Caecilius, but he is, from this day forward, a free man, and able to choose his own path.*'

The praetor clears his throat.

Beside me, Spartacus is quietly weeping. Had he expected this? Perhaps. But it is nevertheless an important event. He faithfully served Uncle Pliny for years. Longer than I've been alive.

'Congratulations,' I say.

The praetor continues, '*As my final act, I adopt as my son and heir, my nephew, Gaius Caecilius. At his election, he is, hence forth, to take my name, and be known as Gaius Plinius Caecilius Secundus. He is to inherit my entire estate, including all land, chattels, human or otherwise, titles, property, save and except for my bequest to Spartacus Plinius.*' The praetor twirls his finger. 'Et cetera, et cetera.'

I feel a painful twist in my chest – grief or joy or possibly both.

The praetor looks up. 'Well?'

Collecting myself, I say, 'I'm sorry. Did I hear that correctly?'

The praetor sighs. I am slowing him down.

'You are to inherit your uncle's entire estate should you elect to be adopted by him. There is more here that I do not have to read, should you elect to do as your uncle hoped you would. It is a great honour, particularly given your uncle's renown and affiliation with the Imperial family. Not to mention his deep pockets.'

'He loved you like a son,' Spartacus says. 'You must elect. It's what he would have wanted.'

'Yes,' I say, struggling with my emotions. 'I will elect.'

'Lovely,' the praetor says. He looks at his secretary. 'Do we have everything we need to handle this now?'

'Yes,' his secretary says.

The praetor has me swear an oath and formally elect to be adopted by Uncle Pliny. I am only half-aware of the words he has me say.

When the praetor is finished he says, 'Well, that covers Secundus here. Shall we formally manumit Spartacus as well?'

Spartacus nods.

'Do we have everything we need for that?' the praetor asks his secretary.

'Yes.'

'Good,' the praetor says. 'Maybe I'll make the baths after all.' He looks at me, then Spartacus. 'Why is everyone crying? You'd think we were at a funeral.'

Barlaas

♦

1 September
The Imperial Palace, Rome

It has been years since I have been invited to the Imperial Palace, let alone the throne room, Caesar's inner sanctum. I had forgotten the majesty of it, the opulence.

It's as good a place to die as any, I suppose.

The Palace hallways are lined with white marble, dappled with darker grey veins, occasionally broken by arches and columns of porphyry. The floor is a rainbow of marble rectangles, green and pink and red. Praetorian soldiers and Imperial freedmen scurry past us like mice, most take the time to sneer at the barbarian who dares to walk the halls of the Palace. The sight of a Parthian hostage, towering over them, is so remarkable that they barely notice I am escorted by the Prefect of the Praetorians himself.

The doorway into the throne room is wide enough for an elephant to walk through. Inside, Titus is on a dais, sitting on a curule chair. He is inspecting the blade of his sword and – for a moment – I wonder if he will chop off my head himself. Before he took the purple, when he was Prefect of the Praetorian Guard and his father's attack dog, Titus was vicious. One day you were his friend, the next you were fodder for his blade. I'd heard he'd softened since becoming Princeps, but chopping off the head of an Aryan hostage would help re-establish the terror he used to inspire. Terror is useful for a king.

Among the dozens of attendants and clients, I see a few familiar faces: the Ulpii, the old blind one and Marcus, and their freedman, Theseus. Did they come to put in a good word or to watch me die?

'Barlaas,' Caesar says, without looking up from his blade. 'Thank you for coming.' Then, in a louder voice, to the gaggle of men and women before him, he says, 'may we have the room.'

The audience leaves, save for Virgilius, the Ulpii and Theseus. Once they are gone, the room feels immense and empty.

Caesar stares at me, his face impossible to read.

My old knees begin to ache. By god, I am too old for this, to stand before a king, waiting to learn my fate.

Fucking Romans.

King Gotarez was the Butcher, but he didn't revel in making a man sweat.

Caesar clears his throat. 'You have been a hostage here in Rome for how many years, Barlaas?'

'Twenty-nine,' I say.

'That is a long time to be separated from one's homeland.'

I nod. Yes, obviously.

'I am sure,' Caesar continues, 'that leads to complicated feelings about Rome. About the empire.'

I shrug.

'Do you hate Rome for holding you hostage all these years?'

I narrow my gaze. What trap is Caesar laying for me?

'In my experience,' I say, 'kings do not wish to know the truth.'

'It depends on the king.'

'That is true.'

'What was your brother like?' Caesar asks. 'Vologases.'

'I never served him as king. I was already in chains when he took the throne. He banished me to Rome as one of his first acts.'

'Yes, I know. But surely you knew him. He was the son of a concubine, was he not? To overcome that and become king ... It is impressive. And Parthia was at peace for nearly thirty years under him. That is the mark of good monarch. Is it not?'

'Did you bring me here to brag about my brother's accomplishments?'

Prefect Virgilius shifts uncomfortably. His hand rests on the hilt of his sword. He does not appreciate anyone, let alone a barbarian, speaking to the emperor like this. It doesn't matter what we went through together on the bay.

Fucking Romans.

'I wish to know where your loyalty lies,' Caesar says.

'Not with Rome,' I say, defiantly. 'Not with you.'

Ulpius sighs.

'I am torn, Barlaas,' Caesar says. 'I am told that I owe you a debt of gratitude. After the attempt on my life, you helped interrogate the captured Parthians. You helped unearth the Toad's involvement. Thanks to you, we know the Parthian emissaries were Artabanus's men in disguise. And you helped storm Sulpicius's villa.'

'I did.'

'You killed Artabanus's men.'

'I did.'

'But,' Caesar says, raising his finger, 'you also failed to speak up before the attack on my family. You could have prevented the entire affair.' I start to interject, but with a look Caesar silences me. 'Now, I know you will say that you knew nothing about it, but I don't believe you. My dear friend Pliny saw you attacked by the Parthian envoys. He was certain you were asked to participate in my murder, and the admiral was rarely wrong. You may have refused, and you may have seen this as a good middle ground, burying your head in the sand, rather than picking a side. But I do not see it that way.'

'Am I to be executed?'

Caesar admires his sword again. He holds the steel close to his face and inspects the quality of its edge.

'Ulpius here says that you can be useful. He predicts that if I offer you the chance for revenge, a chance to regain your honour, that you will help us.'

'Revenge against who?'

'Against Sinnaces, who betrayed you. Against Artabanus, who tried to use you. However, unlike Ulpius, I do not think you will be motivated by hate. I think you cared for your brother Vologases. I think you would welcome the chance to help his proper heir, Pacorus.'

'Help? How? What are you proposing?'

'I am naming Ulpius governor of Asia, and I am sending him and Marcus to Parthia. They are going to track down the False Nero. Once they do, they will kill him. And, if possible, they will kill Artabanus as well.'

'You want to send me home?'

'Yes,' Caesar says. He throws the sword to one of his Praetorians, who catches it by the handle. He walks down from his dais and looks me in the eyes. 'There has been a great calamity on the Bay of Naples. You know that as well as anyone. I am bringing soldiers from across the empire to bring relief to the suffering there. I cannot afford to send an army to Parthia – I need my men here, in Italy. Besides, I do not want to give credence to the False Nero. The Julio-Claudians are better left out of sight, out of mind. I am planning a discreet, yet dangerous mission. One that could benefit from a man with inside knowledge of the country. I am offering you the chance to return to Parthia and to destroy your enemies. Once this mission is complete, you would no longer be a hostage of Rome. You would be a free man, to do as you pleased.'

Despite myself I say quietly, 'I thought I was coming here to die.'

'Not today,' Caesar says. He puts out his hand. 'Do we have a deal?'

I take Caesar's hand in mine.

'We do.'

Ten months later . . .

VI

The Undertaker's Son
A.D. 80

Domitilla

1 May

Reate, Italy

I hear her, from the shallow depths of a restless sleep. The effort – to sit up, to stand – is immense. I have not slept – properly slept – since the Ides.

And yet it is nothing. She needs me. I would do anything for her.

The nurse is at the bassinet before me. But with a gentle touch to her elbow, I signal that the task is mine. The doctors say using my own milk will diminish my energy. Use the wet-nurse, they say. But she needs *me*.

Every time I pick her up, I marvel at how light she is, how small. How is it a human can start like this? As tiny as a starling.

Flavia Domitilla. My little miracle.

Now that I'm up, lamps are lit and black shapes move on the periphery. One materializes into Jacasta, carrying warmed, spiced wine. In the lamplight, the burns along her arm and neck look like the scales of a reptile. She comes close to admire my baby girl.

'Little Flavia,' she says.

'Go back to bed, Jacasta,' I say. 'You need your rest.'

She has not been the same since the fire. She tires easily and tasks she had mastered now overwhelm her.

'Mistress,' Livia says, 'you should let me see to the child at this hour. You need your sleep.'

Livia has taken up the duties Jacasta is no longer capable of. Part of me wonders if I should insist Jacasta leave my service. We could find her something less demanding in the Imperial household. But she would be devastated and consider it a betrayal.

'Thank you, Livia,' I say, 'but it's morning. I have slept enough. A mother's work is never done.'

I sit down to feed my daughter. Her small right hand holds my little finger throughout. When she's finished breastfeeding, I pass her to the wet-nurse and Jacasta helps me change into a warm, respectable forest green stola and matching shawl. Livia looks on, waiting to see if she will be needed.

'I think I will go for a walk this morning,' I say.

I make my way through the house, toward the front door. The staff are busy at work, shuffling from one room to the next. They step aside to let me pass, nodding or bowing.

From the garden comes the sound of wood hammering against wood. The Batavian is already hard at work, practising. His companion is a young Praetorian, barely old enough to be in the legions, who was honoured when, our first morning here in Reate, the famous Batavian asked him to spar with wooden weapons. They have been at it every day since, as the sun rises. I resist the temptation to go and watch from the window. One of my self-imposed rules is that I do not go out of my way to stare at the Batavian. There is no reason to break that rule this morning.

As I enter the atrium, I am surprised to find a woman standing at the front door. Her head is shaved, like a recently sheared sheep, and she is dressed in a robe made from simple linen. She is speaking with the chamberlain. Although her back is to me, I do not need to see her face to know who she is. Only one priestess of Isis would visit me, at this hour, at our family home in Reate.

'Vespasia?'

'Sister,' she says, turning to meet my gaze.

The chamberlain is a little, fastidious fellow. His eyes nearly pop out of his head when I say my sister's name. He must not have recognized her with her shaved head. I cannot blame him. She seems a different person. It isn't just her hair. She has lost a considerable amount of weight and her cheek bones look as though they will burst through her pale skin at any moment. And her eyes do not have the alert, intelligent look they normally do. They are unfocused, detached.

'What are you doing here?' I ask. 'And at such an hour?'

'Lovely to see you too, sister.'

I take her hands in mine. 'I didn't mean it like that. I am surprised. You didn't send word.'

'I came to meet my niece.'

'I'm so pleased. But what are you doing here so early?'

'I walked. This is the time I arrived.'

'Walked?' I cannot help but laugh: the idea is ridiculous. Vespasia was loath to walk across a room, let alone from Rome to Reate. It must have taken her days. 'You can't be serious,' I say. But her silence indicates that yes, she is serious. 'Vespasia, that wasn't necessary. You could have travelled by carriage. It must have been terribly unsafe to travel alone.'

Vespasia may no longer have her striking long hair; but she remains quite beautiful. Travelling by herself . . . She would have been helpless to any man she met along the way.

'I no longer wish to live the life I did,' she says, 'of opulence and sloth.'

What does one say to that? Vespasia – spoilt, vain and lazy her entire life – no longer wishes to be spoilt, vain and lazy? This must be another dalliance of hers. Like the summer she fell in love with chariot racing.

'And,' she continues, 'I did not travel alone. The goddess was with me.'

'Oh, Vespasia. You cannot be' – I bite my tongue. If I condescend, she will only dig in her heels. I feign a smile and say, 'Come. It's time you meet your niece.'

'She's beautiful.' Vespasia rocks little Flavia back and forth.

'You're a natural,' I say.

I cannot get used to Vespasia's shaved head. The missing hair has distorted her appearance. Her skull seems too small, her eyes too large. She looks like a poorly made marble bust, not my sister in the flesh.

'It's not me,' Vespasia says. 'It is the goddess. The healer, the deliverer. She protects suckling babes.'

'I see. And the goddess . . . speaks *through* you?'

'Yes. In a way. After the mysteries of Osiris I have felt . . . different.'

'Oh? You've completed the first one, have you?'

'I have.'

'I don't suppose you're willing to tell your sister what that's like? What's involved?'

'We are sworn to secrecy.'

'How unfortunate.'

'But it would be impossible anyway, sister. It would be like explaining the colour red to someone who has never seen it.'

'That does sound difficult.'

'Yes.'

This truly is a new Vespasia. My sharp, condescending tone would normally draw venom in reply. And my response would inevitably grow sharper. The exchange would escalate, back and forth, until we were in a fight. And then we would make up the next day. But Vespasia – the *new* Vespasia, the Isiac initiate – will not rise to the bait.

'She has your eyes,' she says. 'Do you see any of her father in her?'

I stay focused on my daughter, to make sure my eyes do not drift to the gladiator practising in the garden.

'It has been many months,' Vespasia says, 'since I last saw Cerialis. I would like to compare them, face-to-face.'

I feel an immense weight release from my chest. If Vespasia does not suspect the truth, then maybe the rest of the empire doesn't as well.

'Unfortunately,' I say, 'Cerialis is off on campaign again. I was sorry that you could not come to our wedding.'

'My duty to the goddess would not allow it,' Vespasia says. 'Before the mysteries of Osiris, an adherent cannot be exposed to impurities.'

I'm only vaguely familiar with the cult of the Egyptian goddess, but whatever I do know is impossibly strange. How did she become so devout so fast?

It was only last year that Vespasia was causing Titus and I a different sort of headache. She sat, day and night, by the bedside of Caecina, a co-conspirator in Marcellus's plot to kill Father. She stayed with him for nearly a month, as he slowly died. It was more gossip for the city – the sort Titus couldn't stand. But there was no deterring her. And when Caecina finally passed away, Vespasia's grief was so strong it sent her running to this cult. To Isis. Titus was happy for her to be out of the public eye, especially during those tentative first months after Father's death when he was trying to solidify his position. Titus did not want his sister's grieving for a known traitor on display. Titus thought the cult of Isis was another of Vespasia's dalliances. We both did. We thought it would pass, like all the others.

But I can see it has become so much more than that. She seems to have become a true believer. Neither Titus, nor I, could have predicted this. But maybe it makes sense. She was always so lost. Perhaps she has found something. A purpose.

'Of course,' I say. 'I know you are busy. That you have responsibilities now. I was only sorry you weren't there.'

'And it is important you not call me Vespasia anymore.'

'Oh?'

'Yes,' she says. She is looking at little Flavia, pinching her full cheeks. 'After the mysteries of Osiris, I have no name. I am only an acolyte.'

'I see. Is this also why you've come to see me? To tell me your new . . . title?'

'Yes,' she says, handing my daughter to me. 'And to say goodbye.'

'Where are you going?'

'Soon I will participate in the mysteries of Isis. If I pass, I will no longer be permitted to speak with anyone from my former life.'

'Where will you go?'

'That is for the goddess to decide. I hope to remain in Rome, with the temple in the Campus Martius, but it is not for me to say.'

'So you may well be in Rome but you will not speak with us?'

'Yes.'

'And what of your brother? He is emperor and needs his family more than ever.'

'I was always an annoyance for Titus.'

'That's not true.'

'It is, and he was right to feel that way. I was more concerned with myself than the family. The goddess has helped me see this. It is best that your sister vanishes. It's what Titus would want.'

I try to convince her otherwise, but she can see I lack conviction. Perhaps it is what Titus would want – for Vespasia to be forgotten.

We spend the morning together. We talk about our brothers – what is wrong with them and how they could improve. We remember Father, and lament that the world does not seem the same without him. It is pleasant to speak with Vespasia. But she is detached and passionless, a shadow of my sister.

I walk her to the front door when she says she must go.

'Are you really going to walk back? You've barely rested since walking here.'

'The goddess is with me. I will be fine.'

A tear escapes Vespasia's eye. She grabs me by the shoulders and we embrace. I have the sense that by doing this, by hugging her own sister, she is breaking the rules, exposing herself to the impurities of this world.

She pulls back and holds me in her gaze for a moment, as though she is trying to remember me. 'Goodbye, sister.'

'Goodbye.'

She turns to go. I watch her walk along the road, in the shadow of the poplars.

Dusk. Livia and I are walking through the garden. We cross paths with the Batavian. He keeps his eyes aimed respectfully at the ground.

I stop, so he stops.

'I expect to go to town tomorrow. You and the Praetorians will accompany me?'

He bows.

I will grant him this: he is a man of his word. I told him we must forget what happened in Pompeii, that we must be as we were, master and slave. While he agreed at the time, I wasn't sure if he would accept it. I worried he might push to relive the wonderful few hours we had together.

He's kept his word.

I didn't tell him when I was late that the child was his. Other than Titus and Jacasta, I kept this secret to myself. I told Titus only what I needed to. In private, after he asked how I fared with the Batavian, alone in Pompeii for days, I told him that it was in our family's interest for me to marry Cerialis as soon as possible. Titus knew what I meant. He did not chastise me. He wasn't angry or disappointed. He said, 'Then we shall not waste any time.' I was married to Cerialis by the Kalens. As my belly started to grow and the word spread that I was pregnant, it was assumed the father was my husband, a general and patrician, not a famous gladiator.

If the Batavian suspects he is the father, he's given no sign. He's never made me regret what happened. To the contrary, my daughter is perfect, and if the Batavian and I didn't have our night in Pompeii, I wouldn't have her.

The chamberlain walks past us. He is arguing with another maid. They avoid us by stepping off the white stone path that weaves its way through the garden.

I catch the chamberlain say, 'Oh no, do not use *him*. He's overpriced.'

'He's the only undertaker for twenty miles,' the maid replies.

'Chamberlain,' I say. He and the maid turn to face me. The chamberlain's smile is wide but disingenuous. He is from the old guard, one of father's freedmen who continues to keep watch over our family's home in Reate. He still sees me as the young girl that would race through these halls pretending to be her father's legate. He considers me an annoyance rather than a figure of authority.

'Yes, Mistress,' he says.

'Did someone pass away?'

His smile grows wider. 'No one to concern yourself with, Augusta. One of the maid's children died late last night. We are trying to make arrangements.'

Immediately, I think of Pandora, the maid whose pregnancy overlapped with mine. We had developed a bond before Flavia was born. After giving birth, I'd been too consumed with caring for Flavia that I forgot to ask about Pandora.

'Do you mean Pandora?'

He nods, reluctantly.

'When did she give birth?'

The chamberlain looks at the maid.

'Two nights ago, Mistress,' the maid says.

'And her child died last night?'

The chamberlain and the maid look at the ground. Livia, still at my side, speaks up. 'Yes, Mistress. Unfortunately.'

'Any why didn't anyone tell me?'

'We did not want to scare you, Mistress,' the chamberlain says, 'to worry unnecessarily.'

'We know deaths come in threes,' the maid says.

'How is she doing?' I ask.

'How is *who* doing?' The chamberlain is already bored of this conversation.

'It's the second baby she's lost,' the maid says, knowing who I meant. She leaves it at that.

Poor Pandora. I can't imagine what that is like, to lose your child so quickly after giving birth, after finally meeting the person you've carried for nine months. I understand why no one told me. The last thing a new mother should hear of is the death of an infant.

'Our family will take care of any necessary arrangements. Yes?'

The chamberlain bows. 'Of course, Mistress. However, the local undertaker, Pinarius, is particularly expensive.'

The name nags for a moment.

Then suddenly I feel a jolt. It moves through me like lightning.

Pinarius is the name of the man who tried on several occasions to meet with me in Baiae and then died the day before my wedding.

'Did you say Pinarius?' I think of the bloated corpse on the Baiae pier. 'What does he look like? Is he an older man, black hair and black beard?'

'You have described the father, Mistress,' the chamberlain says. 'I was referring to the son, Sextus Pinarius. He studied under his father for years, until he took over the family business late last year.'

'What happened to his father?'

The chamberlain shrugs. What does he care?

'I wish to be taken to the undertaker. Now.'

The chamberlain's wide, disingenuous smile returns. I am interfering with the orderly workings of his household. 'It's late, Mistress, and the sun is close to setting. The roads are dangerous after dark.'

'He's right, Mistress,' Livia says. 'There is no reason to risk going tonight. He will be there tomorrow.'

'Tomorrow morning then,' I say. 'First thing.'

The chamberlain continues to smile. 'I can draw a map.'

To the Batavian, I say, 'Tomorrow morning you will escort me to this undertaker's home. Find two Praetorians to bring with us. Have the horses ready.'

The Batavian nods.

The chamberlain says, 'May I ask, Mistress, what your interest is in this undertaker?'

'I have a few questions for him. That is all.'

I look for Livia, to ask her to come. She spoke with the undertaker after all. But – although she had been standing beside me only a moment ago – she has disappeared.

'Strange,' I say, 'I wonder where Livia's gone?'

The undertaker's home is a small hovel on the outskirts of town. We arrive on horseback. A woman sees us approaching and runs inside. A younger man, dressed in black, steps out of the hovel. When we are close enough, I can tell he recognizes me. He wants to run – he looks for a means of escape – but thinks better of it. There is nowhere to go.

'Are you Sextus Pinarius?' I ask after we've come to a stop outside. 'Son of Plinius Pinarius, the undertaker?'

The man looks dejected.

'Why would you come now?' His voice is more sad than accusatory.

'You wished I had come earlier?'

'We tried to speak with you. For a month we tried.' He shakes his head.

'Was your father the undertaker who tried to speak with me in Baiae?'

The undertaker looks at the men I am with.

'You fear for your safety?'

He nods.

I dismount and walk toward him. I point at his hovel. 'What if we go inside and speak alone.'

'Mistress, I—' one of the Praetorians tries to voice his concern, but I cut him off with a wave of my hand.

'It's fine; soldier,' I say. 'We are all friends here.'

The undertaker relents. I follow him inside his home. The bedroom, kitchen and dining room are packed into one room. Despite its poor quality, he or his wife takes pride in it. It is swept and clean.

He invites me to sit after dusting off a chair.

'What is it you want to know, Mistress?'

'Everything,' I say. 'Start from the beginning.'

One year earlier,

eight weeks before the eruption
of Vesuvius . . .

24 June
Reate, Italy

The undertaker, Plinius Pinarius, stares at the corpse.

My first deity, he thinks.

The body is laid out on a couch, naked and recently bathed.

No, 'scrubbed' is the better word, Pinarius thinks, given the effort required; given the diarrhoea that plagued him near the end and caked to his skin like Campanian cement.

It often happens this way. As the master's fate becomes clear, his death all but certain, his slaves become lazier, less doting. Tasks are shirked. Particularly those charged with the master's toilette. They begin to dream of their new master, one who is younger, his bowels more intact. And then, once the great man has breathed his last, the dried shit caked to his arse is the undertaker's problem.

Such is the life of the undertaker.

There is good news, however. There are no signs of decay, and the summer's heat has yet to reach the hills of Reate. Thank the gods. Perhaps, Pinarius thinks, we will be able to deliver the corpse to Rome without a legion of hungry dogs marching at our heels.

Pinarius's son, Sextus, is on his knees, slowly removing bottles of unguents from a case. He removes them in the wrong order, crocus oil after rose water, rather than the other way around. The error is of no consequence. Only Pinarius can see it; only Pinarius is bothered by it. Still, it nags. He'd hoped Sextus was ready to handle the dead on his own, which he will need to do before finally taking over the family business. But the boy lacks the necessary rigour. Pinarius stares at the body stretched out on the couch. He thinks: did you have to deal with this, a disappointing son?

The corpse has the large belly and swollen, gout riddled ankles of a rich man – and there were none richer. But he also has the miserable look of a man who fought an illness, gaunt cheeks and flesh that hangs loosely around his bones, skin that is meant for a larger, healthier body. His hair is white and receding, his square chin like a slab of marble.

For a god, Pinarius thinks, he looks remarkably human.

Sextus pours infused oil into the open hands of two slaves, who then rub their anointed hands across the corpse's loose skin.

Sextus opens the dead man's mouth. He uses a cloth, so as not to let the pollution of death infect his hand. Inside, there is a gold aureus, worth a small fortune, about one hundred sesterces. Sextus delves in his pocket and pulls out a single dusty silver coin. This is an old undertaker's trick: switching out the coin in a rich man's mouth, after his family wastes valuable gold on the ferryman, when any coin will do.

It is usually harmless.

Usually.

Pinarius grabs Sextus by the elbow. Sextus turns back, searching for an explanation. This is the boy's problem, Pinarius thinks. Everything must be explained.

'Not this time,' Pinarius whispers. 'You don't take money from the gods. Not unless you want a curse to follow us home.'

The slaves continue to rub oil onto the dead man's skin, but their eyes drift up; they note every word.

Sextus closes the god's mouth and pockets the silver coin.

They finish in silence. A maid brings an expensive silk tunic for her master, and a magistrate's robe, white with a broad purple stripe. The slaves slowly dress the corpse; then they unfurl a coverlet over the body, and drop garlands and flowers on top. Pinarius hands the maid a branch of cypress to pin to the front door of the house to warn of the dead man inside.

The chamberlain is waiting in the atrium. Sextus hands him an invoice and the man's eyes widen.

'This is very expensive.'

'The price includes our travelling from Rome and back again,' Sextus says defensively.

Sextus is too quick to forget our value, Pinarius thinks. No one wants to deal with the dead. This is true of anyone, no matter how rich or powerful the family. A dead man's household will pay what you tell them to pay.

Pinarius explains to the chamberlain that if the price is too high, they would be happy to leave the body here. 'It would be what? Another day or so before you found another undertaker? By the time you get the body to Rome, it will stink like a latrine, and the funeral will be a miserable affair. But you might save a few denarii.'

The chamberlain frowns. It's not his money after all. He forces a smile and says, 'Very well.'

The doors across the atrium swing open and two soldiers rush into the room. The man leading the way is in his fortieth year. Handsome, though balding, and with a stout build, like a pleb working the docks. The second is the physical opposite of his companion, skinny as a grape vine, with thick white hair and a matching beard.

'Am I too late?' the first soldier asks.

The chamberlain – who was fine a moment ago – now looks as though he has lost the love of his life. 'I'm so sorry, Master Titus,' he says. 'He's gone.'

That name, Pinarius thinks, where do I know that name . . .

When it dawns on him who has just barged into the atrium, he quickly removes his green cap and falls to his knees. Sextus watches his father, but remains on his feet. Pinarius swats his cap against his legs. 'To your knees, boy.'

The interaction between father and son is lost on the soldiers. Having learned the emperor is dead, they care not for the embarrassment of an undertaker and his understudy son.

'Where is he?'

The white-haired soldier grabs his companion by the arm. 'We've got to get you back to Rome, Titus. You need the troops to swear loyalty as soon as possible. You need the Senate to—'

'Enough has been put in place already, Virgilius. We have time. I will say goodbye to my father.'

The chamberlain calls for a maid and she takes the two soldiers to the room where the emperor is temporarily interred. Once they're gone, the chamberlain's face is again untroubled.

He says, 'before you go, we have another body for you to see to.'

Pinarius is slow to rise. He can feel his age in his aching knees.

'Another body?' Pinarius asks. 'You've not had much luck here, have you?'

The chamberlain is indifferent. 'He's only a freedman, so he doesn't need the full treatment. But he was one of the emperor's favourites, so we can't just toss him into the woods.'

'What happened?'

The chamberlain shrugs. 'He got sick. He died.'

He leads the undertaker and his son outside, to the stables, where a corpse is lying on top of a bed of hay. The lamplight is weak, but Pinarius can see the freedman has the same gaunt face his patron had, and there is the same stink of dried shit.

'Can you get him finished by morning?' the chamberlain asks.

Sextus pinches his nose, kneels and inspects the corpse. 'Yes. I'd say so.'

'Good. I'll leave you to it.'

After the chamberlain leaves, Sextus looks up from the dead freedman and says, 'Do you think they died of the same illness, Father?'

'It's not for us to say.'

'But look.' Using a cloth, Sextus opens up the freedman's eyes. 'His eyes are as red as his patron's. And the diarrhoea. Perhaps it was the same illness. Perhaps they ate the same—'

Pinarius swats Sextus on the shoulder. 'Shut up, boy!'

What is wrong with him? Pinarius thinks. What is he trying to get us mixed up in?

'Focus on your task,' Pinarius says. 'And keep your mouth shut.'

They have loaded the cargo by dawn. The freedman's corpse is in their wagon. The other is placed in a cart built for a king, painted purple and gold, harnessed to a team of four white horses. Pinarius wonders how much a horse like that would cost. *More than I've made in a lifetime,* he thinks.

Sextus and the slaves are on the other side of the wagon. They're arguing in whispers.

'What's this all about then?' Pinarius asks as he appears from behind the wagon and surprises them.

'Nothing, Master,' one of the slaves says. 'Nothing at all.'

'Out with it,' Pinarius says.

The slaves cast their eyes at the ground. Sextus raises his gaze to the treeline.

Pinarius notices something in Sextus's hand. It looks like a roll of papyrus.

'What's that?'

'We found it,' Sextus says.

Pinarius sighs. 'Where?'

'On . . . the freedman.'

'I thought I'd made myself clear. This is not a family we are going to steal from.' Pinarius swipes the papyrus from Sextus. 'We are going to put this back.'

'Father,' Sextus says. 'Look at it. We can't simply throw it back into the stables.'

Pinarius turns the papyrus over and see what must be the Flavian seal.

The Imperial seal.

'It's a letter,' Sextus says. 'From the emperor, I think. Before he died.'

Pinarius's stomach turns. The papyrus feels as heavy as a thousand pounds in his hand.

'We'll give it to the chamberlain and tell him the truth,' Pinarius says. 'That we found it on the freedman.'

'But Father,' Sextus says, 'the seal is broken.'

Pinarius holds up the letter. Sextus is right. The seal is broken. 'Did you do this?'

'No,' Sextus says.

Pinarius knows his son is lying, but it doesn't matter now.

'Jupiter's fucking arse.'

'Father,' Sextus says, 'this could be an opportunity. We can make a fortune from this letter. Open it up. You'll see it is addressed to the emperor's daughter, the Augusta. She will reward us for delivering the letter to her. I know it.'

With the seal broken, the letter easily unrolls. Other than two Latin names, it's in Greek. Pinarius doesn't speak Greek – none of them do. But it's clearly written to the Augusta. Her name – Domitilla – is there plain as day. There is another Latin name as well, in the body of the letter: Cocceius Nerva. A name Pinarius does not know.

'This could change our life, Father,' Sextus pleads. 'The Augusta has been known to grant fortunes to those she thinks worthy. She will be grateful if we deliver this letter. But if we hand it to the chamberlain – you've seen what he's like. The seal is broken. He could have us punished rather than reward us.'

This damn boy, Pinarius thinks, he's never been content with our family's trade; he's always on the hunt for something more, for some way out.

But he's right, Pinarius thinks. They can't return the letter to the chamberlain. They must destroy the letter or try to make a *profit from it. And perhaps something good could come from this. Fortuna willing.*

Pinarius stuffs the letter inside his cloak.

Sextus grins, victorious.

'We'll get it translated first,' *Pinarius says,* 'before we do anything with it.'

'A most prudent course, Father. In Rome, we are likely to find any number of translators.'

'Check the harnesses on the ox,' *Pinarius says,* 'and, by gods, let's be away from this estate.'

1 July
The Suburra, Rome

Deep in the Suburra, the beating heart of Rome's underbelly, Plinius Pinarius is pacing the length of the tiny apartment.

'Are you finished yet?' *Sextus asks impatiently.*

The translator is an ancient, white-haired Greek with a tiny head. He frowns and looks up from his work. He has been staring through a glass pitcher to magnify the letters on the page and translating each word onto a wax tablet. The effort has been laborious.

'Don't rush me, please,' *the translator snaps.* 'You are not paying me enough to rush.'

'Patience, cousin,' *Cornelius says.* 'Patience. Let the man finish his work.'

Cornelius is Pinarius's nephew and a native to Rome. His worldview is shaped by geography. He believes himself to be sophisticated and cosmopolitan because he was born and raised in Rome, and his uncle and nephew to be rustic and unsophisticated because they were not. Sextus has always looked up to Cornelius. And it was Sextus who insisted on bringing Cornelius aboard when they arrived in Rome two days ago. Cornelius's eyes had lit up at the chance to make a profit. 'A letter from the emperor himself!' he'd said. But, as far as Pinarius is concerned, Cornelius has already become more of a burden than a help. It was his idea to use this this old Greek fellow, who appears to be so out of practice that he is somehow having trouble translating his native language.

The Greek turns back to his work.

Does he have any clue yet whose letter he is translating? Pinarius thinks. He doesn't seem to.

He's the third translator Cornelius found. The first read the letter and thought it was a prank. The second, after he'd read the letter, looked as though he'd seen a ghost. He handed it back and politely said he wanted nothing to do with them or their letter. 'My advice,' the man had said, 'throw your letter into the Tiber.' He refused to say why.

The Greek finishes and looks over the Latin translation etched into the wax tablet; he scratches his bald head. 'Where did you say you got this?'

'We are not paying you to talk,' Sextus says, taking the wax tablet.

Pinarius snaps his fingers and Sextus, the dutiful son, hands the letter to his father. Pinarius sits down to read. Sextus and Cornelius read over his shoulder.

Cornelius finishes first. 'Fucking hell,' he says as he collapses into a nearby chair.

Pinarius reads it once, then a second time.

My dearest daughter, Domitilla,

My health is failing. I fear I am not long for this world and, very soon, I will breathe my last. I've had a good life – one the son of a money lender and a provincial could never have imagined. From soldier to general, from politician to Princeps. It was remarkable. So, in a way, I am content.

But something nags.

I was healthy not long ago, other than my gout, which for years has been painful but manageable. The explanation for my failing health is likely a simple one. I am old and this is what happens to old men. One day you're healthy, the next you're not. But I have suspicions that I have fallen ill by the designs of another, by poison, something subtle, administered slowly, over time.

You will recall that after the attempt on my life in May I was lent by a friend – or someone I believed to be my friend – his personal doctor. The man worked wonders on my gout. I insisted he join me when I travelled north, to Reate. Lately, I have begun to think that my decline in health has corresponded to this so-called doctor's concoctions. My freedman, who drinks everything I drink and eats everything I eat, has lately started to feel ill as well. He is a young man, previously in good health, so that may explain why his health did not decline until recently.

I am reluctant to bring this to your brother. If I die, he will have the weight of an empire on his shoulders. I trust you. Of all of my children, you are the most reasonable, the most judicious.

I have no proof, only suspicion. This could merely be denial of the inevitable, the complaints of a dying man. I will only say this: beware of Cocceius Nerva. It is Nerva who lent me his doctor. There are many unexplained troubles our family has faced. And, as I sit here, slowly dying, miles from Rome, I wonder: is Nerva to blame? Do our family's hardships coincide with the waning of Nerva's star? As I bestowed favour on other men, did he scheme against our family and the Principate?

I do not know the answer, and I doubt I ever will. Perhaps you can discover the truth.

*I love you. I hope these are not my last words to you. If they are,
thank you. Thank you for being the woman you are. Our family
would have been lost without you, its sheen less bright. Truly.*

Your loving father,

Vespasian

Pinarius lowers his head, dejected. No wonder the first two translators thought the letter was a prank or incredibly dangerous.
Throwing it in the Tiber was sound advice.

Sextus, however, doesn't see the danger. He asks, 'who is this
man, Nerva?'

'My word, cousin, you really are from a backwater, aren't you?'
Cornelius says. 'Cocceius Nerva is one of the most powerful senators in the empire. He has been since he helped expose the Pisonian
conspiracy and saved Nero's life. Still not ringing any bells? Nerva
was twice consul, once under Nero, once under Vespasian.'

'And he . . .' Sextus is beginning to understand the letter's
import. The translator is as well. He is looking about for some
means of escape. But these are his customers, this is his apartment.

'Kindly leave,' he says.

'We've got to get this letter to the Augusta right away,' Pinarius
says.

The little Greek taps his finger on the table. 'Kindly leave the
coin you owe me on the table and go.'

'There is another option,' Cornelius says. 'I'm sure Senator
Nerva would be grateful to have this letter. Wouldn't he? I'm sure
he'd pay whatever we asked.'

The little Greek shuts his eyes and plugs his ears with his index
fingers. 'Kindly pay and go away.'

'We are not doing that,' Pinarius says. 'We are simple undertakers, not politicians. We know nothing of that world. The safest,
smartest course is to bring it to the Augusta.'

'Cousin Cornelius is right, Father,' Sextus says. 'The Augusta may not pay us anything. She'll be angry about any delay in bringing her the letter. Nerva would pay a great deal to ensure his name isn't dragged through the mud.'

'Think about this, boy.' Pinarius's voice is both angry and pleading. 'If the letter is true . . . If this man Nerva is capable of such an act. What you propose is too dangerous. We bring the letter to the Augusta. That is final.'

'We'll have to head south, then,' Cornelius says.

'What?'

'The Augusta went south, to Baiae, yesterday,' Cornelius says. 'There was a crowd of well-wishers screaming her name as she set out.'

'When will she be back?'

Cornelius shrugs. 'The Imperial family often spends the summer in Baiae. We'll need to go there. Unless you want to wait until September.'

'May we take this?' Sextus asks the Greek, holding up the wax tablet.

'I care not a whit,' the Greek says, rubbing his arms, like he is cold, though it is stiflingly hot in the apartment. 'Please just go.'

19 August
Outside the Villa Piso, Baiae

They wait for the Augusta's maid to return. Sextus paces along the road's black stones.

'Cousin,' Cornelius says. 'Please stop. You've been pacing since the Kalends. Gods, I am so sick of your pacing.'

Sextus does as he's told. He stops and sighs dramatically.

The two soldiers guarding the door to the Imperial villa watch the three plebs with mild amusement.

We must seem a strange trio, Pinarius thinks.

'Uncle,' Cornelius says, 'do you really think today will be any different than the last time we were here?'

Pinarius finds his nephew's voice unnecessarily smug. It was a mistake to bring him with them to Baiae. But once they had the letter translated and they had recovered from the shock of what it said, Cornelius became even more convinced they could make a profit from it and there was no getting rid of him.

'We have been here twice before,' Cornelius continues, 'only to be sent away. Why do you think today will have a different outcome?'

Unfortunately, Cornelius has a point. Getting before the Augusta has been more difficult than any of them could have imagined. The problem is they have had to go through her attendants and Pinarius is not willing to tell anyone other than the Augusta what's in the letter. 'It's too risky,' *he has told his son and nephew several times.* 'Who knows where a slave's loyalty lies?' *But the Augusta has refused to see them.*

And why would she? Pinarius is thinking as they wait, I'm a lowly undertaker, polluted by the death. And she is the daughter of a god. What was I thinking?

'As I've said before, Uncle,' Cornelius continues, 'we have another option. If the Augusta will not see us . . .'

Pinarius grabs Cornelius by the arm and – casually, so as not to cause alarm, still smiling at the soldiers – whispers: 'Nephew, I know what you are about to say, whose name you are about to utter. We need to be careful. We don't know who is listening.'

Cornelius has enough sense to whisper his reply. 'Honestly, Uncle, aren't you being paranoid? I was only going to say that we should take the letter to Senator Nerva. He would be grateful to learn of any slander aimed at his good name.'

'You think the letter is merely slander?'

'Yes, of course,' Cornelius says. 'Vespasian was old and sick when he wrote it. You remember what our grandfather was like near the end? He thought everyone was trying to kill him.'

A door opens behind them.

They turn and see the Augusta's maid, the pretty girl with the one eyebrow. She steps between the two soldiers and walks towards them.

Pinarius's cap is in his hands. He can sense, but not stop, the look of pathetic expectation on his face, like a dog watching the dinner table. Their livelihoods depend on what she is about to say.

When she shakes her head, Pinarius knows they have failed. Again.

'The Augusta will not see you today. Perhaps you can come back another day.'

Pinarius's shoulders slump. Cornelius swears under his breath.

The Augusta's maid smiles, sympathetically. 'I think the problem is you are not giving the Augusta a reason to meet with you. Perhaps if you told me what it is you need to speak with her about, she might change her mind.'

Cornelius jabs Pinarius in the back with his elbow.

'What is your name?' Pinarius asks.

'Livia,' the maid replies.

'Livia. My name is – as I've said – Plinius Pinarius. I'm very sorry, but I must speak with the Augusta. Face-to-face.'

The maid shrugs. 'Have it your way.'

She turns and leaves.

Cornelius starts to argue with his uncle. 'We need to tell her more . . .'

Pinarius shakes his head. 'No. We stick to the plan. We tell the Augusta and only the Augusta what we know. Come on.' Pinarius starts walking down the street, away from the Imperial villa. 'We'll find a better way to speak with her.'

20 August
Baiae, the Bay of Naples

The night before the gladiatorial games, they debate their next move.

'And how will tomorrow be any different?' Cornelius says.

Sextus nervously chews his fingernails.

'All we can do is try,' Pinarius says, doing his best not to show that his despair matches theirs. 'Maybe if she sees us – the Augusta has never seen us, you know – if she sees us, maybe she will change her mind and speak to us. She will be attending the games tomorrow. We can try to speak to her on her way into the arena.'

'But what if she doesn't, Father?' Sextus says. 'We cannot afford to live here another day. Baiae is expensive – even for this hovel.'

Their cramped rented apartment consists of one bed and a door. Nothing else. Not even a window. But because this is Baiae where the rich vacation, it is shockingly expensive.

'And,' Sextus continues, 'we are running out of money. We are needed back in Reate. If we don't, our business could be ruined. We made a mistake coming here.'

Pinarius shakes his head. He can't admit this. Not yet. 'No we haven't. You were right, Sextus. There is profit to be made from this letter. We just need to speak to the right person.'

Pinarius believes this – or thinks he does. But, in truth, he knows that he has fallen prey to a fantasy. He wants to be the man who saved the Imperial family. He wants the Augusta to kiss his hand and say she is indebted to him for saving her life, and from that day forward he and his family will never want for anything. The fantasy is not without precedent. Nero once rewarded a freedman who helped expose the Pisonian conspiracy. He gave the man a small fortune. Why wouldn't the Augusta do the same for a faithful undertaker?

But the longer they wait in Baiae, Pinarius can feel his fantasy drift away; it is shifting into something he does not like. Failure and destitution.

'If the Augusta will not see us today,' Pinarius says, sombrely, 'We will head home.'

'Uncle,' Cornelius says. 'You cannot ignore the other option. We can take this letter to Senator Nerva. He is here in Baiae as well. He might speak to us. He will pay us for the letter. I know it!'

Pinarius should chastise Cornelius and tell him to never raise the suggestion again. But he doesn't. We have come too far, he thinks, and invested too much. We can't walk away.

'Let us see what happens tomorrow.'

21 August
Outside the amphitheatre, Puteoli

The crowd seethes with excitement, pulsing like the sea.

The Augusta's litter is carried by six slaves, three a side. It is made of gilded, spiralling wood posts and opaque white silk, billowing in the wind. An entourage of slaves and attendants trail the litter on foot. Near the arena, the litter is set down on the ground and Praetorians begin shoving the crowd back with the shafts of their spears.

'Wait here,' Pinarius says to Sextus and Cornelius.

He pushes his way through the crowd.

Over the shoulders of two soldiers Pinarius yells at the girl he has spoken to before. Livia. She turns at the sound of her name. She looks annoyed, but quickly smiles, trying to hide her initial reaction.

Pinarius watches her pull on the Augusta's sleeve and the two of them stare at the undertaker. Livia says something to her mistress and then walks over.

Pinarius is holding his cap in his hands.

Livia scowls. 'Nothing has changed, undertaker. My mistress will not speak with you.'

'Please.'

'I've done all I can. Unless you could tell me more. Tell me what you wish to speak with her about.' Her voice sounds genuine, like she wants to help.

'What I have to say – it must be said to your mistress herself.'

'Then you will have no more luck today than you've had before.'

Pinarius looks over her shoulder at the Augusta. She is the picture of beauty: almond curls, glittering gold wrapped around her wrists and neck, dazzling in the Campanian sunlight. The daughter of a god.

Pinarius doesn't want to go back to Reate empty-handed. It would be a disaster.

He thinks of the Augusta kissing his hand, showing her favour.

The undertaker takes a deep breath.

'It concerns Senator Cocceius Nerva,' he says, 'and the safety of the Imperial family.'

Livia stares at Pinarius a moment. He had expected her to be shocked at what he said. But she is not. Perhaps the Imperial maids hear this type of pronouncement more often than he'd imagined.

Livia pushes her way through the two guards and speaks quietly to Pinarius, so no one can hear.

'It's good you have brought this to the Augusta's attention. She will be very pleased. But here is not the place to speak of it.' She looks around, again making sure no one can hear. 'Does anyone else know of this important information? Did you not have friends with you when you called on the Augusta before?'

Pinarius hesitates. Maybe it's best not to involve Sextus and Cornelius. Not yet.

'No. Only I know of what I have to say to the Augusta.'

'That is good. It is important – for your own safety – that you do not tell anyone about this. Not until you tell the Augusta all that you have to say. There is a canteen in Baiae called the Maid's Knees. Wait there tonight, after sunset. The Augusta will send someone to get you, to bring you to the Imperial villa. These are precautions we must take to ensure secrecy.'

She presses something into Pinarius's hand. A gold coin.

'The Augusta is sure to reward you if your information is valuable. This is only the start of the riches you will receive.'

Pinarius looks up. 'Thank you.'

She smiles and walks back to the Augusta. They exchange words. The Augusta frowns, turns and walks toward the arena.

The Augusta looked . . . she did not appear grateful, as Pinarius expected. But perhaps the need for secrecy is greater than Pinarius knew.

Pinarius finds his son and nephew in the crowd.

'What happened?' Cornelius asks.

'All is well,' Pinarius says. 'Our fortune has changed.'

They reconvene in their rented room.

'Do we need to remain hidden?' Sextus asks. 'I want to meet the Augusta as well.'

'All in good time, son,' Pinarius says, as he scrubs his tunic with a wet cloth. He wants to look his best for the Augusta.

'We should be with you in the canteen,' Cornelius says. 'In case you need us.'

Pinarius pauses to consider this. 'I suppose there is no harm in being cautious. Perhaps you should arrive in the canteen before me. The two of you can sit in the corner and watch when the Augusta's servants come to take me to the Imperial villa. Livia saw your face outside the Imperial villa the other day. So perhaps you should disguise yourselves as best you can. With a hooded cloak.'

'Will you take the letter with you, Father?'

'I will take the original. The Augusta will want it. I'm sure she knows Greek well and can read it without assistance. You hold on to the translation. For now.'

Sextus is smiling. 'It's working as we planned. Thank the gods. We came so close to ruin.'

Pinarius nods, gravely. 'Yes. Thank the gods. We must make the appropriate sacrifices when the time is right.'

Cornelius stares at Pinarius's rumpled clothes. 'Perhaps you should buy a new tunic, Uncle?'

'I would,' Pinarius says as he continues to scrub his tunic. 'But we haven't the time.'

Three hours later, after the sun has set, Sextus and Cornelius go through the doors of the canteen. Pinarius waits a quarter of an hour before following them inside. They are enjoying a cup of wine in the corner of the room when Pinarius walks in. There are three customers drinking wine, a man at the bar and another two at a table. The proprietor and his wife are behind the bar. The festivities of the games are happening elsewhere, in Puteoli, so the crowd here in Baiae is subdued. The customers are not looking to celebrate, but to drink. This must be why the Augusta chose it, Pinarius thinks, because it is discreet.

Pinarius orders a cup of wine and takes a seat at a long table, near Sextus and Cornelius.

The younger men hold cups of wine up to hide their smiles. They are enjoying this skulduggery.

They wait half of an hour. Then Livia walks into the canteen with three large men. Pinarius stands, his cap in his hand. He smiles.

Livia points at Pinarius and says to one of the men, 'That's him.'

She turns and leaves.

The three men walk toward Pinarius.

One of them punches Pinarius in the stomach.

He falls to the floor gasping for breath.

'There . . . ' He tries to speak, but can't catch his breath. 'There must be some kind of mistake.'

A foot collides with his stomach and the pain is worse than the punch. Pinarius curls up in a ball. His eyes water from the pain.

A hand grips his shoulder and hauls him up.

Sextus and Cornelius remain seated at their table, their faces white with terror. The three men attacking Pinarius are twice their size. They wouldn't stand a chance.

One of the three thugs circles the room, flicking coins at the patrons and the proprietors. 'For your trouble,' he says. 'You didn't see anything.'

A rag is stuffed into Pinarius's mouth, a hood is pulled over his head, and then he is thrown over a shoulder and carried to the door.

A coin lands in front of Sextus. It spins three times on the table before toppling over. He looks at it, horrified.

'Remember. You didn't see anything.'

Domitilla

2 May
Reate, Italy

The undertaker's voice cracks as he finishes his story. He shows me the coin he received in exchange for watching his father dragged off to his death.

'And what did you do next?' I ask.

He sobs.

'Nothing. I watched men take my father away and I did nothing. I sat there, helpless. Father was found in the Baiae lake the next day. I came back here, to Reate. I didn't know what else to do. I sold our property to pay our debts and I have tried to . . .' He takes a deep breath, trying to control his emotions. 'I have tried to live.'

'I am sorry,' I say.

He doesn't look at me. My words are empty comfort.

This is my fault. I refused to see his father because I am the emperor's sister and he was a lowly undertaker.

Livia is also to blame. She must be Nerva's spy. I knew Nerva had spies across the empire, but I never imagined one had infiltrated our family. I relied on Livia. I trusted her. She became important to me. It happened so gradually that it never occurred to me she was anything other than a loyal member of our household.

'Do you have the letter?' I ask Sextus.

He shakes his head. 'Father had the original. My cousin has the translation. I wanted to burn it, but he thought it might be useful.'

'But your recollection of it, you're confident the words were as you remember?'

'They are seared into my memory. I will never forget. The words were poison for my father, as much as they were for yours.'

'My father specifically named Nerva?'

He nods.

Last year, there were terrible events that were never satisfactorily explained. The attempt on my life and inexplicable prodigies meant to undermine the Principate. Was Nerva to blame? How blind I've been! Father's intuition must have been right. How many of our family's travails can be attributed to Nerva?

I put my hand on the undertaker's. 'Nerva is behind your father's death. He is a monster. We will bring him to justice. I promise.'

'Justice?'

The word is foreign to him. I will need to show him its meaning.

'Come,' I say, standing. 'Your days of living in this hovel are over.'

He does not believe me. His face is blank. I take his arm, help him stand and walk him to the door. I open it and the bright morning sun is momentarily blinding. 'This is a new day for you,' I say, gently guiding him outside. There is resistance at first, as I press on his back, but then his weight rushes forward, as though he has fallen or is pulled, and I stumble through the door.

I fall to my knees, my hands on the sun-baked earth. I look up and see a large man holding the undertaker against the wall of his home. He's holding his forearm against the undertaker's neck, choking the life out of him.

His wife, the woman I saw when we first arrived, is hidden from view but I can hear her screaming.

I call for help but my voice dies in the back of my throat. I turn and see the soldiers who accompanied me lying dead beside their horses. The Batavian is on his knees. His arms being held behind his back by two rough-looking men. He is bleeding, but I cannot see how serious the wound is.

Livia is sitting on a tree stump. She's leaning forward, her chin in her hand.

More tough-looking men mill around the clearing.

Someone is standing over me. I try to make him out. The man's face is clouded in shadow. He squats closer to the ground, so our eyes are nearly level.

Nerva.

'Are you alright, Mistress? Did you fall?'

He puts out his hand. I slap it away.

I can hear the undertaker's laboured breathing behind me. He's still being held against the wall of his home. His feet are a few inches above the ground and he's furiously kicking the air. 'He is choking. Let him go.'

Nerva stands and adjusts his tunic. 'No, I think not.'

The undertaker's kicking intensifies and then suddenly stops; his body goes limp. Nerva's thug steps back and the undertaker falls to the earth.

I have failed both father and son.

Blinded by rage, I stand and run at Nerva. But two men grab me before I am close enough to make contact.

I curse Nerva's name, spitting with rage. He watches me with cold eyes.

Then I turn my anger to Livia, realizing she is the one who ran to tell Nerva that I meant to speak with the undertaker. She must have left last night. She'd suggested the morning to give her enough time to fetch Nerva.

'How could you?' I say.

Livia does not look at me. She is still sitting on the tree stump, staring into the distance.

'I wouldn't judge her too harshly, Augusta,' Nerva says. 'She did not betray you. She has been working for me all the time you have known her. It was my good fortune that you came to rely on her the way you did.' He turns to Livia and snaps his fingers. 'My dear,' Nerva says. He holds out his hand, expectantly.

Livia stands and pulls from under her tunic a vial of a blue liquid.

Nerva takes it from Livia and then tilts it back and forth, mixing the vial. He holds it up to the light.

'What is that?' I ask.

'I think you know.'

'Is it the poison you used on my father?'

Nerva's smile is emotionless. 'No. The one I had administered to your father worked very slowly, over a series of weeks. It was designed to make his death resemble a gradual illness. This—' he holds up the vial '—is deadlier. It will work much faster.'

'You don't deny it then, murdering my father.'

He shrugs.

'Why?'

He stares at me, as though considering whether to say more. 'Your family has been in power too long. You would not understand.'

'You are a traitor and a murderer. I understand that.'

'A traitor? Who did I betray?'

'Rome. Your emperor.'

'You see, I was right.' Nerva shakes his head and nearly laughs. 'You are blind to your family's hypocrisy. You forget your father's rise. Let me ask you this, Augusta: when Vitellius was emperor and your father raised an army and marched it west to challenge Vitellius for the throne, was he betraying Rome? What about when his men butchered Vitellius's army, or when they sacked Rome, or when they tore Vitellius limb from limb on the Gemonian stairs? Was your father betraying Rome then?

'One cannot betray Rome. It is a series of buildings beside the Tiber. It can be taken by force or by intrigue, but not betrayed. At least when I poisoned your father, one man perished. When your father made his bid for the throne, how many people died? Think of the trail of blood your father's army left across Italy – all so he could be the first man in Rome.

'Politics is a dirty game,' he says. 'Your father played it better than most and he won. And he kept on winning until a better man outsmarted him. But he knew as well as anyone that if you are not winning in politics, you are losing. And in Rome, the stakes are as high as they come. When you lose, you forfeit your life.'

'My father was a good man,' I say.

'Your father was a god, not a man. And, like any god, Caesar demands sacrifices in his name. He desires blood. Jupiter, Apollo, Caesar – it is all the same. A god's thirst for flesh is as constant as the rising sun.'

'No. That is false. If you had been loyal, he would never have hurt you. He trusted you.' My voice is dejected now. I had been struggling against the men holding my arms, but I feel a sense of defeat run through my limbs. 'His trust is the only reason you were close enough to kill him. And you betrayed that trust.'

There is a flash of anger in Nerva's eyes. It only lasts a moment, though; and then he is once again as impassive as a rock face, cold and pitiless. 'Caesar did not trust me. He did not trust anyone but his eldest son. He showed favour to senators and then took it away. He made us senators fight amongst ourselves, so that we would not turn our ire at him. When your father first took the throne, he named me consul – a great honour. But then he cast me aside. He favoured other men. It was insulting. And if I did nothing, so long as I was on the outside looking in, it was only a matter of time before I was offered up to the god for sacrifice.'

'Is that why you poisoned my father?'

Nerva is nodding, glad that I can understand his twisted logic. 'I realized that I would have better luck with a new emperor. First I took steps to undermine Caesar and encouraged a coup. But when Marcellus failed I took matters into my own hands.'

I think of the strange prodigies last year. The dog that inexplicably carried a human hand into the forum. The city talked about it for weeks, claiming it meant power was about to change hands. That so-called prodigy, along with Father's age and failing health – it all worked to undermine the Principate. No doubt it emboldened Marcellus to plan his coup. Titus discovered that the dog had been trained to carry out the task. But we never learned who was behind it.

'The hand in the forum?' I say. 'Last January. That was you?'

Nerva nods. 'Yes. One of many omens I orchestrated to undermine the Principate, to hint at your family's vulnerability. To inspire others to do the unthinkable.'

Father was right. Nerva is to blame for all of our family's unexplained misfortunes.

I think of the man who tried to kill me not long after the incident with the hand. He broke into the Palace and attacked me with a knife. It was only thanks to the Batavian that I lived.

'And is that why you tried to have me killed?'

Nerva shrugs. 'You were engaged to Marcellus. I knew Marcellus had designs on the Principate himself. If he were to marry you, and your father and brothers were killed, he would be the logical choice for emperor. I wanted a new emperor, but not Marcellus. He would have been worse than your father. I couldn't have that.'

'So the simplest way to solve the problem was to kill me?'

'Yes.'

I start to cry.

'My father was a good emperor. He was a good man.'

'You give your father too much credit. He wasn't much better than Nero. His great fortune was the civil war that he won to earn the throne. It was so bad the people didn't have the stomach for another one. They still don't. That is why the Flavians continue to rule.'

I think of Titus. My invincible brother.

'You wanted a new emperor, but Titus will not bring you into the fold. He knows what you are.'

Nerva walks towards me, then nods at one of the men holding my arms. A hand pulls my head back and another pries my mouth open.

'I am not concerned,' Nerva says. 'I know your brother. I know his strengths and weaknesses . . .'

Nerva pours the blue liquid down my throat. It's warm and bitter. My mouth is forced shut and they don't let go until I've swallowed the liquid. It leaves a gritty sediment on my tongue.

'I have plans,' Nerva says, 'and your brother will not stand in my way.'

Nerva's men let me go and I collapse to the dirt. My throat begins to burn. I feel too weak to stand.

I watch Nerva walk away.

My fingers go numb. My mouth fills with saliva. I want to retch.

Nerva points at the Batavian. 'Get him ready.'

One of Nerva's henchmen drags iron shackles through the dirt. The Batavian flails, trying to escape, but a man beats the Batavian with a club until he has no fight left. He's thrust face first into the dirt, put in chains and then gagged.

'What are you going to do with him?' I ask.

'Sell him,' Nerva says. 'He will be blamed for your death. The world will think the Batavian could not stand to live without you. So he killed you and ran.'

Intense pain ripples through my stomach. I am having trouble breathing.

I think of Flavia. My little girl. I'm afraid to mention her name. What will happen to her?

I lie back on the sun-baked earth and stare up at the sun. The pain builds until I don't think I will be able to stand it any more . . .

And then it is gone.

There is only the warm radiance of the sun washing over me. I feel as though I am floating in the balmy, brilliant white light.

I close my eyes and all is dark.

Barlaas

15 May
The Euphrates, the border between
Rome and Parthia

Our guide is a short, blue-eyed Syrian with a dagger strapped to his belt. His name is Moses.

'The river,' Moses says, pointing at the Euphrates. For him, there is only one river. No need to call it by name.

'We cross here.'

I stare at the calm green-blue water, slowly snaking its way south and east. The shore is tawny-brown, spotted with green brush. On the other side is what the Romans call Parthia. The land of my birth.

I had forgotten what it looked like, the river. Living as long as I did in Italy, the memory was muted, just beyond reach, like the face of a loved one long passed. But now that I am here – now that I can see it and smell it; now that I can feel the cool breeze coming off the water – memories long buried are coming back to me.

Carenes and I crossed at this very spot thirty years ago. His expression was grim as he stared at the river for the last time. We had been in chains for months before Vologases sent us west, and my wrists were raw from the manacles. My heart was full of hate for my brother, for banishing me, for sending me to live with our enemies.

There is comfort in seeing it unchanged. To know that while I am getting old, the mountains and rivers will continue as they were.

'Is it as you remember?' Ulpius asks. He is slouched in his saddle, bent over the reins. He looks tired and I cannot blame him. Our journey has been long and difficult. He is rubbing that shard of terracotta he always carries with him.

'Yes.'

He nods.

'Would you like a moment? We have time.'

I look behind me. The column of thirty soldiers are waiting patiently. We were supposed to cross into Parthia with more than two hundred men. But in Antioch dysentery ravaged the ranks and Ulpius refused to wait. We left only with those who could walk. 'Let the others catch up,' Ulpius had said.

Our guide Moses is impatient. 'It is folly to linger,' he says. 'You should cross now and be done with it.'

'No one asked you,' Manlius says. He and Marcus are behind me. They have both been watching Moses like a hawk. Our guide has asked too many questions since leaving Antioch, trying to learn all that he can. Once we cross, he will try to sell information to his Parthian contacts. These men of the border, who spend time in Rome and Parthia, can be duplicitous.

But whatever he says, it won't interfere with our plans. His aim was obvious from the beginning, so we have been disciplined. He only knows what is obvious from looking at us. That we are on a diplomatic mission. (No one goes to war in Parthia with thirty men.) That we have two Aryan prisoners; one is earless, the other with discoloured eyes. That among the Romans travelling to Parthia there is an old Parthian warrior who can speak Latin like an Italian. That is all he knows.

'Manlius is right,' Marcus says. 'Take your time.'

I thank my companions with a nod, then dismount and walk to the shore.

I listen to the river. The sun warms my face.

It is strange to the think of the young man I was when I crossed into Roman lands. I had been in chains for months, underfed and sore from the occasional beating by my guards. Still, I was young. I was skinny and strong as an ox.

Something clenches in my chest. I think of the life I lost living in Rome, the thirty years I could have had as an Arsacid noble and warrior. I think of those closest to me when I left. My wives, my sisters, my brothers. How many will be alive? I haven't a clue. And those that are alive – what will they make of me? Will I be an outcast, like the Toad, a Roman in all but name? Or will they be as happy to see me as I will be to see them?

I kneel at the river's edge and reach my hand into the water. It's cool and clean. I push my hand deeper and pull out a fistful of black earth.

The sleeve of my robe is wet and sticks to my forearm. It's pleasant in the heat.

I have carried a sadness with me, a longing. It grew over my thirty years in Rome and I could never soothe it.

But there is an answer to it here, holding the land of my birth.

I rub my hands together; black earth smears across my palms. I hold my hands to my face and inhale, deeply.

The knot in my chest releases, like a flower blooming in spring.

Tears stream down my face.

I am home.

Epilogue

Caesar receives news of his sister in the morning.

It is nearly summer, bright and warm, and Caesar was excited for the weeks ahead. The last brick was laid in the amphitheatre and soon the games will start. One hundred days to celebrate the opening of the largest, grandest structure in the world. A testament to the power of the Flavians. Nero built his Golden House for himself. The Flavians built a stadium for the people. Caesar knows that for this building alone he will be remembered.

And the devastation in Campania – although he could never hope to undo the damage wrought by the worst and most inexplicable fire the world has ever seen; indeed, what can Caesar do when entire cities are buried? – nevertheless, thanks to Caesar's dedication and resources, much had been done to repair the region. The pain is lessening.

And yes, there was a devastating fire in Rome itself, not long after the fires of Vesuvius. But Caesar has nearly rebuilt the city – at his own personal expense – and the suffering the fire caused is starting to fade.

Caesar's father would have fixed the disaster in Campania and the fire in Rome by raising taxes; he would have made the people pay for it. His son, however, is his own man – or so say the people in the streets. As Prefect, he was his father's attack dog, quick with the sword, heavy handed and ruthless. But his citizens are pleased to see Caesar, now the first man in the empire, proving himself to be a benevolent and understanding Princeps.

And there had been no portents as of late, no dire prodigies foretelling disaster. No one has had to consult the Oracles and hear the sort of oracular pessimism that always sends the Senate and the people reeling. To the contrary, so far this year the augers have been well received.

The year is shaping into a fine one. Caesar is popular; his position strong; his people happy. Caesar has not thought of the Sibyl and her dark cave for many months.

This is the state of mind Caesar finds himself in when he learns about his sister.

It is Caesar's closest friend, the white-haired Prefect of the Praetorian Guard, who delivers the news. Caesar was inspecting the amphitheatre with his architects. The Prefect took Caesar by the arm, pulled him aside, and whispered the news in his ear.

Dead. At the hands of the imperial slave, the famous Batavian. Mad with love for his beautiful master, the Batavian strangled her after she rejected his advances. Her honour was kept in exchange for her life.

Because he receives the news in public, Caesar cannot react as a brother should. He does not cry out or fall to his knees. Caesar must remain impervious. It is tragic when a god's sister dies, but he must rise above it.

Caesar whispered back, 'where is the Batavian?'

'We do not know.'

Caesar does not change his plans after hearing the news. He attends every meeting arranged that day; he goes to the Senate, and then the forum. It is only when he retires to the Imperial Palace, in the evening, when he is finally alone, that the tears come.

And it is only in the dark of night, when mortality – his own and his family's – is top of mind – that Caesar again thinks of the Sibyl's voice, her dark eyes, and her pitiless prediction.

A slave shall rule.

Acknowledgements

Thank you to my editor, Martin Fletcher, and everyone at Zaffre, especially Sophie Orme and Jennie Rothwell.

Thank you to my agent, Sam Copeland.

Thank you to those who read and commented on the various drafts on the road to publication: Jeff Hull, Michael Tonner, Marialena Carr, and Elyse Strathy.

Thank you to my wife, Anna.

28/6/19

BETTWS